"I don't understand what I do that scares you," said Luciente.

"What do you want?" asked Connie. "How do you get in here?"

"Try to believe me," he said. "I'm not from your time."

"Sure you're from Mars and you came in a big green saucer. I read about it in the *Enquirer*."

"No, no! I'm from a village in Massachusetts—Mattapoisett. Only I live there in 2137."

Connie snorted. She tossed her hair back. "And you came flying to me in your time machine."

Luciente shrugged and threw up his hands. . . .

"A stunning, even astonishing novel."
—*Publishers Weekly*

"An ambitious, unusual novel."
—*Philadelphia Inquirer*

Fawcett Crest Books
by Marge Piercy:

THE HIGH COST OF LIVING

SMALL CHANGES

WOMAN ON THE EDGE OF TIME

VIDA

Woman on the Edge of Time

MARGE PIERCY

FAWCETT CREST • NEW YORK

A Fawcett Crest Book
Published by Ballantine Books

ISBN 0-449-20485-5

This edition published by arrangement with Alfred A. Knopf, Inc.

Selection of The Woman Today Book Club, November 1976

Manufactured in the United States of America

First Fawcett Crest Edition: June 1977
First Ballantine Books Edition: June 1983

This is a book that took a lot of help to write, although nobody who helped me should bear the burden for what I made. I owe a great debt of thanks to Michael Galen and everybody else at *RT: A Journal of Radical Therapy;* to Nancy Henley; Phyllis Chesler; Michael Brown; to Mary Waters and others of the Mental Patients Liberation Front; to Dr. Paul Lowinger, especially strong thanks; to Jon Levine; to Mary Lou Shields; to Rosario Morales; to Frank Mirer of Harvard and Bernie Bulkin of Hunter, who helped me with the poisoning; all the people at HEALTHPAC and the Somerville Women's Health Project who fed me information and helped me with contacts.

Above all I am grateful to people I cannot thank by name, who risked their jobs to sneak me into places I wanted to enter; and grateful to the past and present inmates of mental institutions who shared their experiences with me, outside and inside. Thanks to the students at Old Rochester Regional High School, amused but supportive of my interest in Mattapoisett. Finally I'm in debt to the folks from Mouth-of-Mattapoisett who worked so hard to make me understand—who found me dense and slow of wit, but always told me that at least I try.

M.P.

Woman on the Edge of Time

One

CONNIE got up from her kitchen table and walked slowly to the door. Either I saw him or I didn't and I'm crazy for real this time, she thought.

"It's me—Dolly!" Her niece was screaming in the hall. "Let me in! Hurry!"

"Momentito." Connie fumbled with the bolt, the police lock, finally swinging the door wide. Dolly fell in past her, her face bloody. Connie clutched at Dolly, trying to see how badly she was hurt. "Qué pasa? Who did this?"

Blood was oozing from Dolly's bruised mouth and she gasped a wad of matted paper handkerchiefs brown with old blood and spotted bright red with fresh. Her left eye was swollen shut. "Geraldo beat me." Dolly let her peel off the blue winter coat trimmed with fur and press her broad hips in pink pants back into the kitchen chair. There Dolly collapsed and began to weep. Awkwardly Connie embraced her shoulders, her hands slipping on the satin of the blouse.

"The chair's warm," Dolly said after a few minutes. "Get me a handkerchief."

Connie brought toilet paper from the hall bathroom—she had nothing else—and carefully locked the outside door again. Then she put some of the good Dominican coffee she saved for special into the drip pot and set water to boil in a kettle.

"It's cold in here," Dolly whimpered.

"I'll make it warmer." She lit the oven and turned on the burners. "Soon it'll be like that hothouse of yours . . . Geraldo beat you?"

Dolly opened her mouth wide, gaping. "Loo . . . Loo . . ."

As gently as she could she poked into Dolly's bloody mouth. Her own flesh cringed.

Dolly jerked away. "He broke a tooth, didn't he? That dirty rotten pimp! Will I lose a tooth?"

"I think you have one broken and maybe another loose. But who am I to say? I'm no dentist. You're still bleeding!"

"He's crazy, that pig! He wants to mess me up. Connie, how come you wouldn't let me in? I was screaming in the hall forever."

"It wasn't five minutes. . . ."

"I thought I heard voices. Is somebody here?" Dolly looked toward the other room, the bedroom.

"Who would be here? I had the TV on."

"It hurts so much. Give me something to kill the pain."

"Aspirin?"

"Oh, come on. It hurts!"

"Hija mía, how would I have anything?" Connie lifted her hands to show them empty, always empty.

"Those pills they made you take, from the State."

"Let me give you ice." Dolly had heard her talking with Luciente: therefore he existed. Or Dolly had heard her talking to herself. Dolly had said the chair was warm: she had been sitting in the other chair, in front of the plate from her supper of eggs and beans. She must not think about it now, with Dolly suffering. His story was unbelievable! No, don't think about it. She wrapped ice cubes in a kitchen towel and brought them to Dolly. "That prescription ran out a year ago." Not that she had taken the tranquilizers. She had sold the pills for a little extra money, for a piece of pork or chicken once a week, soap to wash with. She found it hard to believe anybody would take that poison intentionally, but you could peddle any kind of pill in El Barrio. Still, there had been the nuisance of going down to Bellevue, since she had been living near Dolly's when she had been sent away and never could get her case transferred.

"Consuleo!" Dolly leaned her swollen cheek on Connie's shoulder. "Everything hurts! I'm scared. He punched me in the belly, hard."

"Why do you stay with him? What good is he? With your daughter, why have such a cabrón hanging around?"

Dolly gave her the mocking glance that would greet any comment she might make for the rest of her life on the subject of the welfare of children; or did she imagine it? "Consuelo, I feel so sick. I feel lousy through and through. I have to lie down. Oh, if he makes me lose this baby, I'll kill him!"

As she supported her niece's weight into the bedroom she felt a flash of fear or perhaps of hope that Luciente would still be there. But the tiny room held only her swaybacked bed, the chair with her alarm clock on it, the dresser, the wine jug full of dried flowers, the airshaft window incompletely covered with old curtains from better days. She undressed Dolly tenderly as a baby, but her niece groaned and cursed and wept more. The satin polka dot shirt was streaked with blood and blood had soaked through her black satin brassiere with the nipples cut out. "But it won't show on your nice bra," Connie promised as Dolly mourned her clothes, her body, her skin. Bruises had already clotted under the velvety skin of Dolly's belly, her soft arms, her collarbone.

"Mira! Is there blood on my panties? See if he made me bleed there."

"You aren't bleeding there, I promise. Get under the covers. Oye, Dolly, it isn't that easy to lose a baby! In the sixth month, if he beat you, maybe. But in the second month that baby is better protected than you are." She put the alarm on the floor and sat in the straight chair beside the bed to hold Dolly's limp hand. "Listen, I should take you to emergency. To Met."

"Don't make me go anyplace. I hurt too much."

"They can give you something for the pain. I'll get a gypsy cab to take us. It's only fifteen blocks."

"I'm ashamed. 'What happened to you?' 'Oh, my pimp beat up on me.' In the morning I'll go to my own dentist. You take me down to him in the morning. Otera on Canal. You call him up at nine-thirty in the morning and tell him to take me right away. Now hold the ice against my cheek."

"Dolly, how do you know Geraldo won't come charging up here?"

"Consuelo!" Dolly drawled her name in a long wail of pain. "Be nice to me! Don't push me around too! I hurt,

I want to rest. Be sweet to me. Give me a little yerba—it's in my purse. At the bottom of the cigarette pack."

"Dolly! You're crazy to run around with your face bleeding and dope in your purse! Suppose the cops pick you up?"

"I had a lot of time to sort my purse when I was leaving! Come on, get it for me!"

She was fumbling through Dolly's big patent leather bag, clumsy prying in another woman's purse, when she heard heavy steps climbing. Men in a hurry. She froze. Why? Men ran up and down the steps of the tenement all night. But she knew.

Geraldo pounded the door. She kept quiet. In the bedroom Dolly moaned and began to weep again.

Geraldo hit the door harder. "Open the door, you old bitch! Open or I'll break it down. Bust your head in. Come on, open this fucking door!" He began kicking so hard the wood cracked and started to give way.

He would break it down. She yelled, "Wait! Wait! I'm coming!"

Not a door opened in the hallway. Nobody came to look out. She undid the locks and hopped back, before he could slam the door to the wall and crush her behind it. He strode in, thumping the door to the wall as she had known he would, followed by a scrawny older man in a buttoned-up gray overcoat and a hulking bato loco named Slick she had seen with Geraldo before. They all crowded into her kitchen and Geraldo slammed the door behind.

Geraldo was Dolly's boyfriend. He had been a vendadero and done well enough, keeping Dolly and her little girl, Nita, from her marriage. But some squeeze in the drug trade had cut him off after he had been busted, although he had not ended up serving time. Now he made Dolly work as a prostitute, selling her body to all the dirty men in the city. He had three other girls that perhaps he had been running all the time on the side. Dolly made four.

Connie hated him. It flowed like electric syrup through her veins how she hated him. Her hatred gave her a flush in the nerves like speed coming on. Geraldo was a medium-tall grifo with fair skin, gray eyes, kinky hair—pelo alambre—that he wore in a symmetrical Afro. He was elegant. Every time her eyes grated upon him he was attired in some new costume of pimpish splendor. She dreamed of peeling off a sleekly polished antiqued lizard high-heeled boot and pounding it down his lying throat. She dreamed of yanking off his finger the large grayish diamond he boasted matched his scheming eyes and using it to slit his throat, so his bad poisoned blood would run out.

"Tía Consuelo," he crooned. "Caca de puta. Old bitch. Get your fat and worthless ass out of my way. Move!"

"Get out of my house! You hurt her enough. Get out!"

"Not anything like I'm going to hurt that bitch if she doesn't shape up." The back of his arm striking like a rattlesnake, he shoved her into the sink. Then he strolled over to lounge blocking the bedroom door. Always he was playing in some cold deathshead mirror, watching himself, polishing his cool. "Hey, cunt, stop blubbering. I brought you a doctor."

"What kind of doctor?" Connie shrieked. She had slid under his blow and caught only the edge of the sink. She cowered, half crouching. "A butcher! That's what kind of doctor!"

"That bughouse taught you all about doctors, um?"

"You leave her alone, Geraldo! She wants to have your baby so bad, she can stay with me."

"So you can cut it up, you nut? Now turn it off or Slick will bust your lip." Geraldo leaned on the doorframe, lighting a cigarette and dropping the lit match on the floor, where it slowly burned out, making a black hole in the worn linoleum. "Time to rise and fly. I brought a doctor to fix you. Up now. Move!"

"No! I don't want him to touch me! Geraldo honey, I want this baby!"

"What shits you pushing? You think I sweat bricks for the kid of some stupid trick with dragging balls? You don't even know what color worm you got turning in the apple."

"It's your baby! It is. In Puerto Rico I didn't take my pills."

"Woman, so many men been into you, it could have a whole subway car of daddies."

"In San Juan I never took my pills. I told you already!"

"You tell me? Not in this life, baby. How you pass the time while I was busy in La Perla, um?" He flicked lint from his vest.

"You wouldn't take me to meet your family!"

Geraldo had taken Dolly with him on vacation. Connie

felt pretty sure Dolly had tried to get pregnant, believing that Geraldo would let her quit whoring. Dolly wanted to have another baby and stay home. Like figures of paper, like a manger scene of pasteboard figures, a fantasy had shone in Connie since her conversation with Dolly that morning: she and Dolly and Dolly's children would live together. She would have a family again, finally.

She would be ever so careful and good and she would do anything, anything at all to keep them together. She would never be jealous of her niece no matter how many boyfriends she had. Dolly could stay out all night and go off on weekends and to Florida even and she would stay with Nita and the baby. As if anyone would ever again leave her alone with a child. The dream was like those paper dolls, the only dolls she had had as a child, dolls with blond paper hair and Anglo features and big paper smiles. That she knew in her heart of ashes the dream was futile did not make it less precious. Every soul needs a little sweetness. She thought of the stalks of sugar cane the kids bought at the fruit and vegetable man. Sweet in the mouth as you chewed it, and then you spat out the husks and they lay in the street. Hollow, flimsy, for a moment sweet in the mouth. Cane with which her grandmother had sweetened the chocolate long ago in El Paso.

"Shut off that fucking kettle!" Geraldo shouted at her and she jumped to put out the flame. The coffee she had never finished making. The kettle had boiled almost dry. She shut off the oven and the burners because now her two small rooms felt stifling hot. How she had jumped to the stove when he rapped out that curt command. She resented obeying him automatically, instinctively jerking at the loud masculine order.

His beauty only made him more hateful. His face with the big gray eyes, the broad nose, the full cruel mouth, the hands like long talons, the proud bearing—he was the man who had pimped her favorite niece, her baby, the pimp who had beaten Dolly and sold her to pigs to empty themselves in. Who robbed Dolly and slapped her daughter Nita and took away the money squeezed out of the pollution of Dolly's flesh to buy lizard boots and cocaine and other women. Geraldo was her father, who had beaten her every week of her childhood. Her second husband, who had sent her into emergency with blood running down her legs. He was El Muro, who had raped her and then beaten her because she would not lie and say she had enjoyed it. She had had the strength then to run, to cut her losses and run. On the evening bus the next day she had left her home in Chicago, her father and sisters, the graves of her mother and her first (her real) husband, Martín. Dolly lacked the coarse strength that had saved her that time.

But Dolly had Nita already and a baby in the oven. "Fíjate, Geraldo," she screamed. "She's carrying your child. She came back that way from San Juan. I told her she was carrying the first time I saw her back here. What kind of tailless wonder are you to have your own child butchered by that doctor of dogs?"

Pivoting, Geraldo cuffed her back into the stove. The hot metal seared her back in a broad line and she clamped her lips tight, unable to scream, unable to issue a sound from the suddenness of the pain. She sank to the floor and could not speak or move.

"Puta, get up and go with Dr. Medias, or I'll have him do it on you right in that witch's bed. Move!"

"No! No!" Dolly was thrashing around in bed, screaming and sobbing. Geraldo stepped into the bedroom, out of Connie's line of sight. She tried to roll to her feet. The scrawny doctor sat on the edge of a kitchen chair. He was in his fifties. His clothes were new and conservative, his manner was tense, and his foot tapped, tapped. Slick was leaning against the outer door smoking a joint and grinning.

Connie asked in Spanish, "You are really a doctor?"

"Of course." He did not look at her but replied as softly as she spoke. At his accent her eyes narrowed.

"Where are you a doctor?" She rolled on one elbow and tried to rise. "My back hurts me, it's burned so bad. You're Mexican."

"What is it to you?"

"Where are you from?"

"Mexico City."

"No. From Chihuahua, no?"

"Leave me alone, woman. You ask for trouble."

"From you? You have enough troubles. Practicing medicine without a license. Why do you want to hurt us? My parents too came from Chihuahua."

"Chihuahua can sink in a pit!"

"Her father's a businessman in New Jersey. He has a

big nursery business. Did that stinking pimp tell you? If you do this thing, her father will make trouble for you, it's the truth."

Dolly let out a long, terrified wail that scraped on the inside of Connie's skull. She had not heard such a desperate scream since she had been in the bughouse. Geraldo called Dr. Medias. Medias rose slowly to his feet and fumbled for a bag he had set beside the chair. Connie pulled herself up by the table leg, kicked him as hard as she could in the shin, and ran into the bedroom. She must stop them!

Dolly's mouth was bleeding again. Blood ran over the tattered nightgown Connie had dressed her in, onto the pillow. Dolly was trying to thrash free of Geraldo, who held her pinned. He would kill her! With his treachery he would kill Dolly and her baby too. Dolly would bleed to death in that bed.

Connie seized a bottle from the corner, the wine bottle that had once contained a half gallon of California burgundy and now held dried flowers and grasses, from a rare picnic with Dolly, Nita, Luis (Dolly's father and her brother) and his current family. With the nostalgic grasses scattering, she waved the jug and ran at Geraldo. He did not let go of Dolly quickly enough to defend himself. She smashed the wine jug right into his face. His nose flattened like a squashed bug on a windshield. He fell back against the wall, bellowing rage in no language. She raised the jug to hit him again, but her arms were caught behind her. She twisted. Someone struck her hard in the nape and she tried to turn. The fist caught her again and she went out.

She lay tied with straps to a bed, staring up at a bare bulb, shot up with meds. Thorazine? It felt worse, heavier. A massive dose. Hospital tranks hit her like a bulldozer when she had taken nothing for a long time. Prolixin? Whenever she sank into unconsciousness, she was tortured by clamps on her hips, her breasts, she was trapped in her old Chicago flat in a fire. The flames licked her skin. Her lungs filled with choking smoke. She tried and tried to pull clear of something that had fallen on her, to escape. She could not move.

Her body ached. All of her ached. Geraldo and his carnal Slick had beaten her twice: once right after she had broken Geraldo's nose, and again on the way to Bellevue in his car. Her ribs hurt terribly on the right side and she suspected one or two might be broken. Probably Geraldo had kicked her as she lay on the floor. In the car she had come to and he had begun punching her again in the face and chest and arms. He had beaten her until Dolly begged him to stop and began to weep and threatened to jump out of the car.

Each breath she drew stabbed her. How could she get the hospital to x-ray her for a broken rib? So far no one had heard a word she said, which of course was not unusual. Geraldo was so damned smart—bringing her to Bellevue, for instance, instead of to Met, on Ninety-sixth. Bellevue had records on her from before. He pretended she had attacked him and Dolly at Dolly's apartment on Rivington. He would take no chance that they might not accept her as a crazy woman.

The doctor had not even interviewed her but had talked exclusively to Geraldo, exchanging only a word or two with Dolly. Geraldo had Dolly gripped by the elbow, her face still swollen. Dolly had lied. Dolly had sold her into Bellevue, and for what? For her own skin, already polluted? For the nose of her precious pimp? For the opportunity to fuck more johns? How could Dolly sit there sniveling and nod when the doctor asked if Connie had done that to her face?

Connie writhed on the bed, pinned down with just enough play to let her wriggle. They had pushed her into restraint, shot her up immediately. She had been screaming—okay! Did they think you had to be crazy to protest being locked up? Yes, they did. They said reluctance to be hospitalized was a sign of sickness, assuming you were sick, in one of these no-win circles. The last time she had not fought; she had come willingly with the caseworker, believing in her sickness. She had come humbly, rotten with self-hatred and weary of her life.

Her left calf began to cramp. She wanted to shriek with the sharp pain. She longed to knead the calf in her hands. The hard ball of muscle formed and held rigid. If she screamed they might never release her from restraint. They had forgotten her, locked her away in this broom closet to starve. She had pissed on herself. What could she do? Now she lay in her own wet stink. Cold at first, creepy cold, now warm from her body. And stinking.

She turned her head, craning to watch the slit in the door. Wide and low, like a mouth. If only she saw an attendant look in, she could signal. Her back festered between her shoulder blades, where it had been burned by the stove. The two attendants had put her neatly into restraint, the injection entering her veins like molten lead. Folding a sheet warm from the machine in the laundry room—flip, flip, bang, fold. Already the processing had begun. The attendant at check-in had held by one corner her worn red plastic purse mended with tape, held it like something dirty, a piece of garbage from the streets. Casually the woman arrayed her fragile possessions on the counter and, with a gesture like emptying an ashtray, dropped them into an envelope and locked them away.

Her purse, her keys, her scrap of brown paper on which she had been figuring April's budget, her rent receipt, the ballpoint pen with the name of a stationery company that she had found in the subway, her black plastic comb, her old loved compact with the raised peacock figure that Claud had given her for her birthday, selecting with his sensitive fingers the "look" of the design, her dime store red lipstick that she wore only for best against the day when it would be used up and she would lack the money for another—unless Dolly gave her a lipstick. Dolly! Who had betrayed her. Who had abandoned her. Who had sold her into bondage. At the desk her counters of identity had been taken: welfare ID, Medicaid, old library card, photos of Dolly with Nita, of Angelina as a baby, at one held by her father, Eddie, at two with herself, at three holding Claud's hand with that grin like a canoe—the way she had drawn mouths. There were no pictures of Angelina at four, or afterward.

Through some bond of blood like a ghostly umbilical cord, could Angelina in Larchmont or Scarsdale feel her mother on the rack? Her back hurt so, her calf ached, her face throbbed, her rib stabbed her as she breathed, her shoulder was wounded where Geraldo had twisted her arm in the back seat of the car until she had thought it would snap. Her tongue was swollen and her mouth full of blood as Dolly's had been. A foul taste: herself. The smell of her own piss rose into her nostrils. She began to weep. Then she choked on her tears and stopped in panic. She could not wipe her nose. The tears ran into her mouth. She was trussed like a holiday bird for the oven.

That doctor. What was his name? Youngish, with fine thin brown hair worn straggling, not quite long, not quite short, he kept yawning and trying to suppress the yawns so that his jaw muscles flexed strangely as he questioned Geraldo and wrote entries on a record form. Geraldo was almost demure. He had a good manner with authority, as any proper pimp should, respectful but confident. Man to man, pimp and doctor discussed her condition, while Dolly sobbed. The doctor asked her only her name and the date. First she said it was the fourteenth and then she changed it to the fifteenth, thinking it must be after midnight. She had no idea how long she had been unconscious.

"Listen to me, doctor—I didn't hit her! You take my niece into another room away from him and ask her if I hit her. *He* hit her!"

The doctor went on making notations on the form. She was a body checked into the morgue; meat registered for the scales.

She tried to tell the nurse who gave her the injection, the attendants who tied her to the stretcher, that she was innocent, that she had a broken rib, that Geraldo had beaten her. It was as if she spoke another language, that language Claud's buddy had been learning that nobody else knew: Yoruba. They acted as if they couldn't hear you. If you complained, they took it as a sign of sickness. "The authority of the physician is underminded if the patient presumes to make a diagnostic statement." She had heard a doctor say that to a resident, teaching him not to listen to patients. She had been through that last time in, when she had had a toothache. It had developed into a full abscess before the nurse and the attendants stopped interpreting her complaints as part of her "pattern of illness behavior."

Fool, poor fool she had got herself locked away again. She had jumped into the fire. Why had she done it? Why?

Yet lying in enforced contemplation, she found that clean anger glowing in her still. She hated Geraldo and it was right for her to hate him. Attacking him was different from turning her anger, her sorrow, her loss of Claud into self-hatred, into speed and downers, into booze, into wine, into seeing herself in Angelina and abusing that self born again into the dirty world. Yes, this time was different. She had struck out not at herself, not at herself in another, but at Geraldo, the enemy. She had not been wrong to try to defend Dolly, her closest one now, her blood, her almost child. How could she allow Geraldo to carve up Dolly's body? She had smashed his nose, yes; for all her pain, she smiled as she saw that moment. She had smashed his nose and he would never look quite the same. Last time in she had accepted the doom of sickness; the weight of the heavy judgment they passed out here she had bowed to. This time she was not ashamed. She would get out fast. She would be clearly competent, sane, together.

How long did she lie strapped to the bed? Day was the same as night. They had forgotten her and she would die here in her own piss. Sometimes she could not stand it anymore and she yelled as loud as she could and begged the walls to open. Moments were forever. She was mad. The drugs made her mind strange. She was caught, she was stalled. She floated trapped like an embryo in alcohol, that awful thing the Right to Life people had in that van on the street. She was caught in a moment that had fallen out of time and would never be over, never be done. She was mad. Yes, now she was crazy. How could she doubt it, lying wet in her own piss while her body screamed and the drug thickened her to lead.

Sometimes she slipped down into a hot, muggy doze and sometimes the pain from her back or her rib or her mouth tore through her sleep and she woke wild with grief and wept. "Please, please, please come. Please let me out. Someone. Please!" No response came. That was madness. To weep and cry out and curse and scream, and it was as if she had done nothing. She was dozing in that feverish half-sleep without rest or relief, when the door banged open. Two attendants came in and untied her.

She pitched forward, weak as string. She could see in their faces disgust, boredom. She smelled bad. She stank! They hauled her along the hall like a bag of garbage and they paid no attention to what she tried to say. "Please, I beg of you, listen. I was beaten before they brought me here. My rib hurts so much! Please, listen!"

"So I said to her, it's all right for you. Yon don't have to deal with these animals all day." The woman was a husky dyed blond who spoke with a slight Middle European accent. "All you do is come in two days and play games with the better ones. It's easy for you to pass remarks."

"Those OT's have it easy." The other woman was six

feet tall, hefty and black. "You better believe it. We just don't live right, Annette. We just the muscle around here."

"But Byrd gives me a pain. She's no better than she ought to be. You know, she lives with a man she's not married to. Lives with him openly in an apartment in Chelsea."

"Mmmmm." The black woman wore a bland, noncommittal look. "Here, into the bath with you, snooks," she said to Connie from over her head. They began pulling her clothes off.

"I can undress myself."

"Whew! Me-oh-my, is this one a mess? Did she jump out the window or something?"

"I was beaten up. By a pimp. Not *mine*," she added quickly. "He was beating my niece. It's him who brought me here."

"Now what have you been into?" the black attendant wondered, shoving her into the shower like a dog to be bathed. "Some gorgeous bruises you got yourself!"

"She'll smell better when she gets out. You wonder how they can live with themselves, never washing. But that's part of being sick," the blond said loftily. "Probably she's been sleeping in the street, in doorways. I see them around."

She wanted to scream that she washed as often as they did, that they had made her smell, made her dirty herself. But she did not dare. First, they would not listen, and second, they might hurt her. Who would care?

Because her clothes were filthy, they gave her a pair of blue pajamas three sizes too big and a robe of no particular color. Rotten luck to have been shoved into restraint on arrival. If she had simply walked up to the ward, she would have been able to keep her street clothes and more things. Here a scrap of paper, a book, a handkerchief, a nubbin of pencil, a bobby-pin were precious beyond imagining outside, irreplaceable treasures.

She found herself walking strangely, not only from the bruises: ah, the old Thorazine shuffle. She could no longer move quickly, gracefully, in spite of her plumpness. The black attendant walked her into the day room, a big bleak room between the men's and the women's sides of the ward, right by the locked door to the hall and the elevators. She looked around slowly. She caught sight of a clock on the way in and she knew it was eleven in the morning.

She was not hungry although she had not eaten for a long time. The drug killed her appetite so that she felt hollow, weak, but not hungry. The rib stabbed her. She felt feverish and might be. Nothing she could do. Her only hope was to catch a doctor as he made his flight through the ward or to persuade one of the attendants that she really needed medical help. Then the attendant would tell the doctor. It would take days to reach that kind of relationship with an attendant, and in the meantime she could die.

How hot the ward was. Steam heat from the old radiators turned on full blast. She fingered the plastic identification bracelet sealed on her wrist. Women in street clothes or the hospital clothes issued to them were sitting vacantly along the walls or staring at the television set placed up on a shelf where no one could reach it to change the station or alter the volume level. It was less crowded than when she had been in last, markedly so. Just opposite her, two old women were chatting animatedly in strong Brooklyn Jewish accents, like two gossips on a park bench instead of two madwomen on a plastic bench in a mental hospital. But they might only be elderly and not mad. At their feet a young girl lay motionless with her hands over her face, like a pet dog snoozing. There were many less old women this time. Was there a new wastebasket for the old?

Four Puerto Rican men were playing dominoes with bits of paper at a card table in a slow motion brought on by all of them being heavily drugged, like everybody else. The game seemed to occur under water. A child, a boy of eight or nine, sat near them picking his nose in the same kind of slow motion with such a look of blank despair on his small face she had to turn away. Most of the women were sitting on the plastic chairs that came in ranks of four against the wall, but there were more women than chairs. Though some were old, some children, some black, some brown, some white, they all looked more or less alike and seemed to wear a common expression. She knew that in a short while this ward, like every other she had been on, would be peopled by strong personalities, a web of romances and feuds and strategies for survival. She felt weary in advance. Who needed to be set down in this desolate limbo to survive somehow in the teeth of the odds? She had had enough troubles already, enough!

"Lunch, ladies. Lunch. Line up now! Come on, get your asses moving, ladies!" The dining room was around a bend in the corridor in the same ward. Back and forth they went, back and forth in the confined space from doorless bathroom to dining room to seclusion (called treatment rooms here) to the dormitories to the day room.

Lunch was a gray stew and an institutional salad of celery and raisins in orange jello. The food had no flavor except the sweet of the jello and she had to eat it all with a plastic spoon. At least the food did not need chewing in her bloody mouth. The objects in the stew were mushy, bits of soft flotsam and jetsam in lukewarm glue. She tried to think about how to get out of here, but her mind was mud.

Lunch was over in fifteen minutes and then they were back in the day room, milling around to line up for medication. She needed her wits to plot how she would get out of here. The effects of the shot had not worn off. Then she held her face rigid when she saw the paper cup with the pills. Gracias, gracias. A pill was easily dealt with, unlike the liquid you had to swallow at once. She slipped it under her tongue, swallowed the water, and sat down on an orange chair. It did not do to head too quickly for the bathroom to spit out the pill. She kept it under her tongue till the coating wore off and she began to taste the bitter drug.

Visiting hour came in midafternoon. Hope stabbed her when the attendant came to say she had a visitor. Dolly!

Dolly was heavily made up. She was not wearing her fur-collared coat but her old red belted coat Connie remembered from the year when Dolly was married and carrying Nita.

"Dolly, get me out of here!"

"Honey, I can't just yet. Be a little patient. By the middle of next week."

"Dolly, por favor! No puedo vivir in esto hoyo. Hija mía, ayúdame!"

Dolly chose to reply in English. "It's just for a couple of days, Connie. Not like last time." Politely reminding her that to be locked up in a mental institution was something she should be accustomed to.

"Dolly, how could you say I hit you? *Me?*"

"Geraldo—he made me."

She lowered her voice. "Did you have the operation?"

"I'm going into the hospital Monday." Dolly fluffed her hair. "I persuaded him not to use that butcher on me. It costs a lot, but it will be a real hospital operation. Not with that butcher who does it on all the whores cheap." Dolly spoke wih pride.

Connie shrugged, her mouth sagging. "You could leave town."

"Daddy won't let me have the baby either, that old . . ." Dolly picked at her cuticle, ruining the smooth line of the crimson polish. "I did ask him. He says he washes his hands of me. Listen, Connie—if I have the operation, Geraldo promises I can quit. He'll marry me. We'll have a real wedding next month, soon as I'm better from the operation. So you see, things are working out okay. And just as soon as I come out of the hospital, I'll get you out. It's only for a week."

"Please, Dolly, take me out before you go in for the operation. Please! I can't stand it here."

"I can't." Dolly shook her head. "You really busted his nose. He's going to have to have an operation himself! It's going to cost a bundle, Consuelo. He looks awful with a bandage all over his nose—he looks like a bird! Like a crazy eagle with that big beak in the middle of his face!" Dolly began to giggle, covering her mouth with her hand.

Connie smiled painfully. "I'm glad I hit him!"

"Well . . ." Dolly turned her eyes up. "I guess they can fix him with plastic surgery. You really lit into him! Mamá, how you slammed him with that wine bottle! I thought he'd kill you."

"I wish I had killed him," Connie said very, very softly. "How can you care about him with your face still swollen from his beating?"

"He is my man," Dolly said, shrugging. "What can I do?"

"Listen, can you bring me some clothes and stuff here before you go in the hospital?" When blocked, maneuver to survive. The first rule of life inside.

"Sure. What you want? Tomorrow I'll bring it to you, around this time."

She went into the bathroom after Dolly left and stayed there as long as she dared. Stalls without doors. In spite of the stink, it was a place to be almost alone, precious in the hospital. How could she scream at Dolly? What use? Dolly chose to believe Geraldo, and if she tried to shake that belief, Dolly would only turn from her. Then Dolly would not help her to get out, would not bring her clothing and the small necessities that could make the passing hollow days a little more bearable. She judged her niece for choosing Geraldo over her unborn baby and over herself; but hadn't she chosen to mourn for Claud almost to death?

Outside, did rain slick First Avenue? Was the sun bleeding through a murky overcast? Was it a rare blue day when the buildings stood crisp against the sky? Here it was time for meds. Here it was time to line up for a paper cup of mouthwash. Here it was time to line up for all starch meals. Here it was time to line up for more meds. Here it was time to sit and sit and sit. Here it was time to greet a familiar black face from the last time.

"Yeah, I was brought in three, four days ago," Connie told her. "Been here long?"

"My caseworker brought me in Monday. Same as last time. You too?"

Connie bowed her head. "Yeah, it was my caseworker."

Here it was time to sit facing a social worker, Miss Ferguson, who looked at the records spread out on her desk rather than at her. Miss Ferguson sat tightly and occasionally she glanced toward the door.

"You don't have to be nervous about me," Connie said. "I didn't do what Geraldo the pimp said. I didn't hit my niece. I wouldn't hurt one hair on her head. Him, I hit, that's the truth. I only hit him because he was beating her up."

"Was that how it was with your daughter?" Miss Ferguson had light brown hair curled at the ends. She wore granny glasses and a pale blue pants suit. A pimple had broken out on the end of her nose that her right hand kept stealing up to touch.

"It isn't the same this time! It isn't!"

"How can we help you if you won't let us?" Miss Ferguson glanced at her wristwatch, shuffling the papers in the folder. Her folder. "Three years ago you were admitted to Bellevue on the joint recommendation of a social worker from the Bureau of Child Welfare, your caseworker from welfare, and your parole officer. You were then hospitalized at Rockover State for eight months."

"They said I was sick and I agreed. Someone close to me had died, and I didn't want to live."

"You have a history of child abuse—"

"Once! I was sick!"

"Your parental rights were terminated. Your daughter Angelina Ramos was put out for adoption."

"I should never have agreed to that! I didn't understand what was happening! I thought they were just going to take care of her."

"It was the clinical judgment of the court psychiatrist that your daughter would be better off with foster parents." The pimple was growing as she watched. Miss Ferguson kept feeling it gingerly, poking it while pretending not to.

"They were wrong to take my daughter!" She saw Miss Ferguson frown. "Imagine—your daughter. I hurt her once. That was a terrible thing to do, I know it. But to punish me for it the rest of my life!"

The social worker was giving her that human-to-cockroach look. Most people hit kids. But if you were on welfare and on probation and the whole social-pigeonholing establishment had the right to trek regularly through your kitchen looking in the closets and under the bed, counting the bedbugs and your shoes, you had better not hit your kid once. The abused and neglected child, they had called Angelina officially. She had been mean to Angie, she had spent those months after she got the news about Claud's death gulping downs, drinking bad red wine. A couple of times she had shot speed. She had thought nothing could hurt her anymore—until she lost Angelina. Maybe you always have more to lose until, like Claud, they took your life too.

"The acquaintance who died—that would be your . . . The black handicapped pickpocket whose assistant you were."

Her face slammed shut. They trapped you into saying something and then they'd bring out their interpretations that made your life over. To make your life into a pattern of disease. Couldn't even say blind. "Handicapped." He wasn't. He was a fine saxophone player. He was a talented pickpocket and he brought home good things for her and her baby. He had been as good to Angie as if she had been his own baby daughter. He had been good to her too, a loving man. The sweetest man she had ever had. As if Claud could be summed up in their rotten records, either the sweetness or the pain of him, his badass fury.

They had killed him too. In prison he had taken part in a medical experiment for the money and hoping to shorten his time. They had injected him with hepatitis and the disease had run its course and he had died. Her probation officer, Briggs, would not let her go to the funeral. That bastard—did he think they would plot together, him from his closed coffin?

"The Porto Rican man you describe as your niece's 'pimp'—is that the same man as her fiancé?"

"He *is* her pimp. That's how he makes a living. He has three other girls." Connie sat forward, giving up. Don't try to win now, just survive. "Look, please, Miss Ferguson, look at my mouth, where he hit me. Would you look at me, please, just for one moment? My side. Here. It hurts awful. After they knocked me down, he kicked me while I was lying on the floor. When I breathe, each time, all the time, it hurts. I think—" She was about to say that her rib was broken or cracked, but they got nasty if you said anything medical. "I think something's wrong inside me. Where he kicked me on the floor."

"Who are the '*they*' you believe knocked you down? Is that your niece, Dolores Campos?"

"No! He came in with a—" She realized she didn't want to say "doctor." How careful she had to be with them. "—with a couple of pals—hoodlums. When I hit him, they knocked me down."

"You do admit, you remember that you struck him."

"Yes! He was beating Dolly."

"Your niece says you attacked her."

"She told me he made her say that. Ask her in a room alone. I beg you, ask her alone. She's scared to go against Geraldo." Her hands clasped in the gesture of praying and she heard her own voice whining. "Please, Miss Ferguson, have a doctor look at me. I hurt so much. Please, I beg you. Look at my mouth."

"You say it hurts you. Where do you believe you feel pain?"

"In my side. My ribs. Also my mouth. And my back is burned. Those are the worse places. The rest is just bruises."

"In your side?"

"It hurts every breath I take. Please?"

"Well, you do have bruises. All right, I'll speak to the

nurse." Miss Ferguson caressed her pimple, pretending to adjust her glasses. With a nod she dismissed Connie.

Finally on Tuesday Connie was x-rayed and her cracked rib was taped and her mouth looked at. They sent her with an attendant to the dentist. She missed visiting hour, so she did not find out whether Dolly was out of the hospital yet. But tomorrow, surely, Dolly must come and talk to them about releasing her. If she could get Dolly to tell the truth to the doctor, the nurse, even to the social worker, then they would let her go. . . . Even figuring the whole process of release would take a day or two, she could be out by Friday night.

She sat in a lopsided chair in the hall outside the dentist's office, with the attendant beside her poring over an astrology magazine. How she would celebrate her release! Her dingy two rooms with the toilet in the hall shone in her mind, vast and luxurious after the hospital. Doors she could shut! A toilet with a door! Chairs to sit in, a table of her own to eat on, a TV set that she could turn on and off and tune to whatever program she wanted to watch, her own bed with clean sheets and no stink of old piss. Her precious freedom and privacy!

Yes, she would rise in the morning when she wanted to instead of when the attendant came yelling. No more Thorazine and sleeping pills, the brief high and the endless sluggish depths. Nights of sleep with real dreams. She would go hungry for a week for the pleasure of eating a real orange, an avocado. All day long nobody would tell her what to do. Miraculously she would walk through the streets without an attendant. She would breathe the beautiful living filthy air. She would walk until she felt like sitting down.

Around her kitchen she would sing and dance, she would sing love songs to the cucarachas and the chinces, her chinces! Her life that had felt so threadbare now spread out like a full red velvet rose—the rose that Claud had once brought her, loving it for its silkiness, its fragrance, and not knowing it was dark red. Her ordinary penny-pinching life appeared to her full beyond the possibility of savoring every moment. A life crammed overflowing with aromas of coffee, of dope smoke in hallways, of refried cooking oil as she climbed the stairs of her tenement, of the fragrance of fresh-cut grass and new buds in Central Park. Sidewalk vendors. Cuchifritos. The spring rhythm of conga drums through the streets.

Waiting in the rickety chair for the dentist, her mouth filled with saliva and she glanced with envy at the coffee the attendant was sipping. White coffee, probably sweet too. To make conversation she asked, "What sign are you?"

The woman gave her a sideways glance. "Sagittarius."

She had no idea when that was. "I'm Aries."

"Your sign is cuckoo, girl." The attendant went back to her magazine, turning slightly away.

She would be out soon. Soon! Swallow all insults. Keep quiet. She would have better things than coffee from a coffee machine! She would make herself the pot of Dominican coffee she had started that night for Dolly. She had such a hunger for Mexican cooking! Puerto Rican food was different. She had learned to eat it, to like it. In fact, she had cooked salcocho, mondongo, asopão, and many plátanos dishes for Eddie, for Dolly too, whose mother, Carmel, was Puerto Rican. But even the staples were not the same, all those root vegetables—yuca, yaulin, taro—the salt codfish, bacalao, instead of the base of corn and beans. She had grown up on pintos and the Puerto Ricans ate more black beans. She had noticed a few Mexican restaurants around New York, but they were too expensive for her. Ridiculous to live in a place where the taste of your own soul food was priced beyond you. She got to eat Chinese oftener than Mexican.

To breathe the air of freedom would be enough. She had not handled the interview well with Ferguson. She would talk about getting a job. She could even try again. Trekking from office to office. Maybe she had given up too easily. Maybe she could get temporary office work. Maybe at least she could persuade the social worker that she would. They liked that, if you could persuade them you were going to get a job. She thought of Ferguson and shrugged. Chances were it would be a different one next time anyhow.

She hadn't typed in . . . four years? five years? Last time in, she had applied for a typing job, but they liked to use the younger women. Maybe they had a machine here she could practice on. She had to figure the angles. Best if she could manage to believe it herself, that she could get a job. Herself with a police record and a psychiatric record, a fat Chicana aged thirty-seven without a man, without her own child, without the right clothes, with her plastic pocketbook cracked on the side and held together with tape. The dental assistant pitter-pattered out to summon them, and the attendant hauled her up like a rag doll and marched her in for treatment.

Wednesday and Thursday went by like long, long freight trains and finally Friday came. On her ward two patients had weekend passes to go home. Three other women were being discharged. Their effects came up in bags and their relatives took them away. More women were brought up. Dolly did not come for her. Then the nurse, whistling a song with a Latin beat that had been on all the stations lately, even the white stations, stopped and spoke to her. "All right, Mrs. Ramos, get yourself together."

"I'm getting out! I knew it. I'm getting out, right?"

"You're going to the country. Trees and green grass, for a rest like you need."

"Don't hand me that!" She clutched herself. "You can't send me up. I'm only in for observation."

"Your family wants you to get well, just as the doctor does—"

"The doctor only spoke to me for five minutes!"

"You're a sick woman. Everybody wants you to get well again," the nurse said with that false sweetness. "Don't you want to get well?"

"Who's signing me in? Did my niece do this?"

"Your brother Lewis. So you won't hurt yourself or anyone else. You've been a bad girl again, Mrs. Ramos."

"Where are you sending me?"

"You just get your things together. You'll find out." The nurse strolled off whistling that catchy song by War that had been echoing in El Barrio for weeks.

The rain came down hard. The day was clammy and gusts of wind splashed the water in breaking waves against the closed sides of the ambulance-bus. She sat so that she could see out through the slit, wearing her own clothes that Dolly had brought her. Rain drummed on the metal roof, assaulting it. Under water. She was drowning.

Here she was with her life half spent, midway through her dark journey that had pushed her into the hands of the midwife in El Paso and carried her through the near West Side of Chicago, through the Bronx and the Lower East Side and El Barrio. The iron maiden was carrying her to Rockover again. Luis had signed her in. A bargain had been struck. Some truce had been negotiated between the two men over the bodies of their women. Luis, who never admitted his oldest daughter was a whore, but made her feel like one whenever he got her in his house. The iron maiden jounced roughly on, battering her. Halfway through the hard years allotted women she found herself stymied, trapped, drugged with the Thorazine that sapped her will and dulled her brain and drained her body of energy.

She had lost some weight and the old yellow dress hung loosely. Her lips and her nails were split from the drug and lack of protein. The dentist had yanked a tooth and filled two others in quick repair. Her rib ached. The tape was tight around her like a corset under the loose dress. Into the unnatural darkness of the April storm she was carried blind in the belly of the iron beast.

The ambulance-bus slowed abruptly. Making sharp turns. Slowing down again. She pressed her eye to the slit and stared at the budding trees, the hedges. At length she saw through the blowing veil of the rain the walls she knew too well, that place of punishment, of sorrow, of the slow or fast murder of the self called Rockover State.

Perhaps she deserved punishment for the craziness none had guessed, the questions no one had asked, the story no one had pried from her: that all of the month before she had been hallucinating with increasing sharpness a strange man. That she had dreamed and then waking-dreamed and finally seen on the streets that same smooth Indio face.

Then the gates swallowed the ambulance-bus and swallowed her as she left the world and entered the underland where all who were not desired, who caught like rough teeth in the cogwheels, who had no place or fit crosswise the one they were hammered into, were carted to repent of their contrariness or to pursue their mad vision down to the pit of terror. Into the asylum that offered none, the broken-springed bus roughly galloped. Over the old buildings the rain blew in long gray ropy strands cascading down the brick walls. As she was beckoned out with rough speed, she was surprised to see gulls wheeling above, far inland, as over other refuse grounds. Little was recycled here. She was human garbage carried to the dump.

Two

THE first time. Was there a once? The dreams surely began with an original; yet she had the sense, the first morning she awakened remembering, that there were more she had not remembered, a sensation of return, blurred but convincing. She lay on her back in the rutted center of the bed, the valley that made her doubly conscious of being alone. One of her braids had come unpinned and lay coiled across her throat like a warm black snake.

Usually a sensation of repetition upon waking was a waking to: again bills, again hunger, again pain, again loss, again trouble. Again no Claud, again no Angelina, again the rent due, again no job, no hope. But now she tasted in her morning mouth something of sweet. The wan light leaked through the window that gave on an air shaft between buildings. "No! No, mamacita, no hágalo!" Something fell hard upstairs. She shut her eyes.

Under the smooth surface of sleep what drifted? Face of a young man, hand outstretched. Pointing to something? Trying to take her hand? Young man of middling height with sleek black hair to his shoulders, an Indio cast to his face. More than her, even. Eyes close together, black and shaped like turtle beans. Long nose. Cheeks clean-shaven, skin smooth-looking as hers . . . had been. Never again. That smooth bronze skin with the touch of peach, the hint of gold: how beautiful her skin had been. Chicanos were more apt to call brown skin beautiful today than when she had that perfect skin. La gente de bronce. Depression rose like fog in her throat and she rolled over, began to cough. Coughing shook her hard. Riding on a back road in the cab of Tío Manuel's truck, with dust stretching an enormous plumy tail behind them for miles across the parched land. She groped for the squashed pack; still one, two cigarettes. Lit it, sucked the sweet smoke and coughed more and then, feet on the floor, stood. Her sight prickled out, then cleared. Cold floor. She fumbled into her shoes bowed out on the sides with age. She would love to have slippers, yes, silly fluffy slippers. Then she saw tiny baby slippers pink on Angie's feet. Present from Luis, who called himself Lewis. Prick! My brother the Anglo. Angelina seven years, four months, twenty-two days . . . eight hours. She sucked smoke hard, burst into coughing and padded into the kitchen, to face the day already bleeding at the edges. Straighten, clean, tidy, make perfect the rotten surfaces. Her welfare worker, Mrs. Polcari, came today.

She had a breakfast of coffee light and sweet with a scrap of stale bread dunked in it, the heel of the last bread in the house. Then carefully she figured her budget, refigured after every trip to the superette brought higher prices. She was still hungry but she played her stomach an old trick and drank two cups of hot water, washing out the last good taste of her coffee cup with it. Then she cleaned her two tiny rooms slowly and thoroughly. Made the bed as smooth as it would go, even picked out of the pretty wine bottle with dried grasses and flowers in it, a few whose stems had broken. At the picnic whose souvenirs they were, Nita, just beginning to walk, had fallen asleep exhausted in Connie's arms. She had sat on the blanket burning, transfigured with holding that small sweet-breathing flush-faced morsel. An orange and black butterfly had lighted on her arm and she had remained so quiet hunched around Nita that for several moments the butterfly stood flexing its wings, opening and shutting those bright doors.

At eleven the knock. Mrs. Polcari was slim, with short brown hair smooth as a polished wooden bowl to her cheeks. Today she wore silver earrings with little green stones that might be jade. Large hazel eyes with long sweeping lashes looked out surprised from gold wire-rimmed glasses. She had once asked Mrs. Polcari why she didn't wear contact lenses and been rewarded with a cold stare. But such pretty eyes. If you had the money, a young girl like her, why not? Her large ripe mouth opened to a glitter of good regular white teeth when she, very occasionally, smiled. Girlish, modish, like one of those college girls she used to see when she had worked for Professor Silvester. Mrs. Polcari smelled of Arpege.

Today Mrs. Polcari was pushing a training program that sounded like someone's bright idea for producing real cheap domestic labor without importing women from Haiti. "Ah, I don't know," she said to Mrs. Polcari. "When you been out of a job so long, who'll take you back?" Cleaning some white woman's kitchen was about the last item on her list of what she'd do to survive.

"You're too . . . negative, Mrs. Ramos. Look at me. I went back to work after my children started school. I didn't work all those years."

"How come you had children so young? You got married in high school?" How unusual for a white woman to have children before she was eighteen.

Mrs. Polcari made a face. "Don't butter me up, Mrs. Ramos. I didn't get married until I was twenty-six. My mother was sure I was going to die an old maid."

"How old are your kids, then, Mrs. Polcari?"

"The older boy is ten now, the younger just turned eight."

So she had to be at least thirty-six.

After Mrs. Polcari left she stared in the mirror over the sink, touching her cheeks. How did they stay so young? Did they take pills? Something kept them intact years longer, the women with clean hair smelling of Arpege. The women went on through college and got the clean jobs and married professional men and lived in houses filled with machines and lapped by grass. She had not looked that young since—since before Angelina was born.

Envy, sure, but the sense too of being cheated soured her, and the shame, the shame of being second-class goods. Wore out fast. Shoddy merchandise. "We wear out so early," she said to the mirror, not really sure who the "we" was. Her life was thin in meaningful "we's. Once she had heard a social worker talking about Puerto Ricans, or "them" as they were popularly called in that clinic (as were her people in similar clinics in Texas), saying that "they" got old fast and died young, so the student doing her field work assignment shouldn't be surprised by some of the diseases they had, such as TB. It reminded her of Luis talking about the tropical fish he kept in his living room, marriage after marriage: Oh, they die easily, those neon tetras, you just buy more when your tank runs out.

At least her dour pride kept her cleaning for Mrs. Polcari, who was not subject to the same physical laws, the same decay, the same grinding down under the scouring of time. Let Mrs. Polcari look down on her as a case with a bad history, a problem case; but no dirt would Mrs. Polcari find on the chair she set her little behind on and no dirt would she find on the table from which she would sometimes agree to drink a cup of instant coffee with no sugar.

After two days of scrubbing floors for the city (welfare work program), she woke very early with morning pain low in her back but found herself smiling from sleep. La madrugada—daybreak—a word that always left honey in her mouth. That taste of sweet. The face of the young Indio smiling, beckoning, curiously gentle. He lacked the macho presence of men in her own family, nor did he have Claud's massive strength, or Eddie's edgy combativeness. His hands as they clasped hers, however, were not soft. Shaking hands? Absurd. Warm, calloused, with a faint chemical odor.

"What should I call you?" the voice had asked. High-pitched, almost effeminate voice, but pleasant and without any trace of accent.

"Connie," she had said. "Call me Connie."

"My name is Luciente."

Strange that she had dreamed in English. Me llamo luciente: shining, brilliant, full of light. Strange that with someone obviously Mexican-American she had not said Consuelo. Me llamo Consuelo.

"Come," he had urged, and she remembered then the touch of that warm, gentle, calloused hand on her bare arm. Trying to draw her along.

Mostly she dreamed in English but even yet she had an occasional dream in Spanish. Years ago she had tried to figure out the kinds of dreams she had in each language, during her precious nearly two years at the community college when she had taken a psychology course. She should not have drawn back timidly from the young man with his high, pleasant voice and his workman's hands. She should have sidled up to him and rubbed her fat breasts against his chest. Even in sleep, she got nothing. She rubbed her arm idly where his warm hand had touched her. Coaxing. She had taken to dreaming about young boys. Maybe as she got older the boys of her dreaming soul would grow younger and more beardless, slender as matches.

She rolled over, began to cough, to choke on phlegm. Cursing, she spat into a square of toilet paper and reached for the crumpled pack on the chair. Then she froze. Her fingers. That scent. She smelled her arm. Yes, her arm gave off that chemical on Luciente's fingers. The hair rose on her nape.

Idiot! They'd soon be locking her up again. So she'd got her arm in something, probably cleaning that office, and dreamed about it, like making the ringing of an alarm into a bell tolling. The phlegm she coughed up was brown. A little blood from her throat; that's what she ought to be worrying about. She was too nervous to stop smoking, even though she knew it was hurting her. Oh, well, a taxi would run her down before she could die of cancer. A mugger would bash her head in. She would get cancer from eating garbage on the little money from welfare.

Her neighbor Mrs. Silva knocked on her door shortly after she came back from shopping, from buying two rolls of toilet paper, bread, bananas, spaghetti, eggs. She wanted hamburger but she hadn't the money for meat. Her niece Dolores, called Dolly, was on Mrs. Silva's phone: Luis's oldest, by his first marriage. Luis had got married a lot and by every wife he had kids. Her favorite was Dolly, who was twenty-two, plump and sweet as a candied yam. When Dolly had to get hold of her, she called Mrs. Silva.

Dolly asked her to come down to Rivington Street and she grabbed her old green coat and her battered plastic purse and headed for the subway. On the express down to Brooklyn Bridge, she had a little piece of luck. As she was getting into the car she saw a ballpoint lying at the foot of a seat, and when she tried it, it worked. It had the name of a midtown stationer on it and wrote with blue ink. She had not had a pen that worked in months. She had to write her letters in pencil. Now she would write in ink, the way it should be. Tonight with her new pen she would write to both her sisters. She tucked it carefully in her purse before she changed to the QJ train, checking that the tape was still making a repair so the pen would not slip out. She also picked up a *Daily News* that a man had left in his seat.

At Essex and Delancey she headed north to Rivington, aware with a heavy lopsided sense of Norfolk a block over, where she had lived that year with Angelina in one room, that bad year after Claud had been sent to prison. That room like a box of pain. Dolly had found it for her after she had been kicked out of the apartment she had shared with Claud, three big rooms with their own bathroom just two blocks from Mount Morris Park. Dolly had lived then with her husband on Rivington, where she lived now with her daughter Nita, and the occasional presence of her rotten pimp, Geraldo. There was the bodega where Connie used to try to get credit till her check came, there was the liquor store she had known too well, with its racks and racks of cheap sweet wine.

It was steamy hot in Dolly's apartment, it always was. Nita was eating in a highchair getting to be too small for her, finishing coconut instant pudding and putting most of it into her mouth by now.

"Ahora comes como una santa!" Connie hovered over her grandniece. "She eats real neat now. She's such a good girl. Give me a smile, Nita? Hazme los ojitos! Yes? Qué preciosa!"

Dolly's face was swollen with tears and she rolled up the ruffled sleeve of her blouse to show a bruise.

"Some john did this to you?"

"Geraldo did it!"

"Why do you put up with him? He's bad to the core."

Dolly sighed and rolled a joint in the licorice-flavored paper she liked. "You know how when I got back from San Juan you told me I was carrying?"

Connie nodded, accepting the joint. As she let the smoke seep out she said, "You knew it already. You wanted a baby real bad."

"I still do! I went, I got one of those tests? I haven't had my time since then."

"What did the test say?"

Dolly patted her belly. "I told Geraldo yesterday. He starts yelling at me, that it's by some john. He starts hitting on me!"

"He makes me so sick. He makes you go with men and then he puts you down for it. It's his kid. You came back from Puerto Rico with that baby." She had known as soon as she saw Dolly.

Dolly drew herself up. "The johns are a business thing. Don't put it down, I make good money. I don't bring the johns here—I do them in hotels or at Geraldo's. Listen, every woman sells it. Jackie O. sells it. So?"

"So how do you like it with them?"

"It's a job." Dolly sucked in the smoke, glowering. The minutes thickened between them. Finally she sniffled. "You hate yourself, you hate the trick. I never met one woman yet who didn't hate every stupid trick."

"Leave him, carita, leave him. Never mind him. He's not worth your little fingernail."

"He's smart, Connie, his mind works like that." She snapped her fingers. "He has style. The other whores all stand on their heads to catch his eye when he comes around. . . . I thought, why not have a baby with him? Then I can quit. It'll be like it was before, only better. A man respects you more if you have his baby. Why not?"

"So you didn't take your pills in Puerto Rico?"

"I left them here. I didn't even put them in my purse. I thought too it might be lucky, a baby made on the island. I want to have this baby, Connie!"

"Why not? One child is lonely. Why not have another? You're a good mother. You quit this whoring and have the baby."

"He won't let me! He says I got to have an abortion!"

"No." Connie banged her fist on the table. A strange gesture for her. Dolly stared. "You have it! Tell him to o.d. and sell his body to the city for rat bait. You come live with me. I'll help you with the children. I'd love that, you know it's the truth—"

The phone rang. It was a john. Dolly ran off to the bathroom to fix her face and get herself together. Connie kissed her, fussed over Nita for a couple of minutes, and then reluctantly picked her way down the stairwell. In the street a damp, jagged wind off the East River scraped her face. She pulled her old green coat closer. The lining was gone. She felt high and loose with the grass, too stoned to endure the subway just yet. She decided to walk all the way over to the Spring Street stop on the IRT and take the local uptown, even though it was ten blocks of walking.

In a playground on Elizabeth, some little girls were playing red light, green light. She hunched against the wind, not deciding to walk closer, to stop and stare, but finding herself pressed suddenly into the fence. Brown-skinned mostly, about the right age. Angie would be one of the lighter, one of the shorter girls. Eddie, her father, had been light and short. She could be that lean quick one with the black hair and creamy skin and big love-me grin. Getting caught and making a big show of kicking herself. Yes, the girl who kicks herself would be mine!

Two men wheeling a cart on the sidewalk looked at her, and one spoke laughing to the other. Tears were rolling down her face. Rotten dope making her sentimental. Crazy Connie. She started to walk while the street bellied out before her. With the sleeve of her coat she tried to rub her face. The tears ran from her sore eyes, faucets that would not be shut off. Warm and wet over her cheeks. She turned onto Prince and sat down in a doorway, on a cement step recessed into the entrance to a loft building, the door big as a barn door behind. She spread the newspaper for her butt. Nobody around. She blew her nose hard in a wad of toilet paper. Anybody would think she had loved her daughter.

A shadow across her. She began to get up but that hand was extended again. "What's wrong? You're weeping. Connie, did I frighten you?"

Shorter than in her dream, just a few inches taller than she would be, standing, he bent toward her, moon face, black turtle bean eyes, that gentle smile.

"I'm going crazy! But it could be the dope. Really powerful—"

"I'm *here*. I've been trying to reach you. But you get frightened, Connie." Luciente grinned. Really, he was girlish. Mariquita?

"What do you want from me?" Childhood scary tales of brujos, spells, demons. A lot of garbage, but how could this boy creep into her dreams?

"Just to talk. For you to relax and talk with me."

"Ha! Nobody ever wants to talk to me. Not even my caseworker, Mrs. Polcari. I depress her." Connie rose stiffly, brushing off the seat of her old coat, and folding her paper, she slipped past him. Her arm grazed his.

He was real enough, his arm muscular through the leather jacket. Her belly hardened with fear. El Muro and the way he would wait for her. Then she had been young and succulent as a roasting chicken. Now she was what Geraldo always called her, a bag—a bag full of pain and trouble. She wanted a cigarette bad but she was scared to open her purse in front of him; so easy for him to snatch. She had the plastic pocketbook tucked along with the newspaper between her elbow and her body on the side away from him as he walked beside her with a casual springy step. No, he didn't walk in a swishy manner. He had a surefooted catlike grace. He moved with grace but also with authority. In her purse were seventeen dollars some pennies and two subway tokens, also her welfare ID and the keys to her apartment. Where would she replace the seventeen dollars? He could steal her little TV set to pawn. She had two weeks to wait till her next check, if she got it on time.

He wasn't dressed like a bum. Although nothing was new or flashy, his clothing was substantial and well made. Big heavy boots like the kids wore, black pants cut something like jeans, a red shirt she could glimpse at the throat, a worn but handsome leather jacket with no insignia of gang or social club but instead a pattern in beads and shells in the sleeves. He was without gloves and his hands she remembered. She would have liked to take the hand toward her and lift it to her nostrils. The skin was stained but not with nicotine. What kind of work would stain hands purple? Like the dye used to stamp grades on meat.

She made her voice harsh. "How long you planning to follow me?"

"I'd rather talk to you at home, if you'll let me." Luciente recoiled as an ordinary truck roared by. He covered his nose.

"No. Why should I? Who are you?"

"You know my name, Connie. Luciente."

"Bright boy. What do you want with me?"

His eyes watering, he took a large bright intricately dyed handkerchief out of his pocket to dab at them. "You're an unusual person. Your mind is unusual. You're what we call a catcher, a receptive."

"You like old women?" She'd heard of that but never

really believed in it. She was scared but slightly, slightly intrigued.

"Old?" Luciente laughed. "Sure, only women over seventy. I'll have to wait on you. Tell me, am I so scary? I'm not a catcher myself; I'm what we call a sender." He kept staring past her at cars, at the buildings right and left, up and down like a jíboro just off the plane; like her own grandmother, who would pass into the street in downtown El Paso by crossing herself, refusing to look at the cars, and stepping straight off the curb as if plunging into deep water.

He's crazy, she thought. That's it. She quickened her steps toward the subway station.

"I'm running hard over too much, but where to begin so you'll comprend? So you'll relax and begin to intersee. A catcher is a person whose mind and nervous system are open, receptive, to an unusual extent. . . . It's a hard ride explaining." A jet passed over and he stopped to gape till a building blocked it from sight. "To explain anything exotic, you have to convey at once the thing and the vocabulary with which to talk about the thing. . . . Your vocabulary is remarkably weak in words for mental states, mental abilities, and mental acts—"

"I had two years of college! Just because I'm Chicana and on welfare, don't try to tell me what poor vocabulary I speak with. I bet I read more than you do!"

"You plural—excuse me. A weakness that remains in our language, though we've reformed pronouns. By your language I mean that of your time, your culture. No personal slinging meant. Believe me, Connie, I have respect for you. We've been trying to get through for three months before I chanced on your mind. You're an extraordinary top catcher. In our culture you would be much admired, which I take it isn't true in this one?"

"Your culture! What are you into anyway—a real La Raza trip? The Azteca stuff, all that?"

"Now I lack vocabulary." Luciente reached for her arm, but she dodged. "We must work to commune, because we have such different frames of redding. But that we *see* each other, that feathers me fasure!" The two cabs met at an intersection and both slammed their brakes. Luciente started muttering.

"So where are you from? The high Andes?"

Luciente grimaced. "In space not that far. Buzzard's Bay."

Every time they came to a street, Luciente acted barely in control. He must have escaped from Bellevue. Her luck. He kept looking up and sideways and then trying not to. They were almost to Sixth Avenue when he said, "Look. I have to leave. This place unnerves me. The air is filthy. The noise shakes me to the bone. I admire your composure. Think about me when you're alone, would you?"

"Why should I? You're crazy as a loon!"

Luciente beamed, capturing her hand in his dry, warm grip. "Ever see a loon, Connie? It's the sound they make that's crazy. They're plain but graceful birds that glide with only the head full out of the water. Like turtles, they swim low. Maybe I can show you loons when they migrate through. . . . Don't fear me. I sense you have enemies fasure, but I'm not one. . . . I need your help badly, but I mean you no harm." And with that Luciente abruptly was not there.

Not till she was standing in the subway, wedged in, did she cautiously raise to her nose the hand he had seized. Yes, that chemical scent. She was afraid.

She stood swaying between people to her right, her left, her back, clutching her purse and *Daily News* against her breasts with one hand while the other just reached the strap above. He was right about the whatever he called it—receptive part. Queasy things happened in her. She never talked about those happenings much—a little to Dolly, who consulted palm readers and bought herbs from the botánica in spite of speaking Spanish almost as badly as her father, Loois, who prided himself on having forgotten. Sometimes Connie knew at once things about others she should not know. She had known Luis was going to leave one of his wives before he knew he had decided. Her husband Eddie had called her a witch more than once—for instance, when he had been with another woman and came home with that presence and his pride and guilt flickering sulfurlike around him in small yellow flames.

"Who tells you this garbage? Those gossiping women! You do nothing all day but listen to lies!'

"You tell me! You tell me yourself when you walk in!"

Wise she wasn't. Never could predict, not for herself,

not for others. She had tried to tell fortunes and always guessed wrong and knew in her heart she was just guessing. The other event was not something she tried to do any more than seeing that there was a rat scuttling away in the hall. The information entered her as a sound entered her ears. Often when Eddie was about to strike her, she knew it and cowered before he drew back his hand for a blow. If this was a gift, she could not see what good it had ever done her. When Eddie was going to hit her, he hit her anyhow. Maybe she had a moment to raise an arm to protect her face, but if he knocked her down it hurt as much. Her bruises were as sore and shameful. Her tears were as bitter.

Her knowing that he had been with another woman did not make Eddie love her, did not give her flesh back that spicy tang it had held for him briefly, did not make him want to carry her off to bed. It only meant that she was deprived of the comfort she might have felt when from time to time he was sweet to her for the sake of getting some small thing he wanted. To read his contempt for her had turned love acid in her veins. It had made their marriage last a little less long than it would have.

She could have used some of her mother's resignation. When she fought her hard and sour destiny, she seemed only to end up worse beaten, worse humiliated, more quickly alone—after Eddie had walked out, alone with her daughter Angelina and no man, no job, no money, pregnant with the baby she must abort. She was late for an abortion, past the third month, and it had gone hard with her. When the doctor told her she had been carrying a boy, she had felt a bitter triumph. In fact, she had gone to the bar where Eddie hung out, marched in and told him. He had for one last time beaten her.

A catcher, that's what the cholo called her. The contemptuous word grated on her, leaving in her mind a trail of sore pride like a snail's slimy track. Like black people calling each other nigger. She was angry at Luciente's airs, his beautiful accent in that high-pitched voice. "By your language, I mean that of your time, your culture. . . ." What scheme was he working on? What could he hope to get out of her? If he wanted her welfare check, that was a matter of a blow on the head. She was scared. He had wiped Dolly from her mind, leaving her almost envious of Dolly's sorrow instead of this mystery that must cover some common evil like a cockroach under a plate.

Receptive. Like passive. The Mexican woman Consuelo the meek, dressed in black with her eyes downcast, never speaking unless addressed. Her mother kneeling to the black virgin. Not of course that her mother, Mariana, had lived her life as a peasant. Mariana had been uprooted from a village near Namiquipa, Los Calcinados, and migrated with her family to Texas to work in the fields. In El Paso Mariana met Connie's father, Jesús, and bore the first three children who lived, Luis, the oldest and most important son, then Connie, then her brother Joe, her favorite, who had died just out of prison in California, closest to her in age and temperament. And in defeat.

When Connie was seven, they moved to Chicago, where Teresa and Inez came and the last male baby, stillborn. That baby had almost carried Mariana with him, and never had she been well again. They took her womb in the hospital. Afterward that was a curse Jesús threw in her face: no longer a woman. An empty shell.

Wearily she hauled herself up the steps at 110th and Lexington. PASAJES SEGUROS, the awning flapped. That was a dream. She looked down at herself in a battered green coat. She too, she was sprayed. They had taken out her womb at Metropolitan when she had come in bleeding after that abortion and the beating from Eddie. Unnecessarily they had done a complete hysterectomy because the residents wanted practice. She need never again fear a swollen belly; and never again hope for a child. Useless rage began to sleet through her, and she turned her face blindly toward a pleasant smell. Cuchifritos, jugos tropicales, frituras. She crossed Lexington by the CHECKS CASHED, FOOD STAMPS, UTILITY BILLS, where she brought her welfare checks. Hell Gate P.O.

Her knees felt rubbery, her back ached low down. Wind off the East River chafed her face. The dark railroad like the walls of an ancient city, the cars going under in tunnels. Home was at least a refuge, as a mouse must feel about its hole. To crawl in and collapse. Yet she was not safe there from Luciente any more than she had been safe in her apartment in Chicago from El Muro, who had simply shaken down the janitor for the key. I have lived in three cities, she thought as she turned on to 111th Street with its three straight lines—and seen them all from the bottom. Kids played in the street outside—P.S. 101; mothers fetched their little ones from the day care center in the sawed-off-looking church across from her, Spanish Methodist. Drumming everywhere. It was spring, although she could hardly believe it, with the mutter of salsa music as loud as the roar of traffic, the growly pulse of the ghetto.

At fifteen she stood in the kitchen of her family's railroad flat on the near West Side of Chicago, braced against the sink in blue jeans and fluorescent pink sweater. She could remember herself at fifteen and it did not feel different, only louder, more definite. "I won't grow up like you Mamá! To suffer and serve. Never to live my own life! I won't!"

"You'll do what women do. You'll pay your debt to your family for your blood. May you love your children as much as I love mine."

"You don't love us girls the way you love the boys! It's everything for Luis and nothing for me, it's always been that way."

"Never raise your voice to me. I'll tell your father. You sound like the daughters of the gangsters here."

"I'm good in school. I'm going to college. You'll see!"

"The books made you sick! College? Not even Luis can go there."

"I can! I'm going to get a scholarship. I'm not going to lie down and be buried in the rut of family, family, family! I'm so sick of that word, Mamá! Nothing in life but having babies and cooking and keeping the house. Mamacita, believe me—oígame, Mamá—I love you! But I'm going to travel. I'm going to be someone!"

"There's nothing for a woman to see but troubles. I wish I had never left Los Calcinados." Mariana closed her eyes and Connie had thought she might burst into tears. But she only sighed. "I've seen hundreds and hundreds of miles of a strange country full of strange and violent people. I wish I had never seen the road out of the village where I was born."

From her mother she inherited that Mayan cast to her face, the small chin, the sensuous nose, the almond eyes. They had all traveled far, and all of it bottom class. She knew her mother's family came originally from Campeche, near Xbonil. Troubles had driven them north, and north again, and again north, generation after generation plodding northward into the cold, into bondage, the desmadrados: taken too early from the mother; or the mother cannot nourish. Her mother had died when Connie was twenty, the year of her first abortion. Year of blood. At fifteen, at seventeen, she had screamed at her mother as if the role of the Mexican woman who never sat down with her family, who ate afterward like a servant, were something her mother had invented. She had shrieked how much better she was going to live her life, until her father came in and gave her the force of his fists. Yes, like the teachers she admired in her high school, she was not going to marry until she was old, twenty-five even. Like Mrs. Polcari, she was going to have only two children and keep them clean as advertisements. Those beautiful rooms, those clean-looking men who wore suits, those pretty sanitary babies, not at all like Teresa and Inez when she had to change them and clean up their spilled food.

Yet she understood now, climbing her stoop, that she had wanted her mother's approval. She had wanted her mother's comfort. She had wanted Mariana to come with her in her pursuit of knowledge and some better way to live. She had never been mothered enough and she had grown up with a hunger for mothering. To be loved as Luis had been loved. Only the very youngest girl, Inez, had had that. After Mariana had been robbed of her womb, she had lavished affection on the youngest.

So who was the worst fool, then—herself at fifteen full of plans and fire, or the woman of thirty-seven who had given up making any plans? Despair had stained her with its somber wash and leached from her all plans and schoolbook ideals.

In her box she found a letter from Teresa, married with four kids in Chicago, several miles farther west than their childhood flat. Teresa lived near the old Midway airport in a little house on a street of identical boxes. That Connie should sneer was absurd! What did she live in but a stinking slum? Teresa wrote in her large handwriting with all letters of one size: "Little Joey is sick with a cold and sore throat again, the poor thing. It seems it is one thing after another. I hate to see him so sick. Laura had it too but not so bad, she is big for her age and strong. The dr. says he may have to have his tonsils out. I hope not, not only the expense but it costs so much and the pain it gives him. For kids to go in the hospital. I have been going to Mass whenever I can except lots of times I can't get away from the house because of children. I don't want to have to take Joey to the hospital and leave him there.

"Marilyn's birthday is April 28, I know you remember. What she likes best is dolls with real hair the kind you wash and set. . . ."

Connie put down the letter on her kitchen table. Now, what did Teresa think she could do? She couldn't come up with money for any kind of present. She hadn't had money for a birthday or Christmas present since she and Claud had been busted, almost four years. Teresa had married young, from high school, and never had she worked. Her man drove a bus. Connie wanted to remember her nieces and nephews, and when she had been working she used to send every one of them presents twice a year, to bring toys and pretty clothes to Luis's various families, all conveniently located in the Greater New York metropolitan area. Number one wife (Carmel, the Puerto Rican) was in the Bronx. Number two (Shirley, the Italian) was on Staten Island. Number three (Adele, the Wasp) was with Luis in Bound Brook, New Jersey. She scanned the rest of the letter for catastrophes and decided to read it carefully later on. She had an urge to go back out, tired as she was. If she lay down she would get more depressed. She turned on the kitchen light. Evening thickened in the noisy streets.

In the refrigerator she found pinto beans in chili sauce, good still. With reheated beans she would fry a couple of eggs. She was tired of eggs and yearned for meat. How she would like to sink her teeth in a pork chop. Her mouth watered in faint hope. She turned on the little black-and-white TV she was always hauling back and forth from bedroom to kitchen. The news came on. She listened with half an ear; she did not have it turned loud. The set was company, a human—or almost human—voice. She tended to leave it on even when she was cooking or reading. It was her family, she had once wryly told Mrs. Polcari, who had not understood.

She stood slowly stirring the beans and waiting for the oil in the black frypan to heat up so she could break the eggs. She was in no hurry. What would she hurry toward?

Below in the street evening hummed to the rhythm of high and low drums, a rising tide of dealing and hustling, the push of the young and not so young to score, to get laid. At a simmer, the slow bubbles rising through the thick air, sex and traffic quickened El Barrio. In thousands of meetings—accidental, accidental on purpose, clandestine, dating and courting—men were picking up women on corners, on stoops, in the family apartments, couples were going down the rotten stairs shoulder to shoulder, to restaurants and movies and bars and dancing. Women with no money were working magic in front of dim mirrors, frowning with concentration, as they waited for men to arrive. Couples climbed into cars and shot off into the night. Couples picked up barbecued ribs and chicharrones, couples carried packages of Chinese-Cuban takeout and beer upstairs to their rooms. Men met their pushers and their dealers, or missed them and turned to ash. On the roofs pigeons were released to fly, to circle together fluttering like clean handkerchiefs among the chimneys where kids turned on and shot up and packages and money were exchanged.

That electricity in the streets brushed static from her. She longed to be moving toward someone. She wanted to have someone to go to, someone to meet, someone to come to her; she wanted to be touched and held. So long! Maybe never again.

What did she live for? The beans were sticking to the bottom of the pot, so she turned the flame low and stirred. Protecting Dolly? Could she protect Dolly, really? A fantasy of someday recovering her daughter? Who would not know her. This is the woman the court saw fit to take you from, your evil and criminal and crazy mother. How Angelina had cried. So small, so thin, and so many tears. So many tears.

"I'm too proud to kill myself. Too proud to watch myself o.d. and die," she said out loud. She turned up Walter Cronkite and seated herself to eat supper with him. Not that he would willingly eat with her, but boxed in her set with his public face hanging out, he had no choice. "Have a bite of chili, Walter?" She held out a fork with bent tines. Ojalá! If only she had a glass of red wine. Even beer would taste good and blur the knife edges, but she had only supermarket-brand cola, and not much of that. At one time she had bought *The New York Times* every night, when she had been working as secretary—let us say, secretary-mistress—to Professor Silvester of CUNY, another short time, like her almost two years in the community college, when she had been happy. She had got the job shortly after she had arrived in New York from Chicago. She had adored being secretary—should we say, secretary-mistress-errand girl-laundress-maid-research assistant—to Professor Everett Silvester. It was civilized. It was, if she shut her eyes just right, almost where she wanted to be.

"In fact, you make me think of Professor Everett Silvester," she said to Eric Severeid, and shut the sound off. Eric made fish faces in the TV and she grinned, wiping up her eggs and the remains of the beans with a slice of bread. Eric had been calling down labor unions, about how they were greedy. Everett Silvester had been fond of calling down the world, one item at a time. A fight was creeping through her wall from the next apartment, a fight in Spanish about money. Even though an oil company ad featuring an oceanful of singing fish was on now, she turned the sound back up. Finally she spread out her *Daily News* and skimmed it.

GIRL SHOOTS M.D.
IN L.A. LOVE SPAT

She smiled, tucking her small chin into her palm. She saw herself marching into Everett's Riverside Drive apartment and pulling out of a ratty shopping bag a Saturday Night Special. Mamá, how scared he would be; he would shit in his pants with terror. Would the newspapermen ask her to sit on a table showing her legs? It would be sordid but not unsatisfying, to pump at leisure and with careful and by no means wasteful aim several bullets into Professor Everett Silvester of the Romance Languages Department of CUNY, who liked to have a Spanish-speaking secretary, that is, a new one every year—dismissed when he went away for summer vacation. He called them all Chiquita, like bananas. So many years had run over her since then, he might not recognize her, he might confuse her with some other year's hot Latin secretary. The anger of the weak never goes away, Professor, it just gets a little moldy. It molds like a beautiful blue cheese in the dark, growing stronger and more interesting. The poor and the weak die with all their anger intact and probably those angers go on growing in the dark of the grave like the hair and the nails.

Ah, she should be thinking about Dolly. Dolly must leave Geraldo; and do what for money? To try to get money out of Luis was squeezing orange juice from a paper clip. . . . Dolly and she would live together. This place was small here for all of them, but it would get Dolly away from Geraldo and then they could look for another apartment together. Money. How to get money? She would wake again in a house with children. She would help Dolly through the pregnancy and cook and clean and rub her back. But would Dolly trust her? Leaving a child-abuser with your little ones—for shame! That's how Luis would make her feel. Carmel would flop back and forth, a little jealous, a little relieved. Carmel worked in a beauty parlor and always her hair was some new neon color and crimped into curls resembling the colored excelsior that used to come in Easter baskets, but she stood on her feet in a blast of hot air for ten hours a day, evenings too, just getting by. Little enough she got from Luis, because she had truly loved him but had not been able to get him to marry her legally. She had been his common-law wife, a consensual marriage the whole family had viewed as a perfectly good marriage until the lawyers of Shirley's family had proved that it never existed.

Her father, Jesús, had brought them Easter baskets one year when Connie was ten, little baskets from the dime store full of shredded cellophane and jelly beans and a chocolate bunny wrapped in foil. Tonight she could use something sweet, a chocolate bunny, even a purple jelly bean. She lit her after supper cigarette and flicked the channels all around. Nothing. Coughing from deep in her chest, she flipped the pages of the rumpled paper, looking for something to touch her mind.

She felt so lonely, so aware of being alone this Friday night with spring percolating through the tenements that when she had smoked the cigarette down to the filter she laid her face on her crooked elbow and shut her eyes. Smell of newsprint. He had asked her to think of him. Who knew what he wanted? To kill her and then it would be over and done. She shut her eyes and tried to think of nothing as debris of the day flickered past. Dolly's face frowning with worry. Then she saw that Indio face.

She did not care. Passive. Receptive. Here she was, abandoning herself to the stronger will of one more male. Letting herself be used, this time not even for something simple like sex or food or comfort but for something murky. It could only be bad. Yet she found herself concentrating on that face, waiting.

Maybe a life could become threadbare enough so that even disaster beckoned, just so it wore a different face than the usual grimace of trouble. "So come, Luciente. See, this time you can come without me being asleep or stoned." She was going crazy a new way. After all, she no longer had a baby daughter to punish for being hers.

Still, she jerked as a tentative hand tapped her shoulder. "Thank you, Connie. Much easier this way."

"Easier for what? To rob me? To kill me?" She sat up, shaking back her hair.

Luciente took the chair where Mrs. Polcari always sat. "Please, you embarrass me. I don't understand what I do that scares you. Tell me how to make you less . . . anxious."

"How? That's easy. What do you want? How do you get in here?"

"Obviously this laying a tablecloth over the compost is doing no good. Try to believe me—I say this, knowing you won't." Luciente laughed like a kid, showing strong ivory teeth. "I'm not from your time."

"Sure, you're from Mars and you came in a big green saucer. I read about it in the *Enquirer*."

"No, no! I'm from a village in Massachusetts—Mattapoisett. Only I live there in 2137."

Connie snorted. She tossed her hair back. "And you came flying to me in your time machine."

"I knew it was going to be like this!" Luciente shrugged, throwing up his hands. Tonight he was wearing a ring of blue stone he played with, turning it round and round as he spoke. "Actually . . . I'm not here."

"You're telling me?"

"We *are* in contact. You are not hallucinating. Whether anyone else can see me, I'm not sure. Frankly, this . . . contact is experimental. It's even, grasp, potentially dangerous—to us, I mean. Please don't get frightened again. You're happier being sarcastic."

"Let me get this straight. You're from the future, and naturally you picked me to visit rather than the President of the United States because I'm such an important and wonderful person."

"Fasure we wouldn't pick that person because of political reasons, as I understand the history of your time. Anyone in the hierarchy that made decisions? The Establishment, you called it? I know that, although I'm not a student of your history. Actually I'm a plant geneticist."

"Staining cells!" Connie pointed at his hands. In her freshman year she had had a biology course.

"I'm working on a strain of zucchini resistant to a mutant form of borer that can penetrate the fairly heavy stalks bred fifteen years ago."

"You're a college graduate?" Maybe he wouldn't beat or rob her. Just genteel slavery, like Professor Silvester.

"What's that?"

They stared at each other in mutual confusion. "Where you go to study. To get a degree," Connie snapped.

"A degree of heat? No . . . as a hierarchial society, you have degrees of rank? Like lords and counts?" Luciente looked miserable. "Study I understand. Myself, I studied with Rose of Ithaca!" He paused for her appreciation, then shrugged, a little crestfallen. "Of course the name means nothing to you."

"Okay, where do you go to study? A college. What do they give you if you happen to finish? A degree." Connie lit a cigarette.

Luciente leaped up and backed away. "I know what that is! I beg you, put it out. It's poisonous, don't you know that?"

Dumbfounded, she stared at him. He seemed terrified, as if she held a bomb, and indeed his hand was fumbling behind him at the locks on the door. Bemused, she stubbed the cigarette out, and after the smoke had cleared, cautiously he approached the table fanning wildly. "We study with any person who can teach us. We start out learning in our own village, of course. But after naming, we go wherever we must to learn, although only up to the number a teacher can handle. I waited two years for Rose to take me. Where you go depends on what you want to study. For instance, if I were drawn to ocean farming I'd have gone to Gardiners Island or Woods Hole. Although I live near the sea, I'm a land-plant person." Luciente clapped his hands to his cheeks. "Blathering about myself! I distract. There must be someplace to begin, if I could blunder on it. Well, at least you're no longer scared of me."

"So you want some cola? Or some coffee maybe? I have no wine. I have no beer. Unless soda scares you too?"

"Nothing, thank you. I ate before I came." Then he grinned sheepishly, touching her hand. "Besides, I confess I am afraid to eat here. It's not true, is it, the horror stories in our histories? That your food was full of poisonous chemicals, nitrites, hormone residues, DDT, hydrocarbons, sodium benzoate—that you ate food saturated with preservatives?"

"Some people—like me when I have any money—are good cooks! I could cook you a meal that would make you beg for seconds."

"I don't mean to hurt your feelings, Connie. I'm sure many of the tales we hear are gross exaggerations. Such as the idea that you—you plural—put your shit into the drinking water."

"I never heard such nonsense!" Connie flounced up and turned on the faucet of the sink. "That's drinking water." Then she hauled him up by the arm and marched him into the hall. He hung back skittishly until she said, "There's no one." Then he scuttled behind her nervously as she opened the door and showed him the toilet. She wished it were cleaner. She felt a little embarrassed. The other people who used it never cleaned it, and she cursed as she cleaned for all of them once a week. She flushed the toilet, pulling the chain for demonstration. "See? It goes down and is flushed away." Following him back to her apartment and routinely locking the door with the bolt, the Yale lock, the police lock with its metal rod that fit into the floor, she sucked her lip with satisfaction. For the first time she had scored a point. Then she realized her reaction made sense only if she was such a naïve idiot as to believe his fairy tale.

"So that's a water closet!" Luciente rubbed his scalp, setting his long thick black hair flying. "I can't believe it! So it's all true."

"What's true? The water comes out of the faucet in the sink. Then you use the toilet and the waste goes away."

"The garbage? Where does the food waste go?"

"I put it downstairs in cans. Believe me, some people

around here just throw it out the window. But why foul your own nest? I could see carrying it downtown and putting it by City Hall, to teach them to improve the garbage pickup. In white neighborhoods, you better believe it, they don't drown in their garbage. In the summer, how it stinks! There in the white apartments, they have a super who picks up the garbage in the hall. Or else they have a dumbwaiter—that's a little elevator—and the garbage goes down to the basement, where the super unloads it."

"The super is the name of the task? The person who does the job of returning the garbage to the earth?"

"He puts it in cans in the street and the city comes and takes it away."

"And what does the city do with it?"

"They burn it."

"It's all true!" Luciente shouted with amazement. More gently he added, "Sometimes I suspect our history is infected with propaganda. Many of my generation and even more of Jackrabbit's suspect the Age of Greed and Waste to be . . . crudely overdrawn. But to burn your compost! To pour your shit into the waters others downstream must drink! That fish must live in! Into rivers whose estuaries and marshes are links in the whole offshore food chain! Wait till I tell Bee and Jackrabbit! Nobody's going to believe this. It all goes to show you can be too smart to see the middle step and fall on your face leaping!"

"All right, smart ass. What do you do with garbage and shit? Send it to the moon?"

"We sent it to the earth. We compost everything compostible. We reuse everything else."

She frowned. Oh, he had to be putting her on. "Are you talking about . . . outhouses?"

"Out houses? Houses isolated from others?" Luciente made a despairing face. "We aren't supposed to bombard you with technology, but this is more than I redded." He raised his wristwatch to his ear to see if it was ticking, his lips moving.

"I mean how it used to be at my Tío Manuel's in Texas, for instance. They were too dirt poor to have inside plumbing. They had an outhouse. Flies crawling all over. You sit on a board with a hole in it and it goes down in the ground."

"That's the idea in very primitive—I mean rudimentary

form. Of course now—I mean in our time—it's composted centrally for groups of houses, and once it is safe, used in farming."

"You're trying to tell me you come from the future? Listen, in fifty years they'll take their food in pellets and nobody will shit at all!"

"That was tried out late in your century—petrochemical foods. Whopping disaster. Think how people in your time suffered from switching to an overrefined diet—cancer of the colon—"

Connie giggled. "You get so serious when you talk about food and shit, you remind me of Shirley—my brother Luis's second wife. She's an Adelle Davis nut."

Luciente shook his head sadly, his expressive dark eyes liquid with sorrow. "I was redded for this, but I can't find the door to what you're meaning half the time." He combed his fingers back through his thick hair. "I worked sixmonth with nine other strong senders. Fasure we're a mixed dish. A breeder of turkeys, an embryo tester, a shelf diver, a flight dealer, a ritual maker, a minder, a telemetrist, a shield grower and a student of blue whales. Youngest eighteen and oldest sixty-two. From James Bay to Poughkeepsie, our entire region. We're called the Manhattan Project—that's a joke based on a group—"

"I know what the Manhattan Project did," Connie said with cold dignity. "What are you fixing to blow up? Just everything?"

"It's a rib, you see, because that was a turning point when technology became itself a threat. . . . Cause we're a mobilizing of inknowing resources—mental? We're the first time travelers fasure—not that I'm actually traveling anyplace!"

"Like the bird that flies in narrowing circles until it goes up its own asshole."

"We have that rib too." Luciente beamed. "We must not chill each other. If you're patient in spite of my bumping along, we'll succeed in interseeing and comprending each other. Alia—that's the student of blue whales—told me that after months with them, Alia can only inknow the grossest emotions or messages. Those long epic operas that are their primary pastime are still garble to per. After a whole generation of communicating with the Yif, we are merely transmitting digital code. We think of the Yif as superrational, a world of mathematicians—and maybe that's how they vision us. . . . Anyhow, if you and I suck patience, can we fail to clear our contact? We have only been at this a few weeks, and look how strong and clear we are talking. If we both work at it, we should hear better and better!"

"Work at it!" Connie chuckled, remembering Professor Everett Silvester in bed, working at sex. Her body was a problem he was solving. He put everything in pass-fail terms. "You're crazy, you know that? If I'm not."

"Crazy? No, actually I've never been able to. Jackrabbit went mad at thirteen and again at fifteen—"

"Who's this Jackrabbit?"

"I am sweet friends with Jackrabbit. Also Bee. Both are my mems too—in my family? If we work at this, I hope you'll meet them soon. Even though you laugh at me for speaking of it so. My own work is velvet for me. And this too fascinates." Luciente took her hands and squeezed them.

"Second best to blue whales and the Yif—whatever they are!"

"Not to me, truly," Luciente assured her, nodding vigorously. "I see you as a being with many sores, wounds, undischarged anger but basically good and wide open to others."

"Ha! You know I'm a two-time loser?" Connie yanked her hands free.

"Encyclopedia: define two-time loser." This time she saw that what she had taken for a watch on Luciente's wrist was not only that, or not that at all. He was not lifting it to his ear to hear it tick but because it spoke almost inaudibly.

"What's that?"

"My kenner. Computer link? Actually it's a computer as well, my own memory annex. I don't quite follow what you mean, but I myself have done things I regret. Things that injured others. I have messed up experiments—"

"Messing up is something I'm an expert on!"

Someone banged on the door. Luciente sprang to his feet, glancing around.

"Who is it?" Connie yelled.

"It's me—Dolly! Let me in! Hurry!"

Luciente kissed her on the cheek before she could duck and ran long-legged into the bedroom, saying hastily over his slender shoulder, "Till when! Graze me when you're free."

She stood a moment collecting herself. Dolly was banging on the door and screaming. It was a funny time for her to arrive, on a Friday night, when she always had to be working. As Connie released the police lock, she felt the sensation of Luciente's presence evaporating. She shook her head like a dog coming out of the water. Once Eddie had remained stoned for twenty-four hours on some strongly righteous grass. . . .

Dolly rushed in past her, blood running from her bruised mouth.

Three

LOCKED into seclusion, Connie sat on the floor near the leaky radiator with her knees drawn up to her chest, slowly coming out of a huge dose of drugs. Weak through her whole useless watery body, she still felt nauseated, her head ached, her eyes and throat were sandpapery, her tongue felt swollen in her dry mouth, but at least she could think now. Her brain no longer felt crushed to a lump at the back of her skull and the slow cold weight of time had begun to slide forward.

Already her lips were split, her skin chapped from the tranquilizers, her bowels were stone, her hands shook. She no longer coughed, though. The tranks seemed to suppress the chronic cough that brought up bloody phlegm. Arriving had been so hard, so bleak. The first time here, she had been scared of the other patients—violent, crazy, out-of-control animals. She had learned. It was the staff she must watch out for. But the hopelessness of being stuck here again had boiled up in her two mornings before when the patients in her ward had been lined up for their dose of liquid Thorazine, and she had refused. Pills she could flush away, but the liquid there was no avoiding, and it killed her by inches. She had blindly fought till they had sunk a hypo in her and sent her crashing down.

Letting loose like that brought them down hard on her. She was still in seclusion, having been given four times the dose she had fought. Captivity stretched before her, a hall with no doors and no windows, yawning under dim bulbs. Surely she would die here. Her heart would beat more and more slowly and then stop, like a watch running down. At that thought the heart began to race in her chest. She stared at the room, empty except for the mattress and odd stains, names, dates, words scratched somehow into the wall with blood, fingernails, pencil stubs shit: how did she come to be in this desperate place?

Her head leaning on the wall she thought it was going to be worse this time—for last time she had judged herself sick, she had rolled in self-pity and self-hatred like a hot sulfur spring, scalding herself. All those experts lined up against her in a jury dressed in medical white and judicial black—social workers, caseworkers, child guidance counselors, psychiatrists, doctors, nurses, clinical psychologists, probation officers—all those cool knowing faces had caught her and bound her in their nets of jargon hung all with tiny barbed hooks that stuck in her flesh and leaked a slow weakening poison. She was marked with the bleeding stigmata of shame. She had wanted to cooperate, to grow well. Even when she felt so bad she lay in a corner and wept and wept, laid level by guilt, that too was part of being sick: it proved she was sick rather than evil. Say one hundred Our Fathers. Say you understand how sick you've been and you want to learn to cope. You want to stop acting out. Speak up in Tuesday group therapy (but not too much and never about staff or how lousy this place was) and volunteer to clean up after the other, the incontinent patients.

"As a mother, your actions are disgraceful and uncontrolled," the social worker menaced, at once angry and bored. Angelina was sitting in an office chair from which her little legs could not reach the floor and she was sucking a pencil from the social worker's desk. Connie wanted to take the pencil from her. Lead poisoning: never chew pencils! But she did not dare touch her daughter in front of the bureaucrat from Child Welfare. Angelina had been given a sucker earlier and now she obviously wanted another; a sucker was a big event to her. That afternoon she was to be taken to a children's detention center while Connie awaited "a determination of the case." Connie's case had been determined, all right. "Willful abuse for injuring the person or health of a minor child," they said, but they also said she was not responsible for her actions.

They kept saying what a pretty child Angelina was, and Connie guessed that partly they were expressing surprise that her child was so light. "It won't be hard to place her, even at four," she heard the social worker tell her probation officer. "She doesn't look—I mean she could be anything."

That was what white people noticed about her baby, but Angelina's features were obviously her own, the ample sensuous hook of Mayan nose, the small mouth, puckered now as she pouted, the delicate chin, the eyes of shiny black almonds. In fact, what Connie saw when she looked at her daughter was a small dose of herself. Herself cowering in a chair, whimpering. Herself trying to stick out that tiny chin and shouting with an enraged monkey scowl, *I will I will! I will too! I will too!* Herself starting all over again with no better odds on getting more or less than a series of kicks in the teeth.

After Claud had died of hepatitis in Clinton, she had mourned him in a haggard frenzy of alcohol and downers, diving for oblivion and hoping for death. She had sat for weeks in a chair, letting Angelina scream and weep herself to sleep in fear and hunger. Connie had torn at herself with her nails, with pills, with bottles, with lack of food and all poisons short of open suicide, until she had a nightmare and awakened shivering with sweat in late afternoon on the couch right under the window on Norfolk Street with the flashing blue light of a police car outside playing on the ceiling.

She dreamed that Claud was being born again: that her mourning hauled him out of the grave and drove his restless soul back into a baby's body. Even now from his junkie mama, Claud was being crushed into the world with a habit, and waiting for him was the pot balanced on the edge of the stove that would blind him and seal his face ever after from the light of the world. Reform schools, the courts, zip sixes for kids picked up on federal raps, those rotten sixty-day-to-six-year indeterminate sentences, all the institutions that would punish him for being black and blind and surviving. All the scorn and meat hooks of the world were waiting to carve off chunks of his sweet flesh. As Claud was crammed into the baby's writhing body, as he was forced into the small flesh and vast terror, he cursed her.

She wakened cold with sweat on the couch, her back

aching, and the first thing she heard was Angelina screaming. Angelina was standing about ten feet away in their one room, screaming and kicking the wall with anger, kicking the leg of the metal table. Connie dragged herself from the bed hung over and strung out, and it hit her that having a baby was a crime—that maybe those bastards who had spayed her for practice, for fun, had been right. That she had borne herself all over again, and it was a crime to be born poor as it was a crime to be born brown. She had caused a new woman to grow where she had grown, and that was a crime. Then she came staggering off the couch and saw that Angie, in kicking the table, in kicking the wall—every blow the blow of a hammer on her aching head—had kicked a hole in her lousy cheap shoes. Those were the only shoes Angie had, and where in hell was Connie going to get her another pair? Angie couldn't go out without shoes. There rose before Connie the long maze of conversations with her caseworker, of explanations, of pleas and forms in triplicate and quadruplicate, and trips down to the welfare office to wait all day first outside in the cold and then inside in line, forever and ever for a lousy cheap pair of shoes to replace the lousy cheap pair Angie had just destroyed.

"You fucking kid!" she screamed, and hit her. Hit too hard. Knocked her across the room into the door. Angie's arm struck the heavy metal bolt of the police lock, and her wrist broke. The act was past in a moment. The consequence would go on as long as she breathed.

As she slumped against the wall of the bleak seclusion cell, tears ran into her lap, soaking the yellow dress, faded from repeated laundering. Tears for Claud dead, for Angelina adopted into a suburban white family whose beautiful exotic daughter she would grow into. Remembering what?

Why had Dolly betrayed her? Well, why had she betrayed her own daughter? She had thrown Angelina away from the pain of losing Claud. She should have loved her better; but to love you must love yourself, she knew that now, especially to love a daughter you see as yourself reborn. She slumped against the wall clutching her knees and tried to concentrate on the pain of the old burn that had never quite healed, to blot out memory.

She felt then that sense of approach almost as if someone were standing behind her wanting to come through, that presence brushing her consciousness. The feeling was at once an irritant and a relief. She wiped her nose on her sleeve, lacking anything else, and made a grimace of disgust at the sloppiness. How she hated to be dirty. She felt ugly, bloated with the drugs, skin deadened and flaking, lips dry and split, hair lank and dirty and bleared with feverish sweat. Her throat was sore and the back of her neck ached all the time.

Vanity before a hallucination? If she could so clearly imagine him, why couldn't she imagine herself clean and beautiful? At least a proper hallucination would be some kind of company, so she let her eyes shut, leaned against the wall, and permitted the presence to fill her. For perhaps ten minutes she remained thus, head back and eyes tightly closed.

"Connie, at last! Fasure it's been three weeks!"

"This is the first time I've been by myself since the first night."

"Are we responsible for your being here?"

She did not immediately open her eyes. "No."

"Fasure? You're not just painting the bones?"

She briefly described the night of her commitment. When she opened her eyes she saw Luciente consulting the watch that whispered.

"It's running hard for me to comprend," Luciente said in his high excited voice. "Might as well be Yif. Your mem has a sweet friend who abuses per and who . . . sold your sister?"

"Her pimp, Geraldo. And she's my niece, not my sister. Geraldo is a pig! He didn't want her to have his baby."

Luciente looked deeply embarrassed. Passing his hand over his mouth, he shifted from haunch to haunch, squatting before her. "Uh, I know you people ate a great deal of meat. But was it common to feed upon person? Or is this slavery, I thought wiped out by your time?"

The urge to cry was still burning her eyes. "Sometimes we have nothing to feed on but our pain and each other. . . . What's that about meat?"

"How did this Geraldo sell per flesh then, and pigs too?"

"She hustles!" Seeing blank incomprehension, she snorted and said harshly, "Puta. Tart. Whore."

Luciente began fiddling with the wrist gadget again till she reached out to stop him. Small bones he had, little heavier than hers. "Who do you talk to with that?"

"My kenner? It ties into an encyclopedia—a knowledge computer. Also into transport and storage. Can serve as locator-speaker." Luciente's face changed suddenly and he smiled. "Oh. Had to do with sex. Prostitution? I've read of this and seen a drama too about person who sold per body to feed per family!"

"I suppose nobody in your place sells it, huh? Like they say about Red China."

"We don't buy or sell anything."

"But people do go to bed, I guess?" Connie sat up, holding herself across the breasts as she shook back her lank hair. "I suppose since you're alive and got born, they must still do that little thing, when they aren't too busy with their computers?"

"Two statements don't follow." Luciente gave her a broad smile. "Fasure we couple. Not for money, not for a living. For love, for pleasure, for relief, out of habit, out of curiosity and lust. Like you, no?"

Like sunshine in her cell, he looked so human squatting there she heard herself ask half coyly, "Do you like women?"

"*All* women?" Luciente looked at her with that slight scowl of confusion. "Oh, for coupling? In truth, the most intense mating of my life was a woman named Diana—the fire that annealed me, as Jackrabbit says in a poem. But it was a binding, you know, we obsessed. Not good for growing. We clipped each other. But I love Diana still and sometimes we come together. . . . Mostly I've liked males."

"I thought so." Why should that make her feel gloomy? He had shown no signs of sexual interest, except for all that patting and hand holding. But shouldn't a figment of her mind at least satisfy her? Perhaps being crazy was always built on self-hatred and she would, of course, see a queer.

"You're lonely here, and I just let you down. Truly, I'm not rigid and I like you." Luciente took her hands between his warm, dry, calloused palms. "What is this place? You seem to be locked in. I've seen holies about your prisons and concentration camps. Is this such a place?"

"No. I'd rather be in prison. Unless you're on an indeterminate, at least you know when you're getting out. They can keep me here till I go out with my feet in the air. It's a loony bin—a mental hospital."

Luciente consulted his wrist. "Oh, a madhouse! We have them." He looked around. "But it seems . . . ugly. Bottoming."

"Are yours so fancy?"

"Open to the air and pleasant, fasure. I never stayed in one myself—"

"Big deal!" She pulled her hands free.

"But Jackrabbit has—just before we fixed each other, and we've been sweet friends three years. Bee and I have been lovers twelve now, isn't that strange? Not to stale in so long. And Diana goes mad every couple of years. Has visions. Per earth quakes. Goes down. Emerges and sets to work again with harnessed passion. . . . But I have to say this—in truth you don't seem mad to me. I know I've never gone down myself, I'm too . . . flatfooted . . . earthen somehow, so it's beyond my experience. Bee tells me that I'm the least receptive person in our base, and person has to scream in my ear to get through. . . . I don't mean to pry or make accusations, but are you truly mad?"

"Here they say if you think you aren't sick, it's a sign of sickness."

"You're sick?"

"Sick. Mad."

"We do not use these words to mean the same thing." Luciente tilted his head to one side. "Could it be you're bluffing? Truly, I have never gone down, but I have been close to Diana when person was far inward, and . . . you seem too coherent. Perhaps you're tired, unable to cope for a while? Sometimes, among us, this happens."

"I don't think there's a thing wrong with me, aside from seeing you—that's the best sign of being crazy I can think of."

"No, I'm in touch with you, really." Luciente scowled at the room. "This place bottoms me. Would you like to take a walk?"

"The door's locked. Or do you have a key?"

"Not a walk here or now. I wish to invite you home with me for a short visit. Say an hour?"

"You mean the way you come here?"

"Wouldn't you like to see my village?"

"I'd like seeing anything but these four filthy walls, believe me. But could I get back?" She hooted with laughter. "Why should I care? Better if I get stuck anyplace instead of rotting here!"

"Sadly, you can't get stuck in my time. A lapse of attent would probably break our contact." Luciente rose gracefully and extended his hand for her to grasp. "As I've remarked, the appearance is not a physical presence, but is . . . as if it were. Now we'll see if this trick works. To confess, I haven't a wispy guess if I can really pull you into my time. But the worst that can happen is that we open our eyes and are still in this drab room. Only fit for a storeroom for machinery!"

"You ought to try it twenty-four hours a day. It breaks you, finally."

"Then why did you come here? It seems inadequate."

"I didn't walk, you can count on that. I was dragged screaming. My brother Luis committed me."

"Our madhouses are places where people retreat when they want to go down into themselves—to collapse, carry on, see visions, hear voices of prophecy, bang on the walls, relive infancy—getting in touch with the buried self and the inner mind. We all lose parts of ourselves. We all make choices that go bad. . . . How can another person decide that it is time for me to disintegrate, to reintegrate myself?"

"Here you get put in if your family doesn't want you around or other people don't, and that's about the long and short of it." She finally stuck out her hand and let Luciente pull her to her feet.

"The first time is supposed to be the hardest, but frankly, we're the first contacts to try. That's the theory anyway, for what it weighs. Here comes the practice. NINO."

"Nino? Niño?"

"NINO: Nonsense In, Nonsense Out—that's the motto on every kenner. It means your theory is no better than your practice, or your body than your nutrition. Your encyclopedia only produces the information or misinformation fed it. So on." Luciente gently drew her against him and held her in his arms so their foreheads touched. "You're supposed to be a top catcher and I'm supposed to be a superstrong sender. . . . As people say, with theory and a nail, you've got a nail."

Pressed reluctantly, nervously against Luciente, she felt the coarse fabric of his shirt and . . . breasts! She jumped back.

"You're a woman! No, one of those sex-change operations."

"If you hop around, we'll never get it right. . . . Of course I'm female." Luciente looked a little disgusted.

She stared at Luciente. Now she could begin to see him/her as a woman. Smooth hairless cheeks, shoulder-length thick black hair, and the same gentle Indian face. With a touch of sarcasm she said, "You're well muscled for a woman." In anger she turned on her heel and stalked a few paces away. A dyke, of course. That bar in Chicago where the Chicana dykes hung out shooting pool and cursing like men, passing comments on the women who walked by. Yet they had never given her that sense of menace a group of men would—after all, under the clothes they were only women too.

"I'm not unusually strong." Luciente's face was screwed up with confusion. She still held out her hands to draw Connie to her. "About middling. We do more physical work than most people did in your time, I believe. It's healthier, and of course you lugs were burning up all those fossil fuels. . . . You seem surprised that I am female?"

Feeling like a fool, Connie did not choose to reply. Instead she paced to the locked door with its peephole and then to the radiator. Luciente spoke, she moved with that air of brisk unselfconscious authority Connie associated with men. Luciente sat down, taking up more space than women ever did. She squatted, she sprawled, she strolled, never thinking about how her body was displayed. It was hard to pace with dignity in the tiny space between the stained mattress and the wall. Connie no longer felt in the least afraid of Luciente.

"Please, Connie." Luciente came over and cautiously put an arm around her shoulders. "I don't understand what's wrong. Let's give it a try. We didn't even carry out our experiment. Do you really want to stay here all day? It doesn't bottom you?"

"To the bone." She stood awkwardly and let Luciente pull her close and lean their foreheads together. Hardly ever did she embrace another woman along the full length of their bodies, and it was hard to ease her mind. She could feel Luciente concentrating, she could feel that cone of energy bearing down on her. It reminded her of the old intensity of a man wanting . . . something—her body, her time, her comfort—that bearing down that wanted to grab her and push her under. But she was weary and beaten and she let herself yield. What had she to lose?

Although she could sense in Luciente a bridled impatience, the woman held her gently. A harnessed energy to be doing drove this plant geneticist with breasts like a fertility goddess under the coarse fabric of a red work shirt. A woman who liked her: she felt that too. A rough ignorant goodwill caressed her.

Then she smelled salt in the air, a marsh tang. A breeze ruffled the loose rag of dress, chilling her calves. Under her feet she felt stone. A gull mewed, joined by another somewhere above her. Luciente relaxed her grip. "Home free. Will you stand there all day with your eyelids bolted down? Look!"

Rocket ships, skyscrapers into the stratosphere, an underground mole world miles deep, glass domes over everything? She was reluctant to see this world. Voices far, near, laughter, birds, a lot of birds, somewhere a dog barked. Was that—yes, a rooster crowing at midday. That pried her eyes open. A *rooster?* Fearfully she stared into Luciente's face, broken open in a grin of triumph. "Where are we?"

"You might try looking around! This is where I live." Luciente took her by the arm and swung around to her side. "This is our village. Roughly six hundred of us."

She looked slowly around. She saw . . . a river, little no account buildings, strange structures like long-legged birds with sails that turned in the wind, a few large terracotta and yellow buildings and one blue dome, irregular buildings, none bigger than a supermarket of her day, an ordinary supermarket in any shopping plaza. The bird objects were the tallest things around and they were scarcely higher than some of the pine trees she could see. A few lumpy free-form structures overrun with green vines. No skyscrapers, no spaceports, no traffic jam in the sky. "You sure we went in the right direction? Into the future?"

"This is my time, yes! Fasure, look how pretty it is!"

"You live in a village, you said. Way out in the sticks. Like if we went to a city, it'd be . . . more modern?"

"We don't have *big* cities—they didn't work. You seem disappointed, Connie?"

"It's not like I imagined." Most buildings were small

and randomly scattered among trees and shrubbery and gardens, put together of scavenged old wood, old bricks and stones and cement blocks. Many were wildly decorated and overgrown with vines. She saw bicycles and people on foot. Clothes were hanging on lines near a long building—shirts flapping on wash lines! In the distance beyond a blue dome cows were grazing, ordinary black and white and brown and white cows chewing ordinary grass past a stone fence. Intensive plots of vegetables began between the huts and stretched into the distance. On a raised bed nearby a dark-skinned old man was puttering around what looked like spinach plants.

"Got through, uh?" he said to Luciente.

Luciente asked, "Can you see the person from the past?"

"Sure. Had my vision readjusted last month."

"Zo!" Luciente turned, hopping with excitement. "Good we were cautious in your time. I may be visible there too—that could bring danger!"

"Why isn't it dangerous for me to be seen here?"

"Everybody knows why you're here."

"Everybody except me." The roofs of the huts—that's all she could call them—were strange. "What's on top? Some kind of skylights?"

"Rainwater-holding and solar energy. Our housing is above ground because of seepage—water table's close to the surface. We're almost wetland but not quite, so it's all right to build here. I'll show you other villages, different. . . . I guess, compared to your time, there's less to see and hear. That time I came down on the streets of Manhattan, I'd thought I'd go deaf! . . . In a way we could half envy you, such fat, wasteful, thing-filled times!"

"They aren't so fat for me."

"Are you what would be called poor?"

Connie bristled, but then shrugged. "I've been down and out for a while. A run of hard times."

Luciente put an arm around her waist and walked her gently along. A gaudy chicken strutted across the path, followed by another. The path was made of stone fitted against stone in a pattern of subdued natural color. Along it mustard-yellow flowers were in bloom. Low-growing tulips were scattered like bright stars on the ground.

She caught the whiff for a moment before she saw them. "Goats! Jesús y María, this place is like my Tío Manuel's in Texas. A bunch of wetback refugees! Goats, chickens running around, a lot of huts scavenged out of real houses and the white folks' garbage. All that lacks is a couple of old cars up on blocks in the yard! What happened—that big war with atomic bombs they were always predicting?"

"But we like it this way! Oh, Connie, we thought you'd like it too!" Luciente looked upset, her face puckered. "We'd change it if we didn't like it, how not? We're always changing things around. As they say, what isn't living dies. . . . I'm always quoting homilies. Jackrabbit says my words run out in poppers." Luciente saw her blank look. "The miniature packaged components of circuitry? Jackrabbit means all in a box." Luciente was still frowning with worry.

"So you have some machines? It isn't religious or anything?"

"Fasure we have machines." Luciente tapped her kenner. She seemed more confident in her native air. "When you see more, you'll like better." Her arm around Connie gave affectionate squeezes as they walked and with her free arm she pointed, she waved, she gestured and struck postures. She talked louder and faster. "We raise chickens, ducks, pheasants, partridges, turkeys, guinea hens, geese. Goats, cows, rabbits, turtles, pigs. We of Mattapoisett are famous for our turtles and our geese. But our major proteins are plant proteins. Every region tries to be ownfed."

"Own what?"

"Ownfed. Self-sufficient as possible in proteins." Luciente stopped short and clapped both hands firmly on Connie's shoulder. "I bump around at this, but I just thought of something important. You're right, Connie, we're peasants. We're all peasants."

"Forward, into the past? Okay, it's better to live in a green meadow than on 111th Street. But all that striving and struggling to end up in the same old bind. Stuck back home on the farm. Peons again! Back on the same old dungheap with ten chickens and a goat. That's where my grandparents scratched out a dirt-poor life! It depresses me."

"Connie, wait a little, trust a little. We have great belief in our ways. Let me show you. . . . *No!* Let our doing show itself. Let people open and unfold. . . . Think of it this way: there was much good in the life the ancestors led here on this continent before the white man came conquering. There was much brought that was useful. It has taken a long time to put the old good with the new good into a greater good. . . . You're freezing. Let's get you a jacket. Then you must come and meet my family at lunch."

"I'm not going to meet a bunch of strangers in this filthy bughouse dress. I'm not! Besides, I'm not hungry. Thorazine kills my appetite."

"We can work on that later. We may be able to teach you to control the effects of the drug. . . . But about the clothing—come, we'll get you some and a jacket. I'm sensitive as rock salt, as Bee and Jackrabbit both tell me. So come to my house a minute and we'll find something." Luciente guided her through a maze of paths and huts and small gardens where people who must be women because they carried babies on their backs were planting seeds. They hurried past a series of covered fish ponds and greenhouses, to a hut near the river where domestic and wild ducks mingled, feeding among the waterweeds. They had come nearer the hill of spidery objects, which had to be windmills turning. Again she remembered windmills on the dry plains, on ranches without electricity. The hut was built of old cement blocks croded in soft contours and overrun with a large climbing rose just opening red sprays of crinkled leaflets. "I bred that. Wait till you see it bloom! Called Diana. Big sturdy white with dark red markings and an intense musk fragrance, subzero hardy. It's popular up in Maine and New Hampshire cause it's so hardy for a climber. I bred back into Rugosa using Molly Maguire stock. . . . Oops! I barge on. Come!"

The door was unlocked and in fact had only a catch on the inside. Windows on two sides lit the room. The cherry and pine furniture was sturdy: a big desk and a big worktable and a big bed, over which a wooden coverlet was casually pulled, hanging down at a corner. The floor was wooden and on it two bright woven rugs lay with a pattern of faces peering like tropical fruit out of foliage. Drawings and kids' paintings were tacked up here and there, as were graphs and charts, stuck on the wall somehow. Obviously Luciente liked red and gold and rich brown.

"Three of you live here?"

"Three? No, this is my space."

"I thought you lived with two men. The Bee and Jackrabbit you're always talking about."

"We're sweet friends. Some of us use the term 'core' for those we're closest to. Others think that distinction is bad. We debate. Myself, I use core, cause I think it means something real. Bee, Jackrabbit, Otter are my core—"

"Another lover!"

"No, Otter's a hand friend, not a pillow friend. We've been close since we were sixteen. Politically we are very close. . . ."

"But if you live alone, who do they live with?"

Luciente looked mildly shocked. "We each have our own space! Only babies share space! I have indeed read that people used to live piled together." Luciente shuddered. "Connie, you have space of your own. How could one live otherwise? How meditate, think, compose songs, sleep, study?"

"Nobody lives with their family? So what about kids? Mothers and kids must live together."

"We live *among* our family. Today you'll meet everybody in my family and my core except Bee, who's on defense till next month. All my other mems are around, I think. . . ." Luciente slid aside a door and took out pants and a shirt. "If these don't suit, take what you like. I was told you have body taboos? I'll wait outside while you dress."

Alone, Connie got into the clothes quickly. Luciente was taller and a little broader in the shoulders, but Connie was broader in the hips and behind, so that at first she could not close the pants. Then she found an adjustment in the seams so that they could be tightened or loosened, lengthened or shortened. A woman would not outwear them if she gained or lost twenty pounds. Well, they'd invented one new thing in this Podunk future. After she put on the shirt, she looked around the room. By the desk a screen was set into the wall. A television? Curious, she pressed the On button.

"Good light, do you wish visual, communication, or transmission? You have forgotten to press your request button," a woman's voice said. When Connie went on staring at it, it eventually repeated itself exactly, and she realized it was recorded.

She pushed T for transmission, she hoped. The screen began flashing the names of articles or talks, obviously in plant genetics. As the screen flashed the meaningless titles, she read the other buttons. One said PREC, so she tried it. A description like a little book review came on and remained there for two minutes.

> ATTEMPTS TO INCREASE NUTRITIONAL CONTENT IN WINTER GRAIN (TRITICALE SIBERICA) SUITABLE SHORT SEASON NORTHERN CROPS MAINTAINING INSECT & SMUT RESISTANCE. PROMISING DIRECTION. FULL BREEDING INFO. JAMES BAY CREE, BLACK DUCK GROUP, 10 PP. 5 DC. 2 PH.

Feeling watched, she shut the set off guiltily and jumped back. Then she saw that a large, long-haired cat the color of a peach had got up from a window ledge—a shelf built on the inside for a row of plants and perhaps the cat itself to sun on. The cat strode toward her with a purposeful air, hopped on a chair, and faced her expectantly. "Mao? Mgnao?" The cat blinked, averted its gaze, then glanced back. It repeated the gesture several times, each time more slowly, with a pause in between when it kept its amber stare fixed on her face. She felt a little scared. Did it think she was some kind of big mouse? Did it expect to be fed? Finally with a snort the cat hopped off the chair and pointedly, she could not help feeling, turned its back and flounced off to the sunny window. But it kept its ears cocked toward her.

As she opened the door, she found Luciente squatting outside in the rough grass like a peon, watching a small dark blue butterfly. She looked as if she could squat there all day. Well, what did I expect from the future, Connie asked herself. Pink skies? Robots on the march? Transistorized people? I guess we blew ourselves up and now we're back to the dark ages to start it all over again. She stood a moment, weakened by a sadness she could not name. A better world for the children—that had always been the fantasy; that however bad things were, they might get better. But if Angelina had a child, and that child a child, this was the world they would finally be born into in five generations: how different was it really from rural Mexico with its dusty villages rubbing their behinds into the dust?

"It's a Spring Azure," Luciente said. "Ants milk them."

"Do you have any children?"

"Below the age of twelve, forty-nine in our village. We're maintaining a steady population."

"I mean you: have you had any children?"

"I myself? Yes, twice. Besides, I'm what they call a kidbinder, meaning I mother everybody's kids." Taking her arm, Luciente nudged her toward the blue dome she pointed out as a fooder. "Let's hurry. I put in a guest slip for you, in case we got through. I'm mother to Dawn. I was also mother to Neruda, who is waiting to study shelf farming. Person will start in the fall; I'm very excited. Course, I no longer mother Neruda, not since naming. No youth wants mothering." All this time Luciente was hustling her along the stone path toward the translucent blue dome.

Connie waited to get a word in. "So how old are your children?"

"Neruda is thirteen. Dawn is seven."

That put Luciente at least into her thirties. "Is your lover Bee their father? Or the other one?"

"Father?" Luciente raised her wrist, but Connie stopped her.

"Dad. Papa. You know. Male parent."

"Ah? No, not Bee or Jackrabbit. Comothers are seldom sweet friends if we can manage. So the child will not get caught in love misunderstandings."

"Comothers?"

"My coms"—she pronounced the *o* long—"with Dawn are Otter and Morningstar—you'll meet them right now."

The room they entered took up half the dome and was filled with big tables seating perhaps fifteen at each, mostly dressed in the ordinary work clothes that Luciente wore, the children in small versions. The pants, the shirts, the occasional overalls or tunics came in almost every color she could name, many faded with washing and age, although the fabrics seemed to hold up. Everybody looked to be talking at once, yet it wasn't noisy. The scene was livelier than institutional feeding usually made for. A child was climbing on a bench to tell a story, waving both arms. At the far end a man with a mustache was weeping openly into his soup and all about him people were patting his shoulders and making a big fuss. People were arguing heatedly, laughing and telling jokes, and a child was singing loudly at the table nearest the door. Really, this could be a dining room in a madhouse, the way people sat naked with their emotions pouring out, but there was a strong energy level here. The pulse of the room was positive but a little overwhelming. She felt buffeted. Why wasn't it noisier? Something absorbed the sound, muted the voices shouting and babbling, the scrapes of melody and laughter, the calls, the clatter of dishes and cutlery, the scraping of chairs on the floor—made of plain old-fashioned wood, as far as she could tell. Unless it was all some clever imitation? She could not believe how many things they seemed to make out of wood. Some panels in the wall-ceiling of the dome were transparent and some were translucent, although from the outside she had not seen any difference.

"No reason to look in. The fooder has to be well soundproofed, or on party nights, at festivals, nobody who didn't want to carry on would be able to sleep. The panes with the blue edge come out. We get the breeze from the river—when it gets too hot, we take the panels out." Luciente was heading for a table on the far side, where everyone except the littlest child stopped eating to watch them approach. "Some you can see through and some not, because some of us like to feel closed in while we eat and some—like me—want to see everything. The fooder is a home for all of us. A warm spot."

On the translucent panels designs had been painted or baked in—she could not tell—in a wild variety of styles and levels of competence, ranging from sophisticated abstracts, landscapes, and portraits to what must be children's drawings. "Where did the art come from?"

Luciente looked surprised. "The walls? Why, from us—or some of us. I don't fiddle with it. I'm one of the sixty percent who can't. We find all the arts fall out in a forty/sixty ratio in the population—doesn't seem to matter whether you're talking about dancing or composing or sculpting. Same curve. Me myself, I drum magnificently!"

Like a child! She could not imagine any woman of the age they must share saying in El Barrio or anyplace else she had lived, "Me myself, I drum magnificently!" Indeed, they were like children, all in unisex rompers, sitting at their long kindergarten tables eating big plates of food and making jokes. "I can see wanting to look at your own child's drawing. But wouldn't other people get tired of it?"

They had reached the table through a sea of spicy

odors that touched her stomach to life. Two places were vacant, set with handsome heavy pottery dishes in earth colors, glass tumblers on the heavy side, and cutlery of a smooth substance that was neither silver nor stainless steel and perhaps not even metal. Someone—slender, young—leaped up and hugged Luciente, held out his?/her? arms to her, checked the gesture, and smiled a brilliant welcome. "You got through! Wait till everybody hears about this!"

"Never mind. Did you save us lunch? I'm thinning by the second," Luciente said, hugging the youth back.

They were literally patted into their seats and she found herself cramped with nervousness. Touching and caressing, hugging and fingering, they handled each other constantly. In a way it reminded her again of her childhood, when every emotion seemed to find a physical outlet, when both love and punishment had been expressed directly on her skin.

Large platters of food passed from hand to hand: a cornbread of coarse-grained meal with a custard layer and a crusty, wheaty top; butter not in a bar but a mound, pale, sweet and creamy; honey in an open pitcher, dark with a heady flavor. The soup was thick with marrow beans, carrots, pale greens she could not identify, rich in the mouth with a touch of curry. In the salad were greens only and scallions and herbs, yet it was piquant, of many leaves blended with an oil tasting of nuts and a vinegar with a taste of . . . sage? Good food, good in the mouth and stomach. Pleasant food.

Luciente was saying everyone's name, leaving her battered. Nobody seemed to have more than one. "Don't you have last names?"

"When we die?" Barbarossa, a man with blue eyes and a red beard, raised his eyebrows at her. "We give back with the name we happen to have at that time."

"Surnames. Look, my name is Consuelo Ramos. Connie for short. Consuelo is my Christian name, my first name. Ramos is my last name. When I was born I was called Consuelo Camacho. Ramos is the name of my second husband: therefore I am Consuelo Camacho Ramos." She left out Álvarez, the name of her first husband, Martín, for simplicity.

They looked at each other, several adults and children

consulting the kenners on their wrists. Finally Luciente said, "We have no equivalent."

She felt blocked. "I suppose you have numbers. I guess you're only called by first names because your real name—your identification—is the number you get at birth."

"Why would we be numbered? We can tell each other apart." The tall intense young person was staring at her. Jackrabbit, Luciente had said: therefore male. He had a lot of very curly light brown hair and he wore the sleeves of his pale blue work shirt rolled up to expose several bracelets of hand-worked silver and turquoise on each wiry arm.

"But the government. How are you identified?"

"When I was born, I was named Peony by my mothers—"

"Peony sounds like a girl's name."

"I don't understand. It was the name chosen for me. When I came to naming, I took my own name. Never mind what that was. But when Luciente brought me down to earth after my highflying, I became Jackrabbit. You see. For my long legs and my big hunger and my big penis and my jumps through the grass of our common life. When Luciente and Bee have quite reformed me, I will change my name again, to Cat in the Sun." He produced on his thin face a perfect imitation of Luciente's orange cat squeezing its eyes shut. "But why have two names at one time? In our village we have only one Jackrabbit. When I visit someplace else, I'm Jackrabbit of Mattapoisett."

"You change your name any time you want to?"

"If you do it too often, nobody remembers your name," Barbarossa said solemnly in his schoolmaster's manner. "Sometimes youths do that the first years after naming."

The old brown-skinned . . . woman?—it confused Connie to be so unsure—introduced as Sojourner was giggling. "They're always trying out fancy new labels every week till no one can call them anything but Hey you or Friend. It slows down by and by."

"All right—you have those things on your wrist. Somewhere there's a big computer. How does it recognize you?"

"My own memory annex is in my kenner," Luciente said. "With transport of encyclopedia, you just call for what you want."

"But what about the police? What about the government? How do they keep track of you if you keep changing names?"

Again a great buzz of confusion and kenner checking passed around the table, with half of them turning to each other instead.

"This is complicated!" The old woman Sojourner shook her head. "Government I think I grasp. Luciente can show you government, but nobody's working there today."

"Maybe next time. I will try to study up on this, but it's very difficult," Luciente moaned.

"We should all study to help Luci," a child said.

"In the meantime, maybe you could ask something easier? You said something about the paintings?"

"It doesn't matter. I just thought it was funny you put up the kid's stuff. I mean everybody wants to look at their own kid's pictures, but nobody wants to look at anybody else's."

A slight blond man, Morningstar, peered into her face with puzzlement. "But they're all ours."

"We change the panels all the time," Jackrabbit said. "For instance, say I make one and later it stales on me. I make a new one. Or if everybody tires of one, we discuss and change. I did that whole big river namelon on the east, cause people wanted."

Luciente put down her fork. "What's wrong, Connie?"

"Connie's worn out," Jackrabbit said. "Strangers, every lug asking questions, holding the contact. You imagine there's no energy drain in catching."

Luciente put an arm around her. "You look gutted. Remember this food will not sustain."

"Why not?" She felt thick with fatigue and the room swayed. "I can taste it."

"As in dreams. You experience *through* me. . . . We better go back."

"Finish your lunch first." The voices seemed to drift around her and her eyelids drooped.

"This exhaustion worries me. I must teach you exercises—"

"Not here. Can't think. Too many people."

"Come! Give me your arm. We'll visit again. This is only a false spring, a January thaw of beginning. Back you go."

She felt leaden, her feet wading through loose sand.

As they shuffled out, Luciente looked worried. Standing at last on the stone walk, Connie mumbled, "Clothing. Must change."

"Your body is where it was, unchanged in dress. Understand, you are not really here. If I was knocked on the head and fell unconscious, say into full nevel, you'd be back in your time instantly. . . ." Luciente drew her into the firm embrace with their foreheads touching. She was too spent to do more than fall into Luciente's concentration as into a fast stream, the waters churning her under. She came to propped against the wall of the seclusion room. The tears had dried on the sleeve of her faded dress. She lay down at once on the bare, piss-stained mattress and fell asleep.

Four

SPRING in the violent ward was only more winter, except for a little teasing of the eyeballs when she stood at the high, heavily barred window. The radiators still pumped blasts of heat into the air that the smell of disinfectant and stale bodies turned into a foul broth. Pain and terror colored the air of Ward L-6. Pain silvered the air; when she was lurching into drugged sleep, pain sloshed over from the other beds. Yet spring finally came to Ward L one April Wednesday.

She was sitting near the station, hoping to do some little job to cadge cigarettes. As one of the functional patients, she got on with the attendants, except for an evil redheaded racist bitch on weekends, and with one of them, Ms. Fargo, she got on well. Ms. Fargo was close to her in color and size and age, but black and free—as free as any woman making that kind of wage with six kids at home could be called free.

"I like the Ms. thing," Fargo told her with a big gap-toothed grin. " 'Cause I got six kids and no man steady, and that puts me ass first to how it supposed to be. Ms. do me fine."

Fargo talked to her almost humanly. When Fargo was working, she often waited around near the glassed-in station and sometimes Fargo would ask her to sweep the floor or take a woman to the bathroom or hold a patient for an injection or sit with a patient coming out of electroshock. Then Fargo would give her extra cigarettes.

She hated being around the shock shop. It scared her. Regularly some patients from L-6 were wheeled out for shock. One morning there would be no breakfast for you, and then you would know. They would wheel you up the hall and inject you to knock you out and shoot you up with stuff that turned your muscles to jelly, so that even your lungs stopped. You were a hair from death. You entered your death. Then they would send voltage smashing through your brain and knock your body into convulsions. After that they'd give you oxygen and let you come back to life, somebody's life, jumbled, weak, dribbling saliva—come back from your scorched taste of death with parts of your memory forever burned out. A little brain damage to jolt you into behaving right. Sometimes it worked. Sometimes a woman forgot what had scared her, what she had been worrying about. Sometimes a woman was finally more scared of being burned in the head again, and she went home to her family and did the dishes and cleaned the house. Then maybe in a while she would remember and rebel and then she'd be back for more barbecue of the brain. In the back wards the shock zombies lay, their brains so scarred they remembered nothing, giggling like the old lobotomized patients.

On that Wednesday she was sitting there hopefully, but Fargo was deep in gossip with another black attendant. Connie had gone up once for a light—the only way inmates could get a match was to beg for one—and had been told to wait a minute, honey, half an hour ago. Four other patients were waiting too with small requests. She knew better than to approach again. On her lap was spread yesterday's paper, a present from Fargo for cleaning up vomit, but she had read through it, including births and deaths and legal notices. Mrs. Martínez approached her, eyes meeting hers and then downcast in a gesture that reminded her suddenly of Luciente's orange cat. Several weeks had passed since she had been in contact with the future, although almost daily she felt Luciente's presence asking to be let through. Here in the violent ward she was afraid to allow contact, for she had to watch her step. She was never alone, not even in the toilets without doors, never away from surveillance.

Mrs. Martínez stood almost in front of her but a little to one side and fixed her eyes longingly on the newspaper, met her gaze questioningly, then glanced away. For months Mrs. Martínez had not spoken. The attendants treated her as a piece of furniture. Many of the withdrawn had their own ways of speaking without words to anyone who was open, and Connie never had much trouble figuring out what Mrs. Martinez wanted. She handed over the paper. "Sure, I'm done reading it. But give it back, okay? For me to sit on." A paper like that made a good pillow and she had no intention of abandoning it.

Mrs. Martínez smiled, her eyes thanked Connie, and carefully, as if bearing off a baby, she took the paper away to the corner to pore over. Connie determined to keep an eye on Martínez and make sure nobody strong-armed the paper from her. Martínez would long ago have been transferred from this acute ward to a chronic ward and left to rot there, except that her husband was on a D.A.'s staff and came up to see her the last Sunday in every month with her children—never allowed inside, although she would stand at the window and weep and weep and hold out her hands to them. He would sign her out for holidays, but always, after a month or two, he would bring her back.

Connie was watching Martínez turn the pages slowly, when two orderlies brought in a woman handcuffed to a stretcher, trundling her past roaring muffled protest. A sheet was tied over her and only her hair was visible, long auburn hair clotted now with fresh blood. Her voice rose out of the sheet, her voice soared like a furious eagle flapping auburn wings.

"Sybil!" Connie cried out and half rose. Then she shut up. Give nothing away. She watched them wrestle Sybil into seclusion and heard the thump as they threw her against the wall. Her tall, bony body would be snapping its vertebrae, bucking with rage, until the dose took and she could no longer move.

Sitting quietly, Connie clasped her hands in her lap. Sybil was here. A slow warmth trickled through her. She had been lonely here, for few of the women on L-6 had energy left to relate, in their anguish of dealing with mommy, daddy, death, and the raw stuff of fear. She hoped the orderlies had not beaten her friend badly and that Sybil would simmer down and get out of seclusion soon. She had to try to get a message to Sybil through the locked door. Patients were not allowed to communicate with those in the isolation cells.

Her last time here they had met, and in the strange twilit childhood of the asylum with its advancements and demotions, its privileges and punishments, its dreary air of grade school, they had twice been confined in the same ward long enough to become friends. Each patient rose and dropped through the dim rings of hell gaining and losing privileges, sent down to the violent wards, ordered to electroshock, filed away among the living cancers of the chronic wards, rewarded by convalescent status, allowed to do unpaid housework and go to dance therapy; but twice they had come to rest on the same step and they had talked and talked and talked their hearts to each other.

Patience was the only virtue that counted here. "Patients survive on patience," she imagined embroidering on a little sampler, like "Dios Bendiga Nuestro Hogar." A week wormed through her soul before they let Sybil on the ward.

That morning she sat away from the station for privacy. When Sybil entered, looking tall and drawn, Connie did not greet her except with her eyes. It did not do to presume too much or to impose. Sometimes the mad behaved toward each other with delicate courtesy. She did not want to intrude on a desperate inner battle or mind loop. Sybil met her gaze, strolled the length of the ward in wary reconnaissance, then let her long body down beside her.

"Hi, old darling! When shall we two meet again? In thunder, lightning, or in rain?"

"It looks like a good day to me, Sybil, seeing you again."

"We're two witches, I mean. With a coven, think what we could do!"

Sybil really did think she was a witch, that she could heal with herbs, that she could cast spells both black and white. They'd had an argument last time about those names. Connie had told Sybil that black magic for bad and white for good were racist terms. Finally Sybil had agreed to name the magics red, for blood vengeance, and green, for growing and healing. She wondered if Sybil remembered, or if she had gone back to the old names.

"How long you been in this time? Do you know?" she asked.

"I just arrived. I was hexing a judge." Sybil held up her bony elegant hands with white marks for the rings she wore, which they always took from her over her roaring protests. "They take them because they sense how potent my rings are. They're in a microwave oven, being bombarded with rays to destroy the power in them. When I recover them, it takes me weeks to restore their strength." Gently Sybil touched a lock of Connie's hair. "Did you just get here?"

She smiled at Sybil and began to tell her the story. "This time I did nothing I'm ashamed for—though like you hexing judges, maybe it wasn't so smart for me to fight." Her telling took them through the supper lines and the supper of what Sybil pronounced Toad Stew, through the evening medication line and the blank space of time until lights out.

"Tomorrow is your turn to bring me up to date."

"Oh, that will take at least a week," Sybil promised.

Sybil was her best woman friend except for Dolly, who was blood, but because she lived in Albany they never managed to see each other outside the hospital. Oh, Sybil was crazy, but Connie had no trouble talking to her. Sybil *was* persecuted for being a practicing witch, for telling women how to heal themselves and encouraging them to leave their husbands, for being lean and crazily elegant and five feet ten in her bare long high-arched feet, for having a loud, penetrating voice and a back that would not stoop and a temper that stood up in her, lashing the tail of a lioness. Sybil did not hesitate to take to her fists against anyone, so she had a scar across her high-domed forehead coming down to take a white bite of her left eyebrow. Sybil had lost a front tooth and she had a little bald spot she could find when she wanted to show Connie where her hair had been pulled out by an attendant, the time before the time before last when she had been forcibly committed.

Why did she like Sybil so much? Her heart warmed when she saw Sybil's long body writhing in fury. Sybil had high carved cheekbones and a square jaw, a haughty nose and eyes of a smoky umber. On the outside she wore outrageous makeup and ringed her eyes with black, but inside they would not let her near her precious kohl. Mainly,

Sybil was a fighter and she fought those who threatened her, instead of hating her own self. She didn't deny herself, she had not sold herself to any man. Connie adored the way she fought and wouldn't give up or go under and wouldn't be broken—not yet. All she could give anyone in here was to have survived this far, this long.

They talked passionately, sitting side by side against a wall, sometimes interrupting the flow by half an hour or an hour, sometimes muttering out of the sides of their mouths as if they were kids talking in school. Too much animation, too obvious a pleasure in each other's company would bring down punishment. The hospital regarded Sybil as a lesbian. Actually she had no sex life.

"Who wants to be a hole?" Sybil asked her. "Do you want to be a dumb hole people push things in or rub against? As for sex, it reminded me of going to the dentist the only time I indulged. Now, when you look at it clearly from the outside, Consuelo, with some measure of detachment, you see how perfectly futile"—few-tile, she pronounced it, loving vowel sounds—"futile it all appears, and how sordid besides."

"But people do it all the time, Sybil." She was grinning. "Must be something in it, no?"

"Consuelo!" Sybil pronounced her name carefully and with a reasonable effort at the Spanish. "People play rummy and hearts and we both know how tedious those pastimes are. People put together jigsaw puzzles too. The attendants like it if you work jigsaw puzzles; they think that's relating to reality, the poor boobs. Everybody who is presently touching"—their word for the state when inmates were responsive to things outside them—"has read every word of that newspaper under you. I know you have too, even the sports pages, although you can't tell tennis from football!"

"It's true, when a person is bored they . . . want to go to bed more. It's like the jokes about the long winter night of the Eskimo. When you have nothing to do, you, yourself, are your own plaything. Look at all the . . . fooling around that goes on here."

"I think we're taught we want sex when we feel unhappy or lacking something. But often what we want is something higher."

"For me, sex has more power than that," Connie said a little sadly. "But I think we often settle for sex when we want love. And we often want love when we need something else, like a good job or a chance to go back to school."

"People talk too much about sex," Mrs. Perlmutter said, her hand inside her hospital-issue dress, feeling her own breast.

At odd moments, the better days, the mental hospital reminded her of being in college those almost two years she had had before she got knocked up. The similarity lay in the serious conversations, the leisure to argue about God and Sex and the State and the Good. Except for college students, who else in the world was sitting around talking philosophy? Outside, whole days of her life would leak by and she wouldn't have one good thoughtful conversation. Sybil was a smart person, not street smart like Claud but thoughtful about the way things were and the way they might be. Outside, who talked to her?

On Ward L-6 every day smelled the same, looked the same, sounded the same. Patients rotated through their private cycles of night and day, touching and withdrawing, snowed by the heavy drugs. She was no longer Fargo's favorite, because she spent too much time with Sybil. Today was Friday, a dangerous day, a day of doors opening and shutting.

A doctor came onto Ward L-6, a youngish doctor with pale hair and bloodshot pale blue eyes. He arrived two hours after the time when the doctor raced through, speaking only to the nurse and attendants, while patients touching that day chased after him pleading for attention, changes in medication, furloughs, privileges, a change of ward. Calling them bird dogs, the attendants ran interference. This pale doctor was showing Fargo some papers and Fargo and the nurse were going over the patient's ward records with him, all those comments written on each of them that could get her sent to shock or raised a niche or two nearer the gates.

Even the patients not talking, not supposed to be in touch, knew something was up. Excitement rose like a hot dry wind and the women began chirping. Mrs. Martínez crawled into a corner and pushed her face against the wall. Joan began talking in what the staff called a word salad about her mother and God and the FBI. "They come and come and come again. Scrape it off the ceiling. Bad girl. Bad! Eat it for breakfast. Knock, knock, who's there. Across it up and cross it off. A double cross. Come in and come out. All over, ugh, dirty. Dirty girl. Knock, knock. It's a dirty bird. The pigeon did it. Bad, bad, ate it again! All comes out. Knock knock knock. Hot cross buns. Bang you again. Bang on the bum. Hot, hurt. Bad again! *Bad!*" Her voice rose high in a shriek of fury but her expression did not change.

From the side of her mouth Sybil asked, "What do you suppose the young inquisitor searches for? Are they hunting witches with needles today?"

Indeed, both the doctor and Fargo looked straight at them and they shut up. Connie turned away, but when she cautiously glanced at the station again, the two of them were still under surveillance. Had they been acting too intimate? Fargo jogged over and hoisted Sybil by an arm. Sybil tried to whip her arm free, but Fargo expertly pinned her. When Sybil got mad she could hold her off easily till she was hypoed, but she was more curious than angry. She drew herself up to eye the doctor along her narrow nose, making him instantly aware that she had two inches on him. "Do you enjoy visiting the zoo? Do you want to be a veterinarian when you grow up?" she cooed.

"She's on the large side," the doctor said. "I don't think she'll do."

Fargo dropped Sybil neatly, knocking her legs out from under her, and hauled up Connie instead. "This one been acting okay. She help some. She trying to cope. But she hang out with that big-mouth."

"Any outbreaks lately?"

"Not since she got on my ward. She was pretty wild when she arrive, but we straighten her out."

The doctor turned away and Fargo let go of Connie. Weak through and through, she felt as if her bones had turned to wet rope. Her knees crumbled and she sat abruptly beside Sybil. She started to speak to Sybil, but Sybil shushed her and crept closer to the glassed-in station where the doctor and Fargo were once again looking over the ward book. Sybil was trying to lip-read through the glass. Finally they emerged and the outer door was unlocked with the usual clatter.

"All right, clean that one up Monday morning and bring her down for Dr. Redding. . . . Oh, she speaks English? I mean reasonably?"

"Sure, no problem, Dr. Morgan. Wouldn't I tell you right off if she couldn't talk?"

"Righto. Clean her up and trot her down early Monday."

Sybil and she looked at each other in the ward boiling with tension. Sybil whispered, "All I could make out was that doctor he mentioned—I never heard of him before—Dr. Redding this, Dr. Redding that. And the phrase 'possible subject.' "

"Oh! Oh!" Joan muttered. She got off her bed and darted over to peer into Connie's face. "Knock, knock! Watch out!" Joan fled back to her bed and pantomimed the locking routine she seemed to hope would protect her.

"What do you think they're going to do to me Monday?"

Sybil shook her head, frowning. "They like you because you're small. They expect to push you around easily."

She was scared but alert. Maybe it was a new kind of therapy? Usually they didn't pull patients out of L-6 for group therapy, the only kind in the hospital. If it was shock, they wouldn't make such a fuss. Maybe they were testing drugs, as they had on Claud. Claud's friend Otis said they had given hepatitis, the dirty disease that had killed Claud, to a whole lot of little kids in Willowbrook, a state institution. Some doctor had injected little kids who hadn't done anything wrong except to be born dim witted, and got a big reward for it. What would they do to her?

Monday morning she was taken from Ward L-6 halfway across the grounds to the hospital building itself—the real hospital in the mental hospital. Normally it was a sleepy, understaffed building, but one floor seemed to have undergone changes. She got only a glimpse of maybe twenty other patients, men and women, waiting on chairs in the hall, before Fargo dragged her off. "Behave yourself now. I want to use the staff john. Now you keep quiet and don't mess around." Fargo installed her by the clean white sinks with liquid soap in a container that worked. Enviously she approached. Fargo was pissing. Over the liquid soap container with its yellow-green ooze, she saw a drab, funny-looking woman in the mirror. Quickly she looked away. Outside, no day passed without her seeing herself in mirrors, in shopwindows, everywhere reflected. The battered tin mirror in the bathroom on L-6 gave up only ripples of distortion.

Her hair looked disgusting: not only uncombed, straggly, dirty, but with white roots grown out along her part. Her hair had turned white down the center like a skunk as soon as she had passed thirty. Dolly gave her money for hair dye, which she hid as carefully from her caseworker as a stash of dope. It was her secret vice, dyeing her hair, but also it was a small act of self-affirmation. As long as her will kept her hair black as it had always been, as it should be, she was some part Consuelo who had won the scholarship to junior college, who had had the guts to depart Chicago for a strange city to get away from a rapist, who had broken Geraldo's nose—yes, she was proud of that. Her definition of Connie included black hair.

Well, at least she was no longer overweight, but she was flabby. At home she had the exercise of running up and down four flights of stairs ten times a day, every time she needed something from the superette or the candy store, every time she checked the mail, took out garbage, got a pack of cigarettes, mailed a letter, went down to welfare, went out to those scrubwoman jobs welfare made her do. She carried her groceries, her laundry, her garbage. She walked many blocks. Here her only exercise was being herded to and from the showers.

Small particles of dead skin gave her flesh an ashy look. If only she had a brush, she could disentangle her hair, brush out the mats and clumps. Ah, she looked like a bundle of institutional laundry!

Fargo hauled her along. The young doctor was bustling around the hall, followed by a secretary and more attendants. Fargo turned her over to one of the new attendants, a fat redfaced man, who inserted her into a row of green plastic chairs where the men and women had been placed to wait. As each new arrival was checked in, all the waiting patients stared in hope that something about the newcomer would make clear their mutual situation.

"Do you know what we're in for? What they're going to do to us?" she whispered to a young man in the next chair.

"I don't know." He was white, skinny, long-legged and tall, with abundant kinky brown hair. "They came on my ward last week and they looked over five of us. That blond doctor and attendant. They only took him and me." He pointed to a short black man beside him.

"They didn't say what for?"

"Some kind of testing, we heard. . . . It looks to me like that room at the end of the hall is fixed up as a lab. Past the offices."

"A lab? What kind of experiments could they do on us?"

He shrugged, "Man, I don't know. Whatever it is, you bet it will hurt." He sighed, combing back his nervous hands through his long, tangled hair. "My name's Skip. This is Orville. . . . You don't have any weed, do you? By some miracle? I can buy."

"I'm Connie. I wish I did. Last time I was in, it was all over the place."

"Some buildings it's around, some it isn't. In some you can get anything. . . . Not ours. God, can you imagine the incredible acts of brutality we might commit if we had a little dope? Monsters like us. You been in before, huh?" He waited for her nod. "Me too. Seven times in various spitals. One for each consecutive time I tried to off myself. Actually that was only five times."

"And never made it?" She laughed.

"I'm persistent. Maybe I have a will to failure. Orville, here, he cut up his girlfriend. Did you do anything like that, maybe?"

Orville said flatly (probably for the sixtieth time, as she well knew), "I was overworked. I had this job as night watchman and then I was delivering pizzas weekends. I couldn't cope with it all."

"Sort of." She clutched herself. "I smashed a bottle in the face of my niece's pimp." She grinned. "I wasn't overworked. I just hated him." Such a light feeling, like floating, to say that truthfully and let it hang there; at the same time the floating feeling was a cutting loose because she had been raised and had lived under a code where a woman never did anything like that, let alone speak of such actions.

"As far as I can tell, we all walk and talk," the boy went on. "We're functioning crazies. We all broke the law. I hope we aren't about to get shipped to some maximum security place—not that this place isn't pretty tight."

"You got a record?"

"Yeah . . . possession. But the shrinks wrote up worse things on my record." He poked her with his bony elbow.

"That doctor's the boss. The other's just his lackey."

Middling height, middling weight, brown hair, thick glasses, in his late forties, he exuded an energetic self-importance like a big Harley-Davidson gunning up 111th Street with a Savage Sheik on top. He washed his hands together with a brisk dry happy sound as he marched by the row of bedraggled patients on green plastic chairs, and in his wake bobbed the pale man, Dr. Morgan, a nurse, a man in student clothing, a woman in a white coat whose hand brushed the student type's hand supercasually, a male and female attendant, and a secretary, who stood holding a sheaf of records and pages and pages of other, ominous paper. Eventually Dr. Redding, as she heard him called, took various papers and cruised them, nodded and handed them all on to Dr. Morgan. "Fine, fine. Let's get the show on the road. Morgan, Acker, and I will do the screening, and Patty and Miss Moynihan will sit in. We should zip through this batch before two, because I have to get back to the university to meet one of those foundation johnnies."

Everyone but the attendants and the nurse bustled after him, as the patients looked at each other and the shut door. One at a time they were called in. The morning passed. No provision had been made for them to get lunch, which was brought in on trays for the staff, so they remained parked in the hall, grumbling, those screened and those not yet processed.

"It's no different from a regular psychiatric interview," said a woman in her forties, who also informed them she was a schoolteacher. "I teach auditorium," she said. That sounded peculiar to Connie, like teaching garage or living room. "The doctors simply ask you the same old questions. They have your records right there, so they know the answers, or they think they do. . . . Perhaps I'm being reclassified, finally. They're going to look into our cases."

At about one, Connie was called in as Skip came out. Clearing her throat with nervousness, she sat in a chair facing them lined up behind a table. Doctors and judges, caseworkers and social workers, probation officers, police, psychiatrists. Her heart bumped, her palms dampened, her throat kept closing over. She could not guess which way to cue her answers. What were they looking for? Would it be better to fall into their net or through it? If only she knew. If only she knew what the net consisted of. She was taking a test in a subject, and she didn't even know what course it was.

The young doctor who had picked her out of the ward did most of the questioning at first, with the type in the denim pseudo work clothes horning in from time to time. The same old stuff about Dolly and Geraldo, her daughter, her time with Claud, her drinking, her drug use, her difficulty in getting a job. It was like saying the responses at Mass. When what she said didn't fit their fixed ideas, they went on as if it did. Resistance, they called that, when you didn't agree, but this bunch didn't seem that interested in whether she had a good therapeutic attitude. What were they listening for, inasmuch as they listened at all? How that Dr. Redding stared at her, not like she'd look at a person, but the way she might look at a tree, a painting, a tiger in the zoo.

They were on her brother Joe now. The holy ghost of poor Joe, who had died of a perforated ulcer just after he got out of the pen for a drugstore holdup. Now they were questioning her about the beatings her father had given her as a child. She kept her face frozen, her voice level. Inappropriate affect, they called that—as if to have strangers pawing through the rags of her life like people going through cast-off clothes at a rummage sale was not painful enough to call forth every measure of control she could manage. Her mother, her father, her brother, her lover, her husband, her daughter, all fingered, sized up, dissected, labeled. Still, their white faces looked bored. The denim type, Acker, and Miss Moynihan in the lab coat were exchanging flirtatious glances. They could eat her for dessert and go on to six others and never belch. They were white through and through like Wonder Bread, white and full of holes.

Suddenly Dr. Redding came to life and took over. "Have you ever suffered headaches? pain anywhere in the head region?"

"Headaches?" Now what was this? "The medication does that sometimes," she said cautiously.

"The medication?"

"The tranquilizers."

"Other times. Outside the hospital. Haven't you had headaches outside the hospital, Connie?"

One of those first-name doctors who reduced you to five years old. "Not often."

"How often?"

She shrugged. What was he getting at? Were they wanting to try out drugs on them? "My back aches. My feet sometimes. I've had female complaints. My eyes, my head never has troubled me much in my life. Knock on wood."

"How about in connection with some of those incidents we've gone over? I notice in the incident where you used violence against your daughter there's a mention in the record of your feeling unwell."

"Doctor, I was hung over. Strung out. I was very bad. I'd been drinking for three months."

"Connie, you're diagnosing, aren't you?" He seemed to suspect she was concealing headaches. "Dizziness? Blackouts?"

"Like fainting? No, I never fainted in my whole life."

"Yet you say you were unconscious the night you were admitted to Bellevue."

"Geraldo and Slick hit me in the head. Slick knocked me out."

"Do you remember any blows to the head previously? Before the last accident when you were readmitted to Bellevue?"

"Sure, occasionally."

"Why don't you describe those occasions?"

"I don't remember them all. . . ." She paused when she saw Dr. Redding making a satisfied note of that. "Eddie, Eddie Ramos, my husband, used to hit me in the head sometimes."

"That's the second husband, the one she's still married to," Acker, the denim type, said.

"He didn't sign the commitment. Where is he?" Dr. Redding demanded of Acker.

"Whereabouts unknown, Doctor."

"I suppose no one has tried too hard to find our pugilist," Dr. Redding said with a slight smile. "Connie, do you remember your head being x-rayed after any of these incidents with your second husband?"

"No. I never got beat up that bad, to go into the hospital and get x-rays." They had to be kidding. When she had been with Eddie she had not been on welfare and who would have paid for x-rays and doctors? The only time she had gone in was when she had been bleeding after the abortion, and that had been terrible in its consequences.

"*Not that badly*, Connie? . . . Did he knock you down?"

"Sure." She had noticed before that white men got off on descriptions of brown and black women being beaten. "Hay que tratarlas mal," Eddie would always say.

"Get a set of x-rays on her before we begin the EEG monitoring," Dr. Redding said to Dr. Morgan. "We'll go with this one in the initial stages. How many live ones does that give us today?"

"Seven, Doctor," the secretary chirped.

"That's all? Let's get cracking. Okay, Connie. Take her out." Dr. Redding was already rummaging through the next set of records as she was whisked out and dumped in her chair again.

At two the staff emerged, Dr. Redding looking irritated. "This won't do. We need more. You've got to scan more records. We might even locate some subjects on the chronic wards."

The first consequences of that interview came within the week, when Connie was told to get herself together for a move. "You got lucky, girl. I put in a good word on you. But I know we be seeing you up here again!" Fargo packed her off Ward L-6 to a more open ward, G-2.

Sybil gave her a sad hopeless look that reminded her of childhood partings from best friends. Connie said, "Try to get off here. Be cagey for a while."

"I'll be docile as a plastic cow," Sybil said without conviction. "After all, I'll never get out of this place if I don't start trying, unless I learn to fly. And I have a lot to do this year."

Ward G-2 was in G building, just as old and sad but in marginally better repair. It was a red brick barracks that stood nearer the medical building, where the doctors had interviewed her. Connie sat on her new cot and looked over the ward, trying to gauge its potentials and threats. The long room with the beds had several windows whose sills were claimed as roosting territory by cliques of women, black women on one window and whites on another. G-2 was a locked ward but a more active one. That big door by the nursing station clattered open to admit occupational therapists, an occasional volunteer, and to let out patients who worked off the ward. Group therapy sessions were held on the ward twice a week. Little cabinets stood beside each of the fifty beds, and at one end of the ward card tables were set up. Along one side ran a long screened-in porch where patients could walk. They shared a day room with a men's ward, a dim room with chairs in rows facing a locked TV. It was strange to see men around again.

As she stood in line for medication, she felt like singing out with joy when she saw the little white cups with the pills inside and the cups of water. No more liquid Thorazine burning her throat hoarse. She bit hard on her cheeks to keep her face immobile. This ward meant less snowing. The line moved so slowly she had time to cover her joy, to crush it into a small corner where she could preserve it intact until she had a chance to examine it in safety. Yes, here her head would be clearer. Not today. She was new on the ward and the nurse watched closely as she took the pill. Afterward she walked slowly through the new ward, slowly as inmates always do. She remembered being horrified by that the first time she had been brought here. The drugs caused it, the heavy doping; but also the lack of anyplace to go and the time, the leaden time, to use up.

Sedately she walked through the sleeping room and into the day room. Here she would get the small exercise of walking, but she must be careful not to make it obvious she was pacing. That was an offense that would go in her record: patient paces ward. Here there was more to do but also here would be informers, spies.

She walked onto the porch. It was chilly, but she did not care. She had caught a glimpse of a coat supply in a closet near the nursing station, which meant at least some patients had grounds privileges. She pressed her face to the rusty screen and stared at the trees just leafing out, the benches, the lawns. She would be real cool, real cooperative. How she wanted to walk on that grass below! Her move down to G-2 must prove to be a small step closer to getting out altogether—closer to the big free open daylight out there.

Five

CONNIE sat on the porch with a towel around her shoulders for warmth. The chilly drizzly June day smelled like a basement under the low gray sky. She was so glad to be outside, even on the porch whose rusted screens gave a sepia wash to the walks and brick buildings, that she did not care if her behind hurt from the chill of the warped floorboards. She felt a keen enjoyment too of being alone for the first time since isolation. No one else had come out in the damp and the cold.

She gloried in breathing outdoor air, in seeing more than four walls, in smelling trees instead of medicine and diarrhea and disinfectant. The gray of the day soothed her. Strong colors would have burned her eyes. Every day was a lesson in how starved the eyes could grow for hue, for reds and golds; how starved the ears could grow for conga drums, for the blare of traffic, for dogs barking, for the baseball games chattering from TVs, for voices talking flatly, conversationally, with rising excitement in Spanish, for children playing in the streets, the Puerto Rican children whose voices sounded faster, harder than Chicano Spanish, as if there were more metal in their throats.

She felt Luciente pressing on her clearly for the first time since they had let her out of seclusion: not those brushes of presence that rose and faded but the solid force of concentration bearing around her. She resisted. To sit on the porch was still new, in a convalescent pleasure like the first time out of bed after a long illness. Still, she felt Luciente pressing on her and it was like, oh, refusing to answer the door to a friend who knew she was at home. How could she think of Luciente as a friend? But she had begun to.

"Me too, in truth," the voice formed in her mind. "I've missed you."

"Why don't you take shape? Nobody's out here but me."

"Shut your eyes. Let's go into my space. Today, in my year, the weather is better."

"Do you control the weather?"

"The sharks did in the 1990s—pass the term. I mean before us. But the results were the usual disasters. It rained for forty days on the Gulf Coast till most of it floated out to sea. Let's see, the jet stream was forced south from Canada. They close to brought on an ice age. There was five years' drought in Australia. Plagues of insects . . . Open your eyes."

They were standing in Luciente's hut in sun streaming through the south window, which was open and covered with a fine-mesh screen. "You must still have mosquitoes!"

"They're part of the food chain. We bred out the irritant. . . . About weather, when it gets disastrous, sometimes we adjust a little. But every region must agree. When a region is plagued by drought, grasp, we usually prefer to deliver food than to approve a weather shift. Because of the danger. We're cautious about gross experiments. 'In biosystems, all factors are not knowable.' First rule we learn when we study living beings in relation. . . . You're looking thin!" Luciente reproved her, leaning close.

"You say that like it was bad. Isn't thin beautiful to you? I've been dumpy for three years. Not that I don't look as lousy as I feel in that bughouse."

"Jackrabbit is thin beautiful. Bee is big beautiful. Dawn is small beautiful. Tilia is creamy orange beautiful." Luciente nodded at her cat, who stood up expectantly. "Tilia told me you're stupid, and I explained that people of your time did not talk with cats."

She remembered the orange cat stalking away. It stared at her boldly now, with malice she felt. "People of my time talk to cats, dogs, hamsters. To parakeets and goldfish. Lonely people talk to the wall. Listen, the bughouse is full of women who started talking to the Blessed Virgin Mary because their old man wouldn't listen."

"I mean in sign languages. For instance, Tilia and I talk sign language based on cat signs but modified—because many things must be said between cat and human different from what is said cat to cat."

"Oh? What do you talk about? The taste of raw mouse?"

"Much is simply expressing affection, anger, disappointment. I want, Tilia wants. Fish, milk, yogurt, to go out, peace and quiet, catch the mouse, don't touch that bird. Groom me. Let me work. Tilia does have a strong aesthetic sense and comments freely on flimsies and even on costumes. The last coverlet for the bed Tilia loathed and buried so persistently—that shit-covering gesture—that I had to trade it for another."

"Could you speak to her now? Ask her if she believes in God or what she thinks about public nudity."

"You don't believe me!"

"Either you're putting me on or you're crazier than I am."

"I'll teach you how to meet a cat. Cats are formal about introductions. I got flack last time. Look, Tilia can express feeling puffed. If Tilia takes a flying leap onto my chest at first dawn from the top of the wardrobe, I get a clear notion that cat is dissatisfied with my conduct." Luciente squinted, held her eyes shut for a few seconds, opened them again, squinted again, repeating the whole sequence, and then looked pointedly away. "This is how you meet a cat if your intentions are friendly. If you mean harm—for instance, you are approaching a cat standing over the body of a local chickadee—then you stare hard, you glare."

Connie sank on the broad bed, giggling. "You look . . . ridiculous."

"To a cat I presume I always look ridiculous. Awkward creatures by comparison, waddling around in clothes. *Come!* Talking is ridiculous to animals who commune through scents, colors, body language—all our minute posturing with the tongue and lips and teeth." Luciente made a wide-eyed pleading face. "Come on, just do it once and we can get on with the day's exploring. Just do it and get it over with."

"You want me to make faces at your cat?"

"Just be introduced. Tilia thinks you're hostile."

"All my life I been pushed around by my father, by

my brother Luis, by schools, by bosses, by cops, by doctors and lawyers and caseworkers and pimps and landlords. By everybody who could push. I am damned if I am going to be hassled by a cat."

Luciente looked back levelly with her eyes like black beans. "Person must not do what person cannot do. Let's go. No," she said to Tilia and reached out. Tilia stalked to the door, raised a paw, and slashed at it. Luciente let her out and on the far side of the screen door she paused and buried the house and its inhabitants with that gesture of disdain.

They followed the cat out. The rose on the hut was in full bloom, its scent spicing the air. The roses were luscious semidouble white cups marked on the skirts with dark crimson. "Your rose is beautiful."

"Let me cut you one." Luciente used a clippers from a knife with many parts. "For your hair."

"My hair. I'm embarrassed. I hate it this way."

"Why not change it, then?"

"I used to dye it along the part where it turned white. But in the hospital I can't fix it."

"When we wish to change our hair color, we change the proteins. It doesn't grow out as it was." Luciente was urging her along, arm around her shoulders. In a summer sleeveless shirt of a muted gold, her body was obviously female. Connie smiled to herself. Perhaps it was the lighter clothing, perhaps it was a matter of expectations—anyhow, Luciente now looked like a woman. Luciente's face and voice and body now seemed female if not at all feminine; too confident, too unselfconscious, too aggressive and sure and graceful in the wrong kind of totally coordinated way to be a woman: yet a woman.

"I wish I could help you with your hair," Luciente said. "Myself, I never alter my appearance except for dressing up at festivals. But many of us play with appearance."

"Tell me about this making faces at animals. You do it with puppy dogs and mice and termites too?"

"We have a holiday, Washoe Day, when we celebrate our new community, named for a heroine of your time—a chimpanzee who was the first animal to learn to sign between species. Now we have rudimentary sign languages with many mammals. Some, like apes, use sign language with each other. Most, like cats and dogs, have other ways of communing and only sign to us."

"Tell me—what do you say to a cow you're about to eat?"

"Exactly. It's changed our diet. So has the decision to feed everyone well. For each region we try to be ownfed and until the former colonies are equal in production, mammal meat is inefficient use of grains. Some regions raise cattle on grasses—"

"You never eat meat? It must be like living on welfare."

"We do on holidays, and we have a lot of them. As a way of culling the herd. We say what we're doing. They know it. In the same spirit, in November we hunt for a short period. That is, our village does. We're Wamponaug Indians. We need some experience with free-living animals as prey and predator, to body the past of our tribe fully. . . . Though I confess I never hunt. Some of us would just as soon lapse that custom, but we lack the votes to do it."

"You're what? Blond Indians? Indians with red beards?"

"Barbarossa dyes per beard, in truth. Isn't it pretty? It was brown before."

"You! You look like me. My ancestors were Mayans, but they were hardly Wamponaugs! That's no more alike than . . . Italians and Swedes!"

"We're all a mixed bag of genes," Luciente said. "Now I know where we'll go." She diddled with her kenner. "G'light, it's me, Luciente. Can you meet us at the brooder? I'm with Connie, the person from the past. Get White Oak to fill for you. We'll work running hard later." She turned back to Connie. "I asked Bee to meet us at the brooder. That's the yellow just-grew on the east. So much to glide over!" Luciente broke into a jog, saw that she was leaving Connie behind, and waited. "You set the pace."

"Bee is your boyfriend just out of the army? Was he drafted?"

"Grafted? Everybody takes turns. We can all use arms, we're all trained in fighting hand to hand, we can all manage facets of more complicated operations. I can shoot a jizer."

"Women too? Did you have to go?"

"Fasure I've gone. Twice. Once at seventeen and once when we had a big mobe. I fought both times."

"Fought? And you won't go hunting?"

Luciente paused, her eyes clouding over. "A contradict. I've gone through a worming on it, yet it stays. Grasp, you never know whether you're fighting people or machines—they use mostly robots or cybernauts. You never know. . . . Still I'd go again. At some point after naming, you decide you're ready to go."

"Ha! I bet lots of people decide never to go. Or does someone decide for you?"

"How could they? It's like being a mother. Some never mother, some never go to defend." Luciente frowned, tugging her hand through her thick black hair. "On defense your life can hang on somebody. If person didn't want to be there, person might be careless and you might suffer. If person didn't want to mother and you were a baby, you might not be loved enough to grow up loving and strong. Person must not do what person cannot do."

"Ever hear of being lazy? Suppose I just don't want to get up in the morning."

"Then I must do your work on top of my own if I'm in your base. Or in your family, I must do your defense or your childcare. I'll come to mind that. Who wants to be resented? Such people are asked to leave and they may wander from village to village sourer and more self-pitying as they go. We sadden at it." Luciente shrugged. "Sometimes a healer like my old friend Diana can help. Diana the rose. A healer can go back with you and help you grow again. It's going down and then climbing a hard path. But many heal well. Like you, Diana catches."

The yellow building was odd, like a lemon mushroom pushing out of the ground. Decorated with sculpted tree shapes, it was windowless and faintly hummed. She realized that except for the creaking of windmills, this was the first sound of machinery she had heard here. Indeed, the door sensed them and opened, admitting them to an antechamber, then sliding shut to trap them between inner and outer doors in a blue light.

"What is all this?" She shifted nervously.

"Disinfecting. This is the brooder, where our genetic material is stored. Where the embryos grow."

The inner doors zipped open, but into space that looked more like a big aquarium than a lab. The floor was carpeted in a blue print and music was playing, strange to her ears but not unpleasant. A big black man leaning comfortably on a tank painted over with eels and water lilies waved to them. "I'm Bee. Be guest! Be guest to what I comprend was a nightmare of your age."

"Bottle babies!"

"No bottles involved. But fasure we're all born from here."

"And are you a Wamponaug Indian too?"

Bee smiled. He was a big-boned, well-muscled man with some fat around his midriff, and he moved more slowly than Luciente, with the majesty and calm of a big ship. He steered placidly among the strange apparatus, the tanks and machines and closed compartments, something that beat slowly against the wall like a great heart, the padded benches stuck here and there. Either Bee was bald or he shaved his head, and the sleeves of his rose work shirt were rolled up to reveal on each bicep a tattoo—though the colors were more subtle and the drawing finer than any she had seen. On his left arm he had, not the cartoon of a bee, but a Japanese-looking drawing of a honeybee in flight. On his right he wore a shape something like a breaking wave. "Here embryos are growing almost ready to birth. We do that at ninemonth plus two or three weeks. Sometimes we wait tenmonth. We find that extra time gives us stronger babies." He pressed a panel and a door slid aside, revealing seven human babies joggling slowly upside down, each in a sac of its own inside a larger fluid receptacle.

Connie gaped, her stomach also turning slowly upside down. All in a sluggish row, babies bobbed. Mother the machine. Like fish in the aquarium at Coney Island. Their eyes were closed. One very dark female was kicking. Another, a pink male, she could see clearly from the oversize penis, was crying. Languidly they drifted in a blind school. Bee pressed something and motioned her to listen near the port. The heartbeat, voices speaking.

"That can't be the babies talking!"

"No!" Bee laughed. "Though they make noise enough. Music, voices, the heartbeat, all these sounds they can hear."

"Light, Sacco-Vanzetti. How's it flying?" Luciente said.

The kid was maybe sixteen. Lank brown hair in braids, swarthy skin, the kid wore a yellow uniform much like everybody's work clothes. "Is this the woman from the past?"

Luciente performed the introductions.

Sacco-Vanzetti, whose sex she could not tell, stared. "Did you bear alive?"

"Come on Sacco-Vanzetti, don't be narrow!" Luciente made a face.

"If you mean have I had a baby, yes." She stuck out her chin.

"Was there a lot of blood?"

"I was knocked out, so how do I know?"

"Was it exciting? Did it feel sexual?"

"It hurt like hell," Connie snapped, turning back to the wall of babies. "Were you all born from this crazy machine?"

"Almost everybody is now," the kid said. "I have to go down to threemonth to check the solutions. I'll be in touch. If you remember more about live bearing, I'd be feathered to hear about it." The kid went out.

Bee closed the viewing port. "Wamponaug Indians are the source of our culture. Our past. Every village has a culture."

The way he picked up on that question as if it had just been asked, the way a question floated in him patiently until he was ready to answer it: a memory of sweet and of jagged pain. Maybe she just had a weakness for big black men soft in the belly who moved with that massive grace, although Claud had moved differently. Because of his blindness Claud had held his head a little to the side. She had always thought of a bird. Birds turned the side of the head toward you because their eyes were on the sides, and Claud saw with his ears. "I suppose because you're black. In my time black people just discovered a pride in being black. My people, Chicanos, were beginning to feel that too. Now it seems like it got lost again."

Luciente started to say something but visibly checked herself.

Bee beamed, ambling toward another tank where he opened the viewing port. "I have a sweet friend living in Cranberry dark as I am and her tribe is Harlem-Black. I could move there anytime. But if you go over, you won't find everybody black-skinned like her and me, any more than they're all tall or all got big feet." He paused, looking intently at a small embryo, fully formed and floating just at his shoulder level. "At grandcil—grand council—decisions were made forty years back to breed a high proportion of darker-skinned people and to mix the genes well through the population. At the same time, we decided to hold on to separate cultural identities. But we broke the bond between genes and culture, broke it forever. We want there to be no chance of racism again. But we don't want the melting pot where everybody ends up with thin gruel. We want diversity, for strangeness breeds richness."

"It's so . . . invented. Artificial. Are there black Irishmen and black Jews and black Italians and black Chinese?"

"Fasure, how not? When you grow up, you can stick to the culture you were raised with or you can fuse into another. But the one we were raised in usually has a . . . sweet meaning to us."

"We say 'we,'" Luciente began, "about things that happened before we were born, cause we identify with those decisions. I used to think our history was exaggerated, but I'm less sure since I time-traveled." Luciente drew them toward the next port.

"I don't think I want to look at any younger . . . babies." The little third-month child the doctor had shown her in the basin. Her stomach lurched. "I don't feel too good."

"We'll leave." Bee took her arm. "Maybe it's the filtered air? Grasp, the plasm is precious. Life flows through here for sixteen villages in all, the whole township."

Outside she took a deep breath of salty air and detached herself from Bee. Claud's sore delicate pride, like an orchid with teeth. What could a man of this ridiculous Podunk future, when babies were born from machines and people negotiated diplomatically with cows, know about how it had been to grow up in America black or brown? Pain had honed Claud keen. This man was a child by comparison. "You saying there's no racism left? Paradise on earth, all God's children are equal?"

"Different tribes have different rites, but god is a patriarchal concept." Luciente took Bee's arm and hers. "Our mems, our children, our friends include people of differing gene mixes. Our mothers also."

"But Bee's kids would be black. Yours would be brown."

"My child Innocente has lighter skin than you do." Bee stopped to admire a walk lined with rosebushes blooming in yellows and oranges and creamy whites. "There's no genetic bond—or if there is, we don't keep track of it."

"Then this kid isn't really your child?"

"I *am* Innocente's mother."

"How can men be mothers! How can some kid who isn't related to you be your child?" She broke free and twisted away in irritation. The pastoral clutter of the place began to infuriate her, the gardens everyplace, the flowers, the damned sprightly-looking chickens underfoot.

Luciente urged her along. "We're walking Bee back to the lab. Where I'd be with the rest of our plant genetics base except for you. Bee and I work together. Maybe that's why we're been sweet friends so long, twelve years already."

"I thought it's cause I'm too lazy to run from you the way any sane lug would. I never noticed other cores who worked in the same base stuck so long."

"We're so ill suited we can't give up. Connie, apple blossom, listen to me—"

"Be on guard when Luci calls you soft names." Bee managed to saunter more slowly than they walked and yet keep up.

"It was part of women's long revolution. When we were breaking all the old hierarchies. Finally there was that one thing we had to give up too, the only power we ever had, in return for no more power for anyone. The original production: the power to give birth. Cause as long as we were biologically enchained, we'd never be equal. And males never would be humanized to be loving and tender. So we all became mothers. Every child has three. To break the nuclear bonding."

"Three! That makes no sense! Three mothers!" She thought suddenly of Three Kings Day and the Anglo Christmas carol that Angelina had learned off the TV. She could hear Angie's fluty voice singing monotonously but with a limpid joy in monotony (the security):

> We three kings of Oregon are
> bearing gifts we travels a far.

Tears burned her lids. Angelina, Angelina, if you had three mothers like me, you'd be dead instead of sold off to some clean-living couple in Larchmont. They said you were lucky to be taken at four. I didn't understand till I got out what they'd done! Lucky to be taken from me.

Angelina, child of my sore and bleeding body, child of my sad marriage that never fit right; like a pair of cheap shoes that sprouts a nail in the sole. But you fit right.

The nurse said I would have to show you, but you reached right for my breast. You suckled right away. I remember how you grabbed with your small pursed mouth at my breast and started drawing milk from me, how sweet it felt. How could anyone know what being a mother means who has never carried a child nine months heavy under her heart, who has never borne a baby in blood and pain, who has never suckled a child. Who got that child out of a machine the way that couple, white and rich, got my flesh and blood. All made up already, a canned child, just add money. What do they know of motherhood?

She was sitting against the wall on the porch, tears trickling from her eyes. Had pain broken the hallucination? She did not care. She hated them, the bland bottleborn monsters of the future, born without pain, multicolored like a litter of puppies without the stigmata of race and sex.

Six

NOW listen, ladies, Mrs. Richard said, wagging her fat forefinger. "None of you are getting off this ward till you tell me who stuck that dope behind the radiator. And I mean it!"

It was an aspirin box of dope that Glenda had got from her boyfriend on the men's side. Glenda was married and so was her boyfriend, but nobody counted that against them. Outside, it would end; they would be stuck back in the frame they had fallen from, with a new glue of fear to hold them there. Romances between patients reminded Connie of grade school affairs, a matter of catching a glimpse at a high window, sending a note on a cart, holding hands briefly in the common day room, touching for an instant at group therapy, dancing together at a Christmas party. Sometimes patients with grounds privileges were rumored to fuck in a storage room or behind a hedge, but that was mostly fantasy. For staff, it was different.

Mrs. Richard and Nurse Wright reminded her of grade school teachers anyhow. Her first school hadn't been that bad. She had gone with Luis hand in hand. All the children had been Mexican and the school within walking distance. No, the grade school she remembered with a shudder was her Chicago grade school.

"Say sit down."

"Seet down."

"*Sit* down. Now say it correctly, Consoola."

"Seet down."

Luis had mastered that Anglo sound and taught it to the rest of them, hitting them with his fists until they said it as he did. Luis punching her in the arm was better than the white teacher looking at her with that bored knowledge that she would fail and fail again to say the sound that seemed to have been invented to shame her. Luis did not teach them to say "sit." Luis's word of choice for his finally successful lesson was "shit."

"Can I go to the bathroom? Teacher, I got to go." Here she approached the nursing station and begged for a scrap of paper, a pencil, a cigarette, a light, a chance for one word with the doctor, permission to make a phone call. Everything but being tied down drugged blind or wheeled off to electroshock was a privilege. A job off the ward, a chance to take a walk, a candy bar.

One of the privileges was a trip to the beauty shop, where they made up women her age to look exactly like women her age made up. She wouldn't come out of there looking like Mrs. Polcari. Last time she had been released, the beauty shop had done a job on her like Dolly's mother, Carmel, did on the Puerto Rican women who came to her to be stuffed and cooked for weddings, important parties. She had looked ten years out of style, covered with funny wry curls and with a quarter inch of mask emphasizing every line, with green eyelids and a bright orange mouth and thickened lashes caked with mascara on the front of her like new awnings on a pawnshop window.

When she had arrived at the welfare hotel where they had her for the first months—junkies in the halls and ten kids to a room with a stopped-up-sink—she was greeted by that garish face of an elderly doll lurid with the grime of traveling. Stretched out on the bed, she imagined Claud's ghost touching her skin with his knowing fingers, those fingers faster than the rest of him and ending in sensitive bulbs. How he would have complained about what was smeared over her cheeks.

"You feel like satin pillows. Like the satin sheets the king of the pimps sleep on. Gonna spend this whole Sunday just lollin around, just rootin around grabbin myself handfuls of that good stuff."

Claud made love as if he had all the time in the world. He might not feel like it for a week, he might disappear, he might feel too low and mean. But when he came to it, he took his sweet time. He loved up every bit of her. He would stroke the silky skin on the underside of her arms until her breasts would begin to burn, he would play with her breasts with light teasing and then he would take great handfuls and nuzzle and suck, until her belly ached with wanting. He would rub his thing against her languidly, slowly, slowly he would slip in and then ease out, slip in and ease out until she was thrusting him in herself with her hand. After he came, he would pause a little but he would stay hard. Then he would go on and go on. He would be so patient and so deliberate with her, so slow and easy, that she could give herself up to loving him back, to enjoying his coming, to the feeling of their skins touching, knowing that she would have her pleasure opening out full and slow in her.

She had gone into a bar on Second Avenue—one of the few bars with a mixed black and Puerto Rican clientele—looking for Eddie, who'd stopped paying child support. She was sitting at a table alone, low in mind, feeling she must look as if she wanted to be picked up. She had noticed Claud at the back having a drink with some friends, just as she warily noticed every man who came and went. She held a newspaper propped in front of her and nursed a warm beer, hoping that Eddie or one of his compadres would walk through the door.

After some banter with the bartender, Claud started to play his saxophone: blues, spirituals, some popular songs. She was glad. He played all right, but she was glad because she had something to be doing sitting there: she could watch the big black man with the opaque glasses playing saxophone and she could be beating time to music, and only from the corner of her eye keep a watch on the door. Not till Claud finished and passed the hat did she realize he was blind. That took her off guard, so that when he came back to her table, returned the quarter she had dropped in the hat and asked if he could sit down and buy her a beer, she had agreed—not to be rude, because his blindness took her off guard.

This rotten place, it gave her nothing to do and too much time to do it in. Here she was brooding on Claud again. She couldn't take it. Remembering him just cut her to bleeding hunks. Dead.

Ten-thirty. She had been up for four hours and the

big event had been waiting in line for breakfast for half an hour. On the ward it was a bad day. Mrs. Richard found the sixteen-year-old black girl, Sylvia, leaning against the radiator with the side of her face burned. She was dragged off to seclusion, numb with drugs, and whatever they did to her would not include treating the burn.

Then old Mrs. Stein came out of the toilet with shit rubbed in her hair, and while one of the attendants was dragging her back in, Sharma suddenly began to punch Glenda. "You goddamn whore! I know you're carrying on with my husband. You both think I'm stupid! Whore of Babylon! You're doing it with all the doctors. Everybody's talking about you, whore! You do it with all of them!"

By eleven-thirty half the seclusion rooms on the ward were full and the patients lined up for an extra-heavy dose of tranks, given in liquid form that burned the throat raw and made her hoarse. She could feel minds stirring like poplars in a storm all through the ward, and occasionally a brittle branch would break off and crash to the floor. They were angry about being kept in, with none of the minute breaks in routine to look forward to that made a life on G-2. She sat on the floor in a place where she could catch a glimpse of a whole window full of nothing but leaves if she held her head just right. If she sat at the right angle, she couldn't see the other buildings and the green could fill her eyes.

The medication was dragging her down, filling her mind with cotton fluff and odd hot pieces of hallucination and memory. Her head felt swollen: the heads of those embryos floating in the brooder, those oversized knowing heads floating upside down behind glass. She wanted to sleep, but patients were not allowed to lie down during the daytime.

Finally an event: time to line up for lunch. They shuffled into line, they wandered about as the attendants made them stand straight. They waited and waited for the door to unlock. All the wards in G building went to lunch downstairs, but on a staggered schedule. Glenda, with a face swollen from Sharma's attack, came and stood next to her. Waited to see if she would speak.

Connie asked, "Does your face hurt?"

"She never does. All the best plastic."

"I know Sharma didn't really mean what she said."

"Something to tell you. She went along the hall—the attendants took her."

She waited. She knew Glenda was talking about herself and had something pressing to say.

"Come on now," Mrs. Richard was braying. She was afraid of the patients and they all sensed it. "Close up that line. Come on now! A straight line!"

"She saw your friend with her feet sticking out."

"Sybil?" She immediately flashed on her body under a sheet, the long auburn hair flying out. "What were they doing with Sybil?"

"Taking her to be burned. Saint Joan. She told me to tell you she was sorry about your friend."

"Shock? They were taking Sybil for shock?"

"They burn it out. Then they fill it with cement." Glenda peered into her face, then fled away farther back into the line.

She wanted to lie down. She wanted to crawl under a table. Would Sybil know her afterward? Sometimes after shock inmates didn't remember friends or lovers. She felt low and mean. Sybil had had shock before. "They've done everything but hang me," Sybil said. Sybil would fight them; but they were knocking her out, they were running the savage bolts through her soul. Sybil unconscious was merely another helpless woman.

Deliberately, quietly she got out of line and sat down on her cot. Mrs. Richard trotted after her, her small mouth pursing up in a pout of alarm. "Mrs. Ramos, get back in line. It's time for your lunch."

"Why should I stand there for twenty minutes waiting?" She tried to speak with quiet dignity but the medication slurred her tongue. "The medication makes me dizzy. I'll wait here."

She read fear in the eyes of Mrs. Richard, who hated the patients, whose hands shook slightly whenever she had to touch one of them, who gave out a sour stench of fear that roused Connie like the smell of gas escaping from the open cocks of a stove. "Mrs. Ramos, you're confused. You're very confused. It's time to line up for your lunch."

"Why do we have to stand around? It's just garbage when we get it. Who wants to stand in line for garbage like that?" She tried to speak distinctly but was disgusted to hear her thick tongue slurring the words as if she were drunk.

"Come along now! Get back in line. You're not cooperating! All the others are waiting in line for their lunch."

Actually Glenda had stepped out and was wandering among the cots. Connie waited to see what Mrs. Richard would do, expecting her to call the nurse and bundle her back in line. But her little rebellion had to be punished. They threw her into seclusion. Lying on the floor, she felt like a fool. But how could she go down to lunch like a sheep while Sybil burned?

She slept awhile, hot fitful sleep. The room stank of old shit. She did not look around for fear of finding it. She banged on the door, hoping they would come and let her use the bathroom, but no one appeared.

She was sitting in the Boca de Oro, Comidas Chinas y Criollas, a small Cuban-Chinese restaurant with family-sized booths on 116th Street. She and Claud liked to go there. Angie was never much of an eater and in restaurants she inclined more to whining than to eating. But Angie liked the Boca de Oro, partly for the plain buttered noodles the waiter would serve her without making a big scene, and partly for a mural she liked. Connie told Claud he was lucky he didn't have to look at it: prancing señoritas in towering mantillas, with a bull that resembled a fat dog about to sneeze.

They sat in a booth, a more real family in their assorted colors and sizes and shapes than Eddie and Angie and she had ever made up, with Claud taking one side of the booth by himself and his cane on Angie's side for her to play with. Connie and Angie sat facing him, while Angie squirmed with pleasure and asked to go to the bathroom every five minutes. "You can't go to our bathroom," she kept telling Claud. Angie was fascinated by men's and women's bathrooms and why they used the same one at home but they couldn't use the same one here. Lately Angie asked questions about toilets for hours. It drove Connie crazy. The more irritated she grew, the more Angie would push her with questions. Angie had a gift for sensing when her mother didn't want to talk about a subject, and a vivid and driving urge to know why.

"You'd make a great cop," Claud told Angie one time. "A special detective captain cop."

Connie was serene with pleasure: pleasure that they had some money, that they were together, that they were being a good family, that Angie was behaving and eating her noodles, that Claud was sitting there vast and beaming and solid and warm. Like the sun his presence shone on her. She ate from his dish, she ate from her own, she nibbled a little of what Angie would not finish. Everything was spicy and good. It was spring, just after Easter, and Claud had given her money for a new dress. The dress was turquoise, fitted at the waist and swinging out when she walked. Claud said it felt good and sleek. She had touched up her hair just Saturday and then used the cream rinse that made it feel soft for Claud. She was bathing in a pool of sunshine. They were busted two weeks later.

She was in isolation, crying. Claud, Angie. The court-appointed lawyer told her to cop a plea and she ended up with a suspended sentence as accomplice to a pickpocket. But she spent weeks in jail before the trial and Angie had been put in the children's shelter for the first time. Her probation officer would not permit contact with the man she thought of as her husband. The State said her husband was Eddie. She'd never had the money to divorce him for desertion. What was the point? Only sometimes she felt as if the name Ramos was a heavy load, a great dead bough she lugged on her shoulders. Its thickness was the body of a thin but bony man, the roughness of skin closed against her. Claud had been open to her and everybody—the judge, the probation officer, Luis, everybody—had tried to make her ashamed of being with him. Black and blind.

She could not stand remembering! She had felt disgusted by Luciente and Bee, but she did not care. She had to get out of here. She had to turn off her memory. She tried to open her mind, to invite. For a long, long time nothing stirred. Nothing but time sticking to her like cold grease.

Then at last she felt something. At once she begged, "Luciente, let me visit!"

The presence grew stronger. "Grasp, you could be a sender too. What a powerful and unusual mix!"

"Don't flatter me."

"Why not praise strengths? Speak good when you can, and critting doesn't sting. Clear, now, clear hard."

She felt Luciente's firm embrace and then she stood in her hut.

"We lost you suddenly last time." Luciente hugged her. "You weren't injured?"

"I think if I remember something too well it breaks this—whatever you call this link."

"Could be you stop catching when your attent shifts. I guess we'll get used to these abrupt discorporatings and hoppings to and fro in time." Luciente was wearing shorts and a sleeveless shirt. She reminded Connie of an athlete, of a woman tennis player; except that they were hardly ever as dark as Luciente. Bee, on the bed's edge, wore a long red and black robe covered with fine embroidery that stiffened it, with a softly rolled hood cast back on his broad shoulders.

"Come!" Luciente urged her, huskiness catching with haste. "Hurry! Bee's coms wait."

Indeed, squatting carefully outside so as not to stain their costumes were two women as dressed up as Bee, women she recognized from the lunch table. One wore a long shirt and leggings of soft pale deerskin much worked with shell and quill appliqué; she had braided her long black hair with strips of dyed leather into a tower precariously fastened. The other's chestnut hair was loose and she wore long filigree earrings and a flowing blue gown. With quick grace both women rose to greet them.

Sitting a little apart on a stone was a fair-haired girl, yes, of thirteen or so. This child was easy for Connie to distinguish because her cotton shirt was open all the way down like a jacket, and her small cups of breasts were visible as she got up and turned toward them. The skin of her chest looked tattooed. Connie stared. As they moved into a close group, she could see it was paint. The girl wore pants and that open shirt and had at her feet a basket, which now she swung up to wear like a rucksack. She also picked up a bow and slung it over her shoulder. Connie could see at her waist a knife sheath, hanging under the shirt-as-jacket.

"This is our child, Innocente. Innocente, here is Connie, from the past." Bee turned to her, stately today in his movements. "This day is Innocente's naming. Otter, Luxembourg, and I are about to leave together by floater to see per safely landed. We've been Innocente's mothers, and this is end-of-mothering."

"As if you won't be tumbled to get rid of me!" Innocente stuck out her tongue at him.

"You guessed it. We plan to drop you in the bay."

"Except that you float like a bladder." Otter, the woman in deerskin, spoke.

"When I'm eaten by a bear, you'll bottom!"

Otter slipped her arm around Innocente. "A skinny bit like you? And tough! Like chewing on locust wood."

"Do you not want to go?" asked Luxembourg, in the flowing blue dress. "Say it—don't comp yourself. If the time isn't ripe, wait. We're not nipping to let you escape us."

Innocente screwed up her nose, kicking at the stone with new-looking heavy boots. "Fasure I want to go. It's not that I'm running eager to get away from you lugs. Only, my two best friends are already youths. I think it's time. I keep dreaming about going. Besides, what a ticky name you stuck me with. What am I supposed to be innocent of?"

"You said that twice you dreamed going," Otter commented. "That sounds right. Nobody ever feels yin-and-yang sure."

"Of that or anything else on earth." Bee stroked the child's shoulder. "You have me to blame. Innocente was a naming from the heart, partly for Luciente, who speaks Spanish. We'd been lovers only a short time. Partly I liked the sound, pretty in my mouth. Finally I'd just finished a task period working on reparations to former colonies, when I came home and put in to be a mother. I'd been traveling for a year in Latin America. It made me brood about those centuries of the rape of the earth, the riches stolen, the brutalizing and starving of generations . . . toward that day when all trace of that pillaging will be healed. . . . That's how you got named. It's up to you now to improve on it." Bee stepped back. "Did you sharpen your knife?"

"Fasure. I checked everything. Canteen, stringing of my bow, arrow points." Innocente looked at Connie. "Are you coming?"

"I don't know," she said. "Just where are you going?"

"Where it's been decided." Innocente gave a dry, choppy laugh.

"Innocente will be dropped into one of the wilderness areas we use," Luciente said. "This is how we transit from childhood to full member of our community."

"Drop her in the wilderness? Alone?" Her voice rose.

"Fasure I'll be alone," Innocente said with indignation. "What point would there be, at now? I've been in the woods plenty."

Connie turned to Bee. "Does she stay out there overnight?" They had to be crazy.

"For a week. Then the aunts person selected—advisers for the next years—return for per. Not us." Otter adjusted her elaborate hair.

"But *they* won't be able to speak to me for threemonth when I come back." Innocente sounded gleeful. "They aren't allowed to."

"Lest we forget we aren't mothers anymore and person is an equal member. Threemonth usually gives anyone a solid footing and breaks down the old habits of depending," Otter went on.

"Suppose she breaks a leg. Suppose she's bitten by a snake. Suppose she gets appendicitis!"

Bee smiled at her almost sadly. "We take the chance. We have found no way to break dependencies without some risk. What we can't risk is our people remaining stuck in old patterns—quarreling through what you called adolescence."

"A rite of passage that doesn't involve some danger is too much a gift to create confidence," Luxembourg said in her soft, rather deep voice.

"I'm afraid to go . . . but I'm willing, fasure. How come you don't talk to me? You only talk to them," Innocente said to Connie.

"How can you know what you're getting into? You're only a child!" She turned to Bee. "It's criminal dropping her with wild animals and poison ivy and who knows what? How is she supposed to eat and clean herself and take care?"

"I know what to eat in the woods! I'm twelve and a half, not four. I can fly a floater myself, you ask if I can't! There's only one other twelve-year-old who flies a floater alone in this whole township. You can't expect me to go through life with an unearned name, stuck on me when I wasn't conscious yet! How can I go deep into myself and develop my own strength if I don't get to find out how I am alone as well as with others? . . . Zo?"

Luciente took Connie's hand. "I see it's strange to you. But your young remained economically dependent long after they were ready to work. We set our children free."

Bee shook out the folds of his robe. "Come see us off. It's time. Come with us in the floater if you like, or stay with Luciente and person can show you the children's house. We have an hour's flight. We want Innocente to have long hours of daylight to fix camp, scout food, and take stock of the area."

Innocente strode off and they fell in behind. Soon they were ambling together, Innocente arm in arm with Luxembourg, who murmured in her ear soft cautions and advice, while Luciente and Otter walked linked, Luciente telling a broad story about Neruda's naming.

"You're just going to toss her out in a parachute into the woods and run away?" Connie asked Bee.

"Parachute? We lower per to the ground and mark the spot with a radio beacon and big red marker."

Luciente leaned close, grinning. "We haven't misplaced a child yet. You're right, accidents happen. . . . But why try to control everything? Grasp, we think control interfers with pleasure and with communing—and we care about both."

"I won't go along. I don't want to see a child abandoned!"

"Connie, can't you see Innocente wants to go?"

"Kids can be brainwashed into wanting any piece of garbage. My . . . own child cried for a week once for a mechanical walking man she saw on the TV that cost so much I couldn't believe it. Should I have let us go hungry two weeks to buy it to stop her tears?"

"We'll see them away. They'll be happier alone. It's tender, end-of-mothering. Comprend, we sweat out our rituals together. We change them, we're all the time changing them! But they body our sense of good."

Gently Bee adjusted Innocente's jacket. "Don't slow or trance till you build your shelter, grasp?"

As they came over a small rise, they faced a bigger hill. Cut into its side was what appeared to be a hangar, its top standing open like a box with the lid up. Three grasshoppery machines the size of police helicopters stood inside. The hangar was built much larger than needed to accommodate them, as if sometimes it might hold more of them or something else besides.

A blond woman wearing overalls came toward them from the floater in front. She was tanned, her cropped hair was shoved up in a bandanna, her nose reddened by the sun, her eyes wide and blue, and her wiry arms were daubed with grease. "Zo, a good naming, Innocente. You're off now?"

"You got the floater ready, Red Star?"

"All checked. You flying today?"

"Ha! They said no. What do you think?"

"You don't even know where you're going, or have you guessed?"

"If I did, they'd change it."

Slowly other people came drifting toward the hangar from the cornfields, the intensively cultivated gardens, from the fooder and brooder, from huts scattered among the gardens, from the free-form buildings they called just-grews. From the river docks where she could see a variety of conventional and odd, high-in-the-water fishing boats, diving gear, nets and winches, more people strolled toward them. They embraced Bee, Otter, and Luxembourg, they waited for Innocente to leave prowling over the machine so they could greet her. Luciente remained with Connie up on the rise, a little apart. This day had the feeling of a slightly formal but familial occasion, of a great big clan saying goodbye to someone going off to the army or getting married. Of course they were far too many for a real family. Not even her own Comacho clan back in El Paso, with additional strength up on a visit from Chihuahua, could muster such numbers to see them off when they left in their old Ford for Chicago and the promise of work in the steel mills, the last time she had seen gathered in one spot so many people related by blood.

Except of course they weren't. Nobody here knew what that meant. They just acted as if they were. They were kissing and hugging and Otter was beginning to weep. Innocente finally turned from her perhaps embarrassed fumbling with the floater to let people greet her. Even she did not seem to find the embraces or the tears upsetting. Luciente had left Connie to hug Bee, and both of them were crying. Big fat tears rolled down Bee's broad face. Imagine Claud crying! Even when they sentenced him, he had grinned and shrugged and said out of the corner of his mouth, "Shit, could be worse. Time's hard, but you do it, and it's gone." Once again they reminded her of children, even the men. Only Innocente did not weep, stubbornly eager.

Blowing her nose on a big multicolored handkerchief,

Luciente clambered back to her. "Ah me, ah my," she was sighing as she came. Bee and Jackrabbit were embracing now, that skinny rambling kid who was Luciente's lover too.

"Luciente, sometimes a child must have to do without mothers. If someone dies? If someone goes away? What would happen to your child if suppose you went to California? Is there still a California, or did it fall in the sea? Are you allowed to go, or do you have to stay here? Anyhow, could you take your daughter, or wouldn't your comothers let you?"

"Ay, so many questions! Fasure I can go if I want to. How would I work well, how would I contribute to my village if I didn't want to be here? We try not to leave when we're mothering. But if I comped I had to go, Dawn would stay. Because to leave would be a terrible uprooting. Then if the child was old enough, person would choose a third mother. If not, we'd volunteer. Every child has three. If we die, the same." Luciente blew her nose again, emphatically, in the handkerchief of complex and gaudy pattern (a gift handkerchief, Connie thought: I bet people still give each other handkerchiefs when they can't think of anything else).

The drifting to and fro, the greeting and well-wishing, the embracing and weeping, the patting and hugging and hand clasping, rose to a frenzied peak and Bee, Otter, and Luxembourg in their finery climbed into the floater with Innocente. Luxembourg was piloting. They all waved and shouted. Baskets of lunch were handed in and what looked like a bottle of champagne. "Come back with a strong name!" "Till when, Innocente! I'm going next week!" "Take care!" "Have a powerful dream!" "Don't fix on lonely!" "See you in a week!"

At last the floater, painted with a swirly design in pastels, put out a bag apparatus above it and rose slowly, gracefully, and quietly. It soared to perhaps a thousand feet and then sailed off, with another device turning and twittering on it. Smoothly it paddled off through the air silent as a balloon and was soon gone. Once again Luciente blew her nose in the handkerchief of many colors and stuffed it in a pocket of her shorts as Jackrabbit strode from the eddies of leavetaking to hug her. Yes, they were not like Anglos; they were more like Chicanos or Puerto Ricans in the touching, the children in the middle of things, the feeling of community and fiesta. Then, after all that carrying on, everybody walked away cheerful enough, serene. Jackrabbit sauntered with his hand cupped on the nape of Luciente's neck.

"Luciente, that handkerchief—was it a present?" Connie asked.

"This one? Fasure, from Dawn for Mothers' Day. Dawn made it p'self!"

"Mother's Day?" She laughed. "You still have Mother's Day!"

"We have tens and tens of holidays," Jackrabbit boasted. "For famous liberators. For important events, like the domesticking of corn and wheat. The turning of the sun north and south. Famous struggles . . . Didn't your society use rituals to body what you thought good? Like your football games, parades, public executings—"

"We didn't do that! That was the old times, way before."

"I thought on your primitive holies—"

"TV, you mean? At least we had regular programs!"

"Didn't you view bombings, burnings, stabbings? Shootings of people? In every group, spectaclers body ideas of good. Always people try to be good as they see it, no?" His free hand waved.

They were strolling down the hill toward the village. "I don't know. We have a religious idea of being good—a bit like what you call good, being gentle and caring about your neighbor. But to be a good man, for instance, a man is supposed to be . . . strong, hold his liquor, attractive to women, able to beat out other men, lucky, hard, tough, macho we call it, muy hombre . . . not to be a fool . . . not to get too involved . . . to look out for number one . . . to make good money. Well, to get ahead you step on people, like my brother Luis. You kunckle under to the big guys and you walk over the people underneath. . . ." She shrugged wearily, passing the huts crawling with grape vines and roses, the orchards hung with small green fruit, the covered tanks where fish were spawning under translucent domes. Growth seemed to swarm over the land. "Good? My mother was good. What did it get her except to bleed to death at forty-four? Looking like she was sixty." She wished sharply for a cigarette, but she had not seen any here and she remembered Luciente's fear. "I was never able to do good enough to feel good, never able to do bad enough to do me any good."

An older woman came up beside them, holding out her hand to Connie. "I'm White Oak. I work in the same base as Bee and Luciente. You've been pointed out to me and, grasp, we gossip about you. But we've never met. My child named perself this month too—I mean the one who was my child. That one is Thunderbolt now, and we can't talk for another seven weeks."

"Thunderbolt!" Luciente savored it. "I hope we're not in for a summer of titanic names. Leaping Lightning. Stupendous Fireball. The Earth Dances, The Stars Stand Still. Heroic Revolutionary Fervor. Mao Susan B. Ferenzi. Freedom Through Constant Struggle."

"I suppose you selected Luciente right off," Jackrabbit crooned, giving her hair a tug. "I suppose you were too sensible, even at thirteen, ever to pick a silly name."

"Actually I called myself White Light when I came from my naming, so you see I haven't drifted far. But to confess, I went through the usual oddities. When I was first with Diana, I called myself Artemis."

"Actually the twin of Artemis was Apollo. Or did you want to *be* Diana?" Jackrabbit moved beside them, loose-jointed, shambling. "You wanted the moon, Luci, instead of recognizing yourself a creature of the broad pragmatic day."

"I was Panther for a while myself," White Oak said. "As if I'd ever see one, except on the holi. And Liriope—that's a plant we were breeding for erosion control on the old blast sites when I was first in our base."

"I fancy that one," Jackrabbit said. "Liriope . . ." He leaped ahead to assume a position as flowering plant, head hung back, mouth open, arms arched above his head.

"Venus flytrap," White Oak said. "Don't tease me. I remember too well when you moved here, you were going through a name a week."

"Lord Byron, One Who Crests the Wave, Dark Moon, Wild Goose . . ." Luciente crooned.

"And I walked into the fooder one day and you told me you were going to give me my name of the week, Wild Porkchop. That was the first time I noticed you. Now you'd better forget—I'm meaner than you are!" He hopped to Connie's side. "Did you never have another name? Or do you just keep changing that second name?"

They were walking a broad path beside the tidal river.

Every twenty feet wooden benches stood. White Oak took a seat at a table, inviting them to stare at the flow of the currents, the tide washing slowly in. A high in the water Goat skimmed past them, going downriver against the tide.

"It's funny, but the way you talk reminds me of people in . . . in the institution where I'm locked up. . . . A lot of the time we don't talk to each other there, but there are . . . fewer fences than outside. Anyhow, in a way I've always had three names inside me. Consuelo, my given name. Consuelo's a Mexican woman, a servant of servants, silent as clay. The woman who suffers. Who bears and endures. Then I'm Connie, who managed to get two years of college—till Consuelo got pregnant. Connie got decent jobs from time to time and fought welfare for a little extra money for Angie. She got me on a bus when I had to leave Chicago. But it was her who married Eddie, she thought it was smart. Then I'm Conchita, the low-down drunken mean part of me who gets by in jail, in the bughouse, who loves no good men, who hurt my daughter. . . ."

When she stopped short, the others were silent but did not seem scared or judgmental. As usual, Luciente spoke first. "Maybe Diana could help you to meld the three women into one."

"I had a warring self in me when I was thirteen. The things I wanted, I didn't think I should want, so I put them out of myself to plague and threaten me." Jackrabbit spoke with an ironic lilt, but not an irony aimed at her. "I tore so, I saddened I'd gone through my naming. I wanted to return to the children's house, with my mothers ready to fuss when I called them. I had begun to train as a shelf diver, but I didn't want to do that; at the same time I couldn't feel what I did want. . . . You don't at core believe you're three women—that's a useful way to talk about your life. But I did believe the ocean was trying to drown me, cause I felt swallowed by the training. . . ."

"What happened to you?" she asked him.

"I went mad with fear. In the madhouse I met Bolivar and he was good for me in learning to say that initial 'I want, I want.' I had played a lot as a child with paints and with holies and I felt . . . most alive then. I had to do that in the center of my life. I had to follow my comp through and even push it. So Bolivar and I went to study with Marika of Amherst. Then I studied in Provincetown with Blackfish. You see, I'm a needy type and every time I lack, I add on. The next time I jagged, I grabbed Luciente."

"You came from Fall River?" White Oak asked him.

He nodded. "I moved here to be with Bolivar."

"Our gain." White Oak grinned. "Not for your winning disposition always, but you make pretty things and strong holies. In the shop yesterday I was screen-batching the new tintos of Luciente turning her belly up to the sun."

"White Oak, you graze me," Luciente said. "How can you say it's my belly?"

"Person has a good belly," Jackrabbit said. "I like good round bellies. Like yours, White Oak."

They were flirting right in front of Luciente and nobody seemed to care. White Oak must have been twenty-five years older than Jackrabbit, although they were so athletic it was hard to tell for sure. White Oak's hair was abundant and worn loose, but she had a network of deep laugh lines around her eyes and mouth.

White Oak's kenner made a noise. "Here I am, White Oak," she said to it.

"Zo, are we running to crack the new test today or not?" A sharp voice rose from her wrist. "We're limping with Bee off till three and Luciente off till who knows when."

"Flying." White Oak sighed. "Since coordinating this six, Corydora watches the clock as if it could couple with per!"

"No slinging mates. Corydora's doing a good job," Luciente said. "Even if person does try to hand me guilt on a plate about being called up for the time proj. Too bad you lugs have to stiff it twice as hard." She made a mock-pious face.

"Corydora's your boss?"

"We coordinate by lot," Luciente explained as White Oak jogged off. "For sixmonth at a time."

"Why do it that way?" Connie asked. "Some people know how to run a lab, and some people don't, right?"

"Whenever we decide we're ripe to join a work base, we fuse as full members. We share the exciting jobs and the dull jobs. We don't think telling people what to do is a real world skill. Now, joining a base . . . Some people stay on where they study. Others go away to study and then come home—"

"Place matters to us," Jackrabbit said. "A sense of land, of village and base and family. We're strongly rooted. People of your time weren't? So I've been told—lacking Luciente's time traveling. On per it's wasted, too. I bet that one talks a blue streak in your century and looks at nothing."

Connie laughed. "Where I am now, there's not much to see. . . . You . . . went mad a second time?"

"Jackrabbit's jealous of my assignment. Jackrabbit catches like you, but person transmutes everything! . . . I always choose catchers!" Luciente frowned at her big strong hands.

"I'm jealous of everybody's gifts. I want to be everybody and feel everything and do everything. Wherever I am, where I'm not plagues me. As long as I don't have to get up too early in the morning to do it all." He stretched languidly. "The second time I was mad, Diana helped me. I'm *sure* Luci has talked about Diana. At great length."

"We're jealous of each other's past," Luciente said with sudden gloom. "We'll have to have a worming someday."

"*I* don't dread a worming, all that attent. . . . Diana was just emerging from per own journey down, and was more helpful than I can easily say. I only needed twomonth and I came out with a stronger healing than the first."

"Do you tell everyone you meet that you've been mad twice?" She resented his casual, almost boastful air. She lugged that radioactive fact around New York like a hidden sore. To find out she had been in an institution scared people—how it scared them. Not a good risk for a job. They feared madness might prove contagious.

Jackrabbit looked into her eyes with piercing curiosity. "Why not? Why keep that from you any more than studying with Marika?"

"In my time you'd be ashamed. . . . When people find out, they pull away so fast I can see it. Jerky. Afterward, if they have to deal with me, they're thinking all the time that I might suddenly go berserk and start climbing the walls or jumping out the window. Or they don't believe anything I say."

"People of your time confuse me, for they seem neither

strongly inknowing nor strongly outgoing. Except in couples. Unstable dyads, fierce and greedy, trying to body the original mother-child bonding. It looks tragic and blind!"

Luciente said quickly, "I've known Connie for some time, and I wouldn't call per blind. Connie has a high capacity to respond to others. We should not sound arrogant because we have a more evolved society—we came from them, after all!"

"More evolved!" Connie snorted. "I'd say things have gone backward!"

"Our technology did not develop in a straight line from yours," Luciente said seriously, looking with shining black gaze, merry, alert in a way that cast grace notes around her words. "We have limited resources. We plan cooperatively. We can afford to waste . . . nothing. You might say our—you'd say religion?—ideas make us see ourselves as partners with water, air, birds, fish, trees."

"We learned a lot from societies that people used to call primitive. Primitive technically. But socially sophisticated." Jackrabbit paced, frowning. "We tried to learn from cultures that dealt well with handling conflict, promoting cooperation, coming of age, growing a sense of community, getting sick, aging, going mad, dying—"

"Yeah, and you still go crazy. You still get sick. You grow old. You die. I thought in a hundred and fifty years some of these problems would be solved, anyhow!"

"But Connie, some problems you *solve* only if you stop being human, become metal, plastic, robot computer. Is dying itself a *problem?*" Luciente got up to cast a last, lingering glance at the river. "Come. Bee prompted I show you the children's house."

"I can't resist that! A house for kids?" Her legs felt heavy. Suddenly she was slipping back into her drugged real body in real time. A surge of sadness flowed through her hips and belly. Worse, finally, than never to be loved again was never to hold a child next to her body. Her child. Her flesh. She felt a slackening through her, that beginning to slip out of her connection with Luciente, back to the asylum. For an instant she breathed the stifling heat of the closed isolation room, she smelled its stale fecal smell, its smell of caged and fearful bodies. She fought like a swimmer going down. She cast a soundless appeal toward Luciente: Help me! For a long nauseated moment she blurred over and she was no place, lost, terrified.

Seven

JACKRABBIT was towering over her, lifting her to her feet. His thin face furrowed with serious intent. He held her against him, supporting her in a close hug with one long bony arm while the other hand gently stroked her hair back from her forehead. "Don't sadden. Little Pepper and Salt, don't fade on us." Her face was level with his unbuttoned work shirt, his tanned chest prickly with brass hairs, and his voice burred through the skin into her. "We'd be stupid not to sense you're confined wrongly. That you hurt and sadden there and no one seems to want to help you heal. That you're fed drugs that wound your body. Enjoy us. Don't fade from old pain and return to present pain. Guest here awhile."

Unmistakably, as his voice burred against her and his hand kneaded her neck, urging her to relax, she felt the rise of his erection, his hardening against her. She tried to wriggle free, and he at once released her.

"I catch sexually." He shrugged. "Don't upset more. Truly I meant to calm you."

"Doesn't he drive you crazy with jealousy? Why do you let him act this way?" she asked Luciente, who was trying to control a giggling fit.

"Jackrabbit means it—person was trying to comfort you. But person wants to couple with everybody."

"Aw, not *everybody*. Not *all* of the time."

"Just most of the people most of the time." Luciente put

one arm through hers and one through Jackrabbit's. "To the children's house."

When was a pass not a pass? When did nineteen-year-old artists throw their arms around women twice their age from the loony bin? Little Pepper and Salt: what a thing to call her, meaning her hair with the white streak along the part growing out raggedy. That reminded her too of her Texas family, for they would give each other blunt nicknames like One Arm and Old Dimwit. Anglos thought that cruel, and she had come to accept the judgment and to expect a veneer of polite refusal to admit seeing.

"Don't you people ever have to work?" she asked irritably. They were passing greenhouses set into the earth, the sound of falling water. "All those adults taking off to watch a twelve-year-old go for a ride. You all have a mañana attitude for real."

"We have high production!" Luciente's black eyes glinted indignation. "Mouth-of-Mattapoisett exports protein in flounder, herring, alewives, turtles, geese, ducks, our own blue cheese. We manufacture goose-down jackets, comforters and pillows. We're the plant-breeding center for this whole sector in squash, cucumbers, beans, and corn. We build jizers, diving equipment, and the best nets this side of Orleans, on the Cape. On top we export beautiful poems, artwork, holies, rituals, and a new style of cooking turtle soups and stews!"

"Why isn't anybody in a hurry? Why are the kids always underfoot? How can you waste so much time talking?"

Jackrabbit waved his arms windmill fashion. "How many hours does it take to grow food and make useful objects? Beyond that we care for our brooder, cook in our fooder, care for animals, do basic routines like cleaning, politic and meet. That leaves hours to talk, to study, to play, to love, to enjoy the river."

"At spring planting, at harvest, when storms come, when some crisis strikes, Connie, we work, we stiff it till we drop. . . . The old folks story about how they used to have to stiff it all the time. How long the struggle was to turn things over and change them. After, what a mess the whole ying-and-yan of it was from peak to sea." Luciente waved off into the distance. "Now we don't have to comp ourselves that hard in ordintime. . . . Grasp, after we dumped the jobs telling people what to do, counting money and moving it about, making people do what they don't want or bashing them for doing what they want, we have lots of people to work. Kids work, old folks work, women and men work. We put a lot of work into feeding everybody without destroying the soil, keeping up its health and fertility. With most everybody at it part time, nobody breaks their back and grubs dawn to dust like old-time farmers. . . . Instance, in March I might work sixteen hours. In December, four . . ."

"You said you made jizers, comforters. Where are the factories?"

"We just passed the pillow and comforter factory."

"Can I see it?" When she met Eddie, she had been working in a loft where many Spanish-speaking women sewed children's clothes.

Jackrabbit bounded ahead and the door opened. Inside the opaque peach cube, she saw no one. The machinery made the most noise she had heard in the village. "Is this all automated?" she shouted.

"Fasure," Jackrabbit shouted back. "Who wants to stuff pillows? I tore one open once hitting Bolivar over the head. What a mess! Gets up your nose. And the padded jackets with down— they're very warm but who would want to stuff every patch?"

"They're stuffed first, then sewn," she said. "So nobody works in this factory? Not even a supervisor?"

"It's mechanical," Luciente said. "The analyzer oversees it, with constant monitoring and feedback. In operations like the brooder, most everything is automated, but we need human presence because mistakes are too serious."

"This runs off solar energy?"

"No, methane gas from composting wastes."

"Okay, you can automate a whole factory," she said as they walked back into the sunshine. "So why do I see people grubbing around broccoli plants picking off caterpillars? Why is everybody running around on foot or bicycles?"

"We have so much energy from the sun, so much from wind, so much from decomposing wastes, so much from the waves, so much from the river, so much from alcohol from wood, so much from wood gas." Luciente checked them off on her fingers. "That's a fixed amount. Manufacturing and mining are better done by machines. Who wants to go deep into the earth and crawl through tunnels breathing rock dust and never seeing the sun? Who wants to sit in a factory sewing the same four or five comforter patterns?"

"There are ten, in fact," Jackrabbit said. "I counted them."

"Only you have been in enough beds to be sure," Luciente said with a tucked-in smile. They walked on toward a joined group of free-form buildings of sinuous curves suggesting a mass of eggs, but with long loops thrown off and high arches and arcades. This just-grew was the color of terra cotta. A vine ran all over the south side, with big velvet flowers that gave off a fragrance of cloves. Bird feeders hung from every protrusion, out of windows, on posts. The roof was studded with birdhouses and a pigeon coop built in, as if the masonry broke into lace through which pigeons went fluttering and cooing.

Small gardens ran right among the clump of buildings, vegetables and flowers intermixed, tomato plants growing with rosebushes and onions, pansies and bean plants. Some were planted in open borders and some were surrounded by a thin shimmery fence like spiderweb. Out over the bay a towering mass of gray clouds was forming as the wind rose.

"Smells like rain," Jackrabbit said. "The day's turning."

"I hope if it's going to rain, Innocente has time to complete a shelter." Luciente eyed the clouds. "Hope Bee and Otter get back before the storm. Lux too, I mean," she added guiltily.

"When I was on my naming, it rained every damned day," Jackrabbit said. "I should have come back Drowned Rat."

In one of the spiderweb gardens an old man with a bush of white hair and a gnarled face, arms like driftwood scoured by salt and wind, was picking peas into a basket and weeding into another, with two kids of nine or ten working on either side.

"How come they aren't in school?" she asked. "Is school out already for the summer?"

"That *is* school," Luciente said, drawing Connie nearer to them.

"This one is lamb's-quarters, no?" one kid was asking. "Can you eat it?"

"Fasure."

"Look at the shape of the pea flowers. Most legumes have irregular flowers with five petals—see, the two lower ones join in a keel, like the keel on the fishing boats. The two at the sides are like spread wings. Then you have one on top. Most legumes have leaves like these."

"Alternate. Compound. With these twisty things that hold on?"

"Tendrils. Some have thorns instead. After we're done weeding, we'll look for a tree that's evolved in a typical legume way, that has thorns a couple of inches long." His fingers showed the size.

As they strolled on, she said, "But they can't possibly learn as much that way as they would in a classroom with a book!"

"They can read. We all read by four or so," Jackrabbit said. "But who wants to grow up with a head full of facts in boxes? We never leave school and go to work. We're always working, always studying. We think, what person thinks person knows has to be tried out all the time. Placed against what people need. We care a lot *how* things are done."

"Every seven years you get a sabbatical," Luciente said. "You're off production for a year and all you're liable for is family stuff. Some go study in their field. Some learn a language or travel. Hermit in the wilderness. Pursue some line of private research. Or paint. Or write a book."

Connie had been craning her head around. "I see a lot of old people here. Is this building like an old folks' home too?"

Outside on the first lawn of grass she had seen here, a circle of small children sat crowding around an old woman with her hair in braids and the face of a defiant eagle. In spite of her age she still had some teeth—they were too yellowed and irregular to be dentures—and she was telling a story in a high quavering dramatic voice. "Then Green Fire came to Box Turtle and when Box Turtle saw, Box Turtle closed per box tight with a hissing of air." Her ancient brown claw hands became the turtle closing. "Green Fire sat down quietly, tucking per feet under, and waited. And waited. And waited. Finally Box Turtle slowly opened the shell a little peek and peered out."

"When I was little, that was my favorite story," Jackrabbit said. "I imagined when I was twelve I would take that name, Green Fire."

"Box Turtle's little leathery head stuck out of the shell and per little red eyes stared at Green Fire. 'What do you want, long-legged one?' asked Box Turtle.

" 'I want to learn to hide as you do,' Green Fire said.

" 'Hiding is easy when you know how,' said Box Turtle. 'But first you must trade me your long legs that run so fast, before you can learn to hide the way I do.' "

"Sappho perself made that tale long ago." Jackrabbit was watching the old woman with admiration. "Many people now tell that story, but none better. At Icebreaking I taped per telling with the latest varia for the holifile. Sappho's tales have great strength and radiance."

Luciente snapped her fingers. "We never answered your question." They passed under an archway into a room full of books on shelves, screens set into alcoves, displays and cameras and sound equipment and art supplies. A dozen kids were busy in the room. An old man—or perhaps woman—with the wiry, brittle body of spry old age was showing a small child how to work television sets that spewed reams of paper at the touch of a dial. Jackrabbit ambled off to see what some kids were doing, working on a small holi projector. Luciente stayed at her side, saying, "We believe old people and children are kin. There's more space at both ends of life. That closeness to birth and to death makes a common concern with big questions and basic patterns. We think old people, because of their distance from the problems of their own growing up, hold more patience and can be quieter to hear what children want. Not everyone who teaches the young is old—we all teach. The kids work with us. We try to share what we have learned and what we don't know. . . . I think maybe growing up is less mysterious with us since the adult world isn't separate. What better place to learn anatomy than in a clinic? What better place to learn botany than a field of corn? What better place to study mechanics than a repair shop?"

"How can Red Star repair a floater with a mob of kids underfoot?"

"A mob of kids?" Luciente shook her hair back roughly. "I puzzle, I admit. . . . We think about kids so different it makes us crosstalk, my friend. . . . We ask a lot of our kids but . . . politely? It's not the one-to-one bind you had with your daughter, from what you say. We have more space, more people to love us. We grow up closest to our mothers, but we swim close to all our mems—or some, at least!" Luciente grinned. "We have handfriends and pillowfriends among other children in the children's house. . . . It's hard for me to inknow what it would feel like to love only *one* and have only *one* soul to love me."

Wandering through the rooms, she found some low-ceilinged, some opening into fisheye windows, into greenhouses and porches. Some rooms crept into nooks and crannies, small staircases. Others led them to courts full of plants, delicate apparatus, sundials and water clocks, star maps and telescopes. A fountain gurgled. In it three naked children waded with a curly puppy. Birds hopped in the vines, carp lazed in a small stream that flowed through a room whirring with machines into a courtyard, where a construction project was going on with children of seven or eight wielding miniature hammers, planes, and saws.

In a dark room that smelled fresh and cool, a naked girl was listening to what she said shortly was a Bach sonata for unaccompanied flute. How . . . fancy it was in here. Room where the walls were mosaics of old bottles. Room of stark white blocks with rude mats on the floor. Room where a thin film of gauze like those spidery fences was all that separated inside and outside. Everywhere children went about their play and their business with adults, with older and younger children, with dogs, with rabbits, children with what Luciente told her were powerful microscopes, spectroscopes, molecular scanners, gene readers, computer terminals, light pencils, lightweight sound and light holi cameras and transmitters that created an image so real she could not believe till she passed her hand through that the elephant in the center of the room was only a three-dimensional image. She walked through the elephant unable to prevent her heart from racing as it raised its huge tusked head and trumpeted.

"You think because we do not bear live, we cannot love our children," Luciente said in a soft, husky voice, cupping Connie's elbow in her big calloused hand. "But we do, with whole hearts."

The nursery: round high room on the ground floor, room with a circle of windows and a small floating dome in the ceiling; here babies babbled, cried, spat, cooed. A young person in a long green loose gown slit up the sides to the thighs sat barefoot, playing a stringed instrument and singing in a sweet alto, and with a treadle board rocking a brace of cradles. A child was playing with one of the babies, tickling and making faces. The infants lay in low cradles with slatted sides that moved on runners to and fro. Connie counted five babies, including one yelling its lungs out, and then three empty cradles, also rocking.

Barbarossa burst in, out of breath. "I hear you, I hear you. You almost blew the kenner off my wrist, you rascal! What a pair of lungs." He picked up the crying baby. "They can hear you ten miles out on the shelf farm, you hairy little beast!" He sat down with the baby on a soft padded bench by the windows and unbuttoned his shirt. Then she felt sick.

He had breasts. Not large ones. Small breasts, like a flat-chested woman temporarily swollen with milk. Then with his red beard, his face of a sunburnt forty-five-year-old man, stern-visaged, long-nosed, thin-lipped, he began to nurse. The baby stopped wailing and begun to suck greedily. An expression of serene enjoyment spread over Barbarossa's intellectual schoolmaster's face. He let go of the room, of everything, and floated. Her breasts ached with remembrance. She had loved breast-feeding—that deep-down warm milky connection that seemed to start in her womb and spread up through her trunk into her full dark-nippled breasts. Her heavy breasts opened to Angelina's flower face, the sweet sunflower cradled in her arm. She had been borne on the currents of that intimate sensual connection, calmer, gentler than making love but just as enormous and satisfying. She had nursed Angelina until Eddie had absolutely insisted that she stop; for eight months she had nursed her. Angie had been a fat healthy baby. Only after Eddie had made her stop breast-feeding had Angie turned cranky about eating and become the thin doe-like child of the photographs.

She felt angry. Yes, how dare any man share that pleasure. These women thought they had won, but they had abandoned to men the last refuge of women. What was special about being a woman here? They had given it all up, they had let men steal from them the last remnants of ancient power, those sealed in blood and in milk.

"I suppose you do it all with hormones," she said testily.

"At least two of the three mothers agree to breast-feed. The way we do it, no one has enough alone, but two or three together share breast-feeding."

"Why bother? Don't tell me you couldn't make formula?"

"But the intimacy of it! We suspect loving and sensual enjoyment are rooted in being held and sucking and cuddling."

"Where are the babies from the empty cradles? Are they sick?"

"Outside with mothers or somebody! Oftentimes when we're working, we take the baby in a backpack. They get fresh air. When breast-feeding ends, everybody who feels like it lugs them around."

"Suppose you took Barbarossa's baby and he wanted it. Wouldn't he get sore?"

"What are kenners for? You ask."

She stared at the room, blue and lemon and grass green. Sunlight melted through the circle of windows and a muted vegetable light passed through the dome. The windows stood open to the breezes now. The person in green was changing a diaper and wiping the cradle. Both diaper and wipe-up went down a chute.

"Well, at least you're not so crazy about ecology that you wash diapers."

"They're made from cornhusks and cobs, and they compost. Very soft. Feel." The diapers tore off a large roll hung from a stand in the form of a snake dancing, with many tinkling bells attached. Over the cradles mobiles turned and twittered. No pink and blue, no Disney animals prancing, no ugly cartoon pigs decked in human clothes. The nursery was airy, soothing, full of rustling and little bells and wind chimes and the sound of the stringed instrument, the cradles rocking. On the window seat, Barbarossa cuddled his baby to his breast, all the stern importance melted from his features. She could almost hate him in the peaceful joy to which he had no natural right; she could almost like him as he opened like a daisy to the baby's sucking mouth.

The person in green was cuddling the baby just changed and singing a slightly mournful lullaby:

"Nobody knows
how it flows
as it goes.

Nobody goes
where it rose
where it flows."

"Where's Jackrabbit?" Connie asked, realizing that somewhere in the maze of rooms and courtyards he had slipped away.

"Gone to play. This house seduces you."

"Nobody chose
how it grows
how it flows.

How it grows
how it glows
in the heart of the rose . . ."

As they went up a broad shallow stairway, that song, plaintive and endless, followed after them.

"Except in the nursery and among the very young, the kids don't have toys," she said suddenly.

"Most of what children must learn, they learn by doing. Under five, fasure they need toys to learn coordination, dexterity; they practice tenderness on dolls. . . . I'm looking for Magdalena." Casually Luciente flicked her kenner. "Magdalena? Ah, person is coming. Magdalena is unusual. Person does not switch jobs but is permanent head of this house of children. It is per calling. Sometimes a gift expresses itself so strongly, like Jackrabbit's need to create color and form, like Magdalena's need to work with children, that it shapes a life. Person must not do what person cannot do—you have heard us say this a hundred times; but likewise, person must do what person has to do."

A small figure with velvety black skin—she had to be a woman from the delicacy of her bones—a long neck, hair cut to her scalp in an austere tracery of curls, descended toward them, smiling slightly. She came drifting down, stooping to pick off dead leaves from the vine that grew over one side of the open stairs. She was no taller than a ten- or eleven-year-old.

"Magdalena has no family. Person wants this instead. Person is chaste and solitary among adults," Luciente said as Magdalena came slowly toward them.

"You mean an old maid?"

"I don't know this term. You speak it with contempt?"

"Yeah, it's an insult. A woman who can't get a man."

"Connie, we don't get each other. And we respect people who don't want to couple. It's per way: the way for Magdalena."

In a high chirpy voice like a cricket, Magdalena greeted her. "Be guest, woman from the past." She stuck out her tiny hand. Her grip was warm, sun-heated ebony. "I'm Magdalena."

"You're the only woman I met here who has a real name. I mean like somebody from my block."

"It's the name of a woman burned to death for witchcraft in Germany many centuries ago. A wisewoman who healed with herbs. I saw per in my naming trance." Magdalena smiled, a blink of ivory in her quick face. Was she sixty? More? Maybe old people here retained an ongoing strength because they felt useful. When she thought of getting old it always made her feel scared and low in her mind, old age as grim as those witch masks kids bought in the candy store and wore in the streets of El Barrio at Halloween.

"I wanted to know about the toys. You have all those gadgets here. Compared to your huts, it's . . . fancy. Nice. But I don't see many toys for the older kids. Can't you afford to get them toys? I see nobody rich here, but I don't see anybody poor. I think of how sad it's been for families like mine who could never give their kids the beautiful dolls with real hair, the sleds, the bikes and racing cars they see advertised. If I had a house of children, I'd give them every toy in the world! I wouldn't hold *nothing* back!"

Magdalena touched her on the cheek. "They play farming and cooking and repair and fishing and diving and manufacture and plant breeding and baby tending. When children aren't kept out of the real work, they don't have the same need for imitation things. I have studied about the care of children in earlier ages, so I understand more than Luciente what you're talking about. In that time, Luciente, they had many toys for teaching sex roles to children. Children were kept in separate buildings all day and even after puberty were not supposed to begin full lives."

Slowly they descended the broad stairs to the bottom and moved off along an arcade. As they turned a corner, in a little nook that was both bower and bench, a rampant twining vine of wisteria ancient and knotted like muscles held in its protective grasp a curved wooden bench that was a lovely size for curling up and napping or reading, for sitting and feeling sorry for oneself, for daydreaming, for imagining voyages and adventures, for whispering secrets to a best friend. There two children, a boy and a girl six or seven, had hung their light summer tunics on the vine like flags and they were seriously engaged in an attempt to have sex together. It did not look like an attempt that would prove immediately successful, but it was one into which they were putting great effort.

The girl gave them a quick indignant glare. Magdalena pulled Connie away by the arm, Luciente having withdrawn even more quickly. As Magdalena dragged her away, Connie asked, "Aren't you going to stop them?"

Magdalena dropped her arm and began to laugh and although Luciente tried for a moment to keep a straight face she began to laugh with her. Connie stopped, furious. "They're babies! If they were . . . playing with knives you'd stop them. What's wrong with you?"

Magdalena shook her head in wonder. "They learn how to use knives. . . . Mostly they learn sex from each other. If a child has trouble, we try to heal, to help, but—"

"They can hurt each other!"

"How? If a child is rough, the other children deal with that. If I notice a child bullying, I try to work with that child, the mothers and family, to strengthen better ways."

Luciente nudged her in the ribs. "Zo, as a child you never played sex with other children? Not ever?"

Connie paced on, frowning. She leaned on the railing of the courtyard. "Oh. Sure." In fact, her brother Luis had taken her pants down under the porch and poked at her with his fingers, finishing with warnings not to tell Mamá. She had not liked the prodding by Luis, who had kept his own pants on, but it had given her an idea. Casually and a lot more gently, she had begun fooling around together with José, her favorite brother, one year and two months younger.

She took care of him often. Luis didn't have to and he would be off with the boys. She would take José by the hand and they would play together. Ninety-nine games out of a hundred they played with paper dolls, with José's wooden duck, with Luis's wagon if he left it there, with dolls made out of wild flowers, games of school, of sitting at imaginary tables eating meals of grass soup and scolding babies, of charros, of detectives, of general bang-bang. But every so often they climbed into the old car up on blocks behind the chicken coop next door and they touched each other where it felt best to touch. They did not need to warn each other not to say anything. Both of them sensed that what felt really good must be forbidden. It was a silent, pleasurable game that had stopped certainly by the time they moved to Chicago. But not one ounce of Connie's flesh believed it had done her any harm.

"Okay," she said slowly. "Maybe it don't hurt. But I know if I saw my daughter playing that way, I'd have to stop her. I'd feel so guilty if I didn't! I'd feel like a bad mother, a rotten mother."

"How interesting," Magdalena said politely, with her head cocked. "Our notions of evil center around power and greed—taking from other people their food, their liberty, their health, their land, their customs, their pride. We don't find coupling bad unless it involves pain or is not invited." She paused before a closed door. "Come. Watch a lesson."

Inside, a little boy with red-brown skin sat curled up in a wooden chair wearing a metallic cap like a gold hairnet. His eyes were closed and he was breathing slowly as if in sleep. Magdalena cautioned her with a tiny hand to keep quiet. The boy opened his eyes and turned to a screen on which a moving light showed waves that slid evenly across.

"Good, Sparrow! Now without the guide." An old man sat against the wall like a bag of bones, with only shreds of white hair clinging to his huge skull.

"What is he learning?"

"Pulse and blood pressure," the boy said. "How do you start in your village?"

"Start what?"

"Inknowing," the child said wonderingly. "Do you call it different where you come from?"

She turned to Magdalena, who said, "In your day some

of it was called yoga, some meditating, some biofeedback, and some had no name at all."

"We aren't mad to control," Luciente said, "but we want to prevent overreacting—heart attacks, indigestion, panic. We want to get used to knowing exactly what we feel, so we don't shove on other people what's coming from inside."

"We want to teach inknowing and outknowing." Magdalena gestured apology and swept the women gently back into the hall, shutting the door. "To feel with other beings. To catch, where the ability exists—instance, so strongly in you. We teach sharpening of the senses. Coning, going down, how to reach nevel, how to slow at will."

"What is all that stuff?"

"States of consciousness. Types of feeling."

"How can you teach somebody to feel? From a book you can learn the multiplication tables. But how can you teach love?"

"But every mother always has. Or failed to." Seeing something in Connie's face, Magdalena went on quickly. "We educate the senses, the imagination, the social being, the muscles, the nervous system, the intuition, the sense of beauty—as well as memory and intellect. Anyhow, we try!" She laughed again, that laugh that picked immediately at Luciente and made her grin too. "People here in our bony skulls"—lightly Magdalena rapped on Connie's forehead—"how easy to feel isolate. We want to root that forebrain back into a net of connecting." She turned back to Luciente, smiling broadly. "Here comes Jackrabbit with Dawn. By the road, your child grows better and better at the arts of defense. You'll be feathered when you see the next demo!"

Long-limbed rangy Jackrabbit came loping through an archway, making high neighing sounds. A brown-skinned girl with dark braids clung to his neck, laughing with a wide-open mouth that showed her small teeth. Avid teeth flashed. Arms hung on tight. She clung to his neck and laughed and laughed and kicked his ribs with her bare feet. She was about seven, wearing a lavender summer tunic, and she had a scab on her small round, her heavily tanned, her kissable knee. How she laughed, like dry bells, like bells partly muffled, how she laughed: her golden-brown eyes met Connie's. Connie's heart turned in her chest. Her heart sharpened into a dagger and stopped.

"Angelina!" she cried out, and her voice burst from her like a bubble of blood from her mouth. Then she was back in the isolation cell, flat against one wall as if she had been thrown there. She held both hands against her striving chest.

Angelina! Or any brown-skinned girl child of seven or so with golden-brown eyes. How did she know what Angelina would look like after three years? She wouldn't be barefoot in Scarsdale.

Suddenly she assented with all her soul to Angelina in Mattapoisett, to Angelina hidden forever one hundred fifty years into the future, even if she should never see her again. For the first time her heart assented to Luciente, to Bee, to Magdalena. Yes, you can have my child, you can keep my child. Even with your obscenities and your talking cats. She will be strong there, well fed, well housed, well taught, she will grow up much better and stronger and smarter than I. I assent, I give you my battered body as recompense and my rotten heart. Take her, keep her! I want to believe she is mine. I give her to Luciente to mother, with gladness I give her. She will never be broken as I was. She will be strange, but she will be glad and strong and she will not be afraid. She will have enough. She will have pride. She will love her own brown skin and be loved for her strength and her good work. She will walk in strength like a man and never sell her body and she will nurse her babies like a woman and live in love like a garden, like that children's house of many colors. People of the rainbow with its end fixed in earth, I give her to you!

Eight

THAT Monday one of Dr. Redding's attendants, a stooped, paunchy man with burst capillaries in his nose that marked an alcoholic, came to fetch Connie. As the nurse shuffled the papers to sign her out to the attendant, she could feel the palpable envy around her. It did not matter what she was going to: she was going off ward. Nurse Wright started to grab a coat for her but the attendant said, "Don't bother. It's raining cats and dogs. I'll take 'em through the tunnel."

Nurse Wright pursed her lips. "You'd better take a coat anyhow. Somebody else might have to bring the patient back."

The coat was so long it hung to her midcalves and the sleeves concealed her hands, but she knew better than to complain. She plodded after the attendant, folding the sleeves back so that she could use her hands on the two surviving buttons.

All the old buildings were joined by tunnels through which equipment, supplies, and sometimes patients were shipped back and forth. Occasionally patients with grounds privileges hung out in the tunnels smoking, talking, flirting, finding a dark place to sleep. No one on staff with a rank above attendant ever seemed to use them.

"Hi, Mack, Tomo. How ya doing?" Her attendant stopped to greet two men wheeling a covered cart.

"Hokay, hokay," the short one said briskly. "How goes with you?"

"Hi, Fats. Man, this place is creepy today," the younger said. "If it keeps on raining like this, the whole damn place is going to grow two inches of mold."

"I hate it when it rains every day," Fats said. "Hey, you got something nice this week?"

"Everything, man. Red devils, yellowjackets, rainbows. Genuine Nepalese hash. The stiffest coke you ever snorted. You don't go for ups—how about sopors? You dig on them, don't you, Fats? Real mellow."

The man with the accent blinked at them with faint contempt and began reading what looked like a sports magazine in Japanese, pulled from his pocket under the white coat. As they bargained, she stood in her huge coat, waiting. The mad are invisible. Neither had any fear she could damage them. Indeed, if she cared to try, she would only hurt herself. Revenge came easily to staff.

"What's under the tablecloth?" Fats poked the bundle on the cart.

"Old geezer from chronic service." Mack cast back the sheet. Sharp gaunt face of an old woman. Her dark flinty eyes in death stared straight up with a look of rage. Mack flipped the sheet over her again but it caught on her hooked nose. He had to free it. "Kicked off last night. Got to truck it down to the meat department."

"Don't know why the doctors want to cut up every crazy that checks out. When you seen one you seen them all."

"They got to put something on the death certificate."

"Heart stopped." Fats punched Mack in the arm. "That's the ticket."

"See you around, man." Mack started pushing the cart and Tomo hastened to take his position, although the cart was obviously light enough for one to handle.

The last time she had been summoned, they had given her the most thorough physical of her life, and as a side effect treated her old burn and sent her to the dentist for work on her battered teeth. As she was thrust in, she looked at the patients lined up on the chairs as usual: the graceful West Indian, Captain Cream; the tiny black woman, Miss Green; Orville; Alvin, who was white, forty-two, and perhaps the closest of those she had met in the hall here to being really mad; Mrs. Ortiz, a thin bouncy Puerto Rican woman, who winked at her; and Skip, who had saved her a place beside him.

"What's coming down today?" she asked him.

"What they fondly call a battery of tests. Rorschachs, draw-a-person, sentence completion, WAIS, Wechsler Memory Scale, MMPI—"

She clutched her shoulders. "What do they do to us? Does it hurt?"

"Only when you laugh . . . I don't believe it! I've been tested since I was eleven. You've never had these mothers play with you?"

She shook her head no. "What will happen?"

"Oh, like they ask you would you rather fly a plane or play with dolls. Follow the stereotypes. But why should I have to pretend I'd rather watch a football game than a ballet not to be labeled queer? The first man I ever had sex with was an attendant at Wynmont—that's a private buzz farm they sent me to when I was thirteen."

"So young. Why did they do that?"

"My parents thought I didn't work right, so they sent me to be fixed. You know, you send the riding mower back to the factory to be fixed if you get a lemon. Why not a son?"

"Did you figure out yet what this whole thing is?"

"Some research project, with us as the guinea pigs. But I'm on the case. I'll break their game soon. Fats is queer on me."

"That Dr. Redding—I don't like him. He feels so above us. He's not even scared of us the way some are—scared of catching what we got. It never occurs to him he might crack."

"Not Morgan, though. If you stare at him a long time, he starts fidgeting. You can get into staring contests with him, and he gets so he wants to win! But Redding, yeah, he's too cool. He looks through us to something on the other side he's aiming at."

A woman was dumped beside her, a tall lean satin black woman with her hair in a big wild Afro.

"I guess we're the final winners of their screening," Connie said to her. "I saw you when they were x-raying us, but we never met. I'm Connie Ramos."

"Alice Blue Bottom, honey. You Puerto Rican?"

"No, Chicana. I was born in Texas."

"No lie? You don't sound like it. Me, I got myself born in Biloxi, Mississippi. You ever been there?"

She shook her head. "I grew up in Chicago from when I was seven."

"You know what, girl? I put in five years on the South Side of Chicago working as a cocktail waitress in the Kit-Kat Club. Left and come to Harlem with a man I stupid to cross the street with."

"I came to New York to get away from a man I was scared of."

"Better reason than mine, sugar, though I never been scared of a man in my whole life. I eat them for breakfast two at a time. Why you scared of him?"

"He . . . forced me. He took my pay check off of me and said he'd give me a little. He bribed the super to let him in my flat—or he just pulled a knife on him, who knows? When I got home from work—I was working in an office then, I had a good job as a secretary to a real estate man, Chicano—he was in my flat."

"No man ever lay a finger on me I didn't ask for, cause I tote a shiv, and I know how to use it. I carve up more men than you count on your both hands, didn't treat me right. You take shit and you is shit, girl. A man good to me, then I good to him. Everybody know that about Alice Blue Bottom."

"How come you call yourself Alice Blue Bottom?" Skip asked, smiling from under his long lashes.

"Long skinny white boy, don't you wish you know that?" She tilted back her tower of a neck and laughed, with her breasts freely jiggling against the red dress. She had her own clothing, for sure. Some attendant had made her sew up the front a couple of inches with the wrong color thread, but the dress was still shorter and fit better than anything else around. "Cause I'm so black, I'm blue—maybe. No way you gonna find out."

"That's Skip," Connie said. "Do you know anything about this project they're using us for?"

"Papermaking. That's all. That's all they ever doing. You know time you be sitting in that jiveassed group therapy, those doctors thinking how they going to write it all up. How they going to tell it on the mountain at they next staff session. Bullshit!"

Alice's name was called and she strolled after the nurse, swinging her broad, high ass across the waiting room. An attendant brought Sybil out of the office, and Connie half rose. Sybil saw her at once and their eyes exchanged messages of hope. Fats placed Sybil in a chair far down the line. As soon as Fats turned his back, Sybil hopped up and quietly slid into the seat Alice had just left.

"Sybil, it's good to see you! I heard they were shocking you?"

Sybil raised an elegant bony hand to her forehead. "I have dreadful headaches. I have trouble remembering words, the names of objects. Yesterday I could not think what one calls the wood around a door! I nearly wept with rage. . . . What ward are you on?"

"G-2. Not so bad. Are you still on L-6?"

"No, D-5. I wish we were on the same ward. Do you have grounds privileges?"

"Not yet. I'm trying."

"Hey, you." Fats marched over to Sybil. "I put you down at the end. Don't go sneaking away on me."

"We know each other," Connie pleaded. Her voice fawned. "We were just talking. Isn't it good for us to relate?"

"Don't sweet-talk me," Fats said. "You're all violent or you wouldn't be here. You do what I say and we'll get along. Otherwise you'll be eating dirt." He marched Sybil down to the chair where he had parked her.

"Are you lovers with each other?" Skip asked her softly.

"No, we're real good friends. I know her from last time in." She did not mind his asking, really. Better than thinking it and never asking.

"They almost didn't include her. I think Dr. Morgan's scared of big women. But Dr. Redding rode right over him. Said he can handle any of us like day-old kittens. That's what he said, that dear man."

"Ummmm." She smiled. "I bet he's never seen Sybil when she's fighting mad. It takes two attendants to hold her down."

"I'd like to fantasize about that. But all I seem to hurt is myself."

"Me too. Except for what got me in here . . . Listen, Skip, if you entirely hated yourself, you'd be dead by now, right? So part of you does love you."

He giggled wildly. "What a valentine. Part of me loves me. Signed, some love, Skip." He unfolded to his feet as Fats came for him.

The next day rain still blew in gusts across the grounds and the porch was too wet to sit on. Sleepy with medication, she went into the day room. Sharma was standing in front of the set, frowning.

"What's wrong?" she asked Sharma as she shuffled past.

"God damn it," Sharma said. Something she wouldn't have said if the attendants had been in earshot. Patients were punished for unladylike behavior. "I like this soap opera, 'Perilous Light.' I always watch it at home. Anyhow, at one-thirty I went to ask Richard to unlock the set and turn it to channel five. I waited for half an hour while they yakked. Then they finally let Lois out to her job and they got out the mop—they even lock up the mop!—for Glenda to use. Then Mrs. Stein had a question about her meds. She said the doctor changed it. They argued with her for ten minutes. Finally they looked it up. They shuffled papers for ten more minutes. Finally they agreed the doctor signed a change. Then they beat that around for a while. By the time I got Richard to put on channel five, it's the end of the serial anyhow. There's this other woman who's after Maggie's husband, I want to see what's happening. It's like my husband—women are always after him."

She mumbled sympathy, half out on her feet. The set flickered, giving a cover to sitting in the dim room. She took a chair at the back and nodded out. She was sinking into the stuffy sleep of Thorazine when she felt Luciente's presence and lurched unsteadily to meet her.

"It's raining here too," she said with disappointment in her thickened voice.

"You don't farm, Connie, or you wouldn't feel bad about rain." Luciente peered into her face. "You're so drugged you're not quite with me. May I help you?" Luciente put her warm, dry hands beside Connie's temples and pressed carefully but firmly. She began a series of exploratory pressures over Connie's head. "Here, sit on the bench." Luciente spoke to her in a low compelling tone. "Relax. Relax. Yes. Open up. Yes. Flow with me. Relax."

She knew she was being hypnotized and that the iron cage around her brain was lifting. The heaviness slid from her.

"Zo. Better?" Luciente handed her a closely woven hat to keep off the rain, broad enough to protect her shoulders and, unlike an umbrella, not requiring a hand to hold it. Off they started along the slick paths of the village. "Come, we'll bike to the Grange—a beautiful three-hundred-year-old wooden building!" On the end of the village beyond the fish breeding tanks stood racks of bicycles.

"But I haven't been on a bike in years! I can't!"

"Good. We'll take a two-seater. I'll pedal and you'll do what you can."

"I've seen lots of wooden buildings, Luciente! I've seen buildings a lot older than that in Texas."

"You wanted to see 'Government.' It's working today."

"The town government? Like a mayor? A council?"

Luciente made a face, throwing her slack-clad leg over the bike. "Look at it and then we'll figure out what it's like, okay?" They set out along a narrow paved way wandering a pleasant route over a high curved bridge across the river, under big and little trees, past roses drooping under the load of the rain, past willows, past boats and corn patches with pole beans and pumpkins interplanted, past the edge of another village marked by a bike rack.

"This is Cranberry," Luciente said, hitting the brakes so they squeaked to a stop. "Everybody's always making lists of what I ought to show you. Every lug in my base, my mems, everybody at council. Even my defense squad—I'm practicing on my belly and everybody's giving me lists what I should show you. Harlem-Black flavor village."

"I see gardens. Windmills. People. Greenhouses. Where are the huts?"

"Below." Luciente left the bike by a big maple and helped her off. "We'll stop by Erzulia." She used her kenner. "Zuli! It's Luci. I brought the woman from the past. Meet us at your space to show a Cranberry dwelling, favor?"

"No such," said a voice that sounded much more like a black from her own time than anybody she'd heard here. "Got a mean pelvic fracture, old person from Fall River. You drop right by my space and show it your own self."

"Erzulia and Bee are sweet friends," Luciente said. "Erzulia has tens of lovers. Person never stales on anybody, just adds on. Over there!" She pointed to a two-story building. "The hospital where Zuli works—hospital for our township. That great big greenhouse is one where they breed the spinners—those single-celled creatures we use for fences and barriers."

"Creatures! They're alive!"

"Fasure. They mend themselves."

As they walked, she saw that courtyards were dug into the earth the level of an ample story, surrounded by dense, often thorny hedges—blackberries, raspberries. An animal or a child couldn't push through. At ground level trees grew, gardens flourished, paths wound, swings hung from trees and people trotted and biked by. Goats and cows grazed, chickens ran pecking, a cat played with a dying baby rabbit. The solar heat collectors and the intakes for rain-water cisterns studded the surface like sculpture, some of them decorated with carved masks, others scalloped, inlaid with shell and glass mosaics.

Luciente led her by the hand down wide steps curving into a submerged courtyard. The yard itself was paved and had in the center a big weather-beaten table with benches all around and a scattering of chairs. A chess game sat on the table half played, under a clear cover like those Connie had seen put over big cakes. The four walls around the court were of glass threaded with spidery lines almost too fine to focus on.

"The glass can be opaqued or made one-way," Luciente explained.

"This whole house belongs to Erzulia?" Maybe they were richer here.

"No! They live in families. Everybody has private space, but they have common space too, for family. For eating, playing, watching holies. The walls are plenty thick for quiet."

Individual rooms opened onto courts and the courts served partly as hallways and partly as common space. Halls joined rooms on other courts. Luciente guided her through the maze, occasionally consulting her kenner to ask permission to open a door. They cut through a kitchen, where Luciente begged a taste of a hot spicy seafood stew. Only two private rooms were occupied at this time of day. In one, Luciente said, somebody was meditating. On the door was hung a paper hand with the fingers held up.

"That's what they use when they don't want you to enter. I say meditating—of course they may be coupling, reading, sleeping, or just pouting."

Erzulia's room faced west. It was spacious, with walls entirely covered in woven and embroidered hangings, texture upon texture and color upon color. Her bed was a high platform reached by a ladder, the space underneath closed in with hangings to make a dark cave of cushions, a small altar, shelves of herbs in bottles. The furniture was of a dark knobby substance that reminded her of bamboo. On the bed a strange blue costume was laid out.

"We should not stay here. That's Erzulia's raiment." Luciente used the old formal word.

"Is she a mother getting ready for a naming?"

"Zuli's never been a mother. Sappho is dying and Erzulia is her friend. They share a sense of old rites. Zuli follows voodoo as a discipline, as many do in Cranberry, while Sappho is an Indian old believer. But they share a closeness to . . . myths, archetypes."

"Sappho? That old woman who was telling stories to the kids?"

"The same. A great shaper of tales. Now person is very old. It's time for per to die."

"Oh?" She saw the sharp face of the corpse in the tunnel. "I wonder if she's so sure it's time."

"Per body has weakened since Wednesday. Time comes for any fruit to fall. It's a good death that arrives when you're ready for it, no?"

They climbed another broad stair to the ground, where the rain was easing and dark clouds scudded over rapidly, going out toward the bay. The air smelled clean and cottony.

In the old white Grange Hall with its octagonal tower, twenty-five or thirty people sat around an oblong table arguing about cement, zinc, tin, copper, platinum, steel, gravel, limestone, and things she could not identify. Many of them seemed to be women, although she often found when she heard a voice that she had guessed wrong. They ranged from sixteen to extreme old age. Few of them looked entirely white, although their being tanned by the sun made that harder to judge than it might have been in the middle of the winter. They spoke in ordinary voices and did not seem to be speechifying. Behind some seated at the table sat others listening closely and at times putting in their comments and questions.

"We have a five-minute limit on speeches. We figure that anything person can't say in five minutes, person is better off not saying." Luciente and she pulled up chairs to sit behind Otter, whom she had not at first recognized with her black hair in a single braid and her body in overalls splashed with mud and salt. Otter flashed them a smile before turning back to the display set in the table between every other delegate that showed figures, allotments, graphs they were discussing.

"This is your government?"

"It's the planning council for our township."

"Are they elected?"

"Chosen by lot. You do it for a year: threemonth with the rep before you and three with the person replacing you and six alone."

"We want to clear some of the woods on Goat Hill." A map flashed on the displays set in the table. The person speaking, with sideburns and a bristling mustache, somehow drew on the map indicating the section he referred to. "We would like to increase our buckwheat crop

Luciente murmured, "Rep from Goat Hill, Cape Verde flavor village upriver."

"Seems to me that cuts into the catchment area for rain water. We have none too much water, people," a person with green hair said.

"We are only thinking of a matter of fifty, sixty acres of second-growth woods and scrub. Our region imports too much grain, we have all agreed on that," the mustache argued.

"Without water we can grow nothing. Our ancestors destroyed water as if there were an infinite amount of it, sucking it out of the earth and dirtying and poisoning it as it flowed," Otter said indignantly. "Let us not be cavalier about water. What does the soil bank say?"

"I'll direct the question."

Luciente leaned close. "That's the rep from Cranberry. That person is chair today."

"Who's that with green hair?"

"Earth Advocate—speaks for rights of the total environment. Beside per is the Animal Advocate. Those positions are not chosen strictly by lot, but by dream. Every spring some people dream they are the new Animal Advocate or Earth Advocate. Those who feel this come together and the choice among them falls by lot."

The computer was flashing figures and more figures on the displays. After everyone had stared at them, the Ned's

Point rep spoke. "The woods in question are fasure catchment. To take these acres from forest would cut our capacity to hold our water table."

"How can we up our grain output if we can't pull land from scrubby woods to farming?" the Cranberry rep asked.

"Then we must up the output of the land we have," the Earth Advocate said. "We're only starting to find ways of intensively farming, so the soil is built more fertile instead of bled to dust."

Otter was still studying the display, her fat braid hanging over one shoulder. "These woods are birch, cherry, aspen, but with white pines growing up. Will be pine forest in ten years. Its history as we have it is: climax forest, cleared for farming, abandoned, scrub to climax again, bulldozed for housing, burned over, now returning to forest."

At her ear Luciente murmured, "We arrive with the needs of each village and try to divide scarce resources justly. Often we must visit the spot. Next level is regional planning. Reps chosen by lot from township level go to the regional to discuss gross decisions. The needs go up and the possibilities come down. If people are chilled by a decision, they go and argue. Or they barter directly with places needing the same resources, and compromise."

A vote was taken and Goat Hill was turned down. The Marion rep suggested, "Let's ask for a graingrower from Springfield to come to Goat Hill and see if they can suggest how to grow buckwheat without clearing more land. We in Marion would be feathered to feast the guest."

Luciente's kenner called. "How long?" Connie heard her say, and then, "We'll come soon."

"The old bridge is beautiful," a middle-aged man was arguing. "Three hundred years old, of real wrought iron. We have a skilled crafter to top-shape it."

"Nobody in your village has bled from the old bridge being out. We need ore for jizers," an old woman said. "The bridge is pretty, but our freedom may depend on jizers. Head before tail!"

"Weren't you advised last year to look out for alloys that use up less ore?" the rep from Cranberry said.

"We're working on it. So is everybody else!"

The Goat Hill rep suggested, "For the bridge, why not use a biological? It'd corrode less. Repair itself."

"We must scamp now," Luciente said, pulling her up. "Fast. We'll hop the dipper."

"What about the bike?"

Luciente looked at her blankly. "Somebody will use it."

The dipper turned out to be a bus-train object that rode on a cushion of air about a foot off the ground until it stopped, when it settled with a great sigh. It moved along at moderate speed, stopping at every village, and people got on and off with packages and babies and animals and once with a huge swordfish wrapped in leaves.

They sat down in a compartment with an old man facing them, wizened up like a sultana, fiddling constantly, with a satisfied air, with the blanket wrapped around his baby.

"Why do you have the bus cut up in little rooms this way? You'd get more people in if it was like we used to have, just one big space inside."

"It's easier to talk this way," Luciente said. "Warmer."

"You're a guest?" the old man said. "From where? Or are you a drifter?"

"From the past," Luciente explained.

"Ah, I heard, I heard. So . . ." He peered at her curiously.

"Where do you live?" Luciente asked.

"Ned's Point, where I just got on, where else? We're Ashkenazi," he told Connie.

"I don't know what that is."

"We're the flavor of Eastern European Jewry. Freud, Marx, Trotsky, Singer, Aleichem, Reich, Luxembourg, Wassermann Vittova—all these were Ashkenazi!"

"They build kenners," Luciente said. "We were just visiting the planners."

"Look, I don't understand," Connie said. "If workers in a factory, say the kenner factory, want to make more kenners and the planners decide to give them less stuff, who wins?"

"We argue," the man said. "How else?"

"There's no final authority, Connie," Luciente said.

"There's got to be. Who finally says yes or no?"

"We argue till we close to agree. We just continue. Oh, it's disgusting sometimes. It bottoms you."

"After a big political fight, we guest each other," the man said. "The winners have to feed the losers and give presents. Have you been to a town meeting?"

When Connie shook her head he clucked and shook a finger at Luciente. "You must take per. How will person learn about us?"

"Fasure," Luciente said sourly. "I'm trying! Grasp, political decisions—like whether to raise or lower population—go a different route. We talk locally and then choose a rep to speak our posit on area hookup. Then we all sit in holi simulcast and the rep from each group speaks their village posit. Then we go back into local meeting to fuse our final word. Then the reps argue once more before everybody. Then we vote."

"You must spend an awful lot of time in meetings."

"Shalom. I get off here," the old man said. "Make per bring you to Ned's Point. I'm Rebekah and I live by the east side the shul."

Luciente waved goodbye. "How can people control their lives without spending a lot of time in meetings?"

"Don't you get sick of each other?"

"Staling usually has a reason. But you can always leave, wander awhile, or find a new village."

"All right, suppose I don't want to go to meetings."

"Who could force you? People would ask why you no longer care. Friends might suggest you take a retreat or talk to a healer. If your mems felt you'd cut them off, they might ask you to leave. If too many in a village cut off, the neighboring villages send for a team of involvers."

"Years ago I was living in Chicago. I got involved that way. Meetings, meetings, meetings! My life was so busy, my head was boiling! I felt such hope. It was after my husband Martín . . . He got killed. I was young and naïve and it was supposed to be a War on Poverty. . . . But it was just the same political machine and us stupid poor people, us . . . idiots who thought we were running things for a change. We ended up right back where we were. They gave some paying jobs to so-called neighborhood leaders. All those meetings. I ended up with nothing but feeling sore and ripped off."

"You lose until you win—that's a saying those who changed our world left us. Poor people *did* get together." Luciente rose and made ready to get out as the dipper settled into the grass. She spoke to her kenner. "Locate Sappho."

"Sappho is located in tent near mill," the kenner said.

They walked the river path to the south end of the village, where a big tent had been set up. The rain slowed to a fine drizzle and the wind came fresh down the stream. The river was eddying at the turn of the tide, not quite flowing in or out. On a cot under a low roof of canvas, the old woman Sappho lay. She wore deerskin leggings and tunic, large on her and aged, though beautifully decorated with quillwork in soft colors. Gaunter than ever, her face seemed to draw back from the beak of her Indian nose. Her lips were thinned almost away. The skull stood out through the scant hair, pressing the withered skin of her forehead and cheeks. Sappho's black eyes were dull and Connie was not sure she could see, but still she turned her head from side to side to follow conversations, the heavy head turning wearily on the tiny neck like a seed head on a dried stalk.

"Sappho, here I am, Luciente, come to be with you. I've brought the woman from the past."

"Luciente, child of earth and fire like a good pot. The other I do not know. Leave it."

"Does she want me to leave?" Connie whispered.

"No, no," Luciente said in her normal loud voice. "Person only wants not to be made to remember who you are."

"Has Swallow come? Where is my child?" Her thin voice scratched the ear.

Squatting near the cot, Jackrabbit spoke to his kenner. Then he answered her. "Bolivar is in a floater forty minutes distant. Person is hurrying, Sappho."

"I go with the tide. Swallow should hasten."

"Bolivar, hurry up! This is Jackrabbit. Sappho wishes to die soon. Can't you push yourself?"

"Ram it, my love, I'm coming faster than I can already!" The male voice sounded irritated. "You tell Sappho to wait. Person has no patience. I'm in heavy turbulence. I'm bucking the wind, and I have to keep climbing. Are you so sick of my sleek body you want me to scatter it all over the Berkshires?"

"Swallow is always late." Sappho smiled into the ceiling of the tent. "Swallow believes nothing will happen without per."

A young woman with a heart-shaped ivory face and

long straight brown hair to her buttocks moved forward suddenly from her position kneeling by the cot. Laying her cheek against Sappho's scarcely moving chest, she began to weep.

"Louise-Michel?"

"No, no, it's Aspen! Can't you recognize me?"

"Aspen? But I remember Louise-Michel and so many I loved. . . . Aspen, do not weep on me. I want to go out with the waters, quietly."

"Don't die! Wait. If you love me, wait!"

A flick of temper crossed Sappho's face. "If you love me, cut off your hair. Yes, I'll be buried with your hair."

Aspen rose and said more composedly, "I'll go at once and cut it." She trotted off.

"Why did you do that, you witch?" Jackrabbit said. "That was mean."

"Person was bothering me. It's *my* dying." Sappho lay breathing hoarsely. "Besides, will make per feel better. You'll see."

"Who was Louise-Michel?" Jackrabbit asked.

"Second lover. Good friend. Person had long hair too, but person was strong. . . . Died diving accident. . . . I should not have taken a pillowfriend so late. It was vanity. Had little to give. . . . Same with Swallow. Too late to put in for another child. . . . Vanity."

"Not true," Jackrabbit said. "The power in you has stayed strong. Bolivar has much of you inside that I love."

"I have made some good tales, no?"

"They will outlive you many generations," White Oak said from the foot of the cot.

"Luciente!" Connie tugged at her elbow. "If she's dying, why is she out in the rain?"

"But Sappho is under a tent. Person wants to die beside the river."

"But why isn't there a doctor? If she was in a hospital, she might not die, Luciente. She might live longer."

"But why not die?" Luciente stared at her, with incomprehension on her broad peasant face. "Sappho is eighty-two. A good time to give back."

"You're just going to let her lie here in the chilly air until she dies?"

"But why not?" Luciente scowled with confusion. "Everybody gives back. We all carry our death at the core—if you don't inknow that, your life is hollow, no? This is a good death. I hope Swallow gets— Now Sappho's got me doing that. Person's so wicked and mischievous; Sappho insists today on using Bolivar's childhood name."

"Auntie Sappho!" A little kid was tugging at her slack hand. "I come to say goodbye."

"Who is it?" Sappho's eyes were shut and she did not open them. "What chipmunk nibbles at my hand?"

"It's me—Luna. Won't you tell us stories anymore?"

"Never! Somebody else. But not like me!" A light spasm shook her and left her with her mouth slightly opened.

"In hundreds, in thousands of children your stories have made strong patterns," White Oak said. "Your stories have altered our dreams."

Sappho did not speak for a long time. Then she said, "Take me nearer the river. I can't hear it."

Jackrabbit and White Oak carried her cot between them. White Oak asked, "Sappho, old darling, is this near enough?"

Sappho did not answer directly but twisted her head. "Take me nearer. I can't hear it."

They carried her cot as near as they dared, but still she complained. "Per hearing is gone," White Oak said. "Lift Sappho carefully and we'll dip per fingers in. Person will understand."

Jackrabbit picked her up gently, with grave care, and then slowly knelt, still holding her, while White Oak brought Sappho's hand down to the water and held it in the current. The fingers unclenched, the hand slowly opened. "Ah," she muttered. "The tide is going out."

"Bolivar's not going to make it," White Oak said softly, although Sappho could no longer hear.

Jackrabbit sputtered into his kenner, "Bolivar! Sappho is dying now!"

"Ten minutes, comrade, ten lousy minutes!"

Aspen returned with her hair cut off. She knelt beside the cot, where Jackrabbit had stretched Sappho's husk of body. Understanding after a moment that Sappho could no longer hear her, she pressed her shorn hair into the old woman's lax hand. Sappho's hand clasped about the hair and again her mouth twitched in a faint grimace of smile. "Aspen, child . . . plant a mulberry tree for the birds that love fruit."

"Sappho's not gonna last till Bolivar comes." A woman's low voice with the penetration of something worked to a lethal point. "Aspen, sit by that pole. Hush your crying—you cloud my cone."

"Erzulia, you should have come sooner!" Luciente spoke with reproach. "You're not in regalia?"

"Person did not send for me. I come only for the death. In respect. Sappho's far, far into the past, the old loving."

White Oak said, "Erzulia, can you hold Sappho till Bolivar comes?"

"Scamp to the floater pad. Put out a speed warning and bring Bolivar by zoomer. I gonna cone hard and try." Erzulia did not watch to see if she was obeyed but sat on the cot's edge and took Sappho's fragile head in her long-fingered black hands. Erzulia's hair was put up in dozens of narrow braids woven into a beehive on her high-domed head. She dressed in a long folded-over skirt of a blue cloth batiked into a pattern of snakes and flowers, leaving her breasts and lithe powerful shoulders bare. Her large eyes glazed over as she grasped Sappho and sweat started out on her broad forehead. Still, rigid, she sat with Sappho's head clasped in her fingers. Sweat broke out and trickled past her cheeks and sweat ran over her conical outpointing breasts, sweat rose from her in a heat shimmer as if from the body of a long-distance runner.

Luciente spoke softly to her kenner. "Bee, you should come to the tent. Erzulia holds Sappho by mind lock till Bolivar comes."

Bee's voice said, "Can't come now. In the middle of a test run. I'll set my kenner for alert when Bolivar lands and run all the way."

"Watch out, then! Bolivar always overschedules. To do too much oneself all the time is a kind of arrogance. *That's* why person is late again."

"Luciente! If person were early, you'd read arrogance into that, Bolivar thinking Sappho could not die without per. Till when."

"It all seems . . . funny to me," Connie said. "A bunch of amateurs."

"Who's professional at dying? We each get only one turn, no practice." Luciente put an arm around her waist.

"In my family in Mexico, people died this way. But in the city poor people die in hospitals. The attendants put up a screen. The nurse keeps an eye on you if she isn't too hassled. . . . My mother died in the hospital in Chicago . . . so scared. Before when she was in the hospital, they took out her womb."

"We don't do much taking out. When we do, we regrow. We program the local cells. Slow healing but better after."

"I haven't met any doctors. How come there's no doctor?"

Luciente pointed. "Look! Erzulia is a healer."

"A witch doctor!"

"You mean that as an insult? Erzulia works in the hospital in Cranberry. They have the hospital for this township."

"What does she do in the hospital?"

"Oh, person teaches people to heal themselves. Does surgery. Manipulating, pain easing, bone knitting. Erzulia's skilled! Person has trained hundreds of healers and pioneered new methods of bone knitting and pain easing. There's a way of setting pelvic fractures in the aged named after per."

She looked at the tall black woman sitting cross-legged on the cot with sweat pouring down her muscular arms and big breasts and she could not see her as a doctor in a white coat in a big hospital. "How can anybody be into voodoo and medicine? It doesn't make sense!"

"Each makes a different kind of sense, no? How not?"

She was lying in bed with the doctor going rounds and cracking jokes for the amusement of his residents over the bodies of the women patients, mostly black and Puerto Rican, whom some female troubles had cast up on this hard white beach, this glaring sterile reef. They were handed releases to sign, carefully vague so that the residents could get practice in the operations they needed. In the bed next to her was a nineteen-year-old black woman on welfare who had been admitted for an abortion in the fourteenth week and been given a hysterectomy instead of a saline abortion. The woman had gone into withdrawal shock, which made her a quiet patient. Nobody bothered about her as she stared at the ceiling. The women with syphilis were treated to obscene jokes. All the doctors ever said to any complaint was, "We're giving you some medicine that will take care of that." They did pelvics and rectals seven or eight times in a row on interesting cases, so all the doctors and residents could get a look, all the time explaining nothing. "You're a very sick little girl," the doctor said to a forty-year-old woman whose intestines they had accidentally perforated in removing an embedded IUD.

Anger began to blur the scene and she moved closer to Luciente for support, feeling the ground solidify again beneath her. Suddenly excitement blew like a wind through the tent. "Bolivar is down," Jackrabbit cried out. A bell began to toll.

"What's the bell?" she asked.

"For death," Luciente said.

"But she isn't dead yet!"

"But person soon will be." Jackrabbit frowned. "Pepper and Salt, it's not always bad to die, is it? Who'd want to be built of steel and go on living after all the people born in your brooder in your time, all your mems and mates and mothers, all your sweet friends, had long gone down?"

Connie snorted and turned away. The bell tolled through the damp air in waves of heavy sound. Slowly more people began to drift into the tent, keeping away from the side toward the floater pad. Finally she heard a high-pitched warning siren and a fast-moving vehicle flashing red lights came shrieking toward them about a foot off the ground. It came to an abrupt halt right outside the tent and settled with a hiss. White Oak hopped out and a person—the voice *had* been male, she thought—about five feet nine, compactly built, slid out of the other side and strode with quick, slithery grace toward the tent. Bolivar, she supposed, had kinky hair worn in braids fully as elaborate as Erzulia's, but his skin was fair and heavily freckled with the sun. He wore a knee-length . . . she could not call it anything but a dress, with stripes on the bias.

Luciente nodded curtly as he swept by. "Erzulia has been holding Sappho for you."

"Why not you? You could have!" he rapped out.

"Not with the person from the past in tow."

"Ummmm." Briefly he glanced at Connie, his skeptical eyes pale gray and cold as rock. Then he rushed to the cot, embraced Jackrabbit briefly and then put his hands on Sappho's head beside Erzulia's hands. After a moment Erzulia seemed to come to and slowly her grip loosened.

She rolled off the cot onto the ground. As Aspen supported her, Bee came forward.

"I'll take Zuli now. Person's weary and must sleep." Gently Bee rose with her slung over his shoulder and carried her off along the river path toward the bridge downstream, whistling softly as he padded off.

Everyone had drawn back to leave Bolivar with Sappho. He held her head with his fingers flexing, moving, and for the first time in a quarter of an hour, her lips groped to form words. "Good . . . Here! Good," was all she said and then in a hoarse shudder she expelled her breath and was still.

Bolivar rose. "The person who was Sappho is dead."

Jackrabbit spoke to his kenner, ceremoniously repeating, "The person who was Sappho is dead."

The bell tolled more slowly. Barbarossa dodged through the gathering people, carrying a plank. He laid it on the ground and Luciente moved forward to help Jackrabbit and Bolivar lift Sappho from the cot and place her on the plank. White Oak and Aspen, shaken with weeping, turned to each other to embrace. Bolivar's knuckles were clenched white on Jackrabbit's arm. The freckles on his hand stood out like the blotches on aged skin. White Oak steadily stroked Aspen's cropped head.

Jackrabbit was one of the four people who lifted a corner of the plank and began to carry Sappho into the filmy strands of rain. Aspen's thick grown hair lay like a bouquet of shiny grasses wedged under the small claw hands folded on Sappho's narrow chest. Aspen, White Oak, and Bolivar stumbled along behind the body, White Oak walking with her arm around Aspen, Bolivar going along ahead of them in stiff dignity, as if the only joints in his body were in his bare knees. Luciente fell in behind them with Connie. "Where are we going? To the undertaker?"

"The family, the lovers, the closest friends sit with the body to loosen their grief. After supper everybody in the village will gather for a wake in the big meeting hall where we politic, watch holies, hold indoor rituals."

"When is the funeral?"

"Funeral?" Luciente consulted the kenner. "We have no such. All night we stay up together speaking of Sappho. Then at dawn we dig a grave and lay the body in. Then we plant the mulberry tree Sappho wanted. Someone will go to the tree nursery in Marion for one. Then before we go to bed, we visit the brooder and signal the intent to begin a baby."

"Right away? That's heartless. One in, one out!"

"Why heartless? In a week traditionally, when we are caught up on work and sleep, we discuss into which family the child should be born and who are to be mothers. We begin by meditating on the dead."

"It just seems . . . cheap somehow. No funeral, no undertaker. Just shovel them in."

"Connie, your old way appears barbaric to us, trying to keep the rotting body. To pretend we are not made of elements ancient as the earth, that we do not owe those elements back to the web of all living . . . For us a good death is one come in the fullness of age, without much pain and in clear mind. A full life is a used life! Person should be tired. . . . You should sit in on the wake with us! You'll see. It feels beautiful, it feels good. You'll see what beauty Jackrabbit makes—person and Bolivar spectacle together. Bolivar is a ritual maker. I myself will perform tonight with my drums—which we should scamp over and get after we set up at the meetinghouse."

"Something is wrong!" She felt a threat shaking her. "Let go, Luciente. Let me go!"

"With haste, Connie!" Luciente stepped back and Connie faded through into the chair in the dim day room. Nurse Wright was slapping her to and fro till her jaw ached.

"Please . . . don't!"

"Thought you'd . . . withdrawn."

"I feel real funny today. I think I slept or passed out. The medication . . . I felt real funny after I took it today."

Nurse Wright was a motherly woman in her fifties, but overworked. She had given up and just drifted along in the ward, leaning heavily on her attendants. Connie liked her but felt she couldn't be relied on. Nurse Wright peered into her eyes. "Ummm. I'll mention it to the doctor. Maybe you're on the wrong dosage."

"I think I'm kind of sensitive to drugs, maybe," she said meekly. She was still shuddering with the force of the transition. Her heart pounded wildly and Nurse Wright, taking her by the wrist, pursed her lips at the pulse.

"I'll mention it to the doctor. You may be on too high a dosage, or maybe not. He'll say in the end. Now, on your feet."

She rose shakily. "I feel funny."

"Come along now. It's time to get in line for your supper."

Nine

THEY'RE moving us all on a special ward, Skip said. "Here in the medical building."

"Who says?" Connie asked. Rumors had galloped back and forth through their little group for two weeks.

"Fats, the friendly attendant. He says pretty soon we'll all be moved onto a ward fixed up for us."

"Men and women both? A locked ward?" Even if it was locked, at least she could get to be on the same ward as Sybil again.

"I think locked." Skip pulled a long face. "They don't act like they're fixing to turn us loose. I got a funny letter from my father, saying they're real proud I've been picked to be in a pilot project for special attention, and they hope I'll cooperate and get well. That we're lucky to have such a famous doctor, written up in *Time* magazine."

"Redding?"

"The same. But they're even more bowled over by a Dr. Argent, who's head of some institute."

"Dr. Argent? There's nobody around here like that."

"Beats me. What bothers me is that the hospital's been after them to sign a permission for something."

She hugged herself, trying to summon up the nerve. Skip had his own clothes, he always seemed to have a little cash, even cigarettes. "Skip . . . could you loan me a little to call my niece in New York City? I haven't had a visit since I got here. I know if I talk to her, I can get her to bring me some money and some of my clothes. They're ashamed, and they're pretending I don't exist since they sent me up."

"My folks guilt-trip over sending me to the state hospital. They don't come either, but they deposit an allowance." Skip fished out a pouch he wore under his shirt. He had made it in Occupational Therapy. She longed for OT privileges but couldn't get them because Mrs. Richard had put down bad things in her record. OT was just an hour every other week (the men went one week and the women the next) playing with clay or cutting out leather, but it was something to do. Of course you couldn't really relax because the OT had to justify her job by writing a report too ("patient withdrawn, made woman with over-developed sexual features"), but it was some kind of change. Skip stuck the pouch back under his shirt and slid a dollar into her hand. "Hope it does you something."

She hid the dollar in the secret compartment under the bottom flap of her shopping-bag-within-a-shopping-bag—both wearing dangerously thin and mended twice on the handles. "Thanks, Skip. Listen, if I can get her, she'll come through. She has to."

"They don't like us, you know, We're lepers. . . . You know what the last experiment was they pulled on me? They stuck electrodes on my prick and showed me dirty pictures, and when I got a hard-on about men, they shocked me. Whatever they're into here, it can't be that painful, right?"

As they sat on the bench waiting for Acker, the denim psychologist, to give them some new test, she felt better. She had a secret key to the world, if only she got permission to use the phone that night.

The time they could make phone calls was fixed: after supper, before roll call. She waited in line to ask permission.

Sharma asked, "Please can I have some toilet paper?"

"Again? What are you doing in the bathroom, Sharma?"

"It's the medication. It makes me have to pee all the time, Nurse, honest."

"It doesn't do that to any other patient. Why would it do that to you? If you didn't play with yourself, you wouldn't have to pass urine every five minutes." Two sheets of toilet paper doled out.

"Please can I make a phone call?" Sylvia asked.

"Who do you want to call?"

The black woman shifted her feet. "My boyfriend."

"What's his name?"

"Duster."

The nurse was still waiting.

Reluctantly Sylvia added, "Duster MacPhee. He's in Yonkers."

"You have the money?"

"Right here, I sure do."

"Okay. The men's attendant is on duty in the hall." The nurse acted out permitting a great favor.

"I need a couple of aspirin. I have a terrible headache tonight." A new patient, Mrs. Souza, held out her hand impatiently.

"Your medication is listed on your chart, and it doesn't include aspirin," the night nurse said.

"But I have a headache. I don't need any . . . medication. Drugs. Just plain, ordinary aspirin."

"You're a doctor now, to prescribe for yourself, Mrs. Souza? Is that what you're doing in the hospital—thinking you're a doctor?"

"I'm not asking for morphine, Nurse. Just aspirin! Like we sell in the drugstore I own with my husband, by sizes up to one thousand! Aspirin!"

"Sweetie, you may or you may not own a drugstore, but you're confused now. You aren't the one who prescribes for the patients in here. Now go sit down! Now! Or I'll have you sedated."

Mrs. Souza could not believe it. She turned to Connie, next in line. "I was only asking for plain aspirin, for my headache! I'll tell the doctor about this."

"Better sit down," she said softly. She could not risk saying more. She stepped past Mrs. Souza and in her best beggar's manner pleaded, "Please, I would really appreciate it if I could call my niece Dolly Campos in New York City?"

"You have the money?"

She showed her the precious dollar, cashed into quarters and dimes from Mrs. Stein. "See? Enough to call her. Please. I would appreciate it, Nurse, ever so much."

"I sure would like to know where you got that, Mrs. Ramos."

"It's mine. See? Please." Again she held out her hand

with the precious coins hot in her palm. "I would really like to talk with my niece, Dolly Campos, in Manhattan. You have her on the list of family, if you want to check it."

"Go ahead. Though I'd like to know what you did for that money. Did you bum it in dimes?"

A man was talking on the pay phone already and four others were ahead of her, including Sylvia. They could all hear, although the man tried to hold his mouth close to the receiver and cup his other hand around it. Still, when his wife could hear him, they could hear him too.

"So how come you haven't brought it? I'm not angry. . . . I can't talk louder , baby. . . . So sell the goddamned house before they foreclose! Never mind what your brother said. . . . Now listen. . . . I'm not yelling! . . . Listen, so call a real estate man—that's what they're for. . . . Never mind what he says, the commission comes out of the price. If they don't sell it, they don't get anything, Margaret. Listen to me!"

"Hurry up, you," the kid next in line said. "I got to call by eight o'clock. You been on ten minutes!"

The whole line wriggled with excitement, anxiety, the dreadful force of focusing all longing on that black object waiting to eat their precious coins. The attendant leaned smoking against the far wall, idly flirting with a woman patient giggling in short nervous bursts, her eyes fixed on his shoes. Dolly might not be home. She might be with a john. Geraldo might be with her, and he would hang up. To get Geraldo would be worse than not to get anyone, because that would alert him to Connie's trying to reach her niece. If she could only call in the morning!

The kid was talking to his mother and father at once, presumably on different extensions. He was about fifteen, with acne run wild in the hospital, a tubby build, hands that shook on the phone. It depressed her to see a kid with hands that shook. She stared at the greasy texture of the wall opposite, like the skin of a dirty old lizard. Geraldo's sharp lizard boots. He would be there, of course, he would answer the phone. She could try to disguise her voice. If he answered and she hung up immediately, maybe her coins would come back. No, that didn't work; once he answered, the money was lost and the chance blown.

The kid left the phone dangling and shuffled off. "Bitch, bitch, bitch," he mumbled and slammed headfirst into the opposite wall. The attendant seized him by the scruff.

Sylvia grabbed the phone for her call. Behind them five others were waiting. Sylvia dialed her number. It was busy. Her face would not accept that. She dialed again. It was busy again. Without a word she went to the end of the line to wait another turn. Her face was wondering who her boyfriend was talking to. Her face was naming women, her face was inventing women he was about to run over to see, hop into bed with, love in total forgetfulness of her.

Connie fumbled at the coins, dropped a dime, stomped it and scooped it up in blurred haste before she could lose her place in line. She dialed deliberately, not too slow, not too fast. The number rang. Third ring. Picked up. Her heart rose like an express elevator.

"Hello, this is Dolly Campos' residence. I am busy right now but I will call you back as soon as I am free. Please state your name and number, and I will get back to you just as soon as I can. That's a promise! Love from Dolly. You have sixty seconds after the tone."

She could not comprehend for a moment and then she realized it was a recording machine. She said quickly, for she had already lost seconds, "Dolly, my baby, it's me, Connie, in the hospital. Please, come to see me! This weekend or next. Please! Bring me a little money and clothes! Write me. Please, Dolly! Don't forget me!" It beeped again before she could get in "Don't forget me," and she spoke to dead air. She hung up the phone and drifted away. A machine. Across the hall the attendant was muttering in the ear of the woman patient, who fidgeted and shook her head limply.

What was Dolly doing with a machine? She must still be in the life. That way could she pick and choose? Fat chance. A machine! She had worked Skip for a dollar to speak to a rotten machine.

Friday she got a letter that had been opened and read, pawed through, inspected, and passed upon by staff, but still it was hers. From Dolly, in English. The staff took an extra week on Spanish; maybe Dolly remembered, or more likely she could not write Spanish.

Dear Connie,

I got yr messag, how do you like my new machine? Isn't is something? I almost fell off the chair, when I hear your voice come out. Saves me loosing calls when I am bussy! Saves $$$$ too.

Nita is prettier every day, wait till you see her. I am ok. Gerardo that no good punk left me stuck with the hospital bill from my operation, I am still paying on it. I have a new man, ~~s-rekly~~ strickly bussyness. This one is ok, you will like him. He is call Vic, he used to be a real pro baseball player. I will ask him to bring me up there this Sunday. Can't come Saturday do to bussyness. Sunday will come with Nita. Will go by Daddy's and get yr things. You don't say what you want, I will pick out what I think. If you think of something call me back and put it on the machine. ~~so I bring it.~~

XXXX
Love, your Dolly

Saturday her excitement strummed like a wire. She noticed every visitor. So that was Sharma's husband, the one she was always accusing other women of sleeping with—that awkward sleepy-faced middle-aged boy who kept gaping around him but never looked into any of their faces. Introduced to him as she passed—Sharma was proud of having her husband visit—she tried to meet his gaze but he stared unwaveringly into her torso, breast high. She mistrusted him instantly. Yes, she felt he had another woman already, who cooked his breakfast and laundered his shirts and lay in his bed. She could feel that coming off him. Sharma knew too. Connie fled.

Weekends were bad unless a patient had visitors. The locked door of the ward hardly budged, not for the unpaid labor called industrial therapy, not for OT, not for group therapy, not for the doctor on his galloping visit.

The evening medication did not work on her. Her

adrenaline hummed in the dark ward like a generator and it burned off the Thorazine and the Seconal like fuel. She was dreadfully alert and bored. How many, many hours must wear away before dawn could stain the high windows? How many more hours of the day must flow, a river of lard, over her before Dolly would appear? Dolly must be persuaded to start trying to get her out of here, before Luis signed whatever release the doctors were after. But don't push Dolly; to reestablish contact was everything. Everybody outside had freedom and power by contrast. The poorest most strung out fucked up worked over brought down junkie in Harlem had more freedom, more place, richer choices, sweeter dignity than the most privileged patient in the whole bughouse.

She opened her mind to Luciente and waited. Nothing happened. Time crawled like ants over her clenched eyelids and nothing stirred. Hey, Luciente! she thought. Oye, where the hell are you? Don't shut me out! She imagined! Luciente in bed with . . . Bee?

A sluggish presence eventually touched her. "Mmmm, it's me—Luciente. A moment."

"Am I interrupting?"

"Not expecting you . . . silly with wine and marijuana. Wait. Will clear and return." The contact faded.

Guiltily she turned on her cot. Butting into Luciente's pleasure. At the same time a dour envy lapped her mind. Saturday night was a big night everywhere, even in the future. Everybody was having a good time, everybody in the world, in the universe, everybody but her, alone and bored. Everybody was loving everybody else, everybody was drinking wine and smoking dope and dancing and sitting on each other's laps and whispering in each other's ears. Everybody was kissing their children good night and tucking them in and going back to the guests at the long table laid out with the remains of roast suckling pig, lechón asado, as at Dolly's wedding, everybody but her.

"Here I am," Luciente said. "Come through now. I'm coning."

"Look, I'm sorry I bothered you. Go back to your party."

"Why shouldn't you come? I didn't think of it, but . . . why not? Everybody here says it would be lovely to invite you." Luciente gave what felt like an abrupt impatient brutal tug on her and she was clutching Luciente by the upper arms and standing in a warm night lit by floating bulbs a few feet over their heads, lights like big pastel fireflies, some steady, some winking on and off as fireflies do, but all with that cool light.

A rabble of kids ran by screaming and laughing, carrying streamers that clittered and clattered in the noise of their running, children in bright butterfly costumes with their faces painted. Two dogs chased them, barking, one with ribbons plaited into its high plumy tail.

"We're entertaining Cranberry. We won a decision about the dipper routes."

She stepped back to examine Luciente, who was wearing a backless dress of a translucent crimson chiffon that tied behind her neck. The skirt was cut diagonally, quite short on one side and medium length on the other. "I've never seen you in a dress."

"It's my flimsy for the evening—Jackrabbit designed it. . . . A flimsy is a once-garment for festivals. Made out of algae, natural dyes. We throw them in the compost afterward. Not like costumes. Costumes circulate—like the robe Bee wore for naming? Costumes you sign out of the library for once or for a month, then they go back for someone else. But flimsies are fancies for once only. Part of the pleasure of festivals is designing flimsies—outrageous, silly, ones that disguise you, ones in which you will be absolutely gorgeous and desired by every body in the township!"

"That must be what yours is for."

Luciente threw up her hands. "At a festival, why not be looked at?"

"What about me? Can you dress me up?"

"I don't have a flimsy for you." Luciente looked grief-stricken. Then she snapped her fingers. "All is running good. You put on Red Star's flimsy. Red Star ordered it but that person had an accident picking cherries and is healing at Cranberry. We'll get per flimsy from the presser for you."

Luciente scooped her along and they dodged through groups wandering the paths of the village, people in wild and bright, in delicate and fanciful flimsies, carrying wine bottles and passing joints and eating small cakes that left a scent of spice on the air, trailing flowers in leis and in hair and beards, playing on flutes and recorders and guitars and stringed instruments strange and twangy, high and shimmery in their sound, beating on drums and sets of drums and carrying along objects that sputtered sound and light and scent.

The rooms of the children's house glittered and footsteps echoed down the stairways, laughter and shrieking flew out of every crevice. Adults and children in their flimsies played a game of catch with floating objects that moved in slow-motion S's. In a room full of tools and devices Luciente addressed a machine. "Produce the flimsy ordered by Red Star."

Out of the slot a garment slowly protruded, like a paper towel feeding itself from a roll. Luciente grabbed it and shook it out. "Here! Put it on."

"Here?" She glanced at the busy hall.

"I'll turn my back," Luciente said with exaggerated patience, and shrugged to the walls.

The garment was a jiggling thing made of small bubbles, weightless and loosely bound together so that they swayed and bounced and gathered the light as she moved. The garment lay lightly upon her shoulders but did not touch her body elsewhere. She felt very naked under it.

"That's clever." Luciente eyed the flimsy, circling her. "Marvelous the way it shivers and moves. You backed into luck."

"It isn't . . . transparent?"

"Transparent? Hardly at all. Come!"

In the fooder many of the panes had been removed so the breeze off the river could blow through the dining room, where small groups still sat picking at the remains of the meal, gossiping and smoking and drinking. One table was singing together in a foreign language, beating time on the tabletop.

"What did you have?" she asked with the passion for food of the institutionalized.

"Would you like leftovers? Of course. I'll set up a plate."

A cold cucumber soup flavored with mint. Slices of a dark rich meat not familiar to her in a sauce tasting of port, dollops of a root vegetable like yams but less sweet and more nutty—maybe squash? Luciente had told her they bred squashes here. A salad of greens with egg-garlic dressing. Something rubbery, pickled, hot as chili with a strange musky taste. Young chewy red wine.

"Remember, this won't nourish you," Luciente said mournfully, stealing a taste from her plate. "The bread is gone. We bake it fresh daily. Was a graham fruit bread and every bit was gobbled."

"Who cooks? What is this meat? she asked between bites.

"Roast goose. We take turns. Hawk—the person who has Innocente, remember?—and I spit-roasted the geese. By rotation every night we have a chef and four assistants."

"Who cleans up?"

"Mechanically done. Nobody wants to wash dishes."

"In my time neither. Does it really work?"

"Better than people, more patient. For washing dishes, we are willing to spend precious energy."

"Couldn't a machine cook too?"

"Fasure. But not inventively. To be a chef is like mothering: you must volunteer, you must feel called. Myself, I have no gift and only help in the kitchen. But Bee is a chef and at the next feast, person will make the menu and direct—the feast of July nineteenth, date of Seneca Equal Rights Convention, beginning women's movement. Myself, I play Harriet Tubman. I say a great speech—Ain't I a woman?—that I give just before I lead the slaves to revolt and sack the Pentagon, a large machine producing radiation on the Potomac—a military industrial machine?"

"Oh, is that how it happened?" she said. "In what century was that battle?"

"Grasp, that's the essence of it. History gets telescoped a little. The kids get restless if the ritual runs too long. They like best the part where they sack the Pentagon. Everybody joins in and then at the bottom are little honey cakes with quotes from revolutionary women baked in them and stories of their lives, so you can have your cake and eat it too. Then we all go party."

"That's only two weeks away. Do you have a big holiday every two weeks?"

"We have around eighteen regular holidays, maybe another ten little ones, and then the feasts when we win or lose a decision and when we break production norms. We like holidays—a time to remember heroines and heros, to loose tensions, to have a good time, to praise the history that leads to us—"

"Like Harriet Tubman sacking the Pentagon?"

"Zo, that does body vital ideas in the struggle. . . . The history you people celebrated—all kings and presidents and Columbus discovered a conveniently empty country already discovered by a lot of people who happened to be living here—was just as legendary. . . . Did you enjoy the food?"

"You eat well here anyhow."

"Very important! Enough food, good food, nourishing food. We care a lot that all have that. Nobody born now anyplace on the whole world, Connie, is born to less in any areas we control. *They* still have the space platforms, the moon, and Antarctica. Myself, my favorite holiday in the whole year is Thanksmaking. Then we fast for twenty-four hours and go around asking forgiveness from everyone we have offended in the year past. It comes right at the end of fall harvest, when all our crops are in except a few root crops we winter over, and the greenhouse stuff. Then we feast and go around the fooder breaking bread together, eating slowly and for hours. Wine and turkey and—oh, it takes another day to sleep it off!"

By the time Connie finished her nibbling, almost everyone had drifted out of the fooder, and they followed after. In the tall trees outside the children's house many swings had been put up, conventional, one-person swings, trapezes, two- and three-person swings like cages, round swings, swings people lay in. From all the swings and trapezes, children and middle-aged people and an old woman with long white hair were hurtling through the air, calling to each other like a forestful of monkeys.

"That's Tecumseh." Luciente pointed to a girl hanging by her bare feet on a trapeze, flipping over and over as if her body had no bones. "Tecumseh won a first today in gymnastics. How graceful and fluid person is!"

"How old is she?"

"Sixteen, I think? Tecumseh waited till only a couple of years ago for naming."

"So you do have sports. You said you taught kids not to compete, but she won a first."

"But to try to do things well! That's fun. . . . A child playing alone will still try to jump higher than that child jumped yesterday, no? We don't keep back from saluting each other for doing well. We want each other to feel . . . cherished? . . . It's a point of emphasis, no? Maybe always some cooperating, some competing goes on. Instead of competing for a living, for scarce resources, for food, we try to cooperate on all that. Competing is like . . . decoration. Something that belongs to sports, games, fighting, wrestling, running, racing, poemfests, carnival . . ."

In the meadow near the floater pad people were playing games that involved contact or a lot of running around or a lot of acting up and yelling. Some were games with things, like soft collapsible swords, pillows that spilled light bubbles when they broke. People were gliding on big wings off the hill by the river, and every so often someone fell in, settling into the water and then swimming to shore as the wings dissolved.

"You make a lot of things that fall apart quickly. They did that in my time also. Called it planned obsolescence."

"Playthings, flimsies, some pretty things we make for a moment. They're called butterflies. But objects we make for daily use, we make to last. It would be a pity to use up scarce copper or steel on a machine that worked poorly."

"Ummmm. Luxury items are made for once only and the necessities to last?"

"Not exactly." Luciente stopped in front of a glass wall that mirrored them to admire her dress, turning to and fro like a child in a new suit. "Luxuries fall into two categories: circulating and once-only. Look, they're playing web. There's Jackrabbit and Bolivar."

About ten people were playing with long luminous cords, which they fixed somehow at intervals and wove in and out so that a great dully glowing web was created in which people got caught. A box would be built around them before they were aware or could dash out, and then they were apparently a prisoner until embraced and let out when everybody was so trapped but one. Jackrabbit was hopping among the strands, leaving a nimble zigzag wake.

"Circulating luxuries pass through the libraries of each village—beautiful new objects get added and some things wear out or get damaged. Costumes, jewels, vases, paintings, sculpture—some is always on loan to our village. And always passing on. Some are for personal wearing, at feasts and rituals. Some are for enjoyment in the children's house, the meetinghouse, the fooder, the labs, the diving gear factory. Outside as we walk around."

"But you have to give them back. You don't get to keep anything for yourself! It all belongs to the government?"

"We pass along the pleasure, Pepper and Salt. Think,

for my birthday last year I wore a sable cloak like the Queen of the Night. I have worn emeralds and for a month a Michelangelo hung where I could see it every day. All the pleasure I can suck from these things I've had and pass on to pleasure others!"

Bolivar was about to be enclosed in a box. Quickly Jackrabbit leaped forward and was sealed in with him. The others laughed and called out. Jackrabbit and Bolivar embraced in the fictitious confines of the cell, the walls of luminous rope. Connie could feel that Luciente was not pleased. Jealousy like a damp wind, she could feel it. She was sad for Luciente. So they did feel jealousy here. Both young men were dressed alike, naked except for knee-length cloaks thrown back. Each had painted on his chest an elaborate flower, Jackrabbit's a lush peony, Bolivar's a trumpeting pale lily. Luciente forgot what she had been saying, forgot her bouncy explanations, and her eyes brooded on them twinned in the web, their slender bodies embracing naked under the rippled backs of the cloaks. Bolivar had been Jackrabbit's lover long before Luciente; Bolivar was older than Jackrabbit but much younger than Luciente, who stood fingering the chiffon of her dress, clumsy before their straight, supple, lithe alikeness, feeling cast out from the luminous web of their play.

She took Luciente's arm, as Luciente had so often seized hers, and pulled her firmly downhill in the other direction. "Show me more. So many people. Are they only from Mattapoisett and Cranberry?"

Luciente peered into her face, and her black eyes said she understood Connie's kindness. Gently Luciente brushed her lips against hers. "No. It was a feast only for Cranberry and us—the dinner part. But the afternoon games were for everybody and this evening people are here from all the towns in Mouth-of-Mattapoisett. Whoever feels like partying with us."

Feeling she had intruded on Luciente's privacy, which she could hardly avoid when they were linked, she wanted to give her friend a piece of her own life. "Tomorrow my niece Dolly is going to visit me for the first time since I been in."

"Niece Dolly . . . Ah, person you protected from per seller in a situation of brutality and exploitation! I recall. You're keening to see per?"

"Yes . . ."

"Good. Let love flow between you. You must forgive Dolly for betraying you, and Dolly must forgive you for trying to save per and failing, no?"

"I'm excited. She's broken with Geraldo! I'm going to get her to work on springing me. Soon I'll be free."

"Free. Our ancestors said that was the most beautiful word in the language." Luciente stopped to beg a swallow of wine from White Oak, wearing a long white tunic slit up the sides and toting a jug of red wine. "Connie! Tell me why it took so long for you lugs to get started? Grasp, it seems sometimes like you would put up with anything, anything at all, and pay for it through the teeth. How come you took so long to get together and start fighting for what was yours? It's running easy to know smart looking backward, but it seems as if people fought hardest against those who had a little more than themselves or often a little less, instead of the lugs who got richer and richer."

"Who can you hate like you hate your neighbor?" Connie reached for the wine.

"If I didn't like my neighbors, I wouldn't live with them."

"We hate ourselves sometimes, Luciente, worse than we hate the rich. When did I ever meet a richie face to face? The closest I ever came to somebody with real power was when I was standing there in front of the judge who sentenced me. The people I've hated, the power they have is just power over *me*. Big deal, some power! Caseworkers, pimps, social workers."

"Much I don't comprend that led to us," Luciente said gently, arm around her waist as they bumped downhill. "But *not inevitably*, grasp? Those of your time who fought hard for change, often they had myths that a revolution was inevitable. But nothing is! All things interlock. We are only one possible future. Do you grasp?" Luciente's hand became iron on her ribs. Her voice was piercing and serious.

"But you exist." She tried to laugh. "So it all worked out."

"Maybe. Yours is a crux-time. Alternate universes coexist. Probabilities clash and possibilities wink out forever."

"What are you talking about?"

"You're learning, how not?" Luciente stooped to peer

into her face. "Our ancestor."

"Me!" Connie hooted. "Honorable ancestor! Sure, pray to my ghost. Don't forget plenty of pork and chicken, for sacrifices!"

Four older people were playing violins and such together under a gathering of those cool floating lights. Others sprawled on the ground listening. Music older than she was.

"Beethoven," Luciente offered. "Quartet in B Flat. The Grosse Fuge."

"Claud's friend Otis used to say that after the revolution, all their Kulchur would be burned in the streets and nobody would bother with all that stuff from Europe."

"We enjoy no one culture, but many. Many arts. All with own inknowing, seeing, intents, beauties. Fasure some of what we inherit feels . . . closed, trivial, bloated with ego, posturings of lugs who had to attract rich patrons or corporate approval to survive . . . but much of it we have to love, Connie."

Beyond the shimmer pool cast by the floating lights, real fireflies slow-blinked their lures on the soft air. At a giant maple a child stood with eyes closed, counting by fives to one hundred: hide-and-seek, a game ancient in her own childhood. Game she had loved as a child in hot dusty Texas streets. Rushing to hide, perhaps alone, perhaps with her best friend Lupe, whose two fat braids always hung before her dark, heart-shaped face. Waiting to be found. Suspense plucked at her with a quasi-sexual thrill as she waited, or as they waited together, giggling and clutched. The worst was not to be found, to go on waiting. The apparent purpose of the game (to hide so cleverly that no one would find you) giving way to the real purpose: to sneak in free. Perhaps, perhaps even better if Neftali, around whose sharp bronze face she had cast a secret ring of fire, was to find her. Yes, hide-and-seek wove into its ritual from generation to generation something of the hidden inner life of children. I'm going to run away from home and you won't see me anymore! But come and search for me. The fear *they* would not care, would not come after. To be hidden away and then found and brought joyfully out to the others. Yet afraid she lay hidden, her heart beating absurdly in the dust under the pickup truck. Who would come? What would they do?

The child turned from the tree and stood blinking into

the darkness, hesitating on one foot. "It's her!" Connie cried.

"My child, Dawn." Luciente spoke softly in the shadows. "Let them play."

The flimsy had a pelt and a furry tail. "Is she a squirrel?"

"Yes! Person has a fix on squirrels lately. Other children feed birds and try to build squirrelproof bird feeders. Dawn built a squirrel feeder."

Dawn darted away into the bushes and a moment later they heard a squeal of discovery. Dawn came racing after a boy who streaked ahead of her toward the tree-safe. Just short of the tree, she launched a flying tackle and brought him down. "Got you!"

"She looks so delicate!"

"Well-coordinated. Good muscles. Fast reflexes. Dawn works hard at martial arts. You should have seen per fighting this afternoon." Luciente's excitement returned and she dragged Connie along a little too fast toward a game consisting of a large board with people on it instead of pieces. The game seemed quarrelsome and noisy, and debate raged over the players, whose faces were hidden by masks. They had just come to one edge of the painted board when Luciente's kenner said, "New holi in meetinghouse. Name: Pageant of the Lost. Duration: one hour. Starts: on the hour in ten minutes."

"That's Jackrabbit's new holi. And Bolivar's. They worked on it all week."

"Bolivar has stayed since Sappho died?"

"Basically Bolivar works as a spectacler. This is per village, but person's gone more than here. Has to be on call for villages that want rituals, feasts, pageants. Bolivar's quite good. When they work together, beautiful events result." Luciente spoke with a stilted justice, carefully fair. "Jackrabbit does rituals alone sometimes, but mostly person works in graphic arts." Arm in arm they strolled toward the meetinghouse, a building long and low like a loaf of bread.

Inside it was larger than she would have thought, for it was built into the hill. "For meetings we use only a part, so we are more face to face. Walls can be dropped at any point. This is the biggest it gets."

The rounded ceiling reminded her of the planetarium, the time she had taken Angie for the Easter show. Angie had been frightened of the dark and the stars that seemed to rush toward them and, crawling into her lap to bury her head, refused to look. Gradually Connie had aroused her curiosity and managed to get her to peep at the sparkling night sky of the ceiling. This ceiling too became a night sky with more purple in its black than the night they had just abandoned, with a pale moth-green moon rising in the south over one of the entrances. Slowly as people came wandering in to their seats, a different color moon rose majestically over each of the doors: white to the north, yellow to the east, red to the west and green to the south. As the moons reached the zenith, the four of them began a stately dance to music welling up. Their shapes began to shift from round to oblong to crescent to wing-shaped like birds, images of dignified flight; now slow hopping courtship of the whooping cranes, extending their broad wings.

As the room filled and the doors shut, the cranes came down from the ceiling and became flesh—although she had learned that these vivid three-dimensional images were a mere trick of projectors and lights. A voice like a bird, a reedy voice, talked over the music about whooping cranes and faded into the music. The image broadened. One enormous crane filled it and then his head spread into clouds and his feet turned to water; little black and white dots came bobbing on the waves toward them, the Labrador duck. Last one shot in 1875 off Long Island.

The great vulture, the California condor glided on twelve-foot wingspan. The bald eagle screamed and carried fish home to stuff into the beaks of its huge fledglings, clumsy in the twiggy nest at the top of a dead pine. The grizzly stood at bay. The humpbacked whale rolled and dived and roamed the lightless depths, singing its epics improvised on the age-old patterns of its vast oral culture —was fired on by a factory ship and its warm flesh carved up on the spot for dog food. The last brown-skinned inhabitant of Tasmania was hunted down and shot on a rocky ledge. Her body smashed on the stark rocks, last of a unique and delicate, small-bodied branch of the human family. Passenger pigeons darkened the sky with their fluttering passage, settled into trees that shone with them like soft blue and gray fruit, their cooing, the feathery warmth of their rosy and buff breasts filling the air. Alarmed, they startled into flight; the whistling of their thousands of wings beat the air to a wind that rustled the trees. They were shot, they were clubbed, they were taken by live decoy nailed through the feet to a perch, they were lumbered out of their homes, they were slaughtered and fed to livestock. Finally they were gone, the last female dying in a Cincinnati zoo. Ishi, last of the Yaqui of California, came out of the woods where he had lived alone, last of his hunted people, to a world where no soul spoke his language, and died in the Museum of Natural History. Archaic stone lions crouching in a row on wind-swept Delos, lions marching across the tiled walls of Babylon, gave way to the last of the Asian lions, sick, starving under the drought-parched tree in India. The lion's body became the western prairies where General Sherman led an extermination campaign against Indians and buffalo together. Heaps of corpses rotted under the alkali sun. The wheat grew up through the bodies and the wind blew the land away in dust-storms that darkened the sky. Briefly they became bones flying and then the sky was empty as a skull.

The bones lay in the dust. Slowly they put out roots that sank deep in ravaged earth. Slowly the bones burgeoned into sprouting wands. The wands grew to a tree. The oak thrust its taproot deep and outstretched its massive boughs. The tree became a human couple embracing, man and woman. They clutched, they embraced, they wrestled, they strangled each other. Finally they passed into and through each other. Two androgynes stood: one lithe with black skin and blue eyes and red hair, who bent down to touch with her/his hands the earth; the other, stocky, with light brown skin and black hair and brown eyes, spread his/her arms wide to the trees and sky and a hawk perched on the wrist. A green and brown web flowed out from them and into them. They stood on the shoulder of a huge ant. Grapevines grew from their finger ends. Bees swarmed through the heads. The animal images felt real: they did not appear animations but living beings. The last image was water flowing, which became a crane flying.

"Only in us do the dead live.
Water flows downhill through us.
The sun cools in our bones.
We are joined with all living
in one singing web of energy.
In us live the dead who made us.

In us live the children unborn.
Breathing each other's air
drinking each other's water
eating each other's flesh we grow
like a tree from the earth."

The crane flew to the ceiling and slowly split into four moons that set in the four directions. The room lightened. She saw Dawn's upturned face two rows away, watching the eastern moon go down. In their real future, she had been dead a hundred years or more; she was the dead who lived in them. Ancestor. Feeling remote from the moment, she fixed her eyes on Dawn's wondering face. A terrible desire to hold that child's body tantalized her flesh with the electrical itch of wanting. To touch her gently. Just once.

Luciente knew or read her gaze. When the room was light she called, "Dawn? Please come a moment?"

Dawn glanced around, saw them and climbed nimbly over the rows that were emptying. "G'light. You're the person from the past!"

"Per name is Connie," Luciente said, kissing the small ear that showed through the tumbled hair.

"May I kiss you?" Her voice shook.

Dawn looked at her with a limpid sandy brown gaze, questioning. Hesitating. The tremor in her voice. Wanting too much. Scary to a kid. But Dawn finally said, "Okay."

Quickly she kissed Dawn's cheek, cupping her small shoulders gently in her hands. Twice the size Angelina had been that last time, but small still. Small-boned. Dawn skipped away then, looking back in open curiosity. Then off at the heels of two other running children.

"Goodbye, little squirrel," she said after her.

"Dawn likes red squirrels better because they're smaller but bolder."

"Like her."

They strolled toward the western entrance. "At four, Dawn was timid. We worried. Me, my coms. We all struggled to bring per out."

"But you say you respect difference."

"Different strengths we respect. Not weakness. What is the use in not actively engaging life? It passes anyhow."

She thought of the asylum. "Sometimes you have no choice."

Outside in the soft night music ticked the air. In the square outside the meetinghouse six musicians were playing. People were beginning to dance alone, in couples, in small and large circles. Bee and Erzulia were leaning together arm in arm on the far side, talking with their heads bent close. The music was subtle over a strong beat and a counterbeat: rhythm crossing rhythm but entering the feet, the legs, the hips, the ass, the shoulders. Dawn was dancing with the two children she had chased outside, turning round and round, pulling hard on each other's taut link of arms.

"The children are still up. It must be ten-thirty, eleven."

"They work hard. They get up early every day except after festivals. Shouldn't they have holidays? When they can't stay awake, they fall asleep. If they doze off in the grass, someone will carry them home."

"You have wonderful faith in other people!"

"Without that social faith, what a burden it would be to have children! The children are everyone's heirs, everyone's business, everyone's future."

A flash of dog food supper. She worried, never being able to afford to serve meat after Claud was imprisoned. The food prices higher each week. She wanted to commit murder in the supermarket and she could not afford a shoplifting charge, being on suspended sentence. The only meat she could buy was in dog food cans. Should have fed Angie from a bowl on the floor. Who knew what they put in those cans? Man's best friend was a big police dog, not a little brown child like Angie. Dogs to defend against poor people like her. "Eat it, Angie, please! It's good stew." She had added chili powder, herbs.

"Why?" Angie pointed to the picture of the dog. "Why they got a picture of a dog?"

"That's just the picture on it. Like Bugs Bunny on the cereal."

It turned out Angie feared it was a dog they were eating. She did not want to eat a puppy dog, she explained. Ay de mi! "It's beef! Like hamburger. I wouldn't feed you a dog!" But wouldn't she, if she found one for sale cheap? She had to feed Angie anything she could find to fill their bellies. What choice had she?

Luciente was holding her by the shoulders. "You're fading out! Come. Stay. Dance with me." Tugging her out onto the square.

"I don't know how you dance!"

"Any way you feel like. It's for pleasure."

She let her eyes half close and her body began to sense the music. Still, it alarmed her, how when she moved her hips the flimsy with all its little bubbles took off and flew away from her body, naked underneath. But nobody was wearing much in the way of clothes. She had not danced since . . . the first time in the bughouse, a sad Christmas party, parody of cheer in old-fashioned polite ballroom dancing, waltzing and fox-trotting and an occasional meek rumba round and round under the watchful eyes of staff and the hungry gazes of the majority not dancing. Luciente was a better partner than any she had enjoyed that evening of excuse me's and wistfulness and an occasional fumbled clutch. Ah, nothing was so sad as looking around at all the black and Latin patients and watching each other trying to boogaloo so zonked with Thorazine they could hardly do the zombie shuffle.

She opened her eyes as the band went into a faster number and saw Bolivar and Jackrabbit dancing. Jackrabbit moved wild and loose and explosive. Bolivar was a little too controlled. He did what he did well, but he was not inventive. He moved with a measured elegance. But Jackrabbit exploded around him. Luciente was dancing to/for Jackrabbit, without ever looking at him. She was performing and Jackrabbit was aware of her too, and so, with resentment, was Bolivar.

She encouraged Luciente, she egged her on. Bee stood now with White Oak, chatting and watching. Erzulia was dancing alone, gone into an absorbed passionate trance state where nothing lived but her and the music centered around the throbbing drums. Someone else watched too, a tall woman standing with two others on the steps that led to the meetinghouse. Her hair was in a white turban and one breast was bare, as were her feet. Around her neck a crescent moon was hung, against the white of her dress. She left the women on the steps nd stalaed among the dancers toward them, approaching Luciente from behind. Bee moved onto the square and began to dance beside them. He smiled at Connie with an amusement she did not understand.

The tall woman paused behind Luciente, her hazel eyes crinkled with mischief. Unwinding her turban so that her auburn hair fell out loose onto her shoulders, she swung the long white scarf around and then cast it over Luciente, catching her by the waist and pulling her backward.

Off balance, Luciente stumbled back against her and remained pinned there, her face silly with surprise. "What happens?"

"You dance just as wickedly as when you were eighteen. Shameless, still, shining on the dark. And that dress, it's decadent. You'll go down like Sappho at eighty, still greedily nibbling young lovers!"

"Diana, it's you. Don't tease me so." She tried to turn her head but Diana had her pinned. "This is Connie, the person from the past."

"I'm Diana, the person from Luciente's past," Diana said flamboyantly, laughing deep in her chest. "That flimsy chills me," she crooned, sighting down her long nose. "Reeks of the same taste that dressed Achilles and Patroclus over there."

"Diana!" Luciente twisted around in the loop of the scarf to put her hands on the taller woman's shoulders. "You didn't come looking for me to crit my flimsy."

"To take it off perhaps?" Diana released the scarf. "Come walk with me . . . It's been a long time since we walked together under the moon."

Luciente gave a short joyful ringing laugh. "You fake! There's no moon tonight. And you can't bring off sounding forlorn with your mob of sweet friends giving me those looks from the steps!"

"Always so literal. Yet you can't tell what looks they give from a hundred feet! I wear my moon—come!"

Bee said in her ear, "Now you'll have to salvage with me."

Luciente turned toward them, her face begging their pardon, blushing like a fifteen-year-old; then she gave her hand to Diana and they went off quickly among the dancers and in to the dark.

Connie looked after them, perplexed. "I'm not a goat for dancing," Bee said at her side. "Came out to collect you when I saw Diana bearing down. When I like music, I want to let my mind sail on it." With that easy comfort, he took her arm and ambled her off the square. His big hand felt warm and heavy on her: an affectionate acceptance of her like Luciente's but not like Luciente's. Because her arm swelled, grew enormous and hot with blood, with his touch on her.

"I don't know you," she said haltingly.

"Only through Luciente we know each other."

"But you remind me of someone."

"Is that so?" Amused and accepting at once. Past the range of the music—loud enough in the square but damped off by baffles beyond it—the night softened to small noises. Someone was singing to a mandolin. People went linked arm in arm, entwining shoulders and waists, to little huts where lights had begun to blink on and off again. Otter, her long hair released from pigtails and hanging straight and black as a flood of satin to her waist, stood under one of the floating lights staring at a youth who stood staring at her. Otter was touching the other's face with her fingertips and then she laughed, breathlessly, as if she could hardly breathe. An old person, drunk, with gnarled face bent back and mouth open to the stars that could be seen now and then through the floating lights, sang with thin voice in a minor key:

"How we loved,
laid in one bed,
while night ran through us
like swift water, sped
onto the teeth of the dawn:
I must let go,
go on.
My side aches.
The bow has shot its
arrow and the twine
breaks."

In the dark another heard and began pushing the song through the bell of a trumpet. The brassy honey and vinegar seeped through her. Her hand clasped Bee's hand harder. He squeezed her hand back and then dropped it, and she felt ashamed until his arm came around her, pulling her closer to him as they strolled still more slowly, her hip bumping his thigh. She could not speak, her flesh heavy and sweet on her bones. She felt swollen equally with old tears and present wanting, the memory of Claud and the presence of Bee. Who was not Claud. But who made her remember. Whose big hand on her waist, the thumb just touching her breast through the flimsy that parted for his thumb hot and fat, asking her and getting an answer as her knees half buckled and her breath sucked in and swayed in instinct faster than decision against him. Thumb messenger of the member she could feel as she pressed against him for his kiss. As his lips moved onto hers in a patient, long, sensual kiss, a voice was singing in a low throaty joyous voice:

"How good to fight beside you,
people of my base.
With you I work
forehead to forehead.
With you I plant corn,
stand in the tree picking apples.
How good to fight beside you,
friend of our long table,
mother of my child.
We share the soup and the bread,
the trouble and the meetings
that last till sharp dawn.
How good to fight beside you.
An army of lovers cannot lose,
an army of lovers cannot lose.
How good to fight for each other."

"How can anybody sing about fighting on such a night?" she asked against his chest, drawing a deep breath.

"On such a night people die at the front, like any other," he said. "This flimsy gets in the way with its bubbles." He gestured into the dark. "Here is my space. Will you come in?"

"You know I will." She laughed. She was startled then to hear that old happy laugh from her chest, that sensual laugh Claud had loved to feel with his hands against her. In the last years she had laughed little and never like that.

They stumbled together along a path and up two steps to his door that opened with a tug. Slam of the screen door behind them. He groped at the wall. "I'll get the light."

"No. Please. Let it stay dark." She did not want to see his space, the strangeness of another time. She wanted to be in the simple space of bed, the space of body against body, constant in any time.

"However you like. I can see you with my fingers."

She felt frightened when he said that, as if he could read her mind, her need, her memories. How much did

Luciente absorb and know of her? Yet she felt his kindness radiating toward her and she relaxed and accepted it as she accepted the breeze flowing through the open window.

"What's that out there?" Bird in the night.

"Whippoorwill." His arm came around her, he was leading her to a low firm bed covered with softness, silky and clinging but thick, as if there could be satin pile. Kneeling, he drew her down and she half fell onto the invisible bed. As he helped her free of the flimsy and nestled down beside her he was naked himself, vastness of his body all about. The substantial velvet shock of skin on skin. Her head fell in. She grasped his back in handfuls. He slowly began to build her body out of the dark, painting her touch by touch so that each windowpane of skin glowed from inside.

Once more night gave her a big, generous mouth on her arched throat, her breasts burning like bonfires, her belly rolling under his hands. The head was different, smooth as warm rock. Flesh where no flesh had been. Skin smooth against her thighs as his head rested there, lips and tongue into her there where only Claud had done that before, so that the pleasure came down wet and she melted into him even before he took his mouth away and moved up on her and entered her. So full she felt. The salty sticky taste of herself on his mouth. Never again had she imagined she would feel that weight, the other, heavy body everyplace upon her, the tongues joined and moving as their sex moved together. So good, so good, every last finger spread on his big firm high buttocks, every finger alive to the tip and sunk in his sleek flesh. She felt huge and swollen with pleasure, so sensitive to each slide of his shaft and head as he rode into her, she felt as if she too were sunk into him. Once again to move joined and whole, full with him, open and throbbing, once again to feel the hot flooding rush of his coming, once again to tighten around him, still big enough, and feel him begin to move for her, moving up into her to increase contact, once again to feel her pleasure deepening and spreading like a chord struck in all octaves at once, sustained, played, and then held and held till it slowly faded into its overtones.

Her hands loosened and fell from him. He slowed in her, waited, ceased. Weight collected on her. They worked loose, eased into separation side by side. When she opened her eyes, she could dimly see objects, shape of table, chair with something slung over it. Trees rippled their leaves with a wet sound outside.

"Soon I must go back. Sleep. They wake us early every day. To nothing."

"Each time when you leave us, we regret. We sadden not to help you."

"This helped." She sat up on an elbow. "But . . . how can I still be here without Luciente?"

"Luciente is helping."

"Helping us . . .?"

His knuckles gently trailed along her cheek. "How not? How else could we be together?"

She sat up straight and clutched the cover around herself. "Aware of us . . . in bed?"

"Pepper and Salt, don't be silly. We all care for you But you're of a society with many taboos. It's easier for me to hold you for all of us."

"You'll tell me next you planned this."

"No, no." Bee chuckled, caressing her shoulder. "But we commune running well with each other."

"She . . . you . . . were giving me back Claud for a night."

"I'm not Claud. Maybe I look like Claud did. Maybe I move like per. You feel so." His voice rumbled. "Maybe I am potentialities in per that could not flourish in your time. But I am also me, Bee, friend of Luciente, friend of yours."

She touched his chest lightly. "For sure. However you do it, whatever it means, it was fine enough. You know."

In the morning she felt groggy and hung over when the Muzak came over the PA system with the male voice saying that it was time for patients to get up. As she stood in line for the showers, sensual memories played over her thighs, her belly. His hands upon her, his mouth, the weight and heft of him, the sleekness of his beautiful skin. Joy cut through the scum of the morning. She felt sleepy, fatigue whined in her skull, but she did not mind. The day for once beckoned. The day had a shape full of hope, the afternoon like a hill with a fine view that she would slowly climb.

It was not impatience she felt as she stood in line for

the usual breakfast slop, wan oatmeal and the rationed cup of bitter coffee more precious than dope. All the day stretched toward Dolly's arrival, but to yearn was to be full. She kept the memory of the evening too rich yet to squander, a candy she could suck and suck during the week and not use up.

Could she tell Dolly about Bee? She could refer to him as if he were a patient she was flirting with. What would Dolly's new man be like? She must get on a better footing with him than she had with Geraldo. Yet from the letter he was her pimp. How could she like a pimp? Parasites of women's sweat. Body lice. Why was Dolly still on the streets? Debts, money, her daughter Nita to feed.

No reproaches! May love flow: Luciente waved her calloused hand. Connie combed and combed her wiry hair. That ugly white parting. How drab she looked, how ashen her skin seemed. Dolly, so young and plump and juicy, how could she help wanting to turn away when she saw her aunt? Madwoman with skunk hair wrapped in a faded dress sizes too big, shuffling to meet them like something that crawled out of the wall.

Mrs. Yoshiko, the weekend attendant, brought her a bright red lipstick, Mrs. Yoshiko, exactly her height, laughed and stuck some pins in her hair so that it looked different and a little better. "Good now." She spoke little English but she smiled sometimes and sometimes she looked at them when they spoke.

After lunch she sat at a card table playing gin rummy with Mrs. Stein and losing lots of little white chips torn out of a magazine they used for money. She waited. One o'clock! Visiting hours began. No one for her.

Of course she could hardly expect Dolly to arrive at one! It took two hours to get here from New York. Longer in heavy traffic. A summer Sunday, say three hours. If there was a traffic jam, three and a half! She could not begin expecting until . . . let's see: suppose Dolly got up at ten. Ten-thirty if she worked last night. Say eleven. Wouldn't get out of the house until noon. Her boyfriend was picking her up. Say twelve-thirty. So they might not arrive until almost four. She would begin allowing herself to expect Dolly at three-thirty.

Yet every time the phone rang in the nurses' station, every time the door lock clacked over, she froze, the cards blurred. She hoped and waited and watched the other visitors come and go. The afternoon bled away. She could not play cards anymore. She paced as slowly as she could force herself to, through the dormitory to the day room, back and forth across the porch. Every time the phone rang or the door clacked over, she rushed back to the nursing station to stand about awkwardly, waiting, hoping.

At five it was all over. The last visitor was shooed out. Dolly had not come.

Ten

MONDAY arrived with a thud. Skip turned out to be right and she was carted off to a new ward, set up like a regular hospital ward in the medical building. A plywood partition divided the women from the men, with a door at the moment open. The outer doors on the ward were locked. It had fewer amenities than G-2: no porch, no separate day room with TV. Fats was still with them, but the woman attendant didn't seem to know where anything was on the hospital grounds and complained loudly she had to get up at five-thirty to come out here. Mrs. Valente was a big woman with something wrong with her tongue or palate that gave her speech a muffled, battered quality.

Sybil was here already, her long legs drawn up cross-legged as she camped on her bed waiting to see what was going to happen. Sybil had thrown a bathrobe over the next cot to save it for her, and she grabbed it gratefully. Near the nurses' station a bed had its sides up. In it a black woman lay with a great white helmet of bandages on her head and a gadget perched on top of the bandage like a metal beanie.

"That's Alice Blue Bottom," Sybil hissed. "Look what they've done to her!"

"What is it? Did she have an accident?"

"I don't think so. Doesn't that look bizarre?"

Connie peered down the ward. "Are you sure it's her?"

"I read the name on the chart at the foot of her bed, Consuelo."

"Is she unconscious?" She noticed a machine up on legs beside the bed.

"No. She made a face at me when I came in, which is why I read the name on her chart. I was embarrassed not to recognize her, so I said, Hello, and she said, Look what they have done to me! She did not put it exactly that way, but that was the gist of her earthy expressions."

"What did she say they did?"

"Valente hustled me past before I could ask any questions."

"It looks like they busted her head. Maybe she tried to get away." Connie stared at the tall barred windows.

"Is Valente so crude she'd leave visible damage? A sock with a soap in it, that's what the attendant used to use on me."

Skip came to the doorway. "Hsssst! Connie!"

"Skip, I can't pay you back yet. My niece didn't come Sunday. But she's coming next weekend," she said quickly.

"They brought me down Friday. Alice was already in bed, bandaged up. She told me they took her by ambulance to the city, where they operated on her, and then they brought her back!"

"Hey, did they beat up on her?"

Skip shook his head. "They did a kind of operation. They stuck needles in her brain."

"Are you kidding?" Maybe Skip was crazy. Nevertheless she felt weak with fear. "What kind of needles? She could talk to Sybil."

"She certainly did," Sybil said haughtily. "She was in better shape than if she'd had shock."

"You don't believe me, but you'll see!" With broken-winged dignity, Skip shambled back to the men's side.

"Needles in the brain . . ." It sounded like a crazy fantasy—like Sybil's microwave ovens that burned out magic. Glenda insisted that electroshock was a dentist's drill. Maybe they had given Alice a shot in the head, a new drug injected directly in the brain? That too was crazy. Those new drugs they tried out made your kidneys turn to rock or caused your tongue to swell black in your mouth or your skin to crust in patches or your hair to fall in loose handfuls, like stuffing from an old couch. Perhaps a drug injected right in the brain could turn you into a zombie as quick as too much shock.

This ward was peculiar, because it was like a hospital ward. The mental hospital had always seemed like a bad joke; nothing got healed here. The first time in she had longed for what they called health. She had kept hoping that someone was going to help her. She had remained sure that somewhere in what they called a hospital was someone who cared, someone with answers, someone who would tell her what was wrong with her and mold her a better life. But the pressure was to say please and put on lipstick and sit at a table playing cards, to obey and work for nothing, cleaning the houses of the staff. To look away from graft and abuse. To keep quiet as you watched them beat other patients. To pretend that the rape in the linen room was a patient's fantasy.

But this was a real hospital, even if an ancient one. There were fifteen women on her side of the ward. Her bed was a hospital bed that went up and down, more comfortable than anything she had slept in for years, since she had been the mistress-secretary-errand girl-servant-housekeeper to Professor Silvester. Feeling like an old hand, she smiled at Sybil as they began figuring how they would make do here, the space that might exist, the fringe benefits that could be squeezed.

Tuesday morning she was confined to her bed, as if she were sick. The doctors were to come in the morning. Monday afternoon they had been sent through a whole battery of tests—blood, urine, reflexes, all fussed over by Dr. Morgan. Redding had not been there. He taught someplace. He was connected with something called NYNPI. He was an important man. She was beginning to feel that his actual appearance was ominous. Better when he was being busy elsewhere. On others. There were others. Patients in the hospital in the city. Unsatisfactory in some way. Outpatients slipped away. They could not be depended upon. Their families butted in. They, tucked now in beds in their rows, were to be in some way more satisfactory.

She dozed in her bed, groggy on drugs. Casually in the early morning ward she cast an invitation to Luciente. She felt shy, embarrassed. Tentatively she opened her mind and sensed Luciente's response. How easy it had become to slip over to Mattapoisett. She did not return exhausted. As if her mind had developed muscles, she could easily draw Luciente, she could leap in and out of Luciente's time.

Luciente's family—Bee with his head tilted back beaming at her, the old woman Sojourner on his left, Barbarossa, Otter in long braids looking Chinese, the slight blond man Morningstar bent over Dawn, Jackrabbit staring at one of the decorated panels with a dreamy frown, Hawk thoughtfully picking her nose, Luxembourg about to say something and visibly remembering she was no longer Hawk's mother and still on the silence taboo—were seated around a table in the fooder, breakfasting on whole grains, nuts, sunflower seeds, blueberries, yogurt. The milk tasted full of flavor, like milk from her grandmother's. The teacher said raw milk made you sick; grandmother said it made you strong. Herb tea in large pots steamed.

"You don't have coffee?"

"To start meetings. In the middle if they run long. Same with tea." Luciente yawned. "When we get up running early, to harvest."

"But you don't drink it every day?"

Bee shifted as if he might respond, but Barbarossa was ready with an answer. "Coffee, tea, sugar, tobacco, they all took land needed to feed local people who were starving. Now some land is used for world luxuries, but most for necessary crops. Imagine the plantation system, people starving while big fincas owned by foreigners grew for wealthy countries as cash crops a liquid without food value, bad for kidneys, hearts, if drunk in excess."

"I couldn't face the day without coffee! That's the worst thing I've heard about your way of living."

Everyone looked glum and even Jackrabbit stopped staring at the offending panel. Five people started at once talking about protein and underdevelopment and the creation of hunger, when Dawn piped up, "People, listen! I have a dream this morning."

Other conversation stopped. She preened in the attention, making her face serious. Morningstar's head bobbed over her like a pale sun. "I dreamed I flew into the past. I flew to that river and kept that nuclear power plant from killing everybody in Philadelphia."

"This was a waking dream or a sleeping dream?" Otter gave her a skeptical smile, arching her brows.

"Well, I was kind of asleep."

"There's nothing wrong with waking dreams," Sojourner said in a reedy voice. "To want to save lives is a good desire."

"Everyone has been making too much fuss about connecting with the past." Luciente exchanged a wry look with Otter. "I myself am guilty." They both smiled.

"Magdalena says it's important," Dawn insisted. "Says we may wink out!"

Bee—whose gaze Connie had carefully not met—rumbled from deep in his chest, "To plant beans correctly is important. To smoke fish so it doesn't rot. To store food in vacuum. To fight well, as you did Saturday. To make good decisions in meeting. To be kind to each other."

"But some things are more important!" Dawn stuck out her soft chin. "I want to do something very important. Like fly into the past to make it come out right."

"Nobody can *make* things come out right," Hawk said, her straight nose wrinkled in disgust. "Pass the honey."

"No one is helpless. No one controls." Sojourner had a flattened leathery face and eyes that twinkled with a lively pleasure. "*We* can't make things come out in the past. We can only speak to those who listen." She winked at Connie.

"Are there many of us?" Connie asked. "Many who come here?"

"Mmmm . . . what?" Luciente was yawning again. "Who come? Only five so far. It's odd." Luciente's hand made boxes in the air. "Most we've reached are females, and many of those in mental hospitals and prisons. We find people whose minds open for an instant, but at the first real contact, they shrink in terror."

"Why are you contacting us? You said I'd understand, but I forgot to think about it. It's kind of a vacation from the hospital."

A surge of discomfort passed around the table. "It's hard to explain," Bee said, frowning. "Nobody's supposed to discuss advances in science with you. It might be dangerous—for you, for us, Your scientists were so . . . childish? Carefully brought up through a course of study entered on early never to ask consequences, never to consider a broad range of effects, never to ask on whose behalf . . ."

"But I'm no scientist. What do you want from me?" Her eyes touched Bee and withdrew as if burned, after-image of black on her retina. Suppose there was a price? Suppose they wanted something from her, something, anything. Vaguely she imagined herself smuggling back a weapon, a bomb disguised as a toothbrush. Why should they have been so nice to her if they didn't want something? In her lap under the table her hands sought each other, coldly sweating.

Barbarossa cleared his throat. "We could put it: at certain cruxes of history . . . forces are in conflict. Technology is imbalanced. Too few have too much power. Alternate futures are equally or almost equally probable . . . and that affects the . . . shape of time."

She did not like to be lectured by him, for he reminded her of other men, authorities in her time, even though she could see that in this setting he had no edge on the others. "But you exist." Still she waited for the price, the stinger.

"Maybe. Maybe not." Luciente smiled, her eyes liquid and sad. "It's not clear. We're struggling to exist."

"I don't understand," she said resentfully.

"You move your hand. You wave it. Do you understand how?" Barbarossa too smiled, his blue eyes asking her to listen. "How does the decision in your brain fire your hand? Yet you move."

Her glance fell on Dawn, pouting in her chair. "I wish I could let you fly away into the past with me. For a visit. You'd fix things for me anyhow. Make me so happy. But not to where I'm kept. No!" That child being wheeled to electroshock, her fine brown hair plastered to her scalp with sweat, her eyes so wide open staring at the ceiling that a ring of white circled her pupils.

"Dawn, it isn't bad to want to help, to want to work, to seize history," Luciente said, getting up to caress her. "But to want to do it alone is less good. To hand history to someone like a cake you baked."

Connie looked across the table at Bee, meeting his gaze for the first time. "Are you really in danger?"

"Yes." His big head nodded in cordial agreement. "You may fail us."

"Me? How?"

"You of your time. You individually may fail to understand us or to struggle in your own life and time. You of your time may fail to struggle together." His voice was warm, almost teasing, yet his eyes told her he was speaking seriously. "We must fight to come to exist, to remain in existence, to be the future that happens. That's why we reached you."

"I may not continue to exist if I don't check back. . . . What good can I do? Who could have less power? I'm a prisoner. A patient. I can't even carry a book of matches or keep my own money. You picked the wrong savior this time!"

"The powerful don't make revolutions," Sojourner said with a broad yellow grin.

"Oh, revolution!" She grimaced. "Honchos marching around in imitation uniforms. Big talk and bad-mouthing everybody else. Noise in the streets and nothing changes."

"No, Connie! It's the people who worked out the labor-and-land intensive farming we do. It's all the people who changed how people bought food, raised children, went to school!" Otter was so excited she leaned far forward over the table till one of her fat braids dipped into the yogurt. As she argued Hawk picked Otter's braid out and wiped it with a cloth napkin without Otter even noticing. Hawk smiled. Her smile still said mother. For a moment her glance rested on Dawn wistfully. "Who made new unions, withheld rent, refused to go to wars, wrote and educated and made speeches."

"But there was a thirty-year war that culminated in a revolution that set up what we have. Or else there wasn't and we don't exist." Luciente held her hands up, her eyes big and laughing.

"You're not talking much this morning," Connie said warily. Was Luciente sore at her about Bee?

"Oh, grasp, Luciente's still half buzzy," Otter said teasingly. "Jackrabbit and I had to go in delegation last night to fetch per home from Treefrog to do cleanup."

Jackrabbit roused and waved in response, traces of paint and something shiny on his arms as if he had not quite cleaned up.

"Take Connie to the museum," Luxembourg said. "Then person can understand us and our history better."

"No!" Luciente woke up. "Guidelines set in grandcil by everyone call for no specific history in this proj."

"How can a person understand without understanding?"

"That argument belongs to meeting," Luciente said fimly. "I wait you to raise it there, Luxembourg. Until, no blurring!"

"Zo, you shook Luciente awake," Jackrabbit said, grinning. "Charging into righteous battle with a grandcil ruling in per teeth."

Luciente rubbed her cheek, embarrassed. "Maybe we can have coffee this morning? All this talk about it. I could use some."

"Should we send a note of complaint to Diana of Treefrog?" Otter asked, and everybody laughed, enjoying their power to embarrass Luciente.

Dr. Redding had arrived on the ward as she slipped back. Nobody was paying attention to her. I could have stayed longer, she thought regretfully, but things looked interesting. Dr. Redding, Dr. Morgan, Acker, the psychologist, Miss Moynihan, the EEG technician, and even the secretary, Patty, and the attendants were gathered around Alice's bed.

"I want you to pay close and careful attention this morning, and I want you to keep in mind in the ensuing months of this project what you're going to witness demonstrated. I expect to see immediate effects in a higher level of confidence among staff," Dr. Redding said coldly.

Dr. Morgan's ears were red sticking through his pale thin hair. He hunched smaller. Misery rose from him like a stench. It was quiet in the women's ward.

"Don't get too sure of yourself, Dr. Ever-Ready." Alice grinned under the hill of bandages. "That fat kid doctor there, he scared. He scared of me. Thinking I be fixing to bite it off." Alice snapped her teeth. Under the sheet she wriggled her long body.

"Behold, Francis," Dr. Redding said genially. "Patients recognize hesitation. You were reluctant to include Alice in the experiment because of the very violence that makes her a suitable subject. Your fears are groundless. Poor impulse control has brought this subject into repeated scrapes with society. The very lack of control that has stunted her development, we can provide her."

"You just saying I do what I want. Don't you wish you just sometime know what you be craving to do? Mr. Beardo there, he poor at controlling impulses too. Making it with Miss White Coat Hot Pants. You all just go have one on me and get this crap out from my head."

A tremor of embarrassment bent them all, grass in the wind. Then they drew mutual strength, gathered around Alice's bed, and silently decided to pretend not to hear her.

Acker muttered something about "random hostility patterns" They clustered around a machine that was writing with pens eight at a time on paper that had been heaping up on the floor in accordion piles.

"All that paper," Alice said, louder. "Running out like toilet paper gone wild. How many trees we use up this morning?"

Redding held out his wrist watch. "Argent and Superintendent Hodges will be here soon. Let us hope. And the camera crew." Morgan and Moynihan were exclaming over spikes. All the time the pens kept writing and the paper kept dropping in its neat diarrhea on the floor. Redding came to a decision. "Nurse, time to get off those bandages. Mrs. Valente, bring us coffee and we'll hang out in the conference room till our guests come to the party, eh?" He sped out, with his staff in pursuit.

The nurse began removing the head bandages. Cautiously Connie and Sybil edged nearer and nearer till Connie called out, "Is it true you got needles stuck in your . . . head?"

"No lie. Electrodes, they call them."

Connie stared expectantly as the bald scalp emerged from the swathing. Like Bee. "But I don't see anything!"

"They inside, girl. What you expect, I look like a goddamn pincushion? They stupid, but they not that stupid!"

"Alice, if they're electrodes, where are the wires?" Sybil asked cautiously.

"You old-fashion. No wires. They use a little radio, and they stick that inside too!"

"Now, you cut this out," the nurse said suddenly. "That's enough. Quiet on the ward. You're disturbing this patient."

"I don't see how we could possibly disturb Alice. It isn't we who put a radio and electrodes in her head," Sybil said loftily.

"Quiet down or I'll give you a shot that will lay you out flat," the nurse said, hands on her hips.

Back at their own beds, Sybil whispered, "The nurse didn't contradict us about the electrodes. Could it be true?"

"But what for?"

"Control. To turn us into machines so we obey them," Sybil whispered.

What nonsense it had to be! They were crazy, they were imagining this. She wished she had stayed in Mattapoisett.

At eleven the staff was back with two more doctors and a video tape crew. One of the newcomers she recognized from the Christmas party of her last commitment as the superintendent of the hopsital. Dr. Samuel Hodges was over six feet tall and in his late fifties, with only a circlet of crisp curly gray hair like a laurel wreath around his ruddy dome. The other man was older, with silky white hair, a radiant tan, a fine gray suit, natty but conservatively tailored. Dr. Redding and Dr. Hodges called him Chip, but Dr. Morgan called him Dr. Argent. Dr. Redding asked him how St. Peter's Island had been, casually throwing at the super that Dr. Argent's family owned an island off Georgia. Scoring, point-counting.

"A very small island," Dr. Argent said. "Used to offer shelter to runaway slaves. Now to runaway slaving doctors." He spoke differently than the others; at first she thought perhaps he was English, and sometimes his voice reminded her of the Kennedys speaking on TV. He wore his white hair a little long and wherever he stood became the center of the room. Redding talked to him with the soft edge of diffidence mellowing his voice. A teasing edge brought a laugh up to Redding's throat and kept it waiting there, like a little warning light.

"We'll be video-taping occasionally over the next two months," Redding said to Dr. Hodges. "Advantages: on-the-spot record of procedures and patient responses. Able to be edited into a film we can use for funding and education. Ne special lights needed."

"The light in here is borderline," one of the crew said. "When we get on the ward in NYNPI we'll get you better tape."

"Don't turn that camera on me!" Alice yanked away from the nurse and flailed in the bed.

"I can, of course, calm her at any point, but I'd prefer to proceed as we've programmed it," Redding said.

Dr. Hodges made him a litle bow, indicating he should continue. "Doctor, it's her head," Mrs. Valente said apologetically. "We've shaved it. She's bald. You know, it makes her be embarrassed? To be photographed bald?"

They looked at Valente blankly. Connie felt embarrassed herself. She had disliked Valente on sight, because of her burliness and her speech impediment. But Valente actually saw them as people; saw Alice as a woman who should not be publicly shamed. Valente went on, mumbling badly. "Could maybe get wigs?"

"Patty." Dr. Redding nodded to the ever-hovering secretary. "Get an assortment of wigs for the women, for use while their hair grows out."

"How soon do you want them, Doctor?" Patty looked dubious. She was a slender woman, always in a mint green or cherry red pants suit, with short blond hair and big round blue-tinted glasses sliding on her nose.

"Alice is just a demonstration. We won't start on the others till we're at the institute. Two weeks, say."

So they were going to do it to all of them. They were going to do it to her—whatever *it* was. Her too.

"Charlie, if I may be so bold," Dr. Argent said, "why not begin with her kicking around? After all, irrational violence is what we're about."

"Right you are." Redding chuckled, looking upstaged. "Certainly. Let's go. Roll 'em."

"One minute, Doc. We're working on the miking. Just keep her going and we'll be with you in a couple of minutes."

Alice did keep going. She succeeded in heaving herself out of the bed and it took both attendants and the nurse to force her flat again. As the struggle proceeded, the crew started filming, a mike dangling over the bed, while the impassive gum-chewing cameraman edged Patty out of the way to get a good angle.

"Welcome to the monkey house at the zoo!" Sybil yelled. All the patients were active now, some talking loudly to themselves or the air, Miss Green lying prone with the pillow pushed over her head, Tina Ortiz watching in a knot of fury. The men were crowding the door to stare in. Alvin made a dash down the ward to bang on the outer door with both fists. Fats grabbed him under the armpits and walked him back to his bed. Alvin did not appear again; probably they snowed him with heavy tranks.

Redding, wearing a small mike around his neck like a pendant, lectured steadily on amperage and voltage. "We will be stimulating points one through ten of the left amygdala with point nine milliamps, one hundred, point two microseconds pulse duration, bidirectional square waves for five seconds." He sounded like a repairman from the telephone company calling in to report on a job. Alice breathed in snorts, letting go a tirade of curses. One of the crew shut off her mike. The two attendants braced themselves, holding her down. Dr. Argent stood with his hands clasped behind his back and his lips pursed as if he might start whistling a tune, watching the whole scene with bright interested gaze. Occasionally he rocked to and fro on the balls of his feet. Dr. Hodges stood farther back, stealing a glance at his watch. Finally he sent Patty for a chair.

"The focal brain dysfunction we see in this patient has resulted in episodic dyscontrol. We believe this kind of hard-core senseless aggression can be controlled—even cured. In layman's language, something is wrong in the electrical circuitry—some wires are crossed in the switchboard of the amygdala. When these circuits 'short out,' as it were, irrational violence is triggered in the patient."

Dr. Argent winced, seemed as if he would speak, muttered to himself. Finally he said softly, "Perhaps we should leave analogies to the poets, Charlie."

"Acker, ready? Morgan? Moynihan? Let's go." Redding turned to the camera crew. "You can film the computer stuff at the institute. Here we're just jerry-rigged."

"In the city, gentlemen," Miss Moynihan said to the crew, "we can show you the complete procedures. We have the best equipment."

"Listen, there aren't many state hospitals in the country where you could get this far," Dr. Hodges said testily.

"Chip, come on in the picture," Redding pleaded, and together they moved toward the bedside. "Turn on her mike. Alice, how are you feeling today?"

"Motherfucker, you let me up! I ain't no guinea pig!"

"Can you bleep some of that out? Okay." He signaled, like a conductor to his orchestra. "Alice, now how do you feel?"

Alice relaxed suddenly. A look of surprise came over her face. She didn't reply. Her mouth remained open, then she shut it.

"Release her," Redding said to the attendants.

They looked uncomfortable and did not let go. Fats whined, "Doctor, she strikes out fast. Like a rattlesnake. She can take you by surprise."

"O ye of little faith," Redding said with a faint smile. "Let her go. Stand back."

Gingerly the two attendants backed away from Alice. She continued to lie still.

"Now how are you feeling, Alice?"

Alice turned her head from side to side. She began to smile. "I feel good. I feel so good."

"Tell us what you're experiencing, Alice."

"I like you, baby. Come here. Come close to Alice. That feel so good. You good to me now."

Redding chuckled. "See? Like taking candy from a baby. Righto. Okay, attendants, hold her down."

Exchanging looks of confusion, the attendants took hold of Alice, who giggled and writhed.

"I mean hold her. I mean carefully!" Redding barked.

A moment later Alice's face broke into a snarl and she jerked upright and lashed out at Fats. The nurse had to pile on to wrestle her.

"Now once again let her go."

"Doctor! We can't."

But Alice collapsed and began to giggle.

"You see, we can electrically trigger almost every mood and emotion—the fight-or-flight reaction, euphoria, calm, pleasure, pain, terror! We can monitor and induce reactions through the microminiaturized radio under the skull. We believe through this procedure we can control Alice's violent attacks and maintain her in a balanced mental state. The radio will be feeding information and telemetry straight into the computer once we're in the institute, and Alice will be able to walk around the ward freely. That concludes our little preview demonstration."

The cameraman said, as they began packing up, "That's pretty impressive, Doc. Can you turn her on and off like that every time?"

"Does the light go on when you press the switch?"

As the video tape crew left, Redding turned to his audience. "Well, Sam, Chip, what do you say? Find that interesting?"

Dr. Argent gave him a wry smile, hand on his shoulder. "Showmanship. Got to control that grandstanding urge. Reminds me of Delgado with his bull. You know, he has a bull charge him in full view of a crowd and then he stops it dead."

"Sometimes you have to show something baldly before people accept it as possible. There's no trickery involved. We *can* control the violent."

"I also think you might consider using the electrodes to

produce calm, sleepiness. We aren't making blue movies, Charlie!"

Dr. Hodges cleared his throat, rising stiffly. "It was interesting, sure. But it's not cost-effective. The computer time. The hardware. A sufficient dose of psychoactive drugs would stop her violence as quickly."

"Sam, listen—with a computer the size of a DEC PDP-10 here you could monitor the outputs from every patient in this whole zoo! You have to administer tranquilizers several times a day. But this way, eventually patients will be cleared out, back to their families, back to keeping house, back to work, out into nursing homes. The state's short of money and they put a lot of pressure on you to get them out through the revolving door. But then you get that fuss in the papers about patients being turned loose. Here's your answer. After the initial outlay, Sam, the cost is more than competitive. Now you know, Sam, with the best wish in the world and all the hard work your staff puts in, you can't cure that many. But with these new techniques, you can turn out real cures. Instead of a warehouse for the socially dysfunctional, you'll be running a hospital. That's why the legislature bought this project, Sam. That's why you'll buy it when the time comes."

Dr. Argent sauntered toward the door, leaving the others to follow him. "Isn't he persuasive, Sam? That's how I found myself knee deep in this gadgetry."

"Nonsense," Redding said, but softly. "Now that you're retiring, you want in to the most exciting project to come down the pike in years. You always wanted to make history, Chip."

"Hmmm," Dr. Argent said, and they all went out.

Above the general uproar of the war Connie spoke to Sybil. "They're going to put a machine in our heads?"

"Poor Alice!" Sybil shook her head. "She must be humiliated! Imagine playing up to that fascist because he presses a button."

"I don't want that done to me!" Connie's voice scooted up with fear. She cleared her throat. "There must be a way to stop them. If only my niece would come!"

Thursday evening she called for Luciente. She could not sleep and they weren't allowed to talk after lights out. Nothing happened. She tried again. She pushed blindly in the direction of Luciente, wanting desperately to talk to her, to tell her what was happening. Maybe they'd know what this business of radios in the brain, needles and control, meant and how to fight it. For a moment she felt something, a sense of a person surprised, groggy and excited at once on some kind of drug, it felt like. For an instant she saw a plastic deck lit from below, under a clear dome with nothing outside but strange yellow fog. Women with their legs painted all over in what looked like layers and layers of enamel that shone and glittered as they very carefully moved, posed in awkward one-legged positions like storks, managing small hookahs and bright vials. Men in silver uniforms. All white faces. Panic. Theirs? Hers? Then she felt Luciente and she was back in her bed and reaching. She felt Luciente sluggishly respond and also somebody else.

"Be guest," said a throaty voice. It was not the presence of a moment ago. And she did still feel Luciente.

"Connie, my rose," Luciente said weakly, "I can't handle you tonight. But I'm holding till Parra takes over. Open your mind to per. Parra will send tonight if you'd like to come through."

"Are you sick, Luciente?"

"No, don't worry. Let Parra send."

It took ten minutes and a nauseating time of drifting, while she had strange flashes of the stork women, before she stood in the meetinghouse. It felt like a different building. Ten people were sitting in a small room around a doughnut-shaped table, about half from Luciente's family. She noticed Hawk, Barbarossa, Jackrabbit, and Sojourner. The person with the deep voice who had brought her through bumpily was a short, plump young woman. Although Parra looked strong enough to carry her up a flight of stairs, they were roughly the same size and complexion. Parra had short dark hair and a broad face. On her left arm she wore an armband with a rainbow worked of beads.

Bolivar seemed tense, sitting with his head in his hands, staring from gray eyes that burned bloodshot. Luciente sat bunched tight across the circle from him. Her hands crouched on the table before her, the knuckles like miniature snow-capped mountains. Luciente flashed a tenuous smile at her and wiped her forehead.

"I'm people's judge for Mouth-of-Mattapoisett this year, and tonight I'm refereeing," Parra said.

"This is a game?"

"No, we're having a worming." Parra turned to the table. "Do easercises while I explain. You look as if you could use relaxing."

Around the doughnut table all began to murmur a sort of chant—making no effort to do it in unison—eyes shut, faces tilted slightly backward and then forward.

"Luciente and Bolivar have not been communing. Meshing badly. Sparks and bumps. Tonight we try to comprend that hostility and see if we can defuse it."

"Aren't people allowed to dislike each other?"

"Not good when they're in the same core. Jackrabbit is close to both. Such bumping strains per. They compete for Jackrabbit's attent. They are picky toward each other's ways. We have critted them for it before, but matters lift only briefly. When they crit each other, it does not hold up under scrutiny as honest—but self-serving." Parra smiled wryly.

"Suppose after a worming they still can't stand each other?"

"Jackrabbit may choose to see neither for some time. Both may be sent into temporary wandering. We may impose invisibility. We resort to that after bad quarreling. Or sometimes when people cease to be sweet friends, one feels bitterness." Parra looked into her face with eyes that reminded her of Luciente's. In old earth she'd have thought them related. She felt a brief glimmer of hope that such a resemblance might make Parra sympathetic to Luciente. "We put a mother-in-law taboo on—drawn from old-time practice? Persons aren't allowed to speak for two months to or about each other. Such a time often releases bumping. Besides, it's such a nuisance, frequently each longs to be done with it and speak to the other again. It becomes silly. That too helps."

Connie grimaced. "Don't you people have nothing to worry about besides personal stuff? Why should you care if Luciente and Bolivar like each other? What a big waste of those resources you all like to go on about!"

"First, they need not like each other to behave civilly. Second, we believe many actions fail because of inner tensions. To get revenge against someone an individual thinks wronged per, individuals have offered up nations to conquest. Individuals have devoted whole lives to pursuing vengeance. People have chosen defeat sooner than victory, with credit going to an enemy. The social fabric means a lot to us. In childhood we all learn a story about how an anthropologist asked a Pawnee to define bravery. Person said that White Cloud was the bravest individual person had ever known because when Laughing Bear slandered per, White Cloud had given Laughing Bear a horse. How is that brave? asked the anthropologist. The Pawnee said, But it was White Cloud's only horse."

Around the table everyone was stretching, sitting back.

"The community is precious. That's what you're saying."

"Just so." Parra nodded, grinning.

"You're a judge? Can you hang a sentence on them?"

"Tonight I'm referee. Here to make sure the group crits each justly. I can point out injustice. Watch for other tensions that may surface, clouding the issues, weighting the reaction. Someone not from this village must play referee."

She frowned at this short, plump woman who called herself a judge. Younger than her and no more imposing, surely. "Is that what you mean by a judge? A referee?"

"No. We act in cases of injury."

"Suppose I stole something?"

"We don't have much private property. Likely I'd give you what you asked. But if you did take something, everyone would give you presents. We'd think you were speaking to us of neglect and feelings of poverty. We'd try to make you feel good—wanted."

"Suppose I hurt someone? What about rape and murder and beating somebody up?"

"We're trained in self-defense. We're trained to respect each other. I've never actually known of a case of rape, although I've read about it. It seems . . . particularly horrible to us. Disgusting. Like cannibalism. I know it occurs and has occurred in the past, but it seems unbelievable."

She imagined herself taking a walk at night under the stars. She imagined herself ambling down a country road and feeling only mild curiosity when she saw three men coming toward her. She imagined hitching a ride with anyone willing to give her a ride. She imagined answering the door without fear, to see if anyone needed help. "Nobody ever takes a knife to anybody? No lovers' quarrels? No jealousy? Don't hand me that." Her voice was brassy with skepticism.

"Assault, murder we still have. Not as common as they

say it was in your time. But it happens. People still get angry and strike out."

"So what do you do? Do you put them in jail?"

"First off, we ask if person acted intentionally or not—if person *wants* to take responsibility for the act."

"Suppose I say, 'No, I didn't know what I was doing, judge'?"

"Then we work on healing. We try to help so that never again will person do a thing person doesn't mean to do."

"Suppose I say I'm not sick. I punched him in the face because he had it coming, and I'm glad."

"Then you work out a sentence. Maybe exile, remote labor. Sheepherding. Life on shipboard. Space service. Sometimes crossers cook good ideas about how to atone. You could put in for an experiment or something dangerous."

She stared. "You're telling me that when I smashed Geraldo's face, I'd tell you what I should do to . . . *atone?*"

"How not?" Parra stared back. "You, your victim, and your judge work it out. If you killed, then the family of your victim would choose a mem to negotiate."

"If I killed a bunch of people, then I'd just sign on as a sailor or herd sheep?"

"You mean a second time? No. Second time someone uses violence, we give up. We don't want to watch each other or to imprison each other. We aren't willing to live with people who choose to use violence. We execute them."

"Suppose I say I didn't do it."

"That happens." Parra waved her hand. "By lot someone is picked to investigate. When that investigator thinks the crosser has been found, we have a trial. Our laws are simple and we don't need lawyers. The jury decides. A sentence is negotiated by all the parties."

"You're Latin, aren't you?"

"Latin? Ancient language?"

"Spanish-speaking?"

"Sí, from down in Río Grande, Tejas del Sur. Pero hace cinco años que he vivido in el pueblo boricua Lola Rodríguez de Tío."

"De veras? De Tejas? Yo tambíen. I was born in El Paso. So—pues—en Tejas ahora. . . . Who's got the power?"

"We're an autonomous region." Parra looked a little confused. "Todos, claro, como aquí, como siempre, no?"

"But you all speak Spanish?"

"For our first language, claro que sí, como no?"

"Why are you here? Why did you come up here?"

"To study with María de Lola Rodríguez. Es experta sobre ríos. En mi regíon tenemos todavía problemas terribles con los ríos, que estaban envenedados por completo en tu época. I've been studying five years. María says I can go back to my pueblo in a year, para ayudarles. Tengo muchas ganas de volver. I miss my people, ai!, me hacen tanta falta! And the winters burn my teeth."

"Ojalá pudiera ver Tejas ahora! How I'd like to see Texas now!"

"Por supuesto! It'll knock your eyes out!" Parra grabbed her by the shoulder. "What we've done with adobe in the last forty years—how it glows. We eat plenty of meat too, not like here, where they think one skinny cow makes a fiesta! We have a wonderful system of little clinics everyplace. And in my departamento, we've bred many races of vegetables resistant to . . . a la sequía, to drought. Verdad, you can ask Bee or Luciente. . . .

Parra turned to the table and her face stilled. To the room at large she said, "Should we begin again?" She linked her arm through Connie's and drew her to a chair, squeezing her shoulder as she seated her.

"I feel that Bolivar's work emphasizes the individualistic, places style over the whole yin-and-yang. When Jackrabbit works with Bolivar, I feel a political thinness in Jackrabbit's work, never there when person works alone." Luciente sat with hands folded.

"Such a crit is too general to be useful," a fat person with a bass voice said. "How can Bolivar respond to such vague slinging?"

"In their recent holi, the image of struggle was a male and a female embracing and fighting at once, which resolved into an image of two androgynes. Yet the force that destroyed so many races of beings, human and animal, was only in its source sexist. Its manifestation was profit-oriented greed."

"Luciente crits justly," Barbarossa said. "In truth, I didn't think of it. But it seems to me the holi should have related the greed and waste to the political and economic systems."

The old person with the glittery black eyes, Sojourner, shook her head. "Every piece of art can't contain everything everybody would like to say! I've seen this mistake for sixty years. Our culture as a whole must speak the whole truth. But every object can't! That's the slogan mentality at work, as if there were certain holy words that must always be named."

"But do we have to be satisfied with half truths?" Barbarossa asked.

"Sometimes an image radiates many possible truths," Bolivar said. "Luciente appears to fix too narrowly on content and apply our common politics too rigidly."

"Our common politics gives running room for disagreement," Luciente said. "I like to be clear about political distinctions."

"A powerful image says more than can be listed. It cannot be wholly explained rationally," Jackrabbit said. "What does a melody mean?"

"Yet a work has gross meaning we can agree or disagree with," Luciente said.

"Our history isn't a set of axioms." Bolivar spoke slowly, firmly. "I guess I see the original division of labor, that first dichotomy, as enabling later divvies into haves and have-nots, powerful and powerless, enjoyers and workers, rapists and victims. The patriarchal mind/body split turned the body to machine and the rest of the universe into booty on which the will could run rampant, using, discarding, destroying."

Luciente nodded. "Yet I can't see male and female as equally to blame, for one had power and the other was property. Nothing in what you made speaks of that."

"You have us!" Jackrabbit raised his eyebrows. "That's so."

"What we made was beautiful," Bolivar said. "Weren't you moved? A holi is composed of an hour's images. You're not respectful enough of beauty, Luciente."

Sojourner said, "Luciente leans far in the direction of one value and Bolivar in the other. Yet instead of looking at each other with pleasure and thinking how much richer is the world in which everyone is not like me, each judges the other. How silly. You could enrich each other's understanding through Jackrabbit, who is drawn both ways—as to everything that moves!"

"I don't think the holies I make with Bolivar are better or worse than I make alone. I think Luciente looks at them more critically," Jackrabbit said.

"We all owe you feedback, and it's a pity Luciente's critting waited until now to come out. We fail you as our artist," Barbarossa said. "If we don't crit you, how will you grow?"

The fat person spoke up. "What do you fear, Luciente, that you watch carefully when they work together? What makes you nervous?"

Luciente covered her face with her hands, frowning with thought. A full five minutes passed. Connie stole a look at Parra, presiding over the table but not butting in. She felt a melancholy belief that she would never see the new Tejas del Sur, departamento de Río Grande, which had borne this woman who had so much simple confidence and dignity early in her life.

"I'm not sure," Luciente said slowly, uncovering her face. "I believe sometimes Bolivar seeks to recreate the earlier time when Jackrabbit and Bolivar were always together, each other's core. To me that's sliding back to a time now past, when growth means going forward. They seem to me to bind each other."

"Like what you and Diana did?" Jackrabbit arched his brows.

"Maybe I fear that."

"But Diana and Bolivar have different gifts. The intensity we slip into together lets us keep up our intimacy although weeks pass apart. Our intimacy has always been centered on work. Even at our most intense and coupled, we turn outward and give to the community."

"True, Luciente," Sojourner said. "Your binding with Diana kept you from working well. Never did you work together, yet you fed on each other."

"Bolivar gets nervous too," Hawk said tentatively. "Bolivar teases Luciente a lot, and it makes per feel silly. That's how Bolivar pays Luciente back or punishes per or something."

A gray-haired person with a deeply weathered face next to Bolivar smiled broadly. "It's true, how not? Bolivar outmaneuvers Luciente. Bolivar's clever, quick-witted. Luciente's talkative but not witty. Luciente can't strike back quick enough to win verbal battles. Now, Luciente thinks through things politically much more carefully than Bolivar. Everybody in Mouth-of-Mattapoisett knows Luciente was recruited for the reaching-back proj not only for per sending, but because of political soundness. Person can rep us clearly and fairly. But Luciente uses that political weight as a weapon against Bolivar. You smite each other with your different gifts. Isn't that perverse, no?" The gray-haired person beamed from one to the other.

"Then Bolivar too is afraid," Parra said. "We go too fast. Let's ask Bolivar what person fears."

"If I'm Jackrabbit's past, how frail. Luciente is the present. The past disappears. Health is Luciente, growth is Luciente—according to Luciente! Yet Jackrabbit and I work well together. What's backward about that? We love each other differently at twenty-five and nineteen than we did at nineteen and thirteen, but—"

Jackrabbit said to Luciente, "You've never stopped loving anybody you loved, you know that. Why can't you inknow how it is for me? You don't think you're stale on Bee because it's years old."

Sojourner narrowed her eyes at Bolivar. "Suppose you won this little war? You have Jackrabbit all to yourself. Luciente goes off. Jackrabbit can't travel with you all the time without giving up per workshop. Jackrabbit just put in for defending and mothering. How can person combine mothering with a wandering life like yours? You're with us maybe a week out of the month."

"I never tried to comp Jackrabbit into traveling with me all the time. Only sometimes we're warmed to work together."

"But it's Jackrabbit's work more than Luciente keeping per here in Mattapoisett, no?" The fat person spoke.

"Fasure." Bolivar sighed. "Jackrabbit is more bound to place. Always when we traveled together, person would get irritable. Would sleep badly, grow a mean temper, and sling me."

"Luciente," Sojourner went on. "Suppose you won your war against Bolivar and whittled per down in the eyes of Jackrabbit. Will you give up Bee and spend all your free time with Jackrabbit? Will you give up the reaching-back proj or your work in the genetics base to work with Jackrabbit, the way Bolivar does?"

"That isn't what I want!" Luciente said hotly. "Bolivar doesn't respect me!"

"Do you respect Bolivar?" Parra asked with interest.

"Why . . . yes."

"Why?"

"Person is a good artist."

"Luciente and Bolivar, sit down face to face inside the ring. Look at each other. Then let's be quiet a few minutes. I'm not sure whether we should continue or just leave you to talk. The source of friction seems to lie in your lack of rapport—no friendship yet constant contact. You must set aside time to speak. To deliver your critting and praising privately."

Luciente and Bolivar pulled the table apart and sat down face to face in the middle, where they looked at each other with itchy embarrassment. Connie turned to Parra to say softly, "Something puzzles me. It seems like everybody is careful not to say what seems real obvious to me—that Jackrabbit and Bolivar have . . . well, they're both men. It's homosexual. Like that might bother a woman more."

"But why?" Parra looked at her as if she were really crazy. "All coupling, all befriending goes on between biological males, biological females, or both. That's not a useful set of categories. We tend to divvy up people by what they're good at and bad at, strengths and weaknesses, gifts and failings."

She felt as if she had run into a blind wall. Yet Parra fascinated her. She could be no more than twenty-one or twenty-two, yet she was serving as people's judge. Doctor of rivers. She herself could be such a person here. Yes, she would study how to fix the looted landscape, heal rivers choked with filth. Doctor the soil squandered for a quick profit on cash crops. Then she would be useful. She would like herself, as she had during the brief period she had been involved in the war-on-poverty hoax. People would respect her. There's Consuelo, they'd say, doctor of soil, protector of rivers. Her children would be proud of her. Her lovers would not turn from her, would not die in prison, would not be cut down in the streets, like Martín.

How she had stood over him in the morgue, shaking with rage—yes, rage—because he was dead without reason. Because everybody was poor and the summer was hot and tempers flared and men without jobs proved they were still men on the bodies of other men, on the bodies of women. They had both been twenty when they married. From the cruelty of the Anglo boy who had got her pregnant and then run in fright, saying she could prove nothing, Martin had healed her. She had told him the truth, yet he had married her. They were both twenty-one when he was dead. A knife in the heart. He had been so beautiful.

Tears flooded her eyes in a hot flush and then eased back. She was lying on the hospital bed. Laughter rattled from the nursing station. "I caught you with your pants down, baby! Gin!"

"Shit! You got me with a mittful of face cards."

Martín had been dead almost half the time she had lived. What was the use of crying now? Yet she mourned him freshly, thinking that in the future they might have lived side by side for half a century. There he could have that respect he longed for, the respect whose lack tormented him like a raging thirst. He loved her enough to marry her soiled by another man but not enough to back down once from a challenge, an insult, a threat. There Martín could have had his respect, his dignity, he could have had his work and his leisure. His life. He had admired in her those months at the community college, paid for in blood. In Mattapoisett she too would have respect. And learning.

"Listen," a female voice was saying from the nursing station, "we only got another week or two stuck over here. Then it's back to K building and we'll have a foursome for bridge again. I get tired playing gin every night."

"I don't know why, sugar. You beat me all the time. If we weren't playing penny a point you'd have cleaned me out!"

Eleven

"We already have your brother's signature on the permission form, Acker told her, rubbing his squared-off beard. "But we want you to give us your permission too. We want to be sure you understand how we're going to help you. We want your wholehearted cooperation." His eyes, the color of milky cocoa, waited on her.

"So you feel less guilty what you're doing to us?" She slumped sullenly on the edge of her bed. He kept pestering her.

"What are we doing? Giving you a chance to get out of the hospital. Make a better life. End these episodes of destructive violence. That as a long-term goal. As a short-term goal, we're going to move all our patients out of this state hospital into a ward in NYNPI—a nice research ward. You don't know what it's like to be in a well-equipped mental hospital. No dormitories. You can room with your friend Sybil. Good food. Your family will visit you when you're right in Manhattan."

"And a chance to get my brains scrambled like Alice."

"In two months Alice will be home, Connie. If you leave us, you think you'll be home in two months?"

"Yeah. I wasn't doing so bad."

"You won't go back to G-2. If you transfer out of here, you'll go back where we found you—on the violent ward, L-6. With comments on your record about how uncooperative you proved to be."

She turned to the wall and would not speak to him and after a few minutes he strolled off. He would be back.

That Sunday, finally Dolly came. Dolly pranced into the ward to embrace her, then held her at arm's length. "You lost so much weight, Connie! How wonderful! It's like one of those reducing farms rich bitches go to."

"Not much like them." Connie smiled. "Is Nita here?"

"They wouldn't let us bring her in. She's outside with Vic. Come on to the window and we can wave."

Down below she saw a tall well-built man in ice cream white holding Nita by the hand. They were watching a woman searching for something in the grass and Vic was laughing and nudging Nita. "Nita! Nita!" Connie hollered out the window, but Nita did not hear her. Instead the weekend attendant gave her a sign to shut up. Reluctantly she obeyed, craning down at Nita.

"Dolly, you look beautiful," she said when she turned from the window. "You lost some weight too?"

Dolly had dyed her hair a fiery orange-red. She was dressed in a sleek green and yellow pants suit without sleeves, and she had kept on her sunglasses. "Oh, carita, it pays more if you look Anglo, you know? And they like you better skinny, the ones with money. Geraldo, that prick, left me with debts and no money. I have to break my behind hustling till I get clear of my debts."

"Dolly, take off the shades. I can't see your expression. It's like talking through a wall."

Pouting, Dally took off the glasses, wincing at the light. A little prickle ran up Connie's neck. "Nevertheless, darling, everything is going fine for me and mine, let me tell you. I've done okay without that big honcho. I work hard but the marks come running and I make better money than ever before, much better than with Geraldo. Listen, Connie—last week I made four hundred! In one week! How's that?" Dolly's words spilled out.

"Dolly, did you maybe bring me a little something?"

"How could I forget? I mean forget to tell you. I didn't forget to bring for you. Now listen—I gave the old bitch at the desk thirty dollars for you in your account. Now, if you hold out your hand casual like, I'm going to slip you another five for extras. This place don't look like no luxury hotel, but you can buy yourself a little something to take the edge off."

She held out her hand and Dolly slipped a bill in it,

folded up. "And my clothes? Did you maybe bring me some clothes?"

"Daddy, he said you were in the hospital and didn't need street clothes. So I brought you two nightgowns, an old one you had and one of my own special ones, with real handmade black lace so you won't be ashamed in the hospital. I wore it when I was having my operation, and it brings me down to look at it!" Dolly chattered as if nothing would ever bring her down. "Also I decided to bring you some dresses anyhow. What do men know what women need? I see you got a dress on, if you can call it that. So I brought you the turquoise and your green print and the red. You could use some new dresses, Connie. You lost so much weight, I don't know if these will fit."

"The turquoise, it's from a long time ago. When I was with . . . Claud. It'll fit."

"If you give me your new size, I can get you a nice dress, the length they're wearing now. . . . Listen to me—I gave the old bitch at the desk thirty dollars for you, and if you hold out your hand, I'm going to slip you another five for extras."

"Dolly, you did that!"

Dolly was folding the bill up. "Come on, don't you get it? Stick out your hand natural like."

Dizzy, she stuck out her hand, and Dolly again gave her a five. Oh, well, she could use it. She stared into Dolly's intense eyes, the pupils too big, too shiny. "What are you on?"

"Me? Like always—a little of this, a little of that."

"You're on more than a little of something."

"I got to stay skinny, carita. The money is with the Anglos and they like you skinny and American-looking. It pays more if you look Anglo, you know. Sometimes I say I'm of Spanish mother and an Irish father, and that's why I have the beautiful red hair. Even the hair on my thing, I dyed it red—Connie, you wouldn't believe it." She giggled.

"Is it speed?"

"A little, once in a while, to keep my weight down. Who can stand those assholes? They drive me crazy. They're all pigs. But I'm much better off without that prick Geraldo, you know? This one, Vic, he was a real ballplayer—no joke." She giggled again. "He played a season with the Cleveland Indians, except he was born in the Bronx like me. He's okay, Connie, it's purely business. He's a good businessman. I'm not crazy about him, but so much the better, you know? I was crazy for Geraldo, and what did I get besides a lot of trouble?"

"Is it Vic's idea you take that poison? It'll burn you out."

"Listen, Connie, I'm in terrific shape! Look at me. I weight one hundred seventeen—you believe it? And last week, you know what I earned on my behind?"

"Four hundred dollars," she said wryly.

"How did you guess? Not bad, hey? Nice clothes, pretty things for my baby. Mamá keeps Nita Tuesday through Saturday and then Sunday I get her and I have her till Tuesday morning."

"Carmel's got her all week?"

"What other mother do I have? Sure, Carmel's got her. It works out better."

"Dolly, this is not good. You don't have your baby inside, your daughter you only see weekends like an aunt, and you're taking poison that burns out your soul."

"Don't be silly, Tía. You forget what the world's like, shut up here. I'm on top now. I know what I'm doing. And last week I made four hundred dollars!"

"Dolly, please. Get me out of here! I beg you. Get me released. Talk to them!"

"Hermana, how can I do that? Luis signed the papers. I didn't have a thing to do with it. You have to talk to Daddy about getting out."

"Please, Dolly, do something. I beg you. Look around this ward. They're operating on us. They're sticking needles in our heads!"

"Yeah?" Dolly looked around vaguely. "Daddy says they're famous doctors from a university. That they're for real helping you so you won't have to go in again. He says you're going to be in a hospital in Washington Heights. I could get to see you all the time. It's real hard to get up here, you know?"

"Dolly, you think I need an operation? Look at me."

"Connie, am I a doctor? What do I know? At least it's clean in here, not so depressing like last time."

"I don't want their help, Dolly. I want to go home! Listen—I'll work. Tell Luis I'll do anything! I'll work in his sweatshop nursery. I can get temporary office jobs. Tell Luis that!"

"You shouldn't go on feeling sorry for yourself, Connie—that's your problem. We can rise above what we are if we have the will. Look at me! After Geraldo, that prick, left me flat, with no money and lots of debts, I didn't cry long. I cried, sure, but then I went out and got myself a white pimp. I lost twenty-two pounds, you know? I took myself in hand and I haven't gained a pound in weeks! I dyed my hair on my head and"—lowering her voice coquettishly—"even the hair on my thing. I say I'm of a Spanish mother and an Irish father. Sometimes I say my mother was a contessa."

"I think that's Italian."

"No, it's Spanish. Anyhow, they're johns—what do they know? I make money hand over fist. Just last week—"

"Dolly, please, listen to me!" Connie interrupted, near despair. "They're going to do an operation on me. You go look at that woman in the corner, the black woman, Alice. That's what they want to do to me. At least let me come home for a weekend. To eat real food. To see you and Nita. Please, Dolly, talk to them."

"Sure, honey. Once you're in New York, why shouldn't you come visit me? A weekend wouldn't be so good, but maybe a Sunday together? It's nice of Vic to bring me up here, but how many times can I get him to do it? He knows the value of money. He used to be a real pro ballplayer with the Cleveland Indians. A white pimp is better than a brother, Connie. It's strictly business, but he brings good customers. Businessmen, buyers, salesmen. When you get out, I'll get you some money and help you set up in a nice apartment. Daddy took your stuff into storage, he threw a lot of it out. But I kept some for you, pictures and stuff I know you want."

She stood at the window watching Dolly emerge from the building and Nita break free of Vic and race toward her, hugging her around the thighs. Dolly pointed up at the window and Nita, looking puzzled, waved obediently at the building. They went off, Vic and Dolly talking at once. She stood at the window, staring long after they had disappeared.

She remembered something she had heard Dr. Redding say to Superintendent Hodges: that they had used up five thousand monkeys before they began doing these operations on patients. Used up. She had heard him say he had wanted to work with prisoners—he thought the results would be more impressive—but there had been such an uproar about three little psychosurgical procedures at Vacaville in California that his team decided to work with mental patients. "After all," he had said, smiling his best ironic smile, "they made a court case and a bleeding heart publicity brouhaha about three procedures, while San Francisco Children's Hospital does hundreds with sound and thermal probes—mostly on neurotic women and intractable children—and no one says boo."

Thus, after the five thousand monkeys, they were being used up one at a time. She marched over to Sybil. "Sybil, they're going to finish us. It's death, no matter what they call it."

Sybil sat cross-legged, facing her. Her eyes questioned.

"It's true this is a locked ward. But the hospital here has lousy security compared to our old wards. I know I could get out of here, if I could get off this ward."

"How? We eat here, we lie here. There's not even a porch."

"If I made them think something's wrong with me."

Sybil's hands rose and floated in the air, graceful and helpless as doves. "You could die of smallpox before they'd do anything."

"Would you try if I did?"

Sybil looked down. She flexed her fingers, sighing. "Without money?"

"I have ten dollars. With that we could take a bus for a ways. Then we could hitchhike. Skip says women can alway get a ride. Just so we get away from the hospital. People are too suspicious here."

"We'd get picked up before we could reach a bus station."

"It's summer. Suppose we sleep in the woods and we walk as far as we can. They can't watch all the bus stations in every town. Please Sybil, if I think up a good plan?"

"Since the last series of shocks, I don't have energy."

Indeed, as she looked into Sybil's face she realized how thin and how drawn Sybil was, with that inmate pallor they all shared.

"But we could help each other. We could keep each other's courage up. . . . My niece won't help; she's too spaced out. But if we got to New York, she'd give us money, I know she would. She'd be real impressed by you, Sybil. She's into astrology and she'd be excited about witchcraft."

"If we'd done it sooner . . . when we were on L-6. I'm tired, Connie, I'm weak. They've drained my power. It consumes all my power just to keep out the evil vibrations on this ward."

"If we got away we'd be safe!"

"Ten dollars! That wouldn't get us far. We have to eat. When they caught us, we'd be ruthlessly punished!"

"Sybil, what are they going to do to us anyhow?" She gestured toward Alice's bed.

"At least they only do it to you once." Sybil looked down. "Is it really worse than electroshock? I still can't remember all kinds of things I know I knew before!"

"Sybil, you're getting to be an . . . old patient." Before her she could see the chronic wards, row on row of metal beds full of drugged hopeless women. A terrible silence. "Don't let them wear you down!"

Sybil smiled, cold as a moonbeam. "I can't do it. I haven't healed. My pride is hollow. . . . But I'll help you."

"They'll punish you if you help me and I get loose."

Sybil shrugged. "Not like they'll punish you when they bring you back."

"I'll ask someone else."

"Don't you dare! Haven't we been friends? Don't you think my loyalty has some value?" Sybil drew herself up. "Perhaps if you do escape, I'll consider it in a new light. It's by far the most intelligent plan for you to escape first with my assistance. Then when you're safe, you can assist me."

That evening after lights out, she lay quietly weeping.

Maybe Luciente could help. When she reached her, Luciente was swimming in the river with Jackrabbit, both of them diving and rising and splashing. Luciente hauled herself onto the bank, her hair plastered to her head and her body naked and dripping. Connie turned quickly away as Jackrabbit too clambered up on the grass. "We'll get dressed, Connie. Don't hide away!" Luciente obviously thought it was funny. Jackrabbit and she dried themselves on big towels and trotted off to Luciente's space, with herself following very slowly behind. They were laughing ahead, and she felt left out and awkward. How could *they* help?

She loitered up the path. When she opened Luciente's door, they were both roughly dressed and between them they were making the bed. "Our family met last night," Jackrabbit told her. "I put in as ready for mothering and military service. But everybody decided I ought to take care of going on defense before starting to mother. I know it's logical, but I feel a little parted. I want to mother a lot more than I feel like marching off for six months to wherever the enemy's pestering us now."

Luciente was eyeing her with a gather of skin between her eyes. "What's wrong, Connie?"

When she described the ward and the project, Luciente grew still. She sat on the not quite made bed with her hands crouching on her spread knees. "So soon. It promises ill."

"It's bad, real bad? That's what I thought. I'm scared."

Jackrabbit, puzzled but interested, curled up with a pillow behind his back. Luciente frowned. "It's that race between technology, in the service of those who control, and insurgency—those who want to change the society in our direction. In your time the physical sciences had delivered the weapons technology. But the crux, we think, is in the biological sciences. Control of genetics. Technology of brain control. Birth-to-death surveillance. Chemical control through psychoactive drugs and neurotransmitters."

"Luciente, help me escape!" Her hand trembling, she touched Luciente's sinewy arm. "Before they do that to me."

Luciente shuddered. "Sticking a log in somebody's eye to dig out an eyelash! They had not even a theory of memory! Their arrogance . . . amazes me." She snorted.

"Can you help me? Please."

"Of course we can!" Jackrabbit said, stroking her shoulder, but Luciente paced with her face screwed up.

"I can't interfere in the past, Connie," she said slowly. "But I can give you advice. That's free as the wind. As we say, nobody asks for it and everybody gets it."

"I thought I might fake a sickness scary enough to make them take me off the ward and then I could escape."

"You'd have to be able to create and sustain a high temperature. I could teach you, but it'd take time. I must discuss these problems with my time-travel proj." Luciente marched over to her television set, fiddled with some dials and spoke into her kenner. In a short while she was meeting with several people. Most of them appeared on the screen as they spoke, but a couple were apparently too far from a set and spoke only through the kenner. Connie strained her ears to hear, but most of the argument was in a weird jargon, about gliding, and fast and slow marcon, flebbing, achieving nevel.

"I'm sorry I bothered the two of you. I guess you were planning to be alone," Connie said to Jackrabbit, his long body curled up.

"It's like my naming. Every time I take a step, I start jagging. I want to go back where I was. Not really. But I need Luci today, I need a clear interseeing of who I am and what I was wanting. I feel lost, a little bottomed."

"You don't want to go on defense?"

"Fasure I do. I put in for it. Only, after I make a decision, I feel thinned. As if I just lost eight other selves." He sighed, writhing restlessly on the bed and casting a baleful glance at Luciente in tense discussion at the TV set.

When Luciente turned to them, she was frowning lightly. "Everybody agrees your pass is urgent. But no one is confident you can learn to control body temperature in a week. Marat recommends acute appendicitis, a common health problem in your time. It wasn't always accompanied by fever and could be easily faked."

"No good!" Connie said. "They wouldn't think it was such a big emergency. Why take me off ward? They'd wait till the doctor came in. Weekend is the time to get out, because they're understaffed. And, Luciente, appendicitis, it's not contagious. They never believe us anyhow when we say we're in pain."

"Zo, what about a head injury? Faking unconsciousness is easy. I could teach you to go into delta in a few lessons."

"Let me think." Connie turned and almost tripped over an object leaning on the wall. "What's that?"

"Careful! It's a weapon. I didn't get a chance to turn it in today. We had practice at noon."

Connie detoured it carefully. "I'm trying to think. Maybe."

Luciente's kenner spoke in a loud, demanding voice. "Corydora here. Thought you were planning to test those results from Tennessee."

"Tonight. I'll do it tonight after supper."

"Thought we were having a town meeting about the Shaping controversy."

"Fasure. Will do it between supper and the meeting. I set everything up." Luciente spoke calmly. Connie could sense she was feeling great pressure. As she spoke into her kenner she stood there flatfooted, with her legs as if braced, and looked from Jackrabbit to her with level measuring gaze. Immediately she flicked her kenner and spoke. "Morningstar, can you take Dawn to have her teeth checked? I'm caught to my neck." Then she spoke to Dawn. "My appleblossom, Morningstar is taking you to Goat Hill. I will see you at supper and tomorrow we'll work together in the upper fields."

Suddenly Connie saw her mother's mother: a peasant woman dressed in black with her hair pulled back tight as if to punish it. With eight children, with close to forty grandchildren, with cows and pigs and chickens, she stood with that calm weighing expression as crisis after crisis broke over her. Everyone would be fed, everybody would be comforted, everyone would be healed, to each would be given a piece of herself. Luciente had some of that in her, Connie thought, but with more control and less ultimate despair.

"I think I want to learn how to play dead . . . or knocked out anyhow. I'll let you know for sure tomorrow."

"I'll ask Magdalena how best to teach you," Luciente said, and smiled at Jackrabbit. "In about an hour I'll ask her. Tomorrow morning, Connie sweetness, graze me and we'll start."

Embarrassed, Connie immediately broke contact.

"Tina, please. Watch for us. I want to talk to Sybil for a minute only. Momentito?"

Tina nodded, looking them over curiously. Perhaps she thought they were lovers. Anyhow, she stood near the door watching for attendants, while Connie whispered to Sybil, "Would you stage a fight with me?"

Sybil touched Connie's cheek lightly. "Why not?"

"They'll give it to you afterward. They'll come down on you."

"Maybe they'll send me off this ward. Outside I know the rules. I'm an old hand."

"Maybe they'll just do you sooner."

"Maybe the saddest person will be the last to be 'done.' Like death row."

She began spending all the time she could safely steal with Luciente, studying control of her own nervous system. In the morning Luciente was walking with Bee and White Oak, pausing at the big board in the square in front of the meetinghouse to read the newest notices, poems, proposals, and complaints.

With you

Well coupled: I could wade
in warm water
and melt like a sugar cube.

ANYONE WHO DOESN'T CLEAN DIVING GEAR DESERVES TO DROWN!

Do you value yourself lower than zucchini? Vote the SHAPERS!

Class starting in bacterial fertilizers, Tuesday 8 P.M., Amilcar Cabral greenhouse.

Cellist wanted, antique music quartet. See Puccini, Goat Hill.

WANDERING PLAYERS: Goose Creek players visiting this week. Thursday: THE ROBBER BARONS (historical satire); Friday: WHO KNOWS HOW IT GROWS (Shaping drama); Saturday: WHEN TIME FRAYED (drama of battle at Space Station Beta).

"What's all this business about Shaping?" Connie asked as they read the notices.

"The Shapers want to intervene genetically," Bee rumbled. "Now we only spot problems, watch for birth defects, genes linked with disease susceptibility."

"The Shapers want to breed for selected traits," Luciente said. "It's a grandcil-level fight."

"What do you think?" she asked curiously.

White Oak said, "Oh, we three are all Mixers. That's the other side. We don't think people can know objectively how people should become. We think it's a power surge."

Luciente pointed. "Look, there's my notice. Two people signed up last night. But we need at least five."

Connie read the notice. "Why do you want to learn Chinese?"

"They do interesting work in my field. On my next sabbatical, I'm going to travel there."

"Bee, will you go too?"

"Not so. I traveled too much when I was involved in reparations to former colonies. I never want to move my body again! I got so weary. No, on sabbatical I want to follow a line of research our base decided against—foolishly."

She turned to Luciente. "Will you really go off to China without him?"

"How not? For half a year. Person won't run away."

"Ah, but without you to argue with day and night, my brain will turn into a jellyfish. You'll come back and find me a Shaper. Who'll keep me politically correct, who'll chew me over?"

White Oak had begun to warble a song that Connie had heard people singing lately all over the village:

"Someday the past will die,
the last scar heal,
the last rubbish crumble to good dirt,
the last radioactive waste decay
to silence
and no more in the crevices of the earth
will poisons roll.

Sweet earth, I lie in your lap,
I borrow your strength,
I win you every day."

Bee sang in his deep base voice and Luciente sang fancy alto harmony until they were up to the door of the base where they all worked.

"Someday water will run clear,
salmon will thunder upstream,
whales will spout just offshore,
and no more in the depths of the sea
will the dark bombs roll.

Sweet earth, I lie in your lap . . ."

Bee and White Oak went inside, still singing, while Luciente squatted down on the patch of grass outside to give her a lesson.

Later White Oak came out to join them and they all went to work in the upper fields where the experimental gardens of zucchini and short-season lima beans were growing. They stopped by the children's house to invite Dawn along, and White Oak took a baby for the ride and the sunshine. As they checked the plants and made measurements and notes, Luciente continued her lessons to Connie. Dawn had become curious about the past and kept interrupting with questions until Luciente said firmly, "Keep quiet now or leave, Dawn. Connie must fix on escaping from the bad place that holds per against per will. Next week, if Connie escapes, person will answer all the questions you can ask."

Dawn shut up. Connie said, "That's the first time I heard anyone say no—you know, discipline a child here."

"I have to explain. Dawn must comprend the situation. And per questions will be given time."

She felt as if she, not Dawn, was pulling on Luciente, yanking her back and forth, and pestering her like a yapping puppy. She understood that what she was trying to master was simple indeed; something every six-year-old learned to do at will. In fact, that summer a child on naming had hurt himself badly on a rock pile and had remained in a form of hibernation until help came, slowing his bodily processes so that he was barely alive. That every six-year-old could zip in and out of delta and slow delta did nothing for Connie's temper. Grimly she plodded through her lessons.

Luciente checked the time. "Noon I meet Bolivar. We are eating a sandwich by the river and communing—or trying to!" Luciente gave a wry grin.

"Do you like per better, Mommy?" Dawn asked, cocking her head.

"I'm trying. Bumpy fasure, but I'm trying. So is Bolivar. But it's like dog and cat."

"What do you talk about?" White Oak asked.

"Childhood," Luciente said with another thin grin. "It's the only thing we have found in common, besides Jackrabbit, so far."

"Half the people I see are yawning today," Connie said.

"Oh!" Luciente groaned. "We were up till past midnight arguing the Shaping question. We had coffee twice. We're taking a night off to catch up on sleep and then meeting again tomorrow night to argue out our village posit. Barbarossa and Luxembourg are on the other side, grasp," she said to White Oak. "Got to work on them."

She stashed Dolly's ten dollars between the upper and lower sole in her shoe and persuaded Valente to loan her a needle and thread to take in her dresses. On another ward her sewing would be considered a good sign—a feminine interest in making her clothes fit would have earned her points—but here no one cared. Only Valente's kindness determined that she could get what she needed to fix her clothes so that people would not stare. People on the street.

How she had dreaded leaving her tiny apartment in El Barrio for the grimy simmering streets! She had been crazy then. She would crawl, crawl on her hands and knees down Lexington, to be free.

Saturday night she made her two extra dresses into a small bundle along with her few necessities and at eight she began pushing it out the window through the grating to fall on the privet hedge below. She had to spend ten minutes forcing it through the bars. She hated to think what the dresses would look like by the time she recovered them. Just don't let it rain! It hadn't rained in two weeks. While she was wiggling the package through, Sybil carried on at the nursing station, where she caused a small commotion, not quite enough to be punished but sufficient to absorb the attention of the Saturday night attendant.

"Why can't we socialize with other wards? On my old ward, every few weeks at least we had a nice social visit with another ward. We had Kool-Aid and cookies. Here we don't have anything. We can't even see movies. We don't get occupational therapy. We don't attend dance therapy. We don't even take part in industrial therapy. Last time I was here, I worked in the laundry. Why not this time? This is exactly like a back ward, that's what it's like. We don't even have group therapy! We must be the only functional patients in the entire hospital who don't go to group therapy at least once a week!" Sybil posed with grande dame haughtiness, arching her brows, her voice, her shoulders, extending a regal arm in bold gestures, and managing to steal a glimpse of Connie's progress.

Connie had finished with the package and run into the bathroom, where she took out of her brassiere a small piece of metal she and Sybil had worked loose from Sybil's bed. Slowly she cut into her thigh until it began to bleed and then she caught the blood in a small paper cup from meds they had carefully preserved. She thinned the blood just a little with water to keep it from coagulating too quickly and then she ran back out, dropping the metal weapon on Sybil's bed. Then she put the paper cup of blood near the leg of the bed. Sybil at once stopped her tirade, making a Bette Davis exit back along the ward.

"Good night, Lady Sybil," the night attendant yelled. "We'll give you a stiff one tonight."

Connie stepped in Sybil's path and ran against her.

"Watch where you're going, you fat cretin," Sybil said.

"Watch who you're pushing, you skinny witch! Shooting your mouth off all the time. Think you're better than the rest of us. But you're just a crazy bitch!"

"You tell her," the night attendant called, laughing.

"Your language is like the rest of you, out of the gutter!" Sybil shrieked.

"At least I don't pretend I can fly. They put you through shock so many times you got burnt toast for brains!"

"Ooooooo!" Sybil flew at Connie. She seized the five-inch metal span and waved it aloft, where everyone could see. Then she began striking at Connie with the span. Some of the blows landed and really hurt. Connie fought back with her fists and nails, flailing at Sybil. Tina Ortiz turned and came running down the ward, to mix in. Finally Sybil struck her in the side of the head, pulling the punch as best she could. Connie toppled at once, falling beside the bed and groping for the blood, pouring it into her ear, jamming her fingers hard up her nose into the tender mucous membrane so that her nose too began to bleed. Then she went into the state of unconsciousness she had been practicing. She could hear but was otherwise out. Sybil kicked the paper cup away under the bed as the night nurse and the attendant and Tina arrived, Tina screaming, "Jesús y María, you killed her, you white bitch!" They hypoed Sybil and then Tina. Skip had pushed open the door from the men's ward and he was screaming in horror.

They turned her over and prodded her and then strapped down Sybil, already fading from the sedation. They moved Connie up on her bed. The night nurse lifted her eyelids and peered, slapped her cheeks. "Well, I guess we better get an orderly to take her down to x-ray. I suppose it might be a fracture. Who's on night duty? Probably Dr. Clausen. That New York smart ass Redding will have our hides if something happens to one of his precious brains, I'll tell you. Put a bunch of the most violent hard cases in the hospital in here without enough security and what do you expect? I better give a call and see if Dr. Clausen's asleep. In the meantime go wake up the orderly. Tell him to take her down to the x-ray till we see if we got anybody to operate it. Oh, shit! Why couldn't they do this on a Monday night? Damn animals! Give them all an extra shot."

The orderly who loaded her on a truck and pushed her down the hallway to the creaky old elevator was bored and sleepy and annoyed. "Creeps," he kept mumbling. Nobody hurried. Parked outside the x-ray room on the truck, she found the minutes oozing slowly as the orderly and the nurse stood around complaining. But eventually the nurse left to make phone calls and the orderly went off to the coffee machine on the floor above, having got the nurse to break a dollar for him.

As soon as the orderly left she climbed down. Wiped the blood off as best she could on a sheet from the truck. Her nose was still dribbling blood. Then she trotted off down the nearest hall, trying every door as she went. In a closet she found a technician's coat. All the labs and offices were locked. A broom closet was open and useless. Finally she turned a corner and saw a door to the outside. It was marked with a sign promising that if it was used as an exit the alarm system would be triggered. "What can I do? Santa Maria! Help me now, just once!" She burst through it and it began ringing fiercely, loud enough to be heard everywhere, everywhere.

She had no idea what side of the building she had emerged on. Quickly she circled, looking for her clothes, but the outside lights flashed on and she gave up and started running. Perhaps she could hide someplace till dawn, till the search quieted, then circle back for her clothes. If only she had planned some better way to get the clothes out with her. She ran as hard as she could pump her short legs across the lawns, hopping low hedges, dodging benches. Soon they would be out looking for her in force. She was outside, she was outside for the first time since April! She ran, panting terribly, coughing, under the sliver of crescent moon, sharp enough to cut herself on. White as the metal span Sybil had pretended to attack her with. Bright as freedom. Skinny as her chances. "Pretty moon, mother, lady of those horns, help me. Luciente, shining one, like my friend, help me."

But the sharp scythe of moon mocked her. Commented in a stagy voice like Sybil's that she had planned, but planned like a madwoman, not thinking past the first stage of her escape. Had panicked when the first doors were locked and seized the outside exit with the alarm. She should have continued to try every door on every corridor to make a safe exit.

They might not find her clothes caught in the privet. If she hid, in the daytime she could shuffle slowly as any other inmate through the walks, meander close to the hospital, and grab the package. Another voice in her said, run, make space between. Escape and worry about clothes later. You have ten dollars. Buy, beg, steal clothes. Monday comes soon. Somebody will be doing a wash. Clothes will be hung on lines. Run! The voice sang that if she didn't seize what chance she had, if she didn't leap into the darkness, if like Sybil she awaited the perfect moment, the perfect moment never came. Alice had not tried to escape, and what punishment could they give her worse than to be turned into a toy, a puppet, a laboratory monkey?

She decided to keep going and forget her bundle. A siren was screaming nearby. Search parties, the police—they would all be after her. She knew where to get over the wall. She dodged among the buildings, along the inside of the hedges. She was glad she had been here before, glad she had had grounds privileges toward the end of her last stay so that she knew the layout. Now she was clambering up and over. Running in her clip-cloppy cheap shoes across the road to the far side. Behind a bush she crouched, panting. Waited for her breath to ease in her side. She coughed and coughed and spat. Used the white smock to wipe the blood from her face. Pulled the lump of bills from her shoe and stuffed it in the smock pocket.

As soon as the pain loosened its grip on her ribs she

rose and walked along the road. She could see headlights approaching. Whenever a car came, she hid in the bushes. She walked quickly. Before she reached the next crossroads at the end of the hospital grounds, four cars passed her. One of them was a police car. Every car had cruised too slowly to be passing motorists. She imagined the description: dangerous lunatic escaped. At the crossroads she paused, staring at the expanse of paving without protection. Then she ran clopping across the naked asphalt. Here was the state highway. She must follow it, but she was afraid to walk on the pavement. To reach cover would take too long. She clambered down into the drainage ditch that ran alongside. When a car approached, she threw herself on her belly. As soon as the car vanished, she rose and resumed a quick trot. Her bruises were aching, her cut thigh chafed, and already her feet burned. She had hardly walked in the past months and her feet were tender; her body was slack and weak from bad food and lack of exercise. She felt spent. She wanted to lie down in the drainage ditch. Sleep would rise slowly around her, sleep would rise around her aching body as warm water filled a tub, yes, warm sweet clean water rising slowly, rising up to cover her nice and warm. She was kneeling, her head bowed to the gravel. She forced herself to rise and march on.

All right, she could run and trot no farther. But she could walk. One foot, two foot. Right foot, left foot. A march played in her mind that people had been singing at militia practice, a song they said was from the time they called the Struggles or the Thirty Years' War.

> Let me live in the sun
> the years I have,
> let me walk in the rain
> the years I have.
> Live long enough to tell my love
> to everyone I love.
> Live long enough to bake a brick
> for the house we share.
> Let me fight like a tiger
> and leave something pretty
> like a moon snail
> on the common beach.

The words formed themselves in her mind and she hummed as she walked. Right foot, left foot. With her head tilted, she looked into the clear sky. Almost overhead a big red star shone. A little to the north, still high up in the sky, she found the Big Dipper. West and a little lower down, a sickle of stars hung. She wished she could remember how to find the North Star. Her father had shown her when she was a child.

To leave the state highway would make her safer, but if she did she had no idea how to get to the next town. Again a police car came shining its spotlight lazily to both sides of the road. In the tall weeds of the drainage ditch she lay on her belly, glad that it had not rained for days. A mosquito settled on her leg and patiently sucked out her blood as she lay waiting for the police to leave. As she came to the next crossroads and raced across under high arc lights, she noticed that her green print dress was stained with dirt. She was less acceptable-looking than ever. A gas station stood on the far corner of the crossroads, dark and shut for the night. She tried the doors of the bathrooms. The men's had been left unlocked.

Blood on her face. She looked like an accident victim. She did not dare keep the light on but sat down to rest with a pile of wet towels and cleansed herself, sponging dirt from her dress as well as she could. Helping herself to a nice big stack of toilet paper and a few paper towels, she tucked them away in the smock, which she put on to protect her dress. It was white and might stand out, but if she was too dirty she would never escape notice when it was time to get on a bus. In the pocket of the smock she found a wad of paper handkerchiefs, a pack of Kools with five left and a book of matches. She turned the latter over in her palm reverently. For four months she had been forbidden possession of this dangerous weapon and scrap of dignity: a pack of matches. The picture on the cover showed a man carrying a briefcase and smiling broadly. It invited her to go back to school and train for a great career through the mail. Even without a high school diploma she could earn $$$$$$$ preparing income taxes after only one eight-week mail order course.

She wished she could go back to school. In Luciente's time everybody studied as long as they wanted to. They took courses all the time in fours and fives and sixes. What would she study? She hardly knew where she would want to begin. She was an ignorant woman; sometimes she pitied Luciente for lighting on her, when what did she know? Reluctantly she rose from the tiled floor. The room stank less than the bathrooms in the hospital. It was wonderful to use the toilet alone, with no one looking at her. To shut the door of the toilet stall. Wonderful to wash her face, her hands, her body and feet carefully in the basin. Her feet were swollen but they felt better after a soak. She took the tiny bit of soap left and wrapped it carefully in a paper towel.

Though she was eager to get back into the dark again and away from the intersection, on the chance that there might be a key left in the ignition, she checked all the cars parked behind the garage. They had taken the keys. In one, however, she found a state map, in another a pair of sunglasses (for disguise, maybe?), and in the trunk of an old white Thunderbird, someone had left a denim jacket. She tried it on. Better than the lab coat. She rolled back the sleeves and transferred her ten dollars, five cigarettes, the precious matches, the map to the pockets of the denim jacket. Then she folded the smock and tucked it under her arm.

Then a panic whirled up in her for spending half an hour at the station and she began trotting down the drainage ditch beside the highway. Fatigue made her weak. As she trotted, then slowed to a walk, she nodded out and dreamed in snatches. Dolly and she were drinking café con leche very sweet in Dolly's steamy kitchen. Nita sat on her lap, cuddling. She was letting Nita take a bite of her doughnut, soaked in the sweet milky coffee.

Car. She fell forward blindly and struck something sharp with her arm. She lay still, her arm hurting, while the car swept slowly past. Something rusty. Luckily it had not cut her but had only bruised the skin. The jacket had protected her. She crawled forward and then shakily rose. She walked and walked. The moon sank into the trees. Trucks passed. She spent as much time lying in the ditch as she did on her feet walking. She stumbled. Fell again.

At the next intersection she waited, looking in all directions before that stretch of pavement. There had been a gas station here too but it had gone out of business and the pumps hauled away. On the corner nearest her a produce stand was shuttered and padlocked for the night. She could find no easy way in. Behind it fruit and vegetables were thrown in the garbage, not good enough to sell. A rat stood its ground, then leisurely waddled into the tall grass as she approached. She was afraid to poke around. What a smell. Rotting fruit, rotting greens. Her stomach humped. She shook her head hard. She must eat. She forced herself to pick through the garbage until she had rescued some carrots, a yellow cabbage, some black but edible bananas, and a few sprouted potatoes. The denim jacket held them all except for the bananas, which she ate as she walked on.

Her hands stank. Patience. Wait. In the drainage ditch on the far side of the intersection, a small stream was running. Water in this drought. Taking off her shoes, she tried to wade in it but the water stank and the bottom was slippery with muck. She chose to walk on the side of the ditch away from the road, nervous because hiding was more difficult and the going rougher. Tall weeds tore at her legs and slowed her. She felt visible when she saw headlights or heard an engine and crouched in the tall grass beside the stream.

Her feet were raw. When she sat on a stone, she discovered her sole had worn a hole. She tried to patch the hole with a paper towel, but that created a lump that blistered her foot. She could not walk farther and the sky was beginning to lighten. She had to get off the road.

Limping now between the stream and a barbed-wire fence with some crop growing on the other side, she could see no escape but forced herself on. The air was a thin gray, watery as institutional soup. She hardly had the energy to drop flat as cars approached, and in fact in her stupor a car came from behind without her realizing until it had gone past. By luck it was not searching for her, for it never slackened its speed. She was too exhausted to march on, but she could see no place to hide. She tried to walk faster on her last strength with oozing feet, through the air that betrayed her, growing thinner at each step. She forced her sore and sweaty legs on, swollen, bruised, stumbling beside the polluted ditch with its water flowing sluggishly in the same unknown direction.

She saw a patch of woods across the road. She had to wade the foul water again and then scramble up the embankment to the road and make a run for it. But she could no longer run. She hobbled across the pavement, vast and gray in the half light. Forever she picked up her leaden hoofs and crumpled forward. Her feet were damp with blood and fluid from broken blisters. She crossed the wide pavement with skid marks etched on it. At last she flung herself down the other embankment without pausing to look, because she heard the sound of an engine. No stream ran at the bottom here. She landed on a pile of broken bottles she rolled over limply. Hunched, she began to make her way forward, falling on her belly as cars approached. Lighter still. Now she could see clearly as far as a city block—and be seen. Then she reached the first scraggly tree of the woods. A barbed-wire fence ran along this side of the highway also, but she found a spot where she could use a wad of weeds and her white smock to push the rusted wires till she could crawl over. Then she thrust blindly through the brush until she was out of sight of the road. She collapsed.

Something crawled on her leg. She picked off a tick and flung it. Got up. With the road behind her, she forced her way through the brush toward taller trees. Finally she stood in a grove of tall feathery white pine with occasional young oaks coming up beneath them. The floor was reddish brown needles, beautiful and sweet-smelling. She picked a spot under a tall tree and spread the smock. Lying down with her head on it, she slept almost immediately, collapsing into the thick sleep of exhaustion.

Twelve

WHEN Connie awoke she lay a moment, confused. Her brain felt swollen. Her head ached as if she had really had concussion. Her legs were stiff, sore, and itchy with bites. The sun stood well into the western sky. Yet she was free, she was still free. She felt bewildered with space and half drunk.

Sitting up, she rubbed her legs. What a mess her feet were. The shoes had begun to fall apart; the soles were parting from the uppers. Rising stiffly, she hung them on a branch to dry. If only she could manage to look neater. If she had a comb. If her dress were cleaner. Clothing made such a difference in how people saw you. Often clothing was all they saw. A clean, neat dress and she could break through and be gone. But in her dirty green dress and borrowed man's denim jacket, with the white smock as second hope, she shook her head ruefully.

Peeling off the yellow outer leaves, she nibbled the raw cabbage from her pocket, while her stomach cringed, not having had anything tougher than stew to work on in months. She chewed and chewed the cabbage. Then she gnawed the carrots. Although this food didn't feel like food, it was something. She dreamed of bread and café con leche—all the breads of New York. French breads in long bakery loaves. The dark Jewish pumpernickels. Then tostadas, tortillas. The spoon bread Claud had liked her to make. Big hot pretzels men peddled on the streets from carts, keeping their hands warm in the winter over the fires.

She leaned back on the trunk of her pine, trying to think what to do. The poor vegetables had eased the dryness in her throat, but she must find water and food. She could not leave her cover until darkness, and in the meantime she would rest her feet. She still had ten dollars, she had a road map, she was free. The woods smelled wonderful. The light slanted between the trunks and trickled through the pines over her: the needles were soft and fragrant under her. But she hadn't the faintest idea how to look for food and drink. She couldn't eat a tree. Her head against the trunk, she watched small birds flit to and fro while a bigger bird kicked up the needles, looking for insects. "Luciente!" she summoned.

"How does it fly? I finally caught the error in our experiment. I stayed up most of last night working, but I caught it. Did you escape?"

"Yes."

"Good. Come over. Today let's take a skimmer and visit the shelf farms."

"You come here instead. I need help."

Luciente came, looking about nervously. "I admit, I prefer it the other way. Your time frightens me. Also makes more sense for you to exist in the future, where at least you may be a memory, than for me to poke around in the past, where I have no right to be!"

"Never mind!" Connie said. "You train for surviving in the woods. Like the boy scouts. Well, here I am. My feet are bleeding, I have nothing to eat but raw potatoes, and I don't know one tree from another!"

"Oh, a wilderness exercise. Haven't done this since I took out some kids two years ago. When Dawn almost mistook water hemlock for Queen Anne's lace."

"It was a test she failed?"

"Test? I don't follow. One is poisonous, one is edible."

She giggled weakly. "I hope you passed that test."

"I myself have not only studied but have also taught such things, I am telling you. Feel no anxiety!" Luciente glanced around with quick enthusiasm. "First of all, white pine is edible if not tasty. The cambium layer. You have a knife?"

"Luciente! I only hve matches because I found them. In

the institution we eat with plastic spoons. I have one of them too." She held it out.

"Okay. First we look for tools. In this Age of Greed and Waste, surely we can find something handy that has been discarded?"

"Is nothing thrown away in your time?"

"Thrown away where? The world is round."

Cautiously they crept back into the second growth beside the roadside and poked through the weeds and bushes. Numerous aluminum beer and soda cans lay there, as did pop strips. They also found intact bottles and jars and some usable sharp pieces of glass.

"Luciente, I am thirsty. I need water soon."

"We'll look running hard. Oh, this reminds me of scavenging," Luciente said cheerfully, grubbing among the weeds and occasionally pulling one with a pleased grimace. "When I was fifteen I went on work crew to the ruins of Providence, where we were demolishing old structures."

"Like with wrecking balls? I've seen that in Harlem."

"We take everything apart a board and a brick at a time for reuse. Fasure that work is tedious but somehow satisfying. We used to sing and tell stories all the time. We camped out in the old warehouses and apartment buildings. We would eat over fires or be invited to eat with nearby villages, and they would want to show us how well they cooked. But we had to improvise, we had to remain alert. Those old buildings, some of them were built well but many were built irrationally and even dangerously. We had to work with great caution, and still we got hurt. Old girders would be rusted through. Walls undermined by seepage. Structures that looked solid would prove hollow. Piling would go down only a couple of feet so that the structure had no support after a slope eroded. Sometimes we came across layers of structures under structures, bones and trinkets. Then we would summon the archaeologist who always works with scavengers and we'd work under per direction, sifting and scraping slowly. That would be a change. Sixmonth I worked on that scavenging project till I broke a leg. I was waiting to study with Rose of Ithaca, who had too many students." Luciente was identifying various weeds as she crawled. "Chickweed. Good raw or cooked. Yes, purslane. No, that one. It's a succulent; you can't miss it. Don't worry, I'll go over everything you pick. Only very inner leaves of dandelions by now; the others will be tough and bitter. Same with chicory."

She crawled after Luciente, barefoot through the brush. Twenty feet away trucks and cars swept past at fifty miles an hour. Occasionally a car would pass more slowly and both women froze. The brush hid them, but there was no point moving the leaves suspiciously. The day was hot and the leaves near the road were dusty and smelled of smoke.

"They doubtless have high lead content." Luciente frowned. "Look, here's sumac. We'll take some bark for your feet."

In spite of the pain, as she stumbled after Luciente she began to enjoy herself. Scrabbling around in the bushes made her feel like a child—a six-year-old playing in the fields near her home. Her legs and back ached, her arms and legs were cut in a dozen places, her wrists and ankles were ringed with mosquito bites. Yet she felt silly with happiness gathering up the weeds that Luciente pointed out. So much exercise made her cough repeatedly and spit.

"Being off the Thorazine makes me cough too much."

"It would be better if you coughed more, not less, and brought up the bad stuff in your lungs," Luciente said. "Now sit under your tree and rest. They've made you weak in that crazy hospital. I'll scout for water. Chew on the chickweed while you wait."

She took a cautious bite and winced. "Ugh. It tastes like grass."

"It's good for you and will relieve thirst. My sweet cherry, I didn't promise you I'd find a roast goose in the bushes. Eat, get stronger, and you can go home and cook good food for yourself."

Leaning against the white pine that had become home, she chewed the chickweed, which tasted exactly as she'd expect a mouthful of weeds to taste, and chewed and chewed and swallowed it. No worse than hospital food, really; just stranger. The sun had sunk to the height when it usually disappeared behind the administration building next to the hospital. About four. She did not even worry. She was too glad to be outside, even in this patch of woods with her feet raw, waiting to graze on the grasses of the field like a cow put out to pasture. She felt happy as a cow was supposed to feel chewing its cud. She knew some of the giddiness, some of the feeling that she could sleep and sleep, was from coming off the medication. She hoped

Luciente would find water. The foul stuff in the drainage ditch would probably kill her. Well, chewing the weeds helped. Luciente had found some wild onions and they made her saliva flow and relieved the soreness in her throat. She noticed her hands had a tendency to shake. That tremor seemed to get worse as the day wore on. Thorazine and barbiturate withdrawal. It would help if she had water. But a strange tranquility filled her. She felt space around her body, the space of privacy and choice. Comparing herself with a cow, she felt more human than she had since . . . oh, since she'd been with Claud.

When she had talked about Claud to Luciente, Luciente had been shocked that Claud was a pickpocket. They had worked the well-dressed crowds, the businessmen, the women who shopped on Fifth Avenue. If she searched herself, she found a pride that she had learned those skills, that she had been useful to Claud. They made a living, they could eat out in the neighborhood and buy clothes and keep Angelina looking pretty the way she ought to be. Money to go to the dentist. Money for a new couch bought on time; Naugahyde it was, just like leather, and Claud liked to stretch out on it.

To feel pride. Oh, she had been allowed to feel that briefly when she had gone to the community college in Chicago to study to be a teacher. How she had studied, spreading out her books on a table in the library (too noisy at home). She did not have a typewriter, and no matter how carefully she wrote out her papers, she noticed that her grades were lower for that. She had learned to type in high school, she had taken a whole year, and now she had a job typing. She asked her boss if she could stay late to use the typewriter for her school papers, but he acted suspicious, as if she wanted to hang around to steal something. Chuck, in her American history course, said she could use his typewriter if she'd type his papers too. He had a fancy electric machine, but he couldn't type. She thought that was funny, but she accepted the bargain. Some bargain. A baby in her belly by March and the end of her schooling, her pride, her hope.

Married to Martín a year later, she had been proud. She swatted a mosquito sitting up on skinny legs about to sink its probe in her thigh. But not proud of herself. No. She felt hollow with shame after her Anglo boyfriend Chuck had deserted her. After she had had to leave school, after her family had thrown her out, after she had spent all she had on a six-hundred-dollar abortion done without anaesthetic. Neither baby nor husband, neither diploma nor home. No name. Nobody. Woman spoiled. Chingada.

Martín's love had given her worth. She had feared the loss of his love every day. She spent her time fearing it, walking the line of decorum like a tightrope, lowering her eyes to all other men, speaking only when spoken to. She had loved him. How she had loved him. It had been easy. He had been beautiful, his body like the molten sun, coppery and golden at once, his body in which strength and grace were balanced as in a great cat. His body had been almost girlish in its slenderness—although she would never have dared to say that in any way, for that very thought expressed would have lost him to her—and masculine in its swiftness, its muscular tight control. No wonder Parra had made her remember him. Beautiful, Martín had been, with his face of sadness and grace, his eyes like brown rivers with something moving warily in their depths. His smile that opened like a box of light. His hands nervous as the little birds that darted through the pine boughs. He used to split matches in two while he sat talking at the kitchen table. In the madhouse inmates did that, on the rare occasions they acquired a match. But he did it just because his hands had to be occupied. He had a car, yes, a Mustang the color of gold, and he stood in the street carefully washing and polishing it on Saturday. After he was killed, the company repossessed it. What would she have wanted with it, the chariot of his pride?

With Martín she had been proud with a tremor like the drug withdrawal now, proud of his love but fearful of losing what she could not deserve. He felt lent; always she had expected his loss to another woman who would not come to him stained. But she lost him to the street.

In this odd moment she recalled him peacefully, her young husband. How he would stare to see her now, used and battered. If he appeared before her, he would seem as young as Jackrabbit. Of all she had lost, he was the sweet one she could least afford to call back from the dead, from the garbage bin where the poor were cast, for she was no longer a mate for him. But once, once she had held him supple and sinewy and hot in her arms, she had trembled under him, shy and shaken. Long ago. She had loved him well. As she should have loved her daughter.

When Luciente came back, walking lightly on the needles, she greeted her: "I wish we could have Dawn with us."

Luciente frowned, sitting down. "Afraid to try. Afraid for per . . . I don't like to disappoint you."

"Just a little while. One hour. Half an hour. Who can bother us here in the woods?"

"Ummm. It makes me nervous."

"We'll be careful! I want to see her so much. Let her come through to us. Just for a little while."

Still frowning, Luciente mumbled, "I'll ask her."

A few minutes later Dawn stood under the pines wearing blue overalls. Her hair had been cut shorter, her skin was toasted brown, and she wore a neat bandage that looked somehow sealed to the skin of her arm.

"What happened to your arm?" Connie asked her.

"Oh, that!" Dawn held out her arm importantly. "I did that diving."

"Diving into the river?"

"No, in the bay. My study group went visiting the fish herds. Then we did free diving and I scraped myself." Dawn stared all around her. "It looks just like a regular woods. I thought there'd be cities and accidents and smokestacks and beggars and pollution!"

"There is a lot of pollution," Luciente said. "There's a paved roadway near here with internal combustion engines running on it, and it's lined with dangerous refuse."

"How come you wanted me to come?" Dawn asked Connie. "How come you look at me the way you do?"

"I'm silly." She found herself apologizing. "You remind me of my daughter. She was taken from me."

"Daughter? What's that?"

"My child. You look like my child. She was called Angelina."

"Magdalena says I can only stay a few minutes. I can't go back without seeing something! Mama, isn't there something to look at?"

"Okay!" Luciente sighed. "We'll creep, quiet and stealthy as ancient Wamponaugs, over to the highway and I'll show you a real autocar."

"Really!" Dawn hugged herself. "That's running good! I can't wait! They're fasure dangerous, aren't they! I mean, they killed millions of people!"

"But quietly," Luciente cautioned.

Dawn babbled with excitement. "I studied about them. I saw them on holi. How the whole society was built around them, they paved over the earth for them to run on and sit on right in the middle of where they lived! Everyone had to have one. And they all set out in their private autocar to go someplace at the same time and got stuck in jams and breathed poison and got sick. Yet people loved their autocars like family. They drove fast in them till they wore out and ran into each other and got broken and burned and mangled and still they would rather drive in their autocars than do anything! Now can I see one?"

"But it felt good to ride in them," she said to the child, not daring to touch her. Small brown arm with the bandage where she must have hurt her tender flesh. "You could get into a car and go riding in the country anytime you wanted."

"But there were so many of you. How could you go riding at the same time without running into each other?"

Martín's golden Mustang. "Sometimes when you're young, oh, just riding in a car, a convertible maybe with the top down and the radio turned on, a song with a beat . . . You feel on top of the world. You feel so . . . alive, so beautiful!"

Mother and child surveyed her blankly. "Often we feel good," Luciente protested, "but it usually has to do with work, as when I found the bug in our experiment. Or when we're together in the fooder talking and in the morning telling dreams. Or after the critting session with Bolivar, when you feel others love and care and we live connected and must struggle to do better together. When Bee was with you, you were pleased. What does that have to do with objects?"

Thoy wriggled through the bushes close enough to the highway so that Dawn could peer out. "Ooooh!" she said when a truck thundered past. "It stinks!"

"Shh." Luciente dropped a warning hand on her finely turned shoulder.

"How could they hear us, making so much noise?" But Dawn whispered.

"See, there's a car," Connie said. "The red one. It's a Chevy Vega."

"How come person inside has the windows all the way up when it's so hot? Is person scared of something?" Dawn asked.

"He probably has the air conditioning on—a machine that makes it cool," Connie said, studying Dawn's hair and ears.

"Only one person in that whole machine! So much energy spent! The sadness of it, the loneliness!" Luciente blew her nose.

"Don't cry, Mama," Dawn said, kissing her cheek. "Why sadden? It just seems stupid."

"All those people in metal boxes, alone and cut off!" Luciente shook her head. "How could you start to talk? Make friends? Once when I was returning from visiting my childhood family, I took ill suddenly. My fever rose and I felt dreadful. A person helped me lower my fever and the dipper rerouted to a hospital for me . . . Traveling I always meet people I exchange pleasure with—a meal, a conversation, a coupling, interseeing, a making of music, drumming to their slide playing. . . . Locked in a metal box, how I could make contact? The accidents they had were bumping of metal on flesh. Our accidents are bumping of flesh against flesh, the brushing of lives—"

"Shhh!" Connie thrust herself flat. A police car went by at less than usual speed. Sinister in its lazy patrol. She cringed against the ground, clammy with fear. When it had gone, she began to crawl back from the highway. "Let's get out of here."

When they reached her tree, Luciente had already sent Dawn back. Luciente took her hand then and held it. "Dawn is too young to comprend why you love per. But *we* love you back."

Connie wanted to speak of the night with Bee, but could not. She looked down, sorry she could not say her feelings. "I . . . I," was all she could stammer. "I . . . pues . . . I want you to know . . ."

Luciente beamed. "I found water and also rumcherries and blackberries. The water is unclean. Has residues of lead, cadmium, copper, and strontium ninety. But the water you drank in your space was also unclean. The bacteria content of this water is little higher than that. Will you drink it?"

"Sure." She gathered up her shoes and smock and followed Luciente. The water oozed from the earth perhaps half a mile farther on, near the edge of the patch of woods. It was dark brown and she feared it, but her mouth was sore and dry, her throat burned again. They put a beer bottle and a jar in the small stream to soak as clean as they could, so that after she had drunk her fill, slowly as Luciente warned her, she could carry away water.

Blackberries grew in great arching brambles at the wood's far edge. Only some were ripe and fell into her hand with their fat juicy weight when she touched them. They were sweet and winy in her mouth. After she had eaten and drunk and picked more for later, Luciente pointed out bouncing Bet to her, pretty pale pink flowers that looked as if they might have escaped from a garden. "Use the leaves for soap."

"I have real soap." She rescued the scrap from the pocket of the denim jacket and finally cleaned herself slowly but thoroughly in the brown water of the spring.

Then Luciente showed her half a dozen other weeds she could eat, all of which she took as samples obediently but without enthusiasm. As dusk thickened, so did the cloud of mosquitoes settling over her. They left Luciente alone. "They know I'm not real," she said. "I hope it wasn't a bad idea to bring Dawn through. Dawn is a little bent to personal heroics. I should've consulted my coms. . . ."

"It's twilight. Do you think we could risk a small fire?"

"Anything. Look at my arms and legs!" Her body was lumpy with bites. The bugs were settling on her in colonies, like rows of oil derricks pumping away. She and Luciente moved a distance from the spring, back among the pines, but the mosquitoes followed them. Finally she tore western New York from the map and together with dry fallen branches and twigs, they set a fire that caught on the fourth match.

"You can roast your potatoes."

"I forgot them." She settled against a tree. "Maybe they've stopped looking for me. If I was them, I'd watch Dolly's. After all, I have to go to her for money."

"This money complicates your lives."

"But you have those credits."

Luciente settled down cross-legged across the fire. "Luxuries are scarce. There is only so much Bordeaux, so much caviar, so much Altiplano gray cheese. Necessities are not scarce. We grow enough food. But there are things no one needs that people enjoy. We try to spread them around. In our region we each get a fixed number of luxury credits. We can spend them all on some really rare luxury—a bottle of great old wine like a 2098 vintage Port for my birthday—or we can have many little treats. We can even save them up for two years. In Parra's region, Tejas del Sur, they do it by productivity. They have a fixed number of credits for the region, and villages are allotted points by how much above their quota they produce. We think they'll get tired of that system. It creates rivalry."

"I think I'd spend my credits on clothes."

"But that makes no sense, Connie. The costumes circulate. You take them out as you want them. The flimsies anybody can design. A flimsy is as good as you can imagine it to be."

"But aren't some clothes better than others?"

"We all have warm coats and good rain gear. Work clothes that wear well. The costumes are labors of love people give to the community when they want to make something pretty. Sometimes I want to dress up beautiful. Other times I want to be funny. Sometimes I want to body a fantasy, an idea, a dream. Sometimes I want to recall an ancestor, or express a truth about myself—that, say, I am a stubborn goat in character." Luciente laughed.

"What do you use your credits for, then? Those carved drums I saw you carrying?"

"No, no! Those were made for me by Otter for my birthday. Me, I like Port. And I love the sweet German wine, especially Mosels and Saars and Ruwers. And I like to give presents. Mostly I make them, which is twice a gift, as we say. But sometimes I like to give something pretty and exotic. I can always think of more things to spend credits on than I have credits."

"Don't you wish you could have more?"

"As we become more productive, world-wide, as we put less energy into repairing past damages, then we'll put more energy into producing the unnecessary—the delightful, the pleasing. It will happen."

Connie smiled, poking the fire idly with a stick that charred at the end. "I ask you about I and you answer me about We."

"Connie, we are born screaming Ow and I! The gift is in growing to care, to connect, to cooperate. Everything we learn aims to make us feel strong in ourselves, connected to all living. At home."

"I'm at home here only because you helped me."

"But this too is a human landscape. Look, someone planted these white pines. Regularly spaced. Look closely at the ground. Beneath the needles you can see marks of old furrows. Plowed ground. As long before you as I am living after you, crops grew here. The earth lives, if it isn't murdered."

"Tonight I have to move on. I can't stay here."

"Where will you go?"

"Down the highway, there's a good-sized town in maybe ten miles. I'm not sure how far I've come. There has to be a bus station there. I'll walk through the night and then in the morning go to the bus station. Then I'll go as far as I can on five dollars. I'll use what I have left for food and some clothes from a thrift shop. A dress, some second-hand shoes, and a purse. Once I get to New York I figure I'm safe."

Luciente required definitions of thrift shop, ticket, purse, and still she looked dubious. "Soaking the sumac in water will give us a poultice for your feet."

When Luciente prepared the sticky mess, she pressed it on her soles. Then Luciente kissed her, wished her success, and left. The baked potatoes were mealy and almost inedible without salt, but she ate them anyhow, slowly. A potato without salt roasted in freedom can taste wonderful. Then she lay on her smock, but she did not sleep. Her brain would not quite shut down. Instead she half dreamed. The fire had burned out to dim coals that still gave off some smoke, some warmth.

The embryos in the brooder swam and sang to her, a fish song that did not bubble but vibrated directly into her body, into her midriff; they were bobbing and schooling and serenading her. All were promising to be her little baby, they would be her baby tonight, tomorrow, maybe on Sunday. She would be comother, she would have a baby again of her own to suckle at her breast, to carry, to rock to sleep. Her robbed body twisted to seize one.

She was watching a birth. The three mothers were ritually bathed in a sauna-sweat house and, dressed in red, they were brought in a procession of family and friends to the brooder. One of the mothers was Sojourner, the old person from Luciente's family with eyes of coal chips, one of the mothers was Jackrabbit, and the third was her. They held each other's hands and she walked in the middle. The robes were heavy, encrusted with embroidery. On hers were doves and eggs. Everyone was carrying bouquets of late summer flowers, asters and phlox and white lilies streaked with crimson and wide as plates that lay down a heavy scent, bouquets of marigold and nasturtium.

Some were drumming, and toward the back of the procession a child was playing one of those flutes that sounded poignant and sad to her, although the melody was gay enough. Her heart felt too large under the robe. She gripped the hands of her comothers tight, tight, till Sojourner gently asked her not to squeeze so much, while Jackrabbit gave her grip for grip. Just behind them Luciente beat on her carved drums a syncopated galloping march. Bee nodded to her, carrying a sheaf of yellow and red and bronze bold-faced sunflowers.

As they came to the brooder, everyone fell back except the three of them, who entered. They stood under the sterilizer, helping each other out of the robes and hanging them on hooks to the side. Naked they went into the center chamber, where Barbarossa, the birther, was waiting for them. Dressed in his brooder uniform of yellow and blue, he embraced each. As she looked down at herself, she felt her breasts, swollen from the shots, already dribbling colustrum. She and Jackrabbit were to breast-feed. Sojourner explained she had decided not to try it.

"I didn't have my first child till I was fifty-five," she said. "I fought in the battle of Space Platform Alpha. And in the battle of Arlington and Fort Bragg. Long, long before we had brooders, I had myself sterilized so that I wouldn't be tempted to turn aside from the struggle. I thought I had left my sex behind me. Now I am seventy-four and my family does me the honor of believing there's enough life in me to make a mother a second time."

Now all three knelt, the old woman getting down slowly but stubbornly on her gnarled knees. Barbarossa stood before them like a priest officiating at Mass. "Do you, Sojourner, desire this baby to be born?"

"I, Sojourner, desire to mother this child."

"Do you, Jackrabbit, desire this baby to be born?" and then "Do you, Connie, desire this baby to be born?"

She said softly, "I do. I, Connie, desire to mother this child."

Barbarossa turned. The gawky teen-age assistant she had met in the brooder was delivering the baby from the strange contracting canal while Barbarossa stood by to tie the cord and hold it squalling up, screaming and squirming. A small black girl whose skin gleamed waxy and bright.

"Do you, Sojourner, accept this child, Selma, to mother, to love, and then to let go?"

Sojourner held out her old black arms for the baby, nestling it to her. "I'll mother you, love you, and let you go, Selma."

"Do you, Jackrabbit, accept this child to mother, to love, and then to let go?"

Jackrabbit received the baby from Sojourner. "I'll mother you, love you, and let you go, Selma."

At last Connie held the baby and its small ruby-red mouth closed around her nipple, sucking deep. Black, like Bee: she was sure she was given this baby from her time with Bee, a baby black and velvety with huge eyes to drink in the world.

She woke in the dark. The fire was dead and cold. Clouds covered the sky. She rubbed her legs till she felt less numb. Then she put on her dry shoes and straightened herself as well as she could and headed for the highway. In the dark she thrashed awkwardly through the brush and for a long time she couldn't find the road, until she stumbled out almost in the path of a car.

Then she got oriented and began walking in the ditch. Here it was shallow and she did not feel well hidden.

"Birth! Birth! Birth!" Luciente seemed to sing in her ear. "That's all you can dream about! Our dignity comes from work. Everyone raises the kids, haven't you noticed? Romance, sex, birth, children—that's what you fasten on. Yet that isn't women's business anymore. It's everybody's."

With a heavy whoosh a diesel, unloaded and going too fast, careened down the road way out in the center. Smell of partly combusted fuel. She stumbled to her feet again.

"Take for instance Gray Fox. Last month that person was chairing the economic planning council of Massachusetts-Connecticut-Rhode Island. What Gray Fox normally does is fish-farming out on the shelf. That's per work, per center. But after a year on the economic council and ninemonth chairing it, Gray Fox may come to identify with that job. A job that affects the lives of many people. May come to feel that it's part of the essence of Gray Fox to make big decisions while others look up to per. May come to feel that being Gray Fox involves being such a decider, such a big visible doer. So right now Gray Fox is on sixmonth sheepherding duty. After we've served in a way that seems important, we serve in a job usually done by young people waiting to begin an apprenticeship or crossers atoning a crime. When you are taking on a coordinating job, you say this pledge: 'The need exists. I serve the need. After me the need will exist and the need will be served. Let me do well what has and will be done as well by others. Let me take on the role and then let it go.' "

A voice in her ears, good-natured, chiding: Luciente as a fraction of her mind, as a voice of an alternate self, talking to her in the night. Perhaps she was mad. Perhaps she was merely close to exhaustion and strung out on Thorazine and barbituate withdrawal. She trudged on, wishing for a clock in the sky, a wristwatch. Wishing for a visible moon to mark time by. She did not even know if the moon would be waxing or waning; Luciente always knew those things. The moon seemed to hang over Mattapoisett the way the street lamps hung over El Barrio till the kids shot them out. The night was muggy. She heard thunder to the west and feared rain, but nothing happened.

All night she walked. The blisters on her feet opened and bled, and she kept walking. Most of the time she walked barefoot, carrying the pitiful shoes. Each time her foot touched the ground, dirt rubbed into raw meat. She kept on. She walked and walked. She kept on. She could not think anymore, could not worry. False dawn thinned the sky and then the sun rose behind low clouds. The sky turned pink and then yellow. She could not tell exactly where the sun stood behind the cloud wall. She kept trudging along.

Now she came into a built-up area and she could not hide when cars passed. She put on the shoes and kept going. She passed stores and gas stations and small factories and a lumberyard, crossed railroad tracks, passed a VW dealer and a Dairy Queen. Nothing was open yet. At every closed gas station she tried the doors of the rest rooms, but they were all locked.

Finally she saw an open gas station and she walked very slowly until a car pulled in. Then she crossed to the office as if she came from the car and asked for the key to the ladies' room. Inside she drank water and drank water, relieved her diarrhea, washed herself all over with paper towels. If only she had a comb! With her fingers and water she tried to make her hair passable. Her clothes looked exactly as if she had slept in them. In the mirror she hung sloppy and ashen. After a summer inside her skin was not dark, but she did not look white. That mattered in these towns. She shrugged. What could she do about it? She left the key in the john and slipped away around the back of the building.

She plodded on toward what she hoped was the center of the small city, finally passing the city limits sign. More traffic now. It was Monday morning, people driving to work. Her stomach gurgled its hunger. The first breakfast place she passed had only men in it, trucks parked outside, and she felt they would notice her too carefully.

She promised herself breakfast. Then she would sit. Her bleeding feet would stop being tortured. But she must choose a breakfast spot carefully. That was her bribe to her weary, aching body, giddy with hunger, rebellious at being fed nothing but weeds and rotten vegetables and blackberries. The next spot looked too suburban, too fancy. The next diner had a police car parked outside. The traffic got heavier. The clouds separated into long clots, a pale blue showing between them. She was limping along a sidewalk now, past a shopping plaza, the huge parking lot almost empty.

Now she walked through a neighborhood of factories and again the occasional diner had only male customers. No one else walked here. She felt conspicuous, prey bleeding into her flopping shoes, the sole peeling off the upper at each step. Dizzy. She could not remember a time when she had not felt dizzy, when her head had been normal, when some drug or the absence of some drug had not been ringing its changes on her blood and nerves. Now she trudged through a district of small houses with smaller backyards, houses no farther apart than the distance a person could reach, asbestos, wood siding, shingled, covered with aluminum. The kind of neighborhood where her sister Teresa lived in Chicago. Working class, but each of the families would say, like her own sister, struggling along with noses just above the water of taxes and debts and finance companies, that they were middle class because they were buying their own house.

The first time she had gone on welfare it had been

bitter to swallow, bitter as vomit. Even after her second husband Eddie had walked out on her and Angelina and pulled his disappearing act, she had managed. She had given a neighbor twenty a week to keep Angelina shut up in her apartment all day with five other squalling kids, stuck in front of a TV set. She didn't like it at all, but there was no public day care and the private centers cost too much.

She had worked in a box factory up in the Bronx for a while. Although she hated to ask him for help, she had gone to Luis and been treated to a lecture on what a failure she was as a woman, couldn't hold on to her husband and only one daughter to show. But he had given her a job in his nursery business. The poisons they sprayed made her sick, but the worst part was the travel, three hours out of the days to New Jersey and back. She got home too tired to pick up Angelina and play with her.

But always she had somehow managed until she had been busted. Then had come welfare, the waiting in line, the humiliating questions, the snooping, the meager, meager dole. Rehearsal for life as an inmate, a ward of the state, a prisoner.

Dizzy, dizzy. Slowly the street swung around her. Her vision riddled with spots and then slowly cleared. The traffic was slowing again. The sky was almost clear of clouds now, a washed-out hazy blue with yellow in it. The sidewalks were dusty. The day was hot already and she felt ridiculous in her denim jacket, but it was cleaner than her dress. No trees. A street not made for people.

Little houses. In each a TV, a telephone or two, one or two cars outside, toaster, washing machine, drier, hair drier, electric shaver, electric blanket, maybe a phonograph, a movie camera, a slide projector, maybe an electric Skilsaw, a snowmobile in the garage, a spray iron, an electric coffeepot. Surely in each an appliance on legs batted to and fro with two or three or four children, running the vacuum cleaner while the TV blared out game shows.

She had envied such women, she had strived to become one. Marrying Eddie, she had hoped to be made into such a housewife in such a house. She had hoped she was being practical at last with the steady man, the steady income. She had lied about her age to him. Then she had still been able to pass for a few years younger than she was:

she had been twenty-eight, and she had pretended to be twenty-five. All her aging had come after getting busted. It had shamed her to lie, but she had done all those things she had always been told to do—the small pretenses, the little laughs. Her natural modesty subtly twisted by nervous fingers into something assumed and paraded. Anything to be safe. Anything to belong somewhere at last!

She was passing an appliance store, open now. Inside, a salesman was opening and closing the door of a stand-up freezer, his mouth going nonstop. Small café next door. The morning rush over, some latecomers were having breakfast or loitering over coffee reading a newspaper. She pushed in, feeling terribly visible. Air conditioned, with a quivering machine over the door. She took a stool at the end and reached for a menu. Ah, to sit down at last! She almost fainted with relief.

She blinked at the prices and fear took her in the belly. She had to grip the counter. This did not look like a fancy café, the people sitting at the counter looked ordinary enough, that man in worn pants and a shirt frayed at the cuffs, that woman in white plastic shoes cracking at the toes, a scuffed plastic purse, a dress puckered at the seams. Had prices risen terribly during the few months she had been hospitalized? She had not eaten breakfast in a restaurant since . . . since Claud. It wasn't a thing she could do on welfare. She tried to make herself get up and walk out, but the sight of people eating made her knees dissolve. So many things! How could she choose? She hadn't had a choice in months. If she had two eggs and coffee only (the toast came with), it would still be $1.59 and that was the special. Her ten dollars shrank in her fist to a crumpled damp ball.

Nevertheless, gripping the counter she ordered the breakfast. The waitress behind the counter gave her a quick disapproving glance, a once-over of her hair and face and denim jacket.

"Where's the bus station from here?" she asked, and the waitress mumbled an answer so quickly she could not follow and had to ask again.

"What's the matter, you don't speak English?"

But the woman with the white plastic purse took over. It was only ten or eleven blocks. The woman seemed shocked that she intended to walk, but patiently explained the directions.

The clock said eleven minutes after ten. The eggs arrived overcooked and the coffee bitter from sitting on the stove, but she ate everything, ate it slowly and gratefully. She ate everything one small bite at a time, down to the last crust of toast wiping up the last smear of egg on the platter, and even the little package that said it was grape jelly. Then she paid and ran out quickly, because she could not leave a tip.

She tried not to limp, nothing to call attention. She watched the street signs and counted the blocks. The bus station was obvious as soon as she saw it.

At the ticket counter she tried to figure out what to do. There were two different schedules for two different lines, and they didn't have prices on them. Finally she had to ask questions. That was awkward, the young man behind the counter bored. She had to find out how far she could get toward New York as soon as possible on five dollars.

He was reading a book. She could not see the title. He wanted to get back to it and kept his finger stuck between pages while he talked to her. When he had to let go to get the schedules out, he was irritated. He stuck a pencil in. On the cover two naked women embraced while a man about eight feet tall dressed all in black leather cracked a whip around them. Why would anyone read a dirty book in a bus station, sitting behind the counter? Could he bring himself off back there? Would he go into the john? She felt embarrassed wondering such things as she looked into his blank young face, sallow under the fluorescent lights.

"Don't you know where you want to go, lady?"

Finally she ended up with a ticket that would take her all the way to the Port Authority depot, on a bus leaving at twelve-thirty. She sat down to wait. It was eleven-eighteen. Someone had left a newspaper on a chair and she began to read it through, from the front page onward. Soon she would be in New York. Running up the street. Otis, first she's try to reach Otis, Claud's old friend. Then Dolly. She read on. She reached an article in the women's section describing the regimen of Countess Rataouille, a beauty from a simple banking family of Park Avenue, Seal Harbor, Palm Beach and Monterey, for remaining gorgeous forever, which involved performing isometric exercises, never taking hot baths above the waist, and rubbing fresh strawberries into the skin daily. As her mouth was watering with the thought of fresh strawberries, a shadow fell on her page and a grip took her arm.

"Could we see your identification, you."

The young man whose dirty book she had interrupted had turned her in. By twelve-thirty she was back in the hospital, on her ward.

Thirteen

BUT you said I could room with Sybil! Connie argued.

"That's before you messed up," Valente said firmly. "Listen, if the two of you had tried to pull that game on me, I'd have had you both in seclusion before you could yell Uncle. You wouldn't fool me for five minutes, and don't forget it."

"How could you sign the permission?" Skip asked her as soon as Valente walked away. "They couldn't make *me* sign!"

"You're not twenty-one. They didn't need you to sign it."

"They didn't need you either. Your brother signed it. Why did you give in?"

Connie shrugged. "I was scared what they'd do to me at Rockover if I didn't. I figured they had the permission anyhow. I want them to think I've given in."

"Haven't you?" Skip flounced away, down the wide hallway.

They had all been moved to the New York Neuro-Psychiatric Institute in Washington Heights, to a ward on the eighth floor specially prepared for them by turning it into a secure locked ward. It was the roomiest and most amply furnished and outfitted ward she had ever been on. They shared double rooms—like the one she and Tina Ortiz had now, with a bed for each of them that even had a bedspread and their own window, although it wouldn't open. Sybil was next door, with Miss Green. The men were on one side of the nursing station and the women on the other. In between was a big day room with a color television, card tables, even some easy chairs and a couple of sofas, with green carpeting on the floor. At the far end of the wing that held their ward, the doctors had their conference room and computer, their lab and offices. The patients fluttered around the first few days, exclaiming about about their new quarters.

"This isn't no jive loony bin," Captain Cream said. "This is a Hilton!" Captain Cream was a light-skinned numbers runner born in Trinidad, who believed he was a comic book hero. Even the doctors called him Captain. He was lean and fastidious and spoke with a lilt and grace that kept her from noticing much of the time that he was walleyed.

Sybil sniffed. "You can be sure it's for their convenience and not ours! They're important gentlemen! Even the laboratory mice must have nice clean cages." Sybil had recovered some energy.

Captain Cream, Sybil, and Tina Ortiz stood gathered in the doorway with Connie to see what the new men's attendant, Tony, was doing to Skip, bending over him with scissors. Skip's fine brown ringlets were falling on white towels. "Alas, Delilah, you do me wrong!" Skip sang to Tony. Snip, snip. The hair tumbled. It looked as if he was being drafted. His big, curiously vulnerable-looking skull showed gray. This too they would do to her in time, this too.

"And will I get a wig, Tony?"

"Only the women, punk," Tony grunted. "Hold still, or I'll cut your ear off."

"Like Van Gogh. He was mad too. But he did it to himself. Why don't you let me have a scissors so I can do it?" Skip made a half-playful, half-serious grab.

Tony clouted him in the chest, and Skip fell back coughing. "Stop trying to hold the doctors up."

Snip, snip, past his left ear, coming around. Only one long cluster of curls clung to his cheek. Tony sliced through that and then swept up. When he returned with a razor, Skip stopped joking. He had been given no breakfast. Soon he would be taken away to a hospital near Columbia, where Redding and Morgan would drill a hole in his skull and insert their electrodes. Skip would return to them violated.

She stood with Tina and Alvin as he was carted out. His eyes were open but without expression. After the outer door had shut on him, the patients hung around, as if by staring at the door they might read something of what was happening.

"You like that kid, uh?" Tina asked her. Her new roommate was about her own age, with a long record of drug busts and commitments and disorderly conducts.

"He loaned me money to call mi sobrina, and he knew I couldn't even pay him back."

"He's got it to loan. Easy to be nice if you can afford it, hey? But I guess he's in plenty trouble now, like the rest of us." Tina was Puerto Rican, born in the Bronx, skinny with only a little extra meat on her hips. She talked fast but her sentences often trailed away as if she did not expect to be listened to. She was scrappy and would not settle down to being a good patient. She never stopped hating the hospital. "Just one more way to get busted," she said, glaring at their room. She was the first one on any newspaper that came into the ward, after the staff, although she would read only the first section, the news, muttering to herself, sneering as if she could not be fooled, "Crooks, big crooks!"

They went off together to visit Alice, who lay on her bed staring at the ceiling, as she did most of the time now. She looked ten years older, she looked her full age and then some, all the sass and vinegar bled from her long body.

"Hey, Alice, you know what them bums are trying to pull now?" Tina asked, trying to rouse her.

But Alice only shook her head. The black pageboy wig was stuck on her head crooked, and she did not straighten it. When it fell off, she did not replace it. When the attendant found it on the floor, she scolded Alice, telling her how ungrateful she was. Alice lay and blinked.

The only time Connie saw her look like her old self was when one of the doctors came to use her for a demonstration to an interested visitor. Then her eyes shone blood red and she sang long chains of bitter curses until the doctor pushed the button that shut her up. Now that Dr. Morgan had lost his fear of her, there was something ugly in his demonstrations. He particularly liked to stimulate the point that produced in Alice a sensual rush, until once she kissed his hand and told him he was good to her.

"I got to fool those wiseasses," she told them, "or they going to stick more needles in. I just stringing them along." But she did not sound as if she believed that. When she tried to fight back, the monitor turned off her rage and left her confused. Alice seemed closer to being mad than she ever had. She made up stories to account for what she did, because she literally did not know what she would do next. Yet she felt as if she were deciding. "You wait and see," she said, winking blearily, "who come out on top in the end."

"You ran away because you want to return to society," Acker was saying to her, his square beard wagging on his chin. "But what you don't understand is that's exactly what we want to help you do!"

Ever since she had run away, she had been of particular interest to Acker. She had the feeling he was an uneasy fifth wheel to the project, the psychologist added for some kind of show. He made up reasons for what the others did in terms not exclusively medical. She did not understand more, but she saw his uneasiness, his slippery footing with the doctors. Even the junior partner, Morgan, tried to patronize him. Now Acker took an interest in her. He was proud he had got her to sign the permission forms, but he did not let up his pressure.

"What you don't see, Connie, is that if it wasn't for us, you'd face spending the rest of your life where we found you. Now, you don't want that. Do you? He waited for an answer. He sat with his hands flexed on his spread knees.

As he seemed prepared to wait all day, she mumbled at last, "No, I don't want to spend my life here. Do you?"

"I certainly wouldn't. So, Connie, perhaps you can see we're working for your benefit. After all, why should society care? You've proved you can't live with others. They locked you away where you can't harm others or yourself. Isn't that so?"

"But I can be harmed here. Isn't that so?" She tossed her head.

"You're together enough to notice what happens to old patients, how they become acclimated to life in the hospital. After a while they can no longer function outside. It's a secure life."

"Maybe for you."

"You know where your next meal is coming from. You have a bed, a roof over your head. All right, you say you don't want that security. You want to go back to society."

"I want to go back to my life!"

"This isn't your life? This admission isn't the first for you. I think this is likely to be your life for some years to come if we don't help you. Instead of just warehousing you, we're prepared to help you. This is the first time in your life you've ever had quality medical attention. The affluent hire psychiatrists, but you've never had real treatment. We want you to function again, but without risk of committing those out-of-control acts. Without danger of your attacking some child again, or some other person near and dear to you."

Connie ground her teeth. "Any person not in a wheelchair can hurt somebody. Haven't you ever hit anybody? Ever?"

"Connie, you're resisting. You're the patient. You know why you're here. The more you resist, the more you punish yourself. Because when you fight us, we can't help you."

The orderlies brought Skip back from his two days off the ward. Acker scurried off to see the results, leaving her in peace for a while.

"Think of the stories of heroic prisoners who tried again and again to escape," Luciente said, clapping her on the back heartily. "One defeat is nothing. You must keep on the lookout for other holes in their security."

"If only I could get out for a weekend furlough! I know I could get away from Dolly easy. Even Luis would have to sleep sometimes."

"Why not? But try! You're important to us, we want you to survive and break out. One attempt, one failure—you have to take that for granted. What works the first time? Poof! If I'm stiffing on a task, I may fail twenty, thirty times to fix the proper gene balance. Each time I neglect some crucial factor. But finally it blossoms! So too you must work at escape. Now you're stronger for the exercise and your feet will heal tougher."

"But they've taken my money away. They watch me all the time. Every time I go near the door, they watch me."

"They have a lot to do besides watch you. You have

only to watch them. Keep up your courage."

"Luciente, mercy! Easy. I'm flat on my back. You don't understand. Never in your life have you been helpless—under somebody's heel. You never lived where your enemies held power over you, power to run your life or wipe it out. You can't understand. That's how come you stand there feeding me empty slogans!"

Luciente bowed her head. "You crit me justly, Connie. Forgive me. I'll try to see your situation more clearly and make less loud noises in your ears."

When they came to play with Skip, the doctors were not satisfied. The violence-triggering electrodes did not cause him to try to attack them, as Alice had. Instead he turned from them and drove his fist into the wall. He pounded his head on the wall and before the attendants could force him down, blood oozed from the bandage.

"That won't do!" Dr. Argent frowned, passing his hand lightly over his silvery locks. "Don't bring any visiting firemen in to inspect this one. Hmmmm." Ever the adminstrator, whenever anything went wrong he withdrew from the other two, his shoulders, his back seeming to disdain them.

"Suicide attempts are what we started with. We could be playing into the hands of a masochist, eh?" Dr. Redding glanced sideways at Dr. Argent, trying to enlist him in his little joke. "Uh, we'll discuss the case at staff today. Other procedures may be indicated."

Dr. Argent linked his hands behind his back and rocked on the balls of his feet. "Not a bad idea. Won't do to leave him around in this condition. The feds will be by next week for a tour. If we want our grant renewed, we'd better be tidy and shipshape."

Dr. Morgan perked up. "Surgical procedures?"

Skip asked loudly, "You going to take these out?"

"If our tests prove that's best for your condition, sonny, maybe so," Dr. Redding said. "We'll do what's best."

"Man, you must think I'm really crazy, to believe that."

As they turned to leave, Connie fled from her post at the door to sit in the day room. As the doctors and Acker passed, they were arguing amiably among themselves.

"Lots of talent in your field are working to retrain sexual inversion with electroshock keyed to slides and films," Redding was saying to Acker. "But the recidivism rate isn't promising. If we could cure inversion surgically, we'd open up a whole new area."

"Let's not get too far off the track, gentlemen," Dr. Argent said. "We can run some tests, but our major concern is violence. Our funding is specific. Within those perimeters, of course, we have some latitude to fool around."

"Six to eight thousand for an operation as against hundreds of thousands to keep an invert under treatment or restraint for decades. You can't tell me that's not cost-effective." Dr. Redding risked touching Dr. Argent's shoulder companiably. "Dear to the heart of taxpayers and public officials alike. If the crime-in-the-streets money dries up, it's something to keep in mind."

Dr. Argent looked at the hand. "I want results on this one, *Doctor.*" That formal address cut like a blade. "I'm an old man. It's now or never. For your sake, it had better be now."

Skip was taken to the other hospital again. When he was brought back, they had removed the electrodes but they had done something else. They had coagulated part of his limbic brain, whatever that was. Amygdalotomy was the word they used. The next day we went to see him. He looked terrible, his face sagging. His eyes were dull and bloodshot.

"Why do you want to know how I am? What's it to you?"

"Don't you remember me, Skip? I'm Connie. Your friend. You gave me money to call my niece."

"Some give and some take. Some take everything."

"Does it hurt? Your head?"

"They say if you lose a leg, if they cut it off—what they call a resection, they have names for everything—the leg goes on hurting."

"At least they don't play games with you, like they do with Alice."

"Different games."

"What are you scared they'll do now?"

"Why should I be scared? Who says I'm scared? You'll see."

"I didn't mean it in a bad way, Skip." She touched his hand.

He jerked back as if she had burned it. "Don't try to

get around me. Now I know better. Give and take, and then it's all taken."

Jackrabbit was showing her a bunch of . . . what? Dream images? Sculptures in light? Shapes that reshaped themselves into other shapes? She felt nervous looking at them with the person who made them, the artist, right there making it happen. She was afraid she wouldn't seem appreciative or wouldn't say the right things or look the right way, and he'd think she was stupid. But there at her elbow was Luciente, eating white grapes from a woven basket and grunting rough enjoyment as if it were just a TV program. If she tried to think about what the images were supposed to mean, she felt miserable. But if she looked with her eyes open and let them happen to her, she could not help getting drawn in.

The holi he was showing now had no words, no story, unlike the one he'd done with Bolivar. It was all images having something to do with the ocean and with sex and with power—not power over people, but natural power, energy. Boundaries dissolving. The sea rising, smashing into the land. Under a clear cold blue sky a sea lashed itself into foam and sprang at the shore. Waves with teeth that glinted and hair that tangled and tossed roiled over itself. Wave breaking over wave showed dark bellies arching before they crashed down in froth and slid on the sand spent and hissed dribbling back.

Jackrabbit's workshop stood near the mill, near enough to hear the wheel turning. There the river ground grains and corn and operated a series of pumps. Four times a day a tidal clock swung the wheel mechanism about so that it was always fixed correctly in the flow of waters. When Jackrabbit did not opaque the window and use only the sliding skylight, ripples danced on his high ceiling. Always, he told her, he could hear the mill wheel, the waves slapping the shore just underneath. The workshop was built out some feet over the river, and the side facing the water had a narrow porch.

"Jackrabbit already has two students," Luciente said, leaning on the railing outside the open door while Connie looked through the drawings and prints Jackrabbit started to show her next.

"Deborah and Orion aren't pleased I'm going on defense. They've been slinging about it all week," Jackrabbit complained, knotting his hand in his curly hair.

"Rough!" Luciente said flatly. "They knew when they chose you you hadn't fulfilled defense. They didn't have to wait for you as teacher. Let them do service work for sixmonth."

"Their slinging saddens me," Jackrabbit said, idly trying to tickle Connie in the ribs as she turned over the stiff sheets. "Rhythm of my life crosscutting rhythms of theirs. They feel they're growing and want to fly faster."

"Can't you work alone? You didn't always study with a teacher." Luciente kicked off her shoes and sat with her bare feet hanging off the porch, but she could not quite reach the water.

"Why do you have to go on defense?" Connie turned from the pages. "I can't look anymore. I'm sorry—I just can't take more in."

"But I have to get defending out of the way before I start mothering. It'd be stupid to do it the other way, I grasp that."

"Your society doesn't think that much of art and artists and all that, do you?" Connie looked away from the radiant male nude that hung on the far wall, along with twenty other paintings, drawings, prints, whatever. A naked male body hung like that—doubly hung—embarrassed her. It did not seem like something she should stare at, yet the colors glowed, the flesh shone from within. She kept glancing at it, nervously, from the corner of her eye. It was beautiful when it should not have been—like Martín, her first husband. She could not imagine him permitting anyone to paint him that way, yet if someone with talent had, his flesh would have shone so. It was neither Jackrabbit nor Bolivar. Unless Bolivar seven years younger with a bushy beard?

Luciente turned, propped her back against a post of the railing. "Why do you say that, Connie love? The great majority of us pursue some art, and sometimes more than one."

"But that's like amateur stuff. I mean real artists. Like Jackrabbit. I don't know anything, but I can see it's for real. Yet he still has to work in the fields and go to the army and cook and all that."

Luciente grinned. "But I myself am a real geneticist and I have to defend and dig potatoes and cook and all that. I also eat and make political choices and rely on those in arms to defend me—as does Jackrabbit. Zo?"

"I comprend," Jackrabbit said with an airy wave. "In Connie's time it was thought some people who were good at some things, like a couple of the arts and sciences, should do nothing else."

"That must have made them a little stupid," Luciente said. "A little simple—you grasp? And self-important!"

"Such people tended to feel that other work demeaned their physics or sculpture or whatever. Isn't that so, Connie?" He ran his fingers along her arm caressingly.

She pulled her arm away, embarrassed again. "Well, if a person can do something . . . important, why should they chop onions and pick caterpillars off tomato plants?"

"Eating isn't important?" Luciente scowled with amazement.

"Connie, we think art *is* production. We think making a painting is as real as growing a peach or making diving gear. No more real, no less real. It's useful and good on a different level, but it's production. If that's the work I want to do, I don't have to pass a test or find a patron. But I still have family duties, political duties, social duties, like every other lug. How not?"

"Everybody? What about Bolivar? He's always traveling."

"Bolivar does it all in a couple of lumps. At spring planting, person does the year's quota and then some! Does two solid weeks of preserving in August or September."

"But going on defense—isn't it dangerous?"

They both laughed together, that merry belly laughter. "How not?" Luciente asked. "The enemy is few but determined. Once they ran this whole world, they had power as no one, even the Roman emperors, and riches drained from everywhere. Now they have the power to exterminate us and we to exterminate them. They have such a limited base—the moon, Antarctica, the space platforms—for a population mostly of androids, robots, cybernauts, partially automated humans, that the war is one of attrition and small actions in the disputed areas, raids almost anyplace. We live with it. It's the tag end. We fear them, but we've prevailed so far and we believe we'll win . . . if history is not reversed. That is, the past is a disputed area."

"I don't understand! And it makes me dizzy! But if Jackrabbit goes in the army, he could get killed. Aren't some people worth sparing?"

"Show me someone who isn't," Luciente said. "Who isn't precious to self? How could we decide who to spend and who to save?"

"Risk, danger . . . we don't find them evil," Jackrabbit said slowly. "I don't twitter to go. I fasure don't want to give back. But I don't want to be ignorant. The creature inside a shell is a soft slug, like a worm. Who should protect me? Bolivar? Luciente? Bee? Hawk? Who'll stand between me and death, me and sickness, me and drowning? I must serve the talent that uses me, the energy that flows through me, but I mustn't make others serve me. Don't you see the difference?"

"Won't you miss him? You must mind his going?" she asked Luciente.

"Mind? How not? I mind too we're still at war. I mind that we can't enjoy peace and push all energies into what people need and want. I'll miss Jackrabbit fasure. And I think it grossly unfair that I should be missing first Bee and then Jackrabbit in one year. . . ." Luciente looked at Jackrabbit, her eyes liquid and somber. Then her face lightened. "But I'm excited about Jackrabbit mothering. I'm a kidbinder. I'll mother away too. . . ." Luciente turned to stare at the rush of the waters. "Deborah and Orion must decide if they're going to go on working here alone this sixmonth without you, or if we should close your workshop till you get back."

"They have a week yet to decide." Jackrabbit took Connie's hand. "Why are you shy with me? What do I do that tightens you?"

"Nothing!" She glared at Luciente in appeal.

"Then why do you tug your hand away?"

"Why do you want to . . . hold it?"

Jackrabbit smiled. "When I come back from defense I'll be running mature. Then you won't be shy with me. Bee is nice, but I'm just as nice." He made an exaggerated face of flirtation, batting his eyes. "Don't you feel sorry for me, exiled for sixmonth? Don't you want to comfort me?"

"Don't tease Connie so." Luciente made a fist at him. "You promised not to tease Connie!"

"Don't you like to be teased? At least a little?"

"When you're a mother," Connie said, laughing for the first time in days, "then you can tease me."

"If you experienced a pain in your abdominal region, if it was diagnosed as appendicitis, you might be afraid of the operation, but you wouldn't resist it. You wouldn't attempt to leave the hospital, because you'd know that you were sick and needed help." Acker had cornered her again in the day room, where she had been watching a serial about a lawyer. Behind Acker's back, Tina made faces to Connie to give support. "Now, you can't see your brain. But you can see the output from the EEG machine. You can't read it, because you aren't trained, but your doctors can. You can't see your appendix either. But you accept the expert's opinion in either case, or condemn yourself to getting sicker and sicker."

"Except for not getting exercise and lousy food and those meds that knock me out, I'm fine. I walked twenty miles, didn't I?"

"And came back with abscesses on your feet. You can see those. But you can't see abscesses in your brain, so to speak. Connie, you're going to thank us. Because thanks to modern medical science, you're not condemned to spend your life in a psychiatric unit."

"Look, I guess it's cheaper to keep me on welfare than in here. But I'll go home tomorrow. I'll kill myself trying to get work. I promise! I'll scrub floors. I don't care anymore. I'd rather do housework for white ladies than be in here!"

"Of course. And we want you to be able to return to useful work, to return to society safely—safely for you and for others. But there's the rub, Connie. No one can trust you. If you had typhoid fever, you wouldn't expect us to let you march out the door untreated and go walking through the streets of Manhattan freely infecting others. Now would you?" Acker waited, beaming, his hands on his slightly spread knees. Behind him, Tina was miming a gruesome death.

"I don't think I got TB or typhoid fever—"

"I was speaking by comparison."

"I understand that!" How stupid he thought she was! "But I don't believe I'm sick. Like you, I've done things I regret and things I don't regret. Since I'm poor, I can't hire lawyers to make things come out right for me when I get across the law."

"Always bad luck. Always a hard-luck story. You haven't learned a thing, to listen to you. But I think you know better, Connie, and you're simply resisting. When you look at your situation clearly, instead of through the eyes of irrational fear, you'll see we're your only real friends. . . . Look at Skip. I think he's on the road to recovery. His attitude has changed since his operation. He's trying, Connie. And that trying is going to pay off, you wait and see. He'll be back in society soon, a productive individual, healed of his illnesses, ready to make a life for himself."

Tina was playing a violin and dropped her hands quickly as he turned to leave.

Connie brooded over what he had said about Skip. It was true, Skip had changed. He parroted back whatever they said to him; he told them he was grateful. When they took him out and tested him with homosexual photographs, he had no what they called negative reactions. Meaning he didn't get a hard-on. He told her he felt dead inside. They were pleased with him; they were going to write him up for a medical journal.

Skip wanted to get out. They promised he would. She wondered. Would they really let him out of their clutches? His bandages were off now and his hair was beginning to grow back. He walked around the ward, helping the attendants. He was playing the game. It was still a game, she sensed that; there was a remnant of strong will gone cold at the core pushing him. She had tried to escape in her way, he was trying in his way, with something gutted in him. Something beautiful and quick was burned out. It hurt her to watch him. Because he was too beautiful and tempted them, they had fixed him. He moved differently: clumsily. It was as if he had finally agreed to imitate the doctors' coarse, clumsy masculinity for a time, but it was mastery with them and humility with him. He moved like a robot not expertly welded. Yet he was no robot, whatever they thought they had done. She could feel the will burning in him, a will to burst free.

"You're playing them along, aren't you?" She came up beside him as he was mopping the day room.

"Why not?" he asked her. He had become friendly again, but he no longer flirted or told her wild stories. He was numb, stripped to a wire of will she could feel. They had not burned out or cut out as much as they thought, she hoped. Something of Skip survived.

Fourteen

JACKRABBIT went on defense. For a week Luciente sank into a low energy state that made it hard for them to connect. Then she took a day's retreat at Treefrog and seemed herself to Connie.

Lunch at Mattapoisett was yellow soup thickened with tidbits of shrimp, crab, clam, and fish. Hawk was eating with them again, after several weeks with her friend Thunderbolt's family.

"It got dull, sitting at the table with mems I can't talk to. Now the taboo's off, I'm back. I think I'd warm to stay in our family. See, today I brought a guest for lunch."

Connie had often seen visitors besides herself, mostly people from nearby villages or others on their way through, traveling on some piece of business. Sometimes a whole troupe of players or musicians stopped for a week. Old friends or former mems came visiting. Then there were the people without village called politely drifters and impolitely puffs. Once she had seen a man with a small tattoo on his palm, which Luciente told her marked a crime of violence. Unlike the other guests, drifters often sat apart. People seemed uncomfortable with them. Sometimes they seemed to know each other, and when Connie passed near them, she heard a slang she did not recognize.

Why did Hawk bring this guest to the table? Connie saw

on his palm that same tattoo, that warning mark. He was a big-boned oversized man with little flesh on him, perhaps in his late thirties.

"Waclaw just got done studying with the Cree!" Hawk bubbled.

"On the Attawapiskat. That flows into James Bay from the west." He spoke in a hesitant voice from deep in his barrel chest.

"How long did you have to wait to study there?" Hawk asked. "Did you have to wait long?"

"Six years," Waclaw said. "I was lucky they took me at all."

"Six years!" Hawk's face sagged. "That's bottoming!"

"If they let everyone come who wants to study with them, they'd be swamped," Waclaw said reasonably. "Most people won't wait and so they don't have to say no."

"Was it worth it, waiting so long?" Hawk asked, still whining with disappointment.

Waclaw nodded. "It firmed me. I almost stayed. I am going to see my old village and decide. They say I can come back if I choose, to the Attawapiskat."

As soon as lunch was over, Connie asked Luciente, "He's a criminal, isn't he? I saw a tattoo."

"Not anymore. Person atoned. Has been studying up north."

"The Cree, he said? Like Indians. You still have real Indians?"

Luciente nodded. "Those lands are strongly protected, under their control. Only hunting, gathering, and some scientific activities go on. . . . The Cree have a mixed way of living. They hunt and fish, they've created some Far North agriculture, some handicraft, limited manufacture. They have to take care, for the land is fragile."

"What's to study there?"

"A discipline, a sense of wholeness. Something ancient. They are often part-time hunters or gatherers, part time shamans, part-time scientists."

"But was that his atoning? Going up north and living that way?"

"Never!" Luciente laughed from the belly. "That's a great privilege. That's why Waclaw had to wait six years. Don't know what person did to atone. Ask, if you must, but we usually don't. We feel it's closed—healed. Forget!"

Connie followed at Luciente's heels into the experimental

fields where Luciente was recording comments on performance. "This chews it up. I think we found some good strains to work on next year."

"How come you leave so much woods?" Connie asked. "Like that argument at the council. All over Mouth-of-Mattapoisett I see patches of woods, meadows, swamps, marshes. You could clear a lot more land.

"We have far more land growing food than you did. But, Connie, aside from the water table, think of every patch of woods as a bank of wild genes. In your time thousands of species were disappearing. We need that wild genetic material to breed with. . . . That's only the answer from the narrow viewpoint of my own science."

Bee waved to them, leading a group of kids through the fields on a combination bug survey and lesson in insect life. "Good luck in Oldtown!" he shouted. "Push us over!"

Connie looked after his broad glistening back, the shirt peeled off and tied around his waist. "What's he talking about?"

"I have to fall by Oldtown later and present our new recks."

"Wrecks?"

"Half word, half rib. Grasp, it's a request but we wish it was a requisition. For what we want to do scientifically this winter."

Connie made a face. She let Luciente burble on awhile about the Shaping controversy, but finally she burst out, "It's so hard for me to think of you as a scientist!"

"How not? I don't comprend."

"I mean the only scientist I know is Dr. Redding. . . . I guess we're his experiments. But I'd hardly ever meet a scientist, I mean, like in East Harlem. Not that I'd want to . . ."

"What's different about meeting a scientist and meeting a shelf diver?"

"Like my sister Inez, she lives in New Mexico. Her husband drinks, she has seven kids. After the sixth, she went to the clinic for the pill. You know—No, you can't! It's so hard for a woman like her—a real Catholic, not lapsed like me, under his thumb too and him filling her with babies one right after the other—so hard for her to say, Basta ya! And go for the pill. See, she thought she went to a doctor. But he had his scientist cap on and he was experimenting. She thought it was good she got the pill free. But they gave her a sugar pill instead. This doctor, he didn't say what he was doing. So she got heavy again with the seventh child. It was born with something wrong. She's tired and worn out with making babies. You know you have too many and the babies aren't so strong anymore. They're dear to you but a little something wrong. So this one, Richard, he was born dim in the head. Now they have all that worry and money troubles. They're supposed to give him pills and send him to a special school, but it costs. All because Inez thought she had a doctor, but she got a scientist."

"All this is really so?" Luciente stared from black eyes hard with wonder.

She looked away to the river, just a stream here with coffee-brown waters. They were heading back toward Mattapoisett now, passing as always older people, children, young people working here and there, weeding and feeding, picking off beetles, setting out new plants, arguing earnestly with scowls and gestures, hurrying by carrying a load of something shiny balanced in a basket on the head or in a knapsack or basket on the back, baby under arm or on hip or back. "They like to try out medicine on poor people. Especially brown people and black people. Inmates in prisons too. So . . . you must test drugs on people too? You have to."

"We use computers for biological modeling. Most drugs are discarded long before the testing stage. In your time I think people talked about effects and side effects, but that's nonsense."

"How? Like when I take Thorazine, the effects are controlling me, making me half dead, but I get lots of side effects, believe me, like sore throat and . . . constipation, dizziness, funny speech."

"But, Connie blossom, all are effects! Your drug companies labeled things side effects they didn't want as selling points. It's a funny way to look at things, like a horse in blinkers."

She thrust out her chin. "But there's a difference. The main effect is the thing you do something for."

"But Connie! The world doesn't know that. Don't you see? Let's go around this way—the bees have been set out today." They walked through part of the Goat Hill complex, where fish were being raised in solar-heated tanks and the water fertilized by the fish was used to grow vegetables. Inside the fish domes, men and women, gleaming with sweat, were working wearing only brief shorts. Outside there was a special cooling-off pool with people splashing and swimming in it. "Instance, a factory makes a product. But that's not all. It makes there be less of whatever it uses up to make that product. Every pound of steel used we have to account for—whether what's made is needed and truly desired. It's a pound less for something else. . . . Let's get a bike."

"You'll have to pedal for me." Connie hung back.

"Fasure I'll tote you like a baby. We're for Oldtown." On a two-seater, Luciente argued over her shoulder a little breathlessly. "A factory may also produce pollution—which takes away drinking water downstream. Dead fish we can't eat. Diseases or gene defects. These too are products of that factory. A factory uses up water, power, space. It uses up the time, the lives of those who work in it. If the work is boring and alienating, it produces bored, angry people—"

"You didn't answer me who drugs are tested on. I want to know. Is it criminals?"

"I'm sorry. I started speeching. We volunteer."

"I'll bet. That's what they say about the prisons. They said Claud volunteered for the hepatitis. But for a buck a day, you'd kill your best friend in prison. Because you got no other way to touch money. Everything in the canteen costs. Your family's in trouble. You want time off. They say maybe you'll get parole if you go along. So you volunteer."

"But nobody lacks here. All you get for volunteering is a little prestige. Local councils may give luxury credits or extra sabbatical. Mostly just time off. If enough people won't volunteer for something, we put it aside. Sometimes people choose such a proj for atoning, but that's between them and whoever you hurt."

"Have you ever volunteered?"

"Not for drugs. I don't like taking drugs, even when I'm supposed to. We don't use them much. We do co-op curing, when the healer helps the person firm better habits of minding, better eating or carriage of the spine." She pedaled at a steady rate. They were cruising past Mattapoisett now, past the weir, and Morningstar, who was loading boxes of pillows and comforters on a boat, stopped to wave. They passed the bridge to Cranberry and pedaled toward the wharves of Oldtown. "I've put in for testing new apparatus. Broke my scapula testing a solar airboat. We do admire each other for taking chances for the common good. Everybody is feathered to be admired, how not? More love, more attent. Besides, everybody always yearns for extra time. Life is short and there's so much to do!"

They left the bike at one of the racks and walked along a path in Oldtown, where the main harbor was. It was a Portuguese village whose main activities were boatbuilding, boat repair, shell-fishing and deep-sea fishing.

"They get up at three or four in the morning when the boats go out, so evening meetings are out for them. They have their meets in the afternoon, so that's why I have to present a reck at three P.M. Isn't it beautiful here? Some of these buildings are four hundred years old!"

They had adapted the old buildings, although between them were the same fields and plantings as everyplace else. An old man with a wispy beard was slowly picking blackberries, eating some, putting most in a basket over his withered arm, on what must once have been the lawn of a resort hotel. With him was a child who was eating rather more than picking and singing with him sometimes in unison and sometimes in a bouncy counterpoint, interrupting with questions every few minutes which he slowly answered.

"Why is life short?" Connie asked. "Your old people are healthy, sure, they live with everybody else. But they age. And they die, not much later than we do. Why not live longer?"

"We decided not to try."

"Who's 'we'?"

"The councils. The town meetings. That's how general questions of direction of science get decided."

"You mean by people like me? How could I decide if they should build an atom bomb or something?"

"Of course you could decide. It affects you—how not? A rep from the base talks. On the local level for a small proj. But if it's a major proj—such as research on prolonging life would be—then everybody decides. What it would cost to begin. What it would use up in the way of resources and labor. All that would be set out. What would be consequences on the whole yan-and ying of it, that we could foresee or guess."

"But how could I know if you're a good scientist or not? I know nothing from nothing about genetics. By the time I figured it all out, I'd be an old woman."

"You couldn't tell. But you could decide whether my base should stiff on breeding borer-resistant zucchini or scab-free potatoes or gorgeous and edible day lilies. As for results, whether experiments are valid, we researchers all put in time checking each other's work. Done by lot."

"But it sounds like some kind of dictatorship. I mean in our time, science was kept . . . pure maybe. Only scientists could judge other scientists. All kinds of stories about how scientists got persecuted by the church or governments and all that because they were doing their science."

"But Connie, in your day only huge corporations and the Pentagon had money enough to pay for big science. Don't you think that had an effect on what people worked on? Sweet petunias! And what we do comes down on everybody. We use up a confounded lot of resources. Scarce materials. Energy. We have to account. There's only one pool of air to breathe. You grasp neurologists made the aplysia extinct by using it up in experiments? Almost did the same to chimpanzees! What arrogrance!"

"But why don't you prolong life? Did old people vote on that too?"

"Fasure. We did a breakdown by age after to make sure young weren't voting extended age away from the old. . . . I think it comes down to the fact we're stirr reducing population. Longer people live, less often we can replace them. But most every lug wants the chance to mother. Therefore, we have to give back. We have to die. Finally, people get tired. After a while people you were sweet friends with, hand friends, they die of accidents or diseases, whatever. The old age of the heart comes."

"You just give up."

"We're part of the web of nature. Don't you find that beautiful?"

"Like dumb animals? No! Dust to dust and all that?"

"We have a hundred ceremonies to heal us to the world we live in with so many others. Listen." Luciente waved toward the child and the old man, who had finished picking blackberries. They sang together as they got ready to leave:

"Thank you for fruit.
We take what we need.
Other animals will eat.
Thank you for fruit,
carrying your seed.
What you give is sweet.
Live long and spread!"

"We learn when we're kids to say that to every tree or bush we pick from."

Seconal or not, she did not sleep that night. The next morning they were coming for her, they were going to take her to the hospital where they performed the actual operations. Night before the electric chair. She stared into the thin dark, the light on down the hall at the nurses' station, where the weekend night crew were playing contract bridge. They had an ongoing game in which the night nurse played partners with Stan the Man, the women's attendant Jean played partners with the orderly Chris. The nurse and Stan the Man were ten years older than Jean and Chris, and they called their game the Generation Gap. They were full of jokes and drank beer all night.

Although their game was noisy, they were not what was keeping her awake, no more than Tina's soft mumbled snoring from the other bed. It was the morning to come. Tomorrow they were going to stick a machine in her brain. She was the experiment. They would rape her body, her brain, her self. After this she could not trust her own feelings. She would not be her own. She would be their experimental monster. Their plaything, like Alice. Their tool. She did not want to pass over to Mattapoisett tonight; she wanted to taste the last dregs of her identity before they took it from her.

Lying in the partial dark, she found anger swelling up in her like sour wind. There wasn't enough! Oh, not enough things, sure—not enough food to eat, clothes to wear, all of that. But there wasn't enough . . . to do. To enjoy. Ugliness had surrounded her, had imprisoned her all her life. The ugliness of tenements, of slums, of El Barrio—whether of El Paso, Chicago, or New York—the grimy walls, the stinking streets, the stained air, the dark halls smelling of piss and stale cooking oil, the life like an open sore, had ground away her strength .

Whoever owned this place, these cities, whoever owned those glittering glassy office buildings in midtown filled with the purr of money turning over, those refineries over the river in Jersey with their flames licking the air, they gave nothing back. They took and took and left their garbage choking the air, the river, the sea itself. Choking her. A life of garbage. Human garbage. She had had too little of what her body needed and too little of what her soul could imagine. She had been able to do little in the years of her life, and that little had been ill paid or punished. The rest was garbage.

Who could ever pay for the pain of bringing a child into dirt and pain? Never enough. Nothing you wanted to give her you ever could give her, including yourself, what you wanted to be with her and for her. Nothing you wanted for her could come true. Who could ever pay for the pain of rising day after day year after year in a dim room dancing with cockroaches, and looking out on a street like a sewer of slow death? All her life it felt to her she had been dying a cell at a time, a cell of hope, of joy, of love, little lights going out one by one. When her body had turned all to pain, would she die? Die and poison the earth like a plague victim, like so many pounds of lead?

Outside the trees were turning early, from the drought. The branches of the pines ended in brown nosegays of dead needles. They were cutting their losses. The maples and oaks sported branches already bronze, a dulled version of autumn color. The sky was a hazy buff blue, as if it were dusty for miles up. By nine o'clock, when they took her over to the other hospital, it was already hot for September.

They did not cut and shave her head until she was on the new ward. Valente had told Dr. Redding it upset the patients. The cold touch of the scissors nudged her nape, her ear with its shivery weight like a shark nosing past. With each clack of the blades, her hair fell from her, to lie like garbage on the floor. To be swept up and thrown away. No blackberry bushes would grow from her head's shearing. Rich in nitrogen and trace elements: Luciente was always saying things like that. But Luciente was not with her this morning.

Sybil had stood at the door watching her go, her face working as she tried not to weep. In her mind now she could see Sybil's auburn hair falling, the long beautiful hair of a fine natural red that varied strand to strand. Often she had brushed Sybil's hair for her and always it amazed her how much yellow and brown and brass and carrot and chestnut there was in Sybil's auburn hair, a spectrum of warm colors.

As they were shaving her head, she tried to think of Bee, whose massive well-modeled head looked handsome that way. But she did not think she would look as strong and fine with her hair stolen. She had had no breakfast. They gave her a heavy sedative but they did not knock her out. They told her she would not really be conscious, but she was. She could hear the orderlies making jokes as they wheeled her to the operating room.

She had been prepared for any horror. Anything except boredom.

First Dr. Redding drilled on her skull. It did not hurt; it was merely horrifying. She could feel the pressure, she could feel the bone giving way, she could hear the drill entering. Then she saw them take up a needle to insert something. She did not understand what it was, because she felt nothing. They seemed to be waiting for it to take effect, whatever it was, and she waited too in gasping anxiety until she caught a reference to "radiopaque solution." They were dyeing her and she was dying. The pun hung in her penetrated brain.

Next they fitted a machine over her, what they referred to as a stereotactic machine, and they pounded it into her head with three sharp metal pins as if she were a wall they were attaching a can opener to. Tap, tap, tap. They seemed to be figuring out at what point they were going to zero in, as they put it. She felt faint and weird. She floated miles above her helpless body propped in green sheets and towels in a sort of operating chair, like a fancy dentist's chair. They were using an x-ray machine. They spoke of target structures and Dr. Redding boasted, "No more than a point-five-millimeter factor of error."

Terror cut through the veils of the drug like a needle penetrating the bone supposed to protect her fragile spongy brain. How much of her was crammed into that space? Perhaps they could wipe out the memory of Claud by the slip of a needle. The brain was so dumb, not like the heart knocking on the breastbone loud and fluttery as a captured bird. It hid in its cage of bone, imagining itself safe.

She wanted to weep, to scream. But she was contained in a balloon way back up through her skull, perhaps floating out through the hole they had cut in her, floating out there above them, lighter than air. How patient they were to take so much of their valuable medical time deciding where to push in. How wonderful that they did not simply use a great big can opener and take off the top of her skull and scrape out the brains with a spoon. Some people ate brains.

"You could eat them. Fried," she said suddenly.

Morgan's eyes above the mask widened. "What did she say?"

"Something about eating," the operating nurse said.

"Doubtless we stimulated an appetite center," Dr. Redding said. "We're down there. The higher you cauterize, the more you involve the intellectual faculties. I don't think these patients have a lot to spare in that department. We're after the centers of aggression, the primitive emotions run amok."

Now they were looking at photographs, like those of the moon taken by astronauts. That unknown precious country of her brain. They had a dummy second machine, like the one sitting on her skull squatting like a mosquito about to draw blood, and they were fiddling with the dummy. She would have loved to try it out on them. Suddenly she thought that these men believed feeling itself a disease, something to be cut out like a rotten appendix. Cold, calculating, ambitious, believing themselves rational and superior, they chased the crouching female animal through the brain with a scalpel. From an early age she had been told that what she felt was unreal and didn't matter. Now they were about to place in her something that would rule her feelings like a thermostat.

Time . . . time. Yes, the surprise was the boredom. She could almost have slept, hunched there. The green masks of robbers covered their faces, but she could easily tell Dr. Redding from Dr. Morgan. Redding was brisk and in control and chipper. Morgan was prissy with worry, his every motion a bureaucratic procedure judged against inner or outer rules.

Now a new object was presented, crowed over. The nurses crowded close to see. The new toy. It was a metal disk embossed like a coin. no bigger than a quarter. with tubes and a miniature dialysis bag attached. She would be a walking monster with a little computer inside and a year's supply of dope to keep her stupid. The whole thing would fit in the palm of her hand; it would fit under the roof of her skull, perched cozily on the brain.

Her head felt wrong as they put it in. Everything felt wrong. Maybe it would feel right again. They were closing with cement. A temporary measure. They said they wanted to monitor the reading for a month or two, they might want to change the chemical she was being fed from that dialysis bag. They kept their options open with a cement plug.

Afterward she had a massive headache. Even her teeth seemed all to ache. She did not want to move. She did not care about anything. She lay in her bed and through half-closed eyes she ignored the patients and nurses passing on the neurology ward.

After they moved her back to her own ward, for a week she lay numb and uncaring. Acker came and talked to her. He tried to get her to perform tests and answer questions, he brought his charts and what she always thought of as his children's games. Why should she answer? They were waiting for her to heal before they played with her, she felt.

Skip, who was being a good patient, brought her food on a tray. Politely, he did not look at her, more nude than if her clothes had been taken away.

Tina read her the newspaper, tried to start conversations. Sybil came in and sat patiently, let her alone and then returned, hoping. Tina's voice, rising like an indignant wasp, buzzed at her. She could not want to talk. She could not care. She was a spoiled orange rotting green. The only person she cared to watch was Skip as he came and went, sweeping the ward and running errands for the attendants and the other patients. He was dressed in his street clothes and his hair had grown short and patchy. He looked younger and older than he had: younger in his angularity, his new awkwardness; older in the wary lack of expression on his face. She felt his will all the time like a knife he was carrying concealed, and she envied him for retaining his will. She wondered, when she could bring herself to think at all, how he preserved the power of his will hidden inside.

They had decided to operate next week on Alice. They felt they knew just what tissue in her brain to coagulate now, where to burn a hole in what was called Alice. Then she would have her electrodes removed, they promised, just like Skip. They were tired of playing with Alice, who had become sullen and passive. At times she giggled a lot, she seemed drunk and slaphappy, sitting on the edge of her bed. Then she slumped into a blank depression.

Skip now had grounds privileges. He went to the canteen and brought back doughnuts, danishes, candy bars, cigarettes for any of the patients who had the money. The doctors had their own coffeemaker near the meeting room, and even the patients were sometimes allowed to make coffee in the afternoon in the small kitchen the lower staff used. Dolly had come by to visit her right after her operation, but had not been allowed in. Dolly had deposited some more money for Connie. Connie pretended to order sweets from the canteen with the others. Remembering Luciente's urging, she withdrew change for an order but then quietly told Skip not to bring her anything. Seventy-five cents at a time, she was accumulating capital for escape. That much energy remained to her.

Wednesday Dr. Redding announced to Skip loudly, so that all the other patients could hear, that Skip was being granted a weekend furlough. He could go home to his parents from Friday night through Sunday afternoon. Dr. Redding rolled out the pronouncement with conscious drama, saying that if Skip proved he could handle himself, this was the first of many furloughs, the first step back into society. They were all to envy Skip; they all did. The doctors were almost done with Skip, unless further surgery should prove necessary, a little phrase they added.

Skip said he was grateful and he'd show them he could handle a visit home. He drooped there, no longer graceful under his shorn hair that spoke of the barracks, of the army, and looking Redding in the eyes, he told him how good he was going to be, how he was their cured and grateful little boy.

She felt a strange pang, like something plucked in her.

Friday, as Skip was organizing himself to go home and waiting for his parents to come to collect him, she got up for the first time since her operation, except for walking to the bathroom and back, and put on her robe. Shaking, she tied the loose cord and stumbled off to the men's side. She sat down on Skip's bed and waited for the dizziness to clear. She wasn't allowed to do that, but the attendants hadn't appeared yet.

Skip looked at her with bloodshot weary cautious eyes. "Hello, monster," he said softly.

"Hello, monster," she said back, and smiled for the first time since before her operation. "There's too little of you and too much of me."

"Can you feel it inside?"

"I feel rotten. Snowed."

"I admire you for trying to get away, you know? I wish you'd made it."

"If I get a chance, I'll try it again," she mouthed softly.

"But . . . with that thing in your head, you might die."

"Maybe it'll just wear out its batteries or whatever it runs on and give up. Use up the drug. I know a guy, Otis, who has a metal peg in his knee from Vietnam."

"I think maybe something in the brain's more dangerous. . . . But why not go down trying?"

"You're going outside today."

Skip grimaced. "Home with my loving parents. Back from the factory where they sent me for repairs, on a trial basis. Like if it's broken, get it fixed. If it's crooked, get it straightened out. If it's kinky, iron it."

"But you still got a will to fight them, I can feel it."

"They won something. I don't feel like fucking anybody. Or loving anybody. I don't feel any love at all. I feel like a big block of ice."

Tony walked by whistling, saw her sitting on the bed, and came in. To avoid his touch, she rose. "Take care, Skip."

"I mean to take care." He gave her a mirthless grin. Then he kissed her lightly on the mouth. "You keep trying." His lips were cool and hard. Shyly she kissed him back.

Tony made obscene smacking noises. "Come on, break it up. No PC. They fixed you okay from being a faggot, but you're crazy anyhow!"

As quickly as she could move on her heavy waterlogged legs, her dizzy body riding its private stormy weather, she lumbered back through the ward to her own bed.

Sunday night Skip did not return. By Monday the rumor crept through the ward as fast as patient could whisper to patient. Sunday morning early, Skip had slit his throat with an electric knife in the kitchen of his parents' home. They had hidden the razor blades, the sleeping pills, the aspirin, but they had not thought of the electric carving knife.

Sybil murmured to Connie that she had heard that his father had been angry at Dr. Redding and called him a quack. They felt it was unacceptable for the hospital to send Skip home to kill himself in their kitchen.

She got up from her bed and moved wearily around the ward, with Sybil at her side. Drs. Redding and Morgan were right thinking they had cured Skip, she thought, fighting the tilting aisle. Before he had only been able to attempt suicide, cries for help carved on his body. They had cured him of fumbling, of indecision. They had taught him to act, they had taught him the value of a quick clean death.

Fifteen

SHA! You're the sharpest piper I ever gaped! The woman was propped on the bed surrounded by mirrors—mirrors on the ceiling, the back of the bed, and one side.

Connie stood flatfooted in the center of the windowless room, staring. She had tried and tried to make contact with Luciente, but she had been unable to feel her presence all day. Finally, in a stubborn fury she had cast herself forward, demanding that Luciente receive her.

The woman's hair, stippled mauve and platinum, was arranged in an intricate tower of curls and small gewgaws, dripping pearls like a wedding headdress. She wore a long dress of slippery substance that changed color as she moved and emitted a tinkling sound; it was slit away up the side and cut out here and there so that her breasts occasionally peeked out or her navel appeared and reappeared. When Connie had materialized, the woman had been lying back on a mound of ball-shaped pillows smoking a pipe and chewing what looked like orange marshmallows from a small bowl on the hairy coverlet. The room was air conditioned cool.

"Someone's playing a joke on me, sending a private trans. I don't think it's even a slightly funny. When I find out, you'll be sorry! Cash won't put up with that! And he has means to find out, you dudfreak. whoever you suppose to be!" She popped off the bed and stood facing Connie, quivering with anger. They were about the same height and weight, although the woman was younger and her body seemed a cartoon of femininity, with a tiny waist, enormous sharp breasts that stuck out like the brassieres Connie herself had worn in the fifties—but the woman was not wearing a brassiere. Her stomach was flat but her hips and buttocks were oversized and audaciously curved. She looked as if she could hardly walk for the extravagance of her breasts and buttocks, her thighs that collided as she shuffled a few steps.

"How'd you get in here anyhow? Nobody but contract girls and middle flacks stack in this complex. It's strictly SG'ed."

"SG'ed?"

"Segregated and guarded—are you cored? How did you get in here? Well?" She stomped to and fro on small—ridiculously small—feet. She looked as if any minute she might fall over through imbalance, the small feet and tiny ankles and wrists, the tiny waist, the small head with the tower of Pisa on top.

Somehow Connie had wound up in the wrong place. She had missed Mattapoisett and hit some other place in the future. "Maybe I am in the wrong place, but they let me in. See for yourself. So where am I?"

"They never let you in. Ha! Nobody would take you for a contracty. You've never even had your first grafts. If you ever had a beauty-op, you've reverted. They'd never leave you with that hair and that skin! You're as dark . . . I mean I'd have been on that side myself. But of course I had a full series! When I was fifteen, I was selected, and I'm still on the full shots and re-ops."

"Where am I, though? I'm not in Mattapoisett, obviously."

"You dud, you're in New York. Where else?"

"Where in New York?" She looked for a window, but there were none. "My name's Connie. I'm sorry I got in here by mistake."

"You bet you're sorry. I'm contracted to a fourth-level SD." She batted her eyelashes, fully an inch long, and waited for the effect of her statement. Her eyes had a tendency to droop, the lids pulling down under the weight. "This is 168th and General File, and this whole plex is reserved for contracties and middle flacks. There's nobody here except medical, legal, security, and transport flacks of the middle level. Anyhow"—she tossed her head carefully, while the tower of hair trembled—"I'm Gildina 547-921-45-822-KBJ. You'd better give me an expla how you got in here or I'm about to beep."

"Time traveling." Connie smiled with sophistication. It was almost fun. She imagined how Luciente must have felt laying down the unbelievable truth to naïve ears. Now she was the visitor from elsewhere. Somehow talking with Gildina was a little like talking with Dolly on speed, and a little like conversation with a poodle. "There's a project, you know."

"Yeah?" Gildina was trying to decide whether she should pretend to know or not. "Cash knows that stuff—after all, he's fourth level. What's that got to do with slamming in to my parment?"

"All the kinks aren't out. I've been in 1976. I was supposed to wind up back here, but not in your parment, believe me."

"Ha! You're a dud and you look old too—you must be twenty-five or six! You're a fem too, even if you aren't opped. They'd never pick you to time travel. They'd pick a Cybo or an Assassin!"

"I was born in 1938. You want to see my welfare ID?" Actually, of course, she didn't have it; it was back in the hospital.

"What eye-dee?"

"What you show—a card so they know who you are."

"But everybody's implanted. What's the good them knowing who, if they don't know where and how?" Gildina threw herself on the bed. "Maybe too much Rapture. I really ride out on Rapture. Cash says I ream it too much. But it makes me float."

"I'm no hallucination." Connie felt like giggling. It was so weird to be reassuring somebody else. "Feel me!"

"Don't be lesby. You got no contract on me."

"What's a contract?"

"Maybe you *are* from the ancient past. Are you quiring serious?"

She nodded, sitting carefully on a roundish object that appeared to be filled with air.

"All the flacks make contracts. Contract sex. It means you agree to put out for so long for so much. You know?

Like I have a two-year contract. Some girls got only a one-nighter or monthly, that's standard. You can be out on your ear at the end of a month with only a day's notice. That's no life. Course once in a while some real bulger, she ends up with a ten-year contract. I never met one, but I heared of them."

"But suppose you get tired of him before?"

"Then he can sue. Besides, you can't get out of a contract unless you're bought out. Unless you get a lot saved, and who makes that much? Course if he breaks it, unless he can prove negligence or adultery, then you got him cold and he has to pay or at least settlement you. My contract isn't just support either. I get enough to maintain my shots and re-ops and clothes and a little for all the Rapture and other risers I like to ream."

"What happens when your contract runs out?"

Gildina shrugged nervously. "Sometimes they renew. The first time I was on a yearly I got renewed by that flack—he was a lower-level ground transport smasher. If you're dropped, sometimes you got a prospect. Sometimes you get by on one-nights or weekends till you turn up a prospect. But it drains you. Always worrying about maybe you'll end up in a knockshop. Sometimes you can't keep up maintaining, and then your chances of getting even a lower-level flack run down."

"Can you get married?"

"This is. I mean you know the richies marry old-style. I heared they figure back generations. But this is how it is for us."

"Suppose you have a baby?"

"If it's in the contract. I never had a contract that called for a kid. Mostly the moms have them. You know, they're cored to make babies all the time. Ugh, they're so fat!"

"But suppose you wanted a kid."

"What would I do with it? It couldn't live here at Cash's. He can't stand noise. I can't requisition housing. Who ever supposed on a contracty living alone?"

"What about your mother?"

"She's gone to Geri. You know, she was over forty! I kept getting transies for a year maybe, but I haven't had one in ages. so I suppose she's ashed."

"Ashed? She's dead?"

Gildina blanched. "Watch the language! What are you

talking about? I didn't hear you. Remember this is my mother we're supposing on."

"But forty—isn't that young?"

"She must've been forty-three. How long do you suppose to live? Only the richies live longer, it's in their genes. Like they say, it's all in the genes."

"How long do the richies live?"

"Oh, maybe two hundred years. Depends on what they can afford—you know, the medicos, the organs. I've never actually met one, of course, I never been off the surface—"

"What do you mean, off the surface?"

"Upstairs! The space platforms. The richies don't live down here. Too much . . . thickness. The air's too thick, like they say. Not in here, of course. Middle- and upper-level flacks are all conditioned. But you should see where I was born! You're born coughing and you pass off to Geri coughing, like they say. I always thought the sky was yellow till I came here. Now I know it's a real pale gray-blue, just the prettiest color. I did my hair like that for a couple months after I came here, I was so silly. . . . Even if you look like a dud, you're not to bad to talk to. It's funny, talking to somebody during the day."

"Don't you ever go out? Or have friends over?"

"Out where? Cash seals me in most of the time, he's a jealous slot. Part of being SD, I suppose. He don't trust anyone. Besides, I have everything I need here. You can't leave the plex, because of security. It wouldn't be safe out there!"

"Not even to take a walk?"

"Walk?" Gildina looked embarrassed, as if she had said something about bathroom functions. "I'm middle level, you know! I suppose on duds walking. I wouldn't remember, myself."

"Duds are below lower-level flacks? Poor people?"

"It's not like they're people. They're diseased, all of them, just walking organ banks, like Cash says, and even half the time the liver's rotten. It isn't like they have any use. I mean some are pithed for simple functions, but they live like animals out where it isn't conditioned. Such a sight—if you could see far, it would stretch forever. It's lucky you can't see more than a few feet."

"But you don't have any women friends to visit? Like from apartment to apartment?"

"What for? I got everything I need. You want a Rapture? Or whatever you float on. Have a gape—I got a good selection." She pointed to an automated pill dispenser beside the bed.

"Drugs?"

"Risers, soothers, sleepers, wakers, euphors, passion pills, the whole works. What's your poison?"

"Nothing right now, thanks. I been on them kind of heavy lately."

"Just so you don't cross out, you know? Mixed reacts? You got to check the combos on the Digitab. So many fems cross out just because they don't check it. Me, I almost CO'ed once when I was a kid. Takes just a minute to Digitab, right?"

"You don't have to see the doctor for pills anymore, huh?"

"*See* a doctor?" Again Gildina looked embarrassed. "I'm only middle level. I been to a medimated clinic, you know, like everybody else middle. You wait in line and then you talk with the computer. But see a doctor! Well, there's service medicos here who repair the medimated clinics and the medimats. Supervise organ collection. Do the actual extractions and vacuum seal for transport upstairs. But I never actually *seen* a doctor. They're high-level flacks and some of them even live upstairs. I see a lot about them on the HG, of course. Some of my favorite shows are about doctors. The fight against senility. Thrusting back the frontiers of life. All that stuff. But they're too busy prolonging life to hang around down here, you know."

"HG. Is that . . . holigraph?" They probably had the same thing they called holies in Mattapoisett. "Every so often you have a three-dimensional ritual or story?"

"It's on twenty-four hours if you subscribe. But we have a Sense-all. See?" Gildina pointed to what Connie had thought was a fancy hair dryer suspended over the bed. "That's much better. If it didn't cost a heart and a kidney, I'd be in it all day. But Cash is at me already for the bill I stacked two months ago. It's much realer. Cause you're in it. Didn't you ever try?"

"Never."

"I'd vite you but Cash is at me already, like I said. It's like dreaming, only you're awake, and it's real exciting. Like, look at the catalog." Gildina passed her a well-thumbed Sense-all catalog for September. It was full of ads for drugs and cosmetics and gadgets, services and knockshops, body designers, protection devices. This could not exist simultaneously with Mattapoisett. Could not. Or else they were at war and she had ended up somehow in the enemy camp. Maybe that was the war they were fighting. She forced herself to calm, using easercises Luciente had taught her, then she scanned the catalog.

> "Hot Dog": A bulgy contracty amuses herself while her man is away with a large boxer dog. HD5.
>
> "Tremors on Platform Texaroyal": A top-level SDman goes after the Assassin who got his zec. Another Studs Jerker extravago with contracty harem, degutting, many explos, and lesby sex. FD 20.

"What's the FD 20 stuff?"
"Time and price—what do you suppose on?"
She read:

> "Sorrinda 777": Story of a love never suppose to be, between a low-level medimat swab and a doctor in service to a nuke fission family; her faithfulness, her suffering, her shining love: will she give the ultimate sacrifice of her heart to replace his legal contracty's coronary dystrophy? FD 15.
>
> "Good Enough to Eat": Top level bulger ignores warnings from family and romps in Roughlands. She is captured by mutes. Mass rapes, torture (inch-by-inch close-up with full Sense-all). Ultimate cannibal scene features close-ups. DD 25.
>
> "When Fems Flung to Be Men": In Age of Uprisings, two fem libbers meet in battle—kung fu, tai chi, judo, wrestling. Stronger rapes weaker with dildo. SD man zaps in, fights both (close-ups, full gore), double rape, double murder, full Sense-all. HD 15.

"Contract Null and Void": A dud woman blackmails a re-op tech into a series of beauty-ops, enters career of social scramble from level to level (costumes by Rang-up, full Sense-all) till she falls for Dirk, Assassin to Spaceport Mobilgulf. FD 15.

"Men and women haven't changed so much," she said, thinking of Times Square. She was surprised by how cheerless that prospect seemed.

"So why go out?" Gildina went on, bouncing a little on her bed. "Unless some contracty lousy with credits is about to loan you her Sense-all. By the bim, the HG's not bad. Lots of trans I watch."

"Show me the rest of your apartment, okay?"

"The rest?" Gildina looked blank. "You mean the cleano?"

The bathroom was bigger than it would have been in her time, with more devices: devices for cleaning shoes and what was probably like dry cleaning. There was no tub, but a shower with many hard sprays of water that would hit different places on the body, and a meter to time the amount of water. The shower had a disinfectant light as well plus nozzles for shooting out hot air. The toilet was big and fancy but still a toilet. Over the wash-bowl hung a device for drying hair instantly. But the bathroom lacked a window.

Around the other side of the mirror along the bed, the walls were of nubbly stuff and the carpeting thick and green like imitation grass. Here she finally saw a window. They were at ground level, looking out on a lake with fancy skidboats scooting to and fro and lots of people in glowing metallic swimsuits sunbathing and climbing in and out of the water.

"There's a lake in Manhattan now? I mean besides in Central Park?"

"What's with you? You talk like a dud from the Rough-lands. Look, it's a picture. We got five of them." She pressed a switch and the scene changed to a mountain with skiers and superfast snowbuggies skimming across the snow and hovercraft hanging in the brilliant air. Gildina flicked the switch again and a bunch of men dressed in

Roman tunics began chasing a lot of women around and pulling their clothes off. She flicked again: hand-to-hand sword combat in medieval costumes, with bloody hands flying off. The last scene was a herd of zebras grazing, while some lions stalked, but something was wrong and it was very speeded up and jerky. "That one's broke." She changed back to the lake.

"Can you make it so we can look out? I'd love to see what New York looks like now."

"What's with you? Out where?"

"Isn't that a window?"

"What's that?"

"So you can look out. Glass."

"Like a viewing port? There's one in the lounge. And from the sun plaza you can look around. There's glass on all sides. At first it made me terribly dizzy—I wanted to hold on. All that space. But I didn't let on. I didn't want them spitting about me being a dud and never saw the sun before. Of course I'd never been in the sun. It scared me but I just made out like I been in the sun every day. I had a tan from my last re-op, so how could they tell anyhow?"

"We used to have windows, everybody did. It was just glass so light could come in."

"Light? How? From outside? Oh, I guess when you get up high enough. This is just the hundred twenty-sixth floor. But even up on the sun plaza what's to see except the sun and you can only look straight at that for a while before you begin to see funny spots—maybe five or ten minutes. The sky's nice when you get used to it—it's that gorgeous pale gray color. Once in a while some real weather clouds. I can ride into them, really—they give me a boost. But if you gape too much, flacks think you're lower. You have to pretend to take it for granite."

"Can't you see the city?"

"You can make out some other towers in this plex. But you can't see down or any farther. How could you? It's thick. It's air. How could you see through air?"

"Where's your kitchen?"

"Huh?"

"Where you cook food?"

"Cook it?" Gildina led her to a corner by the outside door, which looked like a bank vault's. There was nothing in the corner she could identify as a refrigerator or a stove. A drawer opened automatically when a button was pressed, to dispense transparent packets Gildina demonstrated for her. She opened one with a hiss of inrushing air that seemed slowly to soak through the mass inside. She was surprised to see it begin steaming.

At Gildina's invitation she tasted the food on a thin shiny plate. The food was heavily spiced but ultimately tasteless and gummy. "What is it?"

"Vito-goodies ham dinner."

"This is supposed to be ham?"

"What's ham? That's the name of the flavor."

"But it doesn't taste anything like ham."

"Ham?" Gildina made a face of incomprehension. "Everything comes in packets. It's made from coal and algae and wood by-products."

"You're vegetarians?"

"What's that?"

"You eat only vegetables?"

"Who's a vegables?" Gildina swished out of the corner in annoyance. "You're only a dud slot, so don't high-top me."

"Things that grow on plants. You know. Like carrots and peas. Beans. Corn."

Gildina shrugged, waving her hand with its inch-long mauve-and-yellow nails. "I know the richies eat queer things, sort of . . . raw. Stuff from, you know, live things. They practically eat them alive. I can't suppose that's good for you, our stomachs aren't made of Cybernall. I never had any of that . . . strange stuff. You trying to tell me you had that richie food? That live stuff?"

"Sure. Poor people couldn't buy a lot of it, but everybody had it sometimes."

"We got enough troubles. I got chronic colonic malachosis myself and Cash has ulceric tumors. I can't imagine how the richies survive. I heard they eat animal tissue even. The idea makes me dizzy. I mean except as a sexy idea. I mean I seen it on the Sense-all, but it doesn't float me."

"Well, where does your food come from?"

Gildina shrugged. "Out in the Roughlands, big corporate factory-farms. They mine it, you subscribe, and it gets delivered every week." Gildina took the plate and plasticware from her and put them into a box in the wall, where they promptly disappeared.

"Where did they go?"

"How would I suppose on that?" Gildina looked shocked. "It's a service. All middle-flack plexes have platos. You take the clean stuff out and you put the dirty stuff in. Look, I'll show you." She opened another sliding door. But nothing happened. She pressed a button on the wall again. "Double stymie! It's broke again. I hope they get it fixed by the time Cash comes home, that's all I can say. Oh, well, I'll get him to take me to the mutual on the floor. Or even upstairs, maybe, if he's in the spending slot."

"A restaurant? Like a place everybody eats?"

Gildina nodded. "But if I decide to do that I got to start prepping."

"What time does he get home?"

"Not for two hours, but it takes that long, for display. The painting is what counts."

"You mean making up your face?"

"No, leg painting. It costs a heart and a kidney, but if you try to do it yourself, you look like a joke. You have to go to a real artiste. There's a fem on this floor who'll do me even at the last minute. I'll flash her a transie."

"How come she'll do you?"

"She owes me . . . I know a few things about her. She skipped on a contract. She's in the crazy slot, she even paints her walls, but she does a good job cheapo with no appoint. So I should turn her in to the organ banks? It's no silc off my ass! They say the richies take the ones who are real good for the platforms."

"Gildina, the richies—who are they, really?"

"The same as in your time—the Rockemellons, the Morganfords, the Duke-Ponts. They're ancient. I mean some of them were alive in your time, I suppose, if you're for real. Wait till Cash gapes you. He'll figure it out." Gildina paraded past, smirking. "He's had SC, did you suppose on that?"

"What's escee?"

"Sharpened control, reallike. He's been through mind control. He turns off fear and pain and fatigue and sleep, like he's got a switch. He's like a Cybo, almost! He can control the fibers in his spinal cord, control his body temperature. He's a fighting machine, like they say. I mean not really like a Cybo, but as good as you can get without genetic engineering or organ replacement. He's still a woolie—that's what the richies and the Cybos call us, who are still animal tissue. But he's real improved. He has those superneurotransmitters ready to be released in his brain that turn him into just about an Assassin. I mean not really, he's fourth level, but he's in that direction, if you gape."

"Remember, I'm just a dud from the past. They haven't told me a lot of this stuff yet."

"Yeah, the Age of Uprisings and all that stuff. Before they automated the boondocks—the old UD countries, when they had all those useless animals and wild plants and dumb people and stuff."

"But who are Assassins?"

"Sha! You don't talk about them." Gildina looked around. "Of course we're monitored like everybody else, so SG knows I'm talking to you. So like if I'm doing anything wrong, they'll stop us."

"Monitored?"

"From the Securcenter here, what else? For versive acts and talks. They pull you in and put a scanner on you so they can tell what you're thinking to the questions, even if you don't talk. From the electrical impulses in your brain. You can't lie to them, unless you're a trained SD man or an Assassin. Assassins work for the richies. That's how they deal with each other when they're at odds. Every richie clan and all the multies have armies of genetically engineered fighters. Instead of sex drive, they have a basic killer drive and obey center. You can't tell exactly what they are—some are woolies genetically specialized. Some are real Cybos. No animal issue. Entirely improved."

The door opened suddenly with a swoosh, and a man barged in. He was close to seven feet tall, completely hairless as far as she could see. He wore a shiny gray-blue uniform and his voice as he barked at her was extremely deep, beyond the ordinary human range, with strange overtones in it that made her stomach clutch. Fear gripped her through the belly. She had to do the easercises Luciente had taught her, she had to become conscious of her breathing and relax. "Who are you? Remain still. Answer correctly."

"My name is Connie and I'm time traveling. I guess you were listening to us?"

"There is no such thing as time travel. You will be scanned. And *you* will be sealed in here again," the man said to Gildina. "We'll deal with you later. She's a dud, but you talked with her for one hour."

Gildina began to blubber. "Well, how could she get in here if you didn't let her? I thought it was a special project. Everybody before the great split, they were all duds and woolies. Everybody knows that! How could she get in if you didn't let her in?"

"That's not your problem. You're for the organ bank now," he said with savage glee in his strange, artificially deep voice. "You, come." His hand bruised Connie's arm, biting in.

"I can only stay here through her. Gildina has a special mental power, even if she doesn't know it."

"Incorrect. She was born a dud. She's just a built-up contracty. All duds have brain deficiencies from protein scarcity in fetus and early childhood. Their IRP's are negative forty to negative fifteen. Her psych scan tests show negative twenty-five. She has no more mental capacity than a genetically improved ape."

"She's still receptive. I guess you don't measure that! I homed in on her. Break my contact with her and I disappear." It was wonderful to feel so confident facing a sort of cop. That's what he was, supercop, with a weapons belt on his waist and one hand modified into a weapon-tool itself.

"When we get done playing with you, you will wish you could disappear. And then you will." A grin of bright enamel teeth, whiter than scrubbed bathroom tiles. "She's just a chica, exactly like you look to be. Cosmetically fixed for sex use. Like you find in any knockshop."

"How would you know?" Gildina drew herself up in fussy, impotent fury. "What would you do in a knockshop? You don't even have the equipment."

"No appendix either." The guard grinned his mirthless flashing white smile. "That's why we don't need many of you useless cunts now-on. Nothing inessential. Pure, functional, reliable. We embody the ideal. We can be destroyed—not by you duds—but never verted, never deflected, never distracted. None of us has ever been disloyal to the multi that owns us."

Connie asked, "What's a multi?"

He looked shocked now, serious. "The multi is everything."

"What does 'multi' stand for?"

"For what is," he said hollowly.

"Like states, countries?"

"That was before," Gildina said. "Multis own everybody —"

"Was irrational," the guard said. "Overlapping jurisdictions. Now we all belong to a corporate body. Multis. Like that contracty soon to be dismantled into the organ bank, I belong to Chase-World-TT. The multi that owns us." He bowed his head briefly. Then his head jerked upright, his eyes narrowed. "Why are you not afraid?"

She was trying to work her arm loose without success. His metal grip dug into her skin. "How do you know I'm not scared?"

"My sensing devices monitor your outputs. I reg adrenaline but no sympathetic nervous system involvement. You feel anger but not fear?" The hand squeezed harder. "A dud could not react so, after coring and behavior mod. You have no monitor implant. Are you on a drug I cannot scan? Not acetycholine. Something is wrong. You look me in the eyes, unlike a fem. All duds are brain damaged and modded. Therefore you're only disguised as a dud!" His other hand groped toward his belt.

She decided she'd better vanish. Shutting her eyes, she let go of Gildina and tried to shove off. But his grip still ate into her arm. Come on, come on! She pushed with her mind, pushed against the metal grip. She fixed her mind on her own bed—that she should ever call a hospital bed her own! She thrust herself roughly back, and the grip began to fade.

Dizzy, sweating from every pore, she lay on her back in bed. Sybil, Tina, and Valente were leaning over her. Her arm hurt. Her head ached horribly. She was being punished for the anger she had felt; that thing in her head was punishing her with sharp pain and spurts of dulling drug. She felt her head was going to break open like a coconut struck with a hammer. She could feel the line where her skull was about to split.

She would not answer them, but seeing she was conscious, Valente left. She winked at Sybil and Tina then, who stared at her, puzzled but relieved. Connie had to lie back, breathe deeply, relax herself. So that was the other world that might come to be. That was Luciente's war, and she was enlisted in it.

Sixteen

CONNIE was an object. She went where placed and stayed there. She caught the phrase "passive aggressive" from Acker to his girlfriend Miss Moynihan. Exactly, she thought. You got it, Waggle-Beard—now run with it. She would not get up until gotten up. She ate only if fed. She sat in a chair when placed there and got up when hauled up.

Although she was proud of time traveling on her own, she was afraid to try again. She did not want to end up in that other future. All the time the drug leaking into her head was clogging her, slowing her, and whenever she got angry, her head turned her off. Something hurt in her then; a dreadful anxiety out of nowhere beset her with a small seizure and she had to remain still. Covertly she watched the ward and learned what she could about the hospital.

She felt distanced from her own life, as if it had ended with the implantation of the dialytrode. She could not resume her life, Therefore Connie was no more. Yet she lived on. Detached, wakeful, brooding inside the heaviness of the drug, she kept still. She had given up smoking. For the first time in her life she stopped smoking. The craving for a cigarette was a left-over itch from being Connie. At least it kicked up sand on the desert of the hours, that old itch.

She could never guess when Dolly would appear. A couple of times her niece promised she was coming and never showed up, and then without warning she sailed in, bright as a parakeet, sharply dressed in something new with her hair that gaudy red, her sunglasses on, her hands wet with the perspiration of speed. The staff encouraged Dolly to come because Connie talked to her. Dolly slipped her money but would not bring Nita. When she asked about Nita, Dolly's answers were vague. "She's doing all right, all right. Just fine."

Nita's birthday approached, the fifteenth of October. Connie begged Dolly to buy a present for her. Something preciosa. Pretty little slippers with bunnies, a soft animal with plush fur. Dolly promised, but Connie had no way to pin her down. The next time Dolly flashed in, she said Nita had had a lovely birthday. Mamá had given her a party with a cake with candles and ice cream. So Carmel still had Nita.

Connie's tongue spoke before she could stop herself. "Dolly, it's you who needs Nita. Sure, your mamá takes good care. But you need her with you. Without her, you don't love yourself. You use yourself like a rag to wipe up the streets. You turn your body to money, and the money to the buzzing of death in your head."

"I'm doing fine, Connie, real fine. Listen, Daddy and Adele say they're coming to see you. How about that?"

"Sin duda. The day it rains money on Harlem."

"Fíjate, I brought you some perfume. And here's for you to get some coffee, a little something from the canteen." Dolly kissed her cheek and pressed a wadded-up five into her palm. "Smell the perfume, it's the real thing. Aprege cologne. Nice, huh? It came in a oot with the perfume. Splash some on now. Nice? You smell like a rose. I kept the perfume, you couldn't hold on to it here, the staff would swipe it. A john gave it to me. He has a drugstore in Teaneck, he says he's the manager."

"Dolly, you're so thin. Do you eat at all?"

"You lost weight too. The both of us. With your hair done where I get mine, you'll look ten years younger, Connie. I'll treat you to it when you get out. Very short hair is in. I make money hand over fist now, you'll see. You like the Arpege? It's good to be thin, it's chic." She pronounced it "cheek." "When you get out, you'll be all better and you'll get yourself a man in no time. But that wig is ratty! How come they give you such a stupid wig? I'll get you a good one, human hair."

"Dolly, don't fuss about the wig. Please get me out of here! Let me come and visit you."

"Okay, Connie, not to worry. You'll look great. I'll send you to my hairdresser. It's good you lost weight, and without taking pills even! But that wig, it makes you look like a jíbara! I'll get you a better wig so you won't be ashamed." Dolly kissed her. "I had something to give you. What was it? Some perfume . . ."

Her arms where Dolly had splashed the cologne smelled like her old caseworker, Mrs. Polcari. One case unloaded. Maybe she had had a bit of a crush on Mrs. Polcari, at the same time that she resented her youth at the age they shared, her job, her money, her home, her children, her air of being gently but firmly at all times right. She felt sophisticated thinking so about her caseworker; Luciente's influence. Maybe she had wanted to eat Mrs. Polcari with a long spoon, like an ice cream sundae, a pineapple sundae with whipped cream and a cherry. Back in her life before they had made her their monster.

Suppose they said she could trade lives? But who would want hers? Only somebody like Dr. Redding would buy her at auction, cheap by the dozen along with five thousand chimpanzees. Now she was a chimp who smelled of Arpege. Probably the cologne would be stolen. In spite of this being a locked ward, people went in and out all day—doctors and researchers besides the staff, orderlies and aides, volunteers who filtered through the whole hospital, students, graduate students, residents, interns, the chief resident, Argent's assistant director of research, patients' visitors, technicians, even a patient from another ward who flitted in to sputter quickly to Tina that she was dying of cancer but nobody would believe it.

A clam in a green chair, she sat in the day room, unmoving, and all the gossip of the ward trickled through her sore mind. Somewhere in this fund of trivial bits of garbage smelling of rotting shrimp and brown lettuce must be some clue on how to find herself again, how to fight. She sat facing the bronze plaque on the wall that said the ward was named for Mrs. John Sturgiss Baylor. Baylor was Dr. Argent's middle name. Actually it was his mother's name, Valente said. His first wife was dead too, and his second, Elinor, was in her late thirties—a hearty good-looking woman who seemed oddly transparent. Connie could never remember in between her appearances what she looked like. She seemed entirely beige and honey-colored and she would come marching rapidly through the ward for some momentary consultation with Dr. Argent, striding as if across a tennis court and looking at no one, cheerful enough and utterly indifferent to them all. She was the only wife who ever came into the hospital. She was on some committee that had to do with fund raising and managing volunteers. Finally at some point she began to speak to Dr. Redding when she encountered him, giving a measured smile, but she never greeted Dr. Morgan.

Dr. Morgan had married a nurse who stayed home with their children in Rye. Nurse Roditis liked her and they had long conversations on the phone, about Dr. Morgan and his temper and his vanities and whether he was or was not having an affair with a ward secretary named Pauline. Connie found it hard to imagine Dr. Morgan having an affair with anyone, but it sounded like he was meaninglessly but frequently unfaithful, like a nervous twitch.

But patients and staff had no gossip about Dr. Redding, who had four children and had always been married to the same wife nobody had ever seen. More was known about his kids, because he talked about them. Chaz Junior was doing his residency in urology. Betsey was married, expecting. John was studying physics. Karen, the youngest, he was bitter about. He said she was spoiled and he made her go to a psychiatrist. She had run away from home, from school, from him.

Patients and staff talked over the doctors constantly. What could she make of this coffee grounds of gossip? That Redding's family had a ski and summer house in Vermont and everybody commuted back and forth except him usually. That Dr. Argent was an Episcopalian and was always hurrying to a banquet or a fund-raising dinner for a senator or a wedding that would be in the *Times*. Elinor cared for neither New York summers nor New York winters, and Dr. Redding thought Dr. Argent took too many vacations.

Dr. Redding wanted Dr. Argent to invite him to some annual get-together, some bunch of men who went up to his family's old hunting lodge in the Adirondacks to shoot at birds or deer or whatever they shot at. Dr. Redding didn't want to go because he liked to shoot things. He didn't seem to like anything except his work. He wanted to go because of the men who would be there drinking and shooting. Dr. Morgan admired and envied Dr. Redding, as Dr. Redding envied but did not admire Dr. Argent. Dr. Morgan was a nervous sneak who clung to the rules on the job, who loved procedures and methodology and other such words. Dr. Redding loved power and the feeling of success. He said Dr. Argent liked too much to be a man about town. She had no idea what Dr. Argent might have loved, but he was nervous now at the brink of retirement to carry off some final prize. Redding had an ulcer, Argent had a heart condition, and Morgan lied to his wife about where he spent his evenings.

Tuesday as she was being taken to the bathroom, suddenly she felt Luciente in her like a scream. Luciente came through her like a great wound ripping open that knocked her to the floor of the ward. Then Luciente was gone. Yet she felt an after-aura of Luciente's presence. She knew her friend had been with her, there like lightning and gone. The attendant picked her up.

After supper she lay down while the patients were still moving around and talking, while the lights were still on all over the ward, while the laughter of the television set sounded like the pins going down in a bowling alley. She and Eddie had lived at first next door to a bowling alley in the Bronx; oh, maybe twenty blocks from Carmel's apartment and beauty shop. She had been pregnant in that apartment; she remembered lying in the bed with the hollow rattling thunder of the bowling alley coming through the wall. . . . She felt Luciente approaching again. Again it was a wild careening approach, full of pain, and almost she resisted in fear; but what should she fear from Luciente? Something must be wrong. She had to find out. She went with the wave of pain, pushing over, and found herself hugging Luciente.

Luciente's face was wet with tears, twisted with agony.

"What's wrong? What is it?"

"Person is dead!"

"Who? Who's dead?"

"Jackrabbit," Bee said behind her, laying his big hand on her shoulder.

"You heard today? When I felt you in my mind for a moment?"

"I didn't know I'd touched your mind," Luciente mumbled in a low, weary voice. "I did so now because Bee suggested you might want to attend the wake." Gently Luciente disengaged herself and stood apart, her shoulders bent.

She touched Luciente's cheek. "I'm glad you sent for me. Yes. I want to be with you."

"We feel you're family," Bee said. "We thought you should share, if you wished."

"I heard today," Luciente said, and began to weep again. "It happened yesterday." She turned away shaking. Her hands clawed the air. Her back arched on itself and seemed to collapse. Bee caught her. She struck at him, writhed, twisted back and clutched him, pressing her face into his chest.

Bee held Luciente until she had stopped shaking and then started her walking, his arm supporting her. "Come. To the meetinghouse. The wake will start."

"Is he . . . Do you have the body?"

"Yes, Jackrabbit was brought by dipper this afternoon and we laid the body out. The mems, we wept over Jackrabbit this afternoon. Now it's time for everyone."

The room was round and about half the size it had been for the holi. Most of the younger people were sitting on mats, blankets, cushions on the floor, while the older people sat on chairs. The room was full by the time they came in and went toward the center of the circle, where Bolivar sat on the floor beside the body, his back like a flagpole. Jackrabbit lay on a board across trestles with a woolen blanket of light and dark blues thrown over him, woven in patterns of rabbits and ferns. Only his head showed. His eyes had been closed and his face wore a strange grimace, but it was obviously him: obviously Jackrabbit, obviously dead. He looked deader than the embalmed corpses of her own time, her mother painted garishly as a whore in the funeral parlor, shockingly made up.

Globes of light stood at his head and feet. Around him objects were arranged like children's offerings: worn boots, clothing, a leather cap, a wide straw hat woven of rushes in a sea gull emblem, drawings, a pocketknife, carefully arranged piles of papers and cartridges, shiny cubes, a pillow, a woolen poncho, an intaglio belt buckle on a carefully worked leather belt, a few books, letters, a ring with a yellow stone. From what she knew of Mattapoisett, she guessed she was looking at the complete worldly goods of Jackrabbit, arranged around him in the dimly lit room.

All her family had gathered now in the innermost circle: Luciente, Bee, Barbarossa, Morningstar, Sojourner, Hawk, Dawn, Otter, Luxembourg, everyone except Barbarossa's baby. She felt a strange shifting as if her internal earth quaked. What did she mean by calling them family? Well, something warm. They had called her to share their sorrow. They were the closest family she had now.

Everybody around her was wearing those ceremonial robes, long dresses. Bolivar, two other young people, three of middle age, and one very old also sat in the inner circle of mourners. Some people began serving coffee in ceramic mugs. Red Star, the yellow-haired mechanic, poured hot savory coffee for them before the general serving began and returned as everyone else was served to offer more to anyone who wished.

"I'm not dressed right. My nightgown," Conne mumbled.

Bolivar took from a pile beside the body a long shift and helped her pass it over her head. It was much too long to walk in, but for sitting it was fine. "Person had taken it out to wear in a ceremony we performed in Red Hanrahan village last month. Neglected to return the garment to the library afterward. Person was often careless." He spoke monotonously, face blotched and strained tight.

"Oh, Bolivar. This is your second loss. Your mother Sappho and now Jackrabbit," Luciente said. She walked over, touched her forehead to his. "Bolivar, you're getting use to grief, and your pain must be great, recalling old pain not yet worn out."

"Nobody gets used to grief. Yet I feel numb."

"Before this night be over, your pain gonna loosen and come down." Erzulia spoke, in a robe of sky blue. "I am ready to lead this ritual. Bolivar, you and Jackrabbit made so many good holies here. Many times you give us pleasure and the healing of conflict, the easing of hard edges, the vision that pick us up and carry us. I hope we able to bring you through this night. All the sweet friends and handfriends, the basemates and old family and mems. We gonna try hard to make the passing of Jackrabbit beautiful as person made other giving backs. We begin now. It gonna be done in truth and beauty and kindness." On that last phrase her voice boomed forth. Her voice for a moment colored the air and hung there. "We gonna speak now and remember our friend. We gonna speak of the good and of the bad Jackrabbit done. We gonna remember together Jackrabbit."

A girl stood. She began to sing:

"A hand falls on my shoulder.
I turn to the wind.
On the paths I see you walking.
When I catch up
person wears another face.
In dreams I touch your mouth.
When new friends ask me of my life
I speak of you
and words turn to pebbles
on my tongue.
I turn from them
to the wind. . . ."

Connie could hardly hear the ending because the girl was crying by the time she finished. "Jackrabbit was my teacher. I felt so close to per! I was angry person chose to defend while I was learning in torrents."

Luciente too began to cry again, but Bolivar sat like a scarecrow, his freckles drawing all the color in his face to them and the rest of his skin pallid.

"I'm Arthur of Ribble, a Lancashire village in Fall River." A heavy-set person of forty or so with cropped light hair rose. "Jackrabbit was my child. Gave me joy and hard worry. Person was running in seven ways at once from five on. Such beauty. Such a pile of beginnings! Jackrabbit wanted to do everything. Person could not, would not choose. Instead Jackrabbit would begin to weave a rug, would launch a complicated genetic experiment, would begin studying spiders, would start glazing a namelon, would demand to be taught how holies function, would begin cartography lessons, all in one week. A month later the rug would be a beautiful fragment, the namelon would be half painted and abandoned, person would know a bit about spiders, something of how holies function, would have had three cartography lessons and would have abandoned the genetics experiment in the third generation of fruit flies. Person drove me wild! I would yell and bluster and my child would sulk and withdraw. But person would forgive me—yes, that's the way to body it. In sunny excitement my child would forgive me and come tell me how person—then named Peony—wanted to learn theory of wind power, construct a mill, learn lithography, study Japanese and vertebrate anatomy. I comped Peony to choose something. Much pressure. I wore out just listening. I could not grasp such trying on of subjects and roles was learning also. When Peony began to think seriously of shelf diving, I bound per into making a commit. I obsessed Peony into being ashamed of flightiness—which was excessive curiosity. I didn't do this alone. Others reacted same way. Including the head of the children's house." Arthur sat down.

The old person rose, still strongly made, with a squat pyramidal body ending in a head whose iron gray hair was worn in a knot. "I became Peony's mother when that child was eight. Peony bumped on per original mother, Elima. Elima felt overwhelmed by Peony's energy and truly began to dislike per child. So Peony and Elima brought the sticky up in council. I'm an old kidbinder and I spoke out and said I'd be feathered to have Peony for my old child. I was old then. Now I'm seventy-nine. In our village it isn't common for people over sixty to mother. But Peony liked the idea."

Arthur spoke again, grinning. "Peony jumped up and down, shouting, 'Yes, Crazy Horse is for me!' "

"I'm an old hard-bitten comrade. I spent ten years in the war. I stiffed it all over Latin America working on reparations—I was one of the teams that worked out the details, in the early days when there were still endemic diseases raging. For a whole year after I could digest no fat. I didn't settle down in Fall River till I was fifty-five. I'd had a child at fifteen, live-born child of my own body, and saw my baby die of tularemia when they loosed the plagues on us. . . . Peony—Jackrabbit—was like wine to me. Didn't care for the right and wrong. I figured you grow through things. I can still remember being hungry as a child, always hungry. . . . What a pretty child person was—gawky, long-limbed, awkward, but coltish and gifted in giving joy. I had only three years of mothering but years I loved. I didn't give dandruff if Peony was irresponsible. We were each comping Peony in opposing ways. No wonder person went mad at naming. I was gobbling up every prank like candy and Arthur here was pushing the straight and narrow. . . ."

"What of the third mother?" Bee asked.

"In Oregon now. Gentle, quiet. Couldn't fix Peony against our heaving and hauling," Crazy Horse said. "Still, Jackrabbit grew strong, and rough times can shake a body down. I never met a kid I liked better."

Arthur shook his head. "Jackrabbit used to fall by to see Crazy Horse whenever person worked near us, and we'd talk. Even last year we were arguing. Somehow we could never leave off arguing. I loved Jackrabbit, yet I think I must have spent ninety percent of the time we had insisting person was always wrong. Clipping, binding." Arthur sat down abruptly and blew into a big orange handkerchief.

At the back someone rose to play a sad melody on a flute. The flutist played for perhaps ten minutes, joined by a guitar, a flat twangy instrument, a drum. After the others stopped, the guitar played a song many joined with that muffled blurry sound people have when they're not trying to sing in unison:

"I feel like dry grass
combed by the wind, the wind.
I feel like last year's grass
raked by the salty wind.
The tides creep in the marsh,
the water rises,
the water falls,
but the old grass finally breaks
under the wind."

After the singing died into silence and they sat on for a while, White Oak rose. "I came here fourteen years ago to work in the plant genetics base just firming. Jackrabbit and I have been friends since sixmonth after person came here to be with Bolivar. Jackrabbit ate with us awhile, deciding what family to join. Especially we shared a love for the sea. What I want to tell is something two—no, three years ago. Now, you know my loving with Susan-B was not good. Never in balance. We all critted on that and tried, but it never flew and always I felt unvalued in the end. Susan-B is gone now and I confess it's easier for me with person living at Portsmouth. For a long time I couldn't want to be loving with anyone, waiting for Susan-B to want to be as close to me as I wanted with per. A long saddening. When Susan-B left, I had to face the failure of the whole long struggle. I withdrew even more. I worked hard—"

"Fasure, day and night," Bee said. "You coordinated and did the work of three."

"I feared being close. My family suggested a healer, but I was too proud. Zo, one day Jackrabbit and I took out the green boat and spent all afternoon and evening on the bay. It was fine—the wind, the salt, the water. I felt loosened. I had not taken a day free in months. I know Jackrabbit sensed my mood, for person could easily catch changes. Doors opening, doors closing. Everyone had eaten. We scraped leftovers and Jackrabbit came along to my space. . . . How easy and insinuating person could be. Without deciding to, still addressing Jackrabbit in my mind as if person were half a child, we ended up coupling that night. After, I felt for the old knot, and it was melted. Only the feeling I'd been a great fool. I'd scorned what was easy, the affection of my own family, for what I couldn't have. Since then I have tried to be simpler, better. . . . It wasn't that Jackrabbit worked healer's entrance, but person loosened the knot that pride kept tight. Once loosened, I couldn't want to bind myself again. Even I had that much sense." White Oak smiled and sat down. Her gaze rested on the wall.

"Person's way of insinuating into other people's beds was not always productive," a young person said, standing on one foot. "Jackrabbit came to me once after a dance and then never again. I felt I was an apple person had taken a bite of and spat out."

"Person was so curious, began far more friendships than could be maintained," Bolivar said dryly, without raising his head.

"How can you carry on about a small thing?" Connie burst out. "Can't you forgive him for something small that wasn't even intended to hurt?" Joined to Luciente, how strongly she could feel her pain raw against the breastbone.

Bee spoke in his deep, gentle, careless-sounding voice. "We recall what we can. Good and ill, doings and undoings. We want to hold person entire in our minds before we begin slowly to forget."

A short brown man rose. "Last year I studied History of Jazz at Oxford. Even there in Mississippi, they had a painting of Jackrabbit's traveling from village to village. That's from my home, I told them, and felt proud."

Luciente rose, swaying. Words came in gouts. "Was good to be with Jackrabbit. I was selfish, selfish over that good. Now it's gone. Person is gone!"

"How did it move, Luciente? Speak of Jackrabbit," Erzulia commanded in a high, carrying voice.

"Person made me able to be . . . careless. Silly."

"Was that good or bad, Luciente?"

"At first I feared maybe bad. I cramped at forgetting meetings, experiments, issues. Gradually I felt that loosening gave me energy. Jackrabbit was water, I could float. Jackrabbit was wine, making me tipsy and glad of the moment. We were always laughing. We never stopped flirting. Person was full of grace. Person made me want to know things that on my own I would never have grazed. Now, nothing . . ." Luciente stopped, choking into tears. She remained standing, her hands inscribing shapes on the air, but she could not sort words. Otter sat her down gently.

After a space of minutes of soft crying and shifting about, a child rose. "Jackrabbit worked with me a whole lot, teaching me how to handle a boat and swim. Person didn't always suck patience, but person laughed a lot—not at me. Person made . . . even picking the Swallowtail caterpillars off the carrots fun. Person made them put out their horns. . . .. I'll miss Jackrabbit a lot!"

Another child stood. "Person was teaching me holi work. Now nobody will have—will ever—grasp, believe in me when I can't do what I mean. Person made me feel my—the pictures I saw in my head were good even when they came out—so stupid!" Abruptly the child sat, red in the face.

Magdalena of the children's house came forward on bare feet, small as a child and black as the blackest cat. "We think old people have a special kinning with children. But sometimes young people hold a strong sense of how it was, so that they stay in touch with the child inside and therefore with real children. Jackrabbit was so. Could enjoy children as people and want to work with them.

Find their ideas interesting, their visions real, their problems worth mulling. . . . I worried about Jackrabbit's wandering sexuality. Person knew of my mistrust and teased me. Ran circles around me. Now Jackrabbit is gone many more children will miss per than will speak of it tonight. I too will miss Jackrabbit! A good strong holi is a powerful tool of learning. Many artists who make ceremonial and artistic holies, if they turn to making instructional holies at all, do so as in a lesser medium. Condescending. They simplify . . . in the wrong dimensions. Children sense the falsity and turn away, bored. The holies Jackrabbit made for us we'll use long past the lifetime that should have been pers."

A big man, grizzled and bald, stood. "Blackfish of Provincetown. I taught Jackrabbit. There's no keener—or more dubious—pleasure than having a student you know will surpass you. I can't stay, I have to go back on the dipper tonight, we're in the middle of harvest. But what a waste! Person did nothing of what person could have. Nothing. We're all poorer."

A person in a mottled green and brown jumpsuit rose and spoke loudly. "I want to tell you how Jackrabbit died. Then I must leave too. I wish I could stay the night. . . . The fighting's been fierce. They have new flying cyborgs, can go rocket speeds and cruise at twenty kilometers. . . . We suffer heavy losses. . . ." The person in green and brown paused to look around as if to recover a lost intent. "At now, you all grasp from the last grandcil more of us are going to have to fight for a while. . . . Jackrabbit was no born fighter. Person would have been happier staying home. But fought well. Jackrabbit was wounded running out to move a sonic shield to protect our emplacement. Was dying when we got to per. Damage to chest and organs was too extensive for us to save the life. We blocked pain. Jackrabbit died within fifteen minutes. We corded a last message. Should I play it?"

Erzulia rapped out, "Play it now."

Minor scufflings with equipment. Then Jackrabbit's unmistakable voice spoke in brief, broken sentences, half swamped in crackling and background noise. "Luciente: weep and work. Was good. You have to help people prepare. . . . Bolivar: break open. Go to Diana for help. Finish our holi with browns, reds, greens. Glim into uprush. Earth itself moving. Armies of trees. See? Armies of trees.

. . . Bee: bring Luciente through. Never got to mother. Mother for me. . . . Corolla: regret what will never fuse now. . . . Orion: have faith in visions and patience with matter—" The voice choked in midsentence. Only crackling followed.

The person in uniform continued apologetically: "Jackrabbit meant to give more messages, but couldn't. We could tell person intended to speak to more of you. . . . At first we were trying to save per. We should have grasped at once the wounds were too severe. Otherwise we'd have started cording sooner. We wasted time while we didn't want to admit Jackrabbit was dying. Our tardiness robbed many of you of a message."

Bee said, "You did well. We'd rather have had Jackrabbit than any message."

The person in uniform bowed slightly and walked out. A voice began to sing:

"The tree quivers
wetly
in no wind.
I cone upon you.
How the light breaks
like arrows
through my eyelids.

Connie stopped listening, catching Erzulia's gaze on Bolivar, his dry narrowed eyes and brooding forehead. Rigid he sat with his legs crossed and his head at the top of the pole of spine slightly inclined. His eyes burned. His hands lay abandoned on his thighs like a pair of old kid gloves.

Others were speaking their remembrances, recounting an episode, embarrassed or nostalgic. Otter said, "I remember stiffing it all night when a hurricane was coming, to bring in the harvest, to batten things down. How Jackrabbit kept us singing and made everything funny, even when the waves came over the sea wall and we were really scared."

Diana and Erzulia conferred. Diana rose and came back with three women of her core. Lovers, sisters, daughters of the moon, they wore the knee-length white tunics of healers. Their hair was bound back and they bore as decoration the crescent of the moon. Now they carried a cello, a flute, and a drum. After tuning up, they began to play, sitting to one side of Diana, who stood to sing . . . or keen. Her voice began softly, sobbing, wordless but musical, used like a fourth instrument higher than the cello but lower than the flute. Her auburn hair fell over one shoulder. Tall and bony and commanding, she swayed. Her voice crooned, soared, ululated, wailed, and mourned over the rhythm of the drum. Finally Erzulia rose. She cast off her blue robe and stood in something like a dancer's leotards, black against her black skin so at first Connie thought her naked. She stood still and then she seemed to grow taller.

She began to dance, but not as Connie had seen her dance the night of the feast. She did not dance in trance but consciously, and she did not dance as herself. She danced Jackrabbit. Yes, she became him. She was tall, bony but graceful, shambling and limber, young and awkward and beautiful, talented and bumbling, pressing off at once in four directions, hopping, leaping, charging, and bounding back.

Bolivar's head slowly lifted from his chest. He was staring. Suddenly Erzulia-Jackrabbit danced over and drew him up. Slowly, mechanically, as if hypnotized Bolivar began to dance with him/her. Erzulia possessed willfully by the memory of Jackrabbit led Bolivar round and round. He danced more feverishly, responding, his body became fluid and elegant as he had danced that night of the feast with Jackrabbit—that night she had spent with Bee. Slowly tears coursed down her own face, perhaps more for Skip than for Jackrabbit, perhaps for both, perhaps for old losses and him too and above all for Luciente and the pain tearing her.

The music ended and Bolivar embraced Erzulia. They stood a moment clasped and then Erzulia's body relaxed. Bolivar jumped back. "But I felt per!" he cried out.

"You remembering," Erzulia lilted gently, wiping her forehead.

Bolivar crumpled to the ground in a spasm of weeping so sudden that for a moment no one moved to support him. Then Bee and Crazy Horse gently held him, murmuring.

"Good. At last your grief come down." Erzulia signaled to the people who had served the coffee, and they began carrying around jugs of wine and glasses and picking up the coffee mugs. This time they served everyone else first, to let the pitch of emotion ease among the close ones.

The wine was strong, fiery, with a heady perfume of grape. The jugs were gallons marked "Egenblick of Cayuga Fortified After Dinner Wine," and they passed around plenty of jugs. Enough to get everyone well drunk, she thought, noticing there were many other jugs waiting. In fact, the tension did seem to be lightening. People were chatting quietly, blowing noses, wiping tears, and putting handkerchiefs away, hugging and talking more. Bolivar sat down and cried in short but lessening spasms. His spine had relaxed. His face was crinkled. His head lay on the thigh of Crazy Horse.

Erzulia said something to the three musicians with Diana, and they began playing a different kind of tune, bittersweet, sweet and sour, it ran. Erzulia and Diana sang together, their voices turning and crossing in the air like swallows. Diana's voice was deeper, Erzulia's sweeter and more piercing. They twined and separated in easy counterpoint in the song Connie remembered from the nursery:

"Nobody knows
how it flows
as it goes.

Nobody goes
where it rose
as it flows."

That lullaby. Everybody began to sing it, they all seemed to know it. It made a slow wave of soft singing over which the voices of Erzulia and Diana rose and dipped.

"Nobody knows
how it chose
how it grows. . . ."

The children joined in, swaying back and forth as they sang words that seemed familiar to all, from babyhood, from mothering and caring for the young. The flute skipped off in a dance of its own high over the voices, and Erzulia and Diana fell back to listen. Other instruments joined in here and there in the hall. The improvising rose in intensity, trailed off, seemed to stop, and then began again in a guitar or recorder.

Finally the song dwindled. Barbarossa spoke thoughtfully. "The holi Jackrabbit made that warmed me most was the one for green equinox, with all the speeded-up plant growth. For days after I kept remembering the little sprouts wriggling out of the seeds, the tulips unfolding, shutting, opening, shutting. It was funny and beautiful at once. Those images kept coming back when I was working and I'd smile. It gave me a good connected feeling."

"The smile on the faces of *kores*, the youth and maidens, the archaic smile. Jackrabbit was . . . moved by that smile," Bolivar mused. He had stopped crying. His face was soft. He leaned on Bee, his head lolling like a sleepy child. "Was my sabbatical and Jackrabbit had not yet settled down. We went to Greece for threemonth. Person was fifteen, more like a cricket than a rabbit. Skinny. Person could eat and eat and nothing would show. Was spring—end of March. Wildflowers everyplace. Crete was velvet to us. We worked on reforesting, we stayed with shepherds, and Jackrabbit was sketching everybody and giving the drawings away. I remember vermilion poppies under gray-green olives, young and black kids that wanted their foreheads rubbed where the horns were going to come through. Dittany growing wild. The pigment factory where we stayed a week, doing odd jobs. We were in love with Minoan wall paintings. An outbuilding at Minos had ridiculous imaginative birds on the murals. Marvelous. Pure velvet. We decided we too would invent unlikely creatures in holies we were even then starting to plan. . . . We decided to build a house, such a house as that one at Minos. A distance away from the others and with a view of the mountains and vineyards. Painted all over and open to the sun."

Bolivar smiled weakly. "A few days later we were traveling by donkey up near Dicty, when we saw those birds. They're called hoopoes in English. There they were, exactly the birds in the Minoan guesthouse. A pinkish brown with black and white striped wings and tail like flying zebras, just flashing at you as they undulate ever so slowly, fluttering across clearings. On their heads an Indian-chief headdress of brown- and black-tipped feathers stands straight up when they want it to. We laughed so hard we fell off the donkeys. And they fluttered away slowly and tantalizingly, rebuking us for not having believed in them. Pooh! Pooh! they cried at us. Ah, the imagination of those ancient Cretans, Jackrabbit said, and for years that was a catch phrase between us. . . ."

He sighed, shrugging. "We saw the work of a holist in Agios Nicolaus who fluttered us. Something . . . fluid about per work. A top spectacler with eight students studying there. I could see Jackrabbit was tempted. That obsessed me jealous, for I viewed myself as Jackrabbit's teacher as well as lover. I bound more jealous yet when Jackrabbit coupled with per. I had believed, I'd wished, that Jackrabbit would also be drawn only to the male body—so that we'd be alike. . . . I remember those months so vividly, day by day. We were never closer. Yet the differences stuck out. Always I wanted Jackrabbit to be more like me than person was. . . . That must have been a strength of your friending, Luciente, that you didn't want per to be like you. That was almost unique for Jackrabbit."

"Ah, Bolivar!" Luciente stirred as if shaking herself. "We each loved Jackrabbit and had great richness and great pleasure and now how we ring with pain. What more could we have asked? Except that it last! But what we had . . ."

The wine went round, the makings of joints began to be passed, marijuana and several other weeds they smoked, the trays with delicate papers and carved pipes. One of the healers was playing the flute again and Diana sang. Luciente was leaned propped sideways against Diana, humming with them. The pressure of her grief was gradually softening. Connie could feel Luciente's pain flowing like a stream rather than a waterfall smashing on her.

Some of the children had fallen asleep. Occasionally an adult or an older child would carry out a sleeper or lead one stumbling home. More than a few adults had dozed off where they sat, stretched out on the floor unashamed. From time to time a song would start, someone would say a poem, someone would rise with a memory.

"I remember one feast day—maybe it was Haymarket Martyrs or Halloween? Jackrabbit helped me design a flimsy that was all dream. I was a luna moth, pale green with yellow veins and a margin of lavender, with plumy antennae. . . ." Luxembourg spoke.

"Up among the grapevines
someone is playing the flute
and the song
calls my name.
Among clusters of grapes
half hidden by leaves
like palms beckoning,
someone waits whose mouth
is sweet as ripe grapes,
whose touch makes me bleed
like ripe purple grapes
in the press.
I am in bed with somebody else.
I was too jumpy.
I'm caught with the wrong person,
the whole night to crawl through
long as a tunnel to France.
All over the hillside lovers couple.
Here I am stuck
with the wrong one
while up among the grapevines
you call my name."

The songs, the poems were more cheerful: love songs, drinking songs, work songs, poems about sailing and farming, political sallies, topical songs she could not follow. Little cakes were passed. More people fell asleep and some went home. Erzulia and Been were singing in another language, accompanied by drums and the laughter of those who understood the words.

When silence settled again, Luciente spoke gently. "I met Jackrabbit through Diana. Jackrabbit had retreated to the madhouse at Treefrog. I came to visit Diana, who kept teasing me and wouldn't sleep with me. Although Jackrabbit was staying in our village, I hadn't got to know per well. All I had noticed was that person kept changing names, and that bumped me a little. Jackrabbit had gone down but by the time I came visiting, was integrated again. . . . Diana had a moon dance, on the grass there. It was green moon, the moon after the green equinox, and at first I was comping jealous, Diana was fused with per mems and only watching me. And then I wasn't jealous."

"Was not like the first time person went mad," Diana said in her beautiful husky voice, stroking Luciente's hair off her forehead. "Not a complete going down. Basically Jackrabbit had come to feel taken over by Bolivar. Wanted to work with you," Diana said to Bolivar, "but also to work alone. To be freer to grow as a person. You knew so much, you have traveled so much, you had worked out your own style, made a reputation. Jackrabbit felt as if per own work and visions were disappearing into yours—perhaps what was happening at Agios Nicolaus too. Jackrabbit lacked a center. Instead was an enormous uprush of vision and great hunger for experience. Balancing came from others. Needed someone to balance you. I also felt Luciente had been wholly sensible too long." She tugged Luciente's hair.

"Yet we both saw through your plotting," Luciente said with sulky dignity.

"What good did it do you? My plotting was healing, old friend."

Luciente leaned her cheek into Diana's shoulder. "It would have happened anyhow, when Jackrabbit came back to the village, but then it would have been shorter. . . . Person died well. That's a good death, a useful one. Just . . . too soon!"

A bass voice was singing softly:

"I am dreaming of a baby
floating among others
like a trout in a stream.
I am dreaming of a baby
whose huge eyes
close over secret promises.
I am dreaming of a baby
who drifts in the throbbing
heart of the brooder
growing every day
more beautiful,
closer to me."

"Sun up," Erzulia said, and signaled for the doors to be flung open. "We have to give our loved friend to the earth. The day here now. This wake over."

Slowly the hall stirred like a dog rousing, shaking. People wakened each other. The cups, the glasses, the jugs, empty and partly empty and still full, were carried off.

"Whoever wants a membrance from Jackrabbit, come and take one. Family and sweet friends first," Erzulia called. Quietly they gathered over the small circle of objects. Luciente took a worn book. "Jackrabbit used to say these. Every poem reminds me of times and times gone."

Bolivar took the ring with the yellow stone. "I had a crafter make this when Jackrabbit turned fifteen."

Everything was carried away except the letters and personal papers, which were placed under the blanket by Erzulia. Then Bee, Bolivar, Barbarossa and Luciente got ready to carry the body. People were going off to work if they could keep awake, or to sleep if they couldn't. About thirty people fell into the procession to the grave.

The bell was tolling again over Mattapoisett. They walked slowly through the paths of the village, with Diana's friends playing a death march. The leaves were just beginning to turn, the maples reddening and one young sapling already vermilion as if dipped in bright blood. It would be a clear day. The air was chilly. Dew wet the stones, making Connie's feet slip. Chrysanthemums and asters glowed along the walks. Frost had not come here yet. Red and green tomatoes still weighed down the tall vines. Pumpkins planted along the edge of gardens grew out into the grass or climbed the corn. Sojourner fell in beside her, asking if she might lean on her arm, as she was weary from the long night. Slowly they ambled well back in the procession.

A deep and narrow grave gaped on the edge of the woods. They gathered around it and used ropes to lower Jackrabbit, with his papers and blanket, down into the hole. As they made to lower him, Erzulia adjusted the blanket to cover the face. The body reached bottom with a soft thud that sent a shiver through Connie. A few, Luciente, Bolivar, Crazy Horse, began to weep again softly, but Connie could sense they were about wept out.

"Friends, we mourn for our comrade Jackrabbit, who died defending us. 'Only in us do the dead live. Water flows downhill through us. The sun cools in our bones. We are joined with all living in one singing web of energy.

In us live the dead who made us. In us live the children unborn. Breathing each other's air, drinking each other's water, eating each other's flesh, we grow like a tree from the earth.' Cast in the dirt and go. We must work on till we give our bodies back. Goodbye, Jackrabbit." Erzulia took up a shovel and cast in a load of dirt. Then she passed the shovel to Bee.

Each in turn said goodbye and cast in the dirt, then walked back toward the village. Standing with its root ball in burlap, a young sassafras tree waited to go into the grave. After the others had finished the ritual casting of soil, Erzulia remained with two volunteers to finish the grave. Luciente, who had waited to one side for Connie, slipped her arm through hers, leaning on her as they walked.

"Now we go to the brooder," she said. Connie could feel the slack of her grief. It remained. A pain that would wear itself down slowly. But the first refusal was over. She would live with the pain and live her life. Connie too felt loosened, weary but released, lighter than air but heavy through all her limbs with fatigue. She felt as if she had cried out years of grief.

Bee, Barbarossa, Otter, Sojourner, Hawk, and Bolivar too were waiting already outside the brooder. Then they all entered in groups of four through the double sets of doors. Sacco-Vanzetti was waiting for them.

"We come to ask that a new baby be begun, to replace Jackrabbit, who is dead and buried," Bee said.

"I have news for you." Sacco-Vanzetti sputtered excitement, trying to speak with dignity. "I have great news. That is, grasp, the council met. Decided to honor Jackrabbit. That genetic chance will be born again."

There was a moment of silence. Then Luciente spoke. "We thank the council. Though we will never know where or who, we know some part of Jackrabbit lives."

After they had returned to the sun slanting bright over the fields, the huts, the yellow hump of the brooder, she asked Luciente, "What was that? I don't understand."

"What? . . . Oh, the decision." Luciente swayed slightly. "Very rarely that is done. When somebody dies young who was unusually talented, as a kind of living memorial their exact genetic mix is given to a new baby. You never know where. Nobody knows. Records are not kept. We know nurture counts more heavily than genetics once you've weeded out the negative genes, but still it is a memorial. It eases the mind strangely to know that a baby Jackrabbit will again be born somewhere, nine months from now."

"I suppose . . ."

"I am too weary to send more, Connie, my sweetness. I must sleep. So must you." Luciente embraced her. "Let go."

She felt herself slowly sinking into her bed. A nurse was sitting beside her and as soon as her eyelids fluttered, the nurse called out. "She's coming around. Quick, tell Dr. Morgan. He's sleeping down the hall."

Her ability to stay in the future amazed her. They had been trying to rouse her since the evening before. This time, locked into Luciente, she had not even felt them. She watched the fuss through narrowed eyes. They were scared. She could feel Dr. Morgan's fear whining like a saw blade cutting wood. What they had stuffed into her head was experimental and they did not want a death.

Morgan and Redding muttered long, and Argent, when he dropped by late in the morning, looked glum and edgy. He eyed her, questioned the nurses briskly, frowned and frowned. Redding paced and muttered and then went in with a hypodermic and a local anaesthetic and changed the medication the dialysis bag was leaking into her.

"That ought to settle it," Redding said cheerfully, but he frowned at her skull as if he would like to take it all apart.

A new watchfulness surrounded her. She was sorry to see that Tina and Sybil were genuinely frightened. Tina nagged her to eat and buzzed between window and door like an angry fly. When Tina was in the day room, Connie tried to give Sybil reassurance.

"All right! You were unconscious for twelve hours! How can that be all right?"

"Sybil, don't worry! Please. The only thing wrong with me is what they got stuck in my head. And I'm doing what I can to get it out. Believe me."

"They're frightened." Sybil's eyes were somber. "They put off the implants scheduled for Monday, until they figure out what's happening to you."

"Good! That's my first victory. Tina was scheduled for

Monday." With Luciente's help, she might be able to scare them again. What else could she do? It was the only way she could see to struggle.

Seventeen

EVERY day for a week she tried to summon Luciente, but without success. Once she felt herself slipping into that other future, till she drew back with horror. Why couldn't she call Luciente? Since they had implanted the dialytrode, she had not been able to reach over on her own, not to the right future, the one she wanted.

She was more lightly doped and time blurred by less dimly. Tina was caught trying to slip out of the ward in a laundry cart, and put into seclusion for two days. When Tina was let out, dizzy and twitching with drugs, Connie rose shakily and touched her shoulder. "Too bad you didn't make it," she whispered. "Try again."

"I only got four days. I'm scheduled for Monday."

In the orange and beige patient lounge, Alice sat in front of the TV, smiling in a slack way. She watched whatever moved in front of her. Connie thought that if she crept up to shut the set off, Alice would go on watching the blank screen with that same blank smile. The staff kept telling Alice she would be released soon, but they were cautious because of Skip. Alice ate a lot. She would not start eating until the attendant got her started, but then she methodically ate everything. She was gaining weight.

The next Monday, after they had wheeled out Captain Cream and Tina to be implanted, she cast herself on her bed and flung herself toward Luciente, she did not care how. The going over was rocky. For a time the ward dimmed and yet she did not arrive in the future. She passed out. It was more like fainting than falling asleep. But at last she stood with Luciente's hands on her shoulders in a small clearing. Outcroppings of gray-green stone. Pine needles lay everywhere, drifted against the rocks. Luciente wore a brown and green jumpsuit uniform.

"Where are we?"

"Near the front," Luciente said. "We've gone up."

"Is that why I couldn't reach you?"

"Communing's been harder. Something is interfering. Probability static? Temporal vectors are only primitively grasped. . . . I tried to reach you before we shipped out, but since then I've been too jammed."

"Where's your kenner?" She stared at a band of pale brown skin on Luciente's left forearm.

"Back at the foco. We take them off for fear we'll use them without thinking. They can home on the frequencies. We use these for locator-talkers." Luciente touched a small netted egg around her neck. "I myself, I confess, I feel naked without my kenner. It's part of my body. I only take it off to couple or sleep."

"Suppose it got lost?"

"I'd lose two-thirds of my memory. . . . Marigold at Treefrog had an accident in which both left arm and kenner were destroyed. Arm we could restore but not kenner. Marigold killed perself. . . . For some it's only a convenience. For others part of their psyche."

Bee came pacing along a trail toward them, carrying a piece of equipment on his back. He looked larger than ever here, and unusually alert. His smile still spoke of luxurious calm and sunny energy. "G'light, Pepper and Salt. I forgot to tell you last time I believe you should trade that wig in on a porcupine."

"It's beginning to grow out. It kind of itches." On impulse she took off the tipsy reddish-brown wig and showed him her crew cut. She could feel a bald spot at the plug of cement, but the rest of her scalp was growing hair straight up.

Both Bee and Luciente giggled without malice and petted her, exclaiming how stiff and bristly the half-inch hair felt. She did not mind their teasing because it carried affection and besides, she knew how funny she looked. This ward had a real mirror in the bathroom.

Bee clucked over the plug in her scalp. "This can't be good. What have they in there?"

"Something to control me. A machine."

Bee looked wasted with sadness, that expression from the beginning of Jackrabbit's wake. "We're all at war. You're a prisoner of war. May you free yourself." Gently he hugged her.

She laughed shortly, disentangling herself. "How can I?"

"Can I give you tactics?" Bee turned her chin back toward him. "There's always a thing you can deny an oppressor, if only your allegiance. Your belief. Your co-oping. Often even with vastly unequal power, you can find or force an opening to fight back. In your time many without power found ways to fight. Till that became a power."

"But you're still fighting. It isn't over yet!"

"How is it ever over?" Luciente waved a hand. "In time the sun goes nova. Big bang. What else? We renew, regenerate. Or die."

"But you don't seem to believe really in *more*—not more people, more things, or even more money."

Luciente leaned against a pine, her fingers playing with the ridged bark. "Someday the gross repair will be done. The oceans will be balanced, the rivers flow clean, the wetlands and the forests flourish. There'll be no more enemies. No Them and Us. We can quarrel joyously with each other about important matters of idea and art. The vestiges of old ways will fade. I can't know that time—any more than you can ultimately know us. We can only know what we can truly imagine. Finally what we see comes from ourselves."

"Do you think I don't know you, Luciente?"

"Grasp, as people. I mean you can't fully comprend our society, any more than I could one a hundred years past us. What new arts will our great-great-grandchildren invent? What old arts discover? What musical instruments will they build? What games? What inknowing? What new foods, what styles of cooking? What sciences we can't imagine? What new ways of healing? Will they sail far into our galaxy? Travel on the submicroscopic strata? When each region is ownfed, when reparations are completed, what then? Sometimes . . . sometimes I want to live forever!" Luciente flung back her head. "But I know I'll find my death ripe. I'll want to lay my body down, I myself, and be done. But now I'd like to travel forward into that future as you traveled to us. I know there's no real point to it. Now suffices. Yet I'm very glad to be knowing you, Connie."

A strange high whistling came through the air, nearer and nearer. Bee and Luciente froze; then they motioned to her and began trotting swiftly in the direction Bee had just come from.

"Fast! Run!" Luciente mouthed at her over her shoulder. Bee dropped back to urge her forward as they ran.

The high penetrating screech grew louder and louder still. It bored through her ears and seemed to whine round and round in her skull. Pain like a drill sang in her marrow. No longer did the pain seem to enter only through her ears; her bones seemed to vibrate at a pitch too high to bear. She was a tuning fork shivering in pain.

"Run, Connie! Run!" Bee urged. "Sonic sweeps kill. The reflectors are over the bridge. Run!"

She tried to keep up, but she could not run as fast. Panting, her sides stabbing, she fell farther and farther behind. They paused to wait. Luciente ran back to drag her along. The high drill of the whining shook her. She crumpled to the ground, clawing at her head. "Go on! Save yourself!"

"There. Her eyelids fluttered. She's coming out of it."

She opened her eyes. The nurse stood over her. An aide bustled off with a message.

"What were you trying to say when you came to?" Nurse Roditis bent close. "Something about going on."

"I don't know." She closed her eyes.

"Were you hallucinating?"

"She doesn't have a history of hallucination." Acker was hanging around the foot of her bed.

"That injection worked. Dr. Morgan will be pleased. But I don't know what they're going to do if this keeps happening." Nurse Roditis sounded stern and judgmental. She made tsk-tsk sounds as she straightened the covers over Connie.

Luciente gripped her arm, pulling her down into the dugout. Behind decorative-looking screens and small pieces of equipment, some like the one Bee had been carrying on his back, the ground had been scooped out to rock. Her friends were occupying a slight rise over a stream. "Baffles and reflectors," Luciente explained tersely. "Keep down! They'll be attacking our line."

"Where is everyone?"

"We're on the right flank. The line curves to our left, all the way to the river."

Otter was cuddled in the dugout next to Connie, examining a bright fallen leaf from one of the maples growing along the stream. Pines stood behind them and a fringe of brilliant maples before. Their red and gold leaves were just starting to fall in drifts on the banks, to float past borne on the rocky stream, to collect in patches of color in eddies and pools.

"How does this touch you?" Otter asked and read off:

"One leaf
webbed gold with fawn
fluttered to my feet
and fragile as a dead moth's wing
was shattered."

She looked at Otter in confusion. Otter was dressed in the same mottled jumpsuit, her hair in two long braids. From her broad nose to her glittering slits of eyes she looked proud of herself. Connie asked, "Is it a code message?"

"Code? It's a poem—a cinquain. You don't like it?"

"But . . . how can you write poems about leaves now!"

Otter's brows wrinkled. "How not? We're close to death. Then it's natural to write poems, no? And we fall like leaves. . . ."

"Here they come," Luciente said calmly, and they all settled into alert poses with their weapons.

The ground shook violently under her, yet she heard no explosion. In effect, nothing seemed to cause what was happening, yet the ground shook again and she felt sick. Again the ground shook and a tree split and toppled in front of them. Other trees were falling, while a boulder crashed from its perch and rolled fifty feet to lodge in a small basin. Cones pelted them as the birds fled crying terror, the jays shouting Thief, Thief as they flew. To their right someone screamed.

Then she saw the enemy coming: tall figures entirely encased in seamless metallic uniforms, clanking with heavy metal and wearing helmets that enclosed their heads. They dodged from tree to boulder, from boulder to bush on the other side of the stream.

"Hold your fire," Luciente whispered.

She found she was gripping something like a gun, although it was aimed by peering through a scope and focusing her eyes. Nervously she practiced with it. It responded quickly but she could not quite get the knack of stopping it. She was supposed to lock it in position somehow before she looked away from the target, but she kept stopping it too late.

More and more metal figures flitted clumsily through the trees, getting ready to attack in force across the water. "Hold your fire," Luciente whispered again emphatically. "Pick off the ones that get through the barrage." Then she added in the tone of a prayer, "Forgive me, if you are living and I kill you."

Bee and Otter mumbled a similar prayer, before Otter whispered, "Do you suppose any of them are people?"

The troops were massing in the far woods, preparing to break cover. More and more moved up into position. Finally they came clanking out, running pell-mell in waves down the shallow embankment to jump the small stream. Silently they came, except for the clanking of their metal parts. They did not scream or whoop.

Suddenly she was standing in the living room of the apartment where she had lived with Martín. Hot. Sweat ran down her back and collected under her breasts. The air was so thick and sulfurous she began to cough. She was frightened, her stomach ached with fear. Why? Martín was down there somewhere. Yes, in the street he was barricaded behind turned-over cars, throwing bottles and rocks at the police. The riot police, the TPF, armed with rifles and shotguns and pistols and tear gas canisters and gas grenades, came clanking down the street, stiff and mechanical. But their voices bouncing off the houses were coarse with the joy of fury: *Motherfuckin cocksuckin nigger spics*!

She stood at the window watching, clutching herself across the breasts in her flower print summer dress. Martín was out there somewhere, screaming helpless rage and about to be murdered, as the police gunned down a fourteen-year-old they said had stolen a car, starting this riot. Then one of the police had turned and, seeing her at the window, raised his gun and shot right at her. The window shattered inward. In terror she screamed and fell to the floor among the breaking glass. For two days she had picked bits of glass out of her arms. But he had missed her. They had missed Martín too that time.

"I think she's coming to, Doctor."

"Patty, did you get hold of Redding? Get on it. Find him."

"Doctor, his secretary says he's on the way over."

"If we lose this implantation, it won't look good," Dr. Morgan muttered. "When did she say he left?"

"Ten minutes ago, Doctor."

"Did she say he was driving straight uptown?"

"She didn't say, Doctor."

"And you didn't ask," he said with sour satisfaction, glad to find somebody to blame for something. "What about Dr. Argent?"

"I couldn't get hold of him, Doctor. He's guest lecturer this morning at Dr. Sanderman's pathology class. His secretary expects him in his office around eleven-thirty."

"She expects! Why doesn't she trot her . . . self over there and give him the message. You call her back and tell her to step on it. She can speak to him as soon as he finishes the lecture. These women are too lazy to get off their chairs and stop powdering their noses. You tell her to hand-deliver that message to Argent."

Nurse Roditis cleared her throat. "Doctor, should I do something about an operating room downtown?"

"That has to be Redding's decision. . . . Where is he? I bet he stopped with one of those university types for coffee. He drinks coffee all day long, it's a medical miracle he has kidneys left. I drink it by the gallon when I'm around him. If I keep it up, I'll end up with ulcers like his. Where the bleeding hell is he?"

"If you do want to operate, she had breakfast this morning, but she hasn't taken anything since." Nurse Roditis popped a thermometer under Connie's tongue. "Now don't bite down, that's a good girl."

Hawk gripped the controls of a floater. Luciente hunched poised at the forward weapon and Connie was in the back seat with another weapon, mounted so that it could swivel through one hundred eighty degrees in any plane.

Hawk was making the floater climb abruptly. They were over the sea, gray waves far below like scales of an enormous fish. The sky was overcast; the puffy bellies of clouds hung over them. They skimmed along just beneath, dodging through fog banks. The floater bobbed corklike in the tides of the air, and she felt a little ill. Hawk looked happy at the controls, singing something Connie remembered hearing before, yes, the night of the feast. She had been walking with Bee, his arm around her. Abruptly her flesh recalled his big warm hand, the thumb gently brushing her breast naked under the flimsy. "How can anybody sing about fighting on such a night?" He had answered her that on such a night people died fighting, as on any other.

"How good to fight beside you
friend of our long table,
mother of my child."

Hawk warbled in her high thin voice and the floater banked, dipped, leaped while Connie's stomach quavered and fell. Sea gulls crossed under them. Fog closed in the horizon. Nothing could be seen but clouds and once in a while another floater bobbing in and out of clouds, as if on an upside-down sea of thick gray air.

"An army of lovers cannot lose,
an army of lovers cannot lose!"

Hawk warbled in her squeaky soprano, cheerful in the closed cabin, and banked the floater right into a cloud that melted around them, shutting off the world till everything was gray cotton fluff and she could not tell up from down. Connie felt dizzy and gripped hard the levers that controlled her sleek weapon.

Luciente grinned over her shoulder. "Don't start shooting clouds, sweetness! Relax. Just enjoy the ride! Whee!"

"Enjoy? My stomach sticks in my teeth! Do we have to scoot along upside down?"

"We're like the sea gulls, winging along," Hawk cried. "How can you not like to fly?"

"You moved this week, Hawk?" Luciente interrupted tactfully.

"I turned over my old space to Poppy. It's kid-sized, the bed and chairs are little. Poppy's been waiting for space for twomonth. Was planning to go to council for building supplies if something didn't break soon. But I'm taking Jackrabbit's old space, and Poppy can take mine." She swung the floater at a ninety-degree turn and scudded across clear space—a ravine dropping to the sea—into another mass of soft nothing. "My old space is great for a kid. Poppy's ten. Near enough to the children's house so you can run over when you want, if you don't like spending the night alone sometimes. But the floater pad's handier to where I'm moving. I love the sound of the waters—I'm sorry! You know what it's like. I'm so sorry," she sputtered to Luciente.

"Today we carry on Jackrabbit's fight." Luciente made herself busy with her weapon. Luciente was operating the jizer and Connie, in the tail, the scanner.

"If we survive," Luciente said conversationally five minutes later, "have you redded what you'll do now you're adult? Bee said you're dreaming on traveling. Will you apprentice yourself?"

"I'd rather work with floaters than anything. But I want to travel awhile. Never hopped farther than the top of the bay. Thunderbolt and I've chewed on taking off for some wandering—after the current phase of the war is over, of course."

"How do you know it'll be over?" Connie asked. "Do you expect to win soon?"

"Win? It comes in spurts." Luciente made a face over her shoulder. "Like sun spots."

"We thought we'd go south. We figure we have a few useful skills to trade and we can always stiff it on any passing work. Bolt is a skilled pollinator. I'm a good beginning mechanic. I don't mean to wander forever, like those puffs. No family, no base. I'd never get to fly. But I want to look around first."

"Forty degrees north of east," Luciente's voice whipped out. "Two hundred feet lower than present elevation. Dogfight. I count eight objects."

Hawk canted about, then lurched off through the gray flab in a direction Connie trusted was north of east. Their speed increased till she felt dizzy and scared once again. During the talking she had forgotten to be anxious. None of them spoke now. Hawk was maneuvering sharply. Luciente was checking her own weapon. Then she unbuckled herself, reached over the seat to make a couple of adjustments on the scammer. Then she buckled in again and quickly read their position on the instruments.

"Almost on them," she said softly, although of course no one outside could hear them through the cabin walls. "Safeties off. Let's get them!"

Their floater lurched free of the clouds and straight into the melee. Four of the floaters were decorated like all the machinery at Mattapoisett. The other five (nine, not eight, she counted) were khaki-colored and leaner in construction. Their motors were loud and they left a trail of dark exhaust whenever they climbed.

Hawk carried them right into the midst of the fracas. The noise deafened her, clutching the scammer. When she saw one of the khaki floaters making at them, she shot the weapon and hoped for the best. A bolt of light ribboned out. Hawk kept them twisting, climbing, dipping, she turned upside down and flipped over and came about again till Connie had no idea what was up and what was down. A floater fell in flames into the sea, but she could not tell whose it was. They were fast, supremely maneuverable. It felt like a contest of hummingbirds. It felt like a scrap of dragonflies glinting and humming, turning over and round with their terrible teeth and claws. The floaters were beautiful even in mortal combat. The soft furry bellies of the clouds hung into the fight. The cold gray scales of the flank of the sea tipped and angled. Sometimes Hawk brought them so low that Connie could see the foam on the crests of the waves, see the spreading stain where the floater had gone down.

Piloted into death by a twelve-year-old, she thought. Between the clouds and the vast sea sweeping off into a fog bank, she felt tiny. They were shrunken to the size of insects, of midges and gnats turning in the air. Then she stared at Luciente and her sense of size and proportion returned.

With a red scarf tied around her head to keep her unruly hair from her eyes, Luciente was calm, cheerful at the jizer. She rode out the twists and turns, the plummetings and the shuddering escalations of the floater with apparent pleaure, as if she were riding a spirited horse. Her body moved easily, not freezing in panic as Connie's did in a futile effort to maintain some reference point of up and down. Luciente swayed and rolled, constantly adjusting her aim.

Hawk carried them down through the center of the fight again. Another floater fell past, broken, burning. This time she could see it was a khaki machine. She tried to count the floaters as they bore in. Perhaps there was one less of each.

Then they were careening in and out among the floaters, spouting forked lightning. She aimed and fired and tried not to lose her way in the twists and turns. Suddenly a khaki floater ran dead at them from five o'clock, straight as if it meant to ram. Just as it came as close as the distance across a ward, the enemy turned abruptly and hung there like a huge mosquito, the jizer preparing to fire on her as she took aim herself and fired. She caught a clear glimpse of the enemy through the bubble glass: the thick glasses, the aquiline nose, the satisfied twinkly blue gaze of Dr. Redding as briskly, efficiently, he shot off the jizer.

As the blasts met in the air, the air itself seemed to buckle and time to pause, humped up in a wave that could not yet fall. She saw that the pilot of the enemy floater was pasty Dr. Morgan, clutching the controls with white knuckles and secretively wetting his lips. Dodging about in the back seat, trying futilely to bring the scammer into action, meticulous Dr. Argent glowered, tossing his silvery hair and dressed in a morning coat, elegant down to the red carnation in his lapel.

She glanced around and saw all the enemy floaters zeroing in on them as if summoned to this attack. As she stared to left and right she saw that they were piloted and manned by Judge Kerrigan, who had taken her daughter, by the social worker Miss Kronenberg, by Mrs. Polcari, by Acker and Miss Moynihan, by all the caseworkers and doctors and landlords and cops, the psychiatrists and judges and child guidance counselors, the informants and attendants and orderlies, the legal aid lawyers copping pleas, the matrons and EEG technicians, and all the other flacks of power who had pushed her back and turned her off and locked her up and medicated her and tranquilized her and punished her and condemned her. They were all closing in, guns blazing. Then the air burst into golden-red flames and she heard Dr. Redding crow, "Right on the button. That does it. Okay, into the ambulance with her."

She was rushed south to the university hospital again and injected for the operation. They shaved her head clean of its bristling mat and once again she was bald as an onion.

The operation took less than half the time of the one before. They removed the dialytrode entirely and closed the wound with dentist's cement. They were going to leave her alone for a while. But they were not done with her, she sensed that.

Two days later she was back on the ward, her bald head bandaged but the evil machine gone from her body and her soul. She beamed thanks to Luciente if she was still alive. Could Luciente have died in the burning floater? But the scene made no sense. Her head still ached and she had trouble remembering exactly.

But she did know something new. The war raged outside her body now, outside her skull, but the enemy would press on and violate her frontiers again as soon as they chose their next advance. She was at war.

She strove to display good patient behavior. She cooperated, she smiled and played up to the staff. She played the nice polite eager humble patient game for all she was worth, because she wanted that damned machine to stay out of her head.

"I do think it helped me," she lied earnestly to Acker. "I feel much calmer. Those blackouts scared me."

"Well, that won't happen again. We try one course of treatment, but we stand ready to switch to a better one if the first has unexpected side effects," Acker said importantly, playing doctor for Miss Moynihan, who was standing behind him. "Sometimes a patient may express an allergy to penicillin. We have to use another antibiotic. Similarly, you proved to be, let's say, allergic to the dialytrode. . . . " He trailed off as he saw Dr. Redding standing in the doorway with his eyebrows raised.

"Allergic, mm?" he said. "How's our problem this morning?"

"I feel fine," Connie said desperately. "Ever so much better!"

Redding put down the mug of steaming coffee he had been carrying and peered into her eyes and poked her. "There's evidence repeated stimulation of foci in the amygdala can produce results," he muttered. "Still . . . probably temporary."

Connie got up as soon as they left and sat in the lounge, ready to start conversations with one and all. She combed her wig and tidied her clothes. She ate her food, she took an interest, she spoke to the staff politely and with deference. She sat with Tina, whose head hurt and hurt and hurt. She held Tina's limp small brown hand, scarred and calloused from who knew how many jobs and battles, the tip of a finger missing. Tina roused herself to say soggily that it had been caught in a machine in a box factory. She had been only temporary, so she hadn't got anything for it. Instead she was fired. "Oh, how my head hurts. Make them give me something! Go to them and ask!"

Staff were relieved to see Connie on her feet again. She had been more work in withdrawal. Now she was not only caring for herself, but volunteering constantly. They finally gave Tina morphine or something like it, letting her drift over into doper's heaven, that still, high place she had entered too many times before when she had been hurt and defeated. Then Tina was as gone from the room as if she had died.

"You're doing much better," Nurse Roditis said approvingly to Connie, and actually smiled. "Now you want to get better."

"Oh, yes." She forced a stiff smile. "I want to get well now." War, she thought, I'm at war. No more fantasies, no more hopes. *War.*

Eighteen

IF it isn't Ms. Model Patient, knocking herself out for a kind word from Nurse, Sybil hissed as she came upon Connie sweeping the day room.

She winced and held her tongue, but the injustice fretted her. How could Sybil lack faith? She wanted to turn and shout after Sybil's back that when she, Connie, had tried to escape, Sybil had been scared to go with her. But Sybil had been put in isolation for helping her. Sybil was still untouched. The staff was watching Captain Cream and Tina carefully to see how their implantations worked out before they proceeded with more, even thought it set back their schedule. Still, all stages were present on the ward, before, during and after: the casualties, the experiments, and the fresh material. Five thousand chimpanzees in their cages.

"I don't dream no more," Captain Cream complained. "How come I can't dream? Something missing."

Tina was high on pain killers and complained only when the magic pills were delayed.

Taking a shrewd and wary interest, volunteering for every task defined as women's work, cleaning, sweeping, helping with the other patients, picking up clothes, fetching and carrying for the nurses, Connie tried to gauge her chance for escape. This was a fancy teaching hospital, less grim, less grimy and overcrowded than Bellevue or

Rockover. Most of the patients were short-term and all the other wards were unlocked. If the hospital could not process the patients in a couple of months, they were shipped off to state or private hospitals, depending on means. Most of them seemed to be middle-class white people with marriage or job problems. All wore their own clothes and had doctors assigned.

This was the only mental hospital she'd ever been in where doctors actually saw patients. She had no idea what went on. The first time she'd been committed, when she belived herself truly sick, she had expected treatment. A kindly gray doctor, a sort of Marcus Welby of the mind, would sit behind a desk asking her questions in a learned but soothing voice, explaining to her exactly how she had gone wrong. She would weep and understand. Confessional. Priests that healed. But all the doctor asked in the five minutes granted her had been the name of the President, the date, why she thought she was there. Then he had told her to count backward from one hundred by sevens.

That counting backward gave her trouble. Somehow, in changing schools from Texas to Chicago, she had missed some arithmetic. Never could she figure a tip or catch the cashier at the superette cheating her, even though she would count over her change, squinting at her palm to con the cashier into thinking she knew what was going on. Let's see—one hundred, ninety-three, eighty-six, seventy-nine, seventy-two . . . A pang of fear tweaked her. Shouldn't it have been seventy? She'd done it wrong again. Seven tens were seventy; she knew that. She had gone wrong again. . . .

If she could get through the locked ward door, she was convinced she could escape the hospital. A guard stood on duty in the lobby, but he hardly ever stopped people. Many outpatients came and went, and furloughs for inpatients were common. She knew she could make it, once past that ward door. But because she had run away, they watched her even more closely than the others. Whenever she loitered near the door, the attendants or the nurse would ask what she thought she was doing. She ran out of excuses. Sometimes she would hang around the nursing station making conversation with staff in order to keep an eye on the door, trying to shape a plan for getting through it, but if she looked at the door too much they got suspicious. Then she would try to redeem herself by offering to make coffee for them. The doctors had their own fancy automatic coffee machine in an alcove outside the conference room. Redding drank ten to fourteen cups a day, and the secretary Patty or one of the aides or attendants made it fresh every couple of hours. The lower staff sometimes drank the doctors' coffee, but mostly used an electric percolator in the little kitchen. Sometimes patients were allowed to use the percolator or to drink an occasional cup of coffee in the afternoon. For Connie that made a big difference, keeping her awake enough to plot and think.

"I'm sorry you didn't make it out," she said to Tina as they got ready for bed.

Tina did not answer for a while. Then she said in a soft, remote voice, "My man, the only man I ever loved all the way through and through. Down to the pit of my stomach. They sent him up for thirty years. It might as well be life. Twice a year I get up to see him. Fifteen minutes through a grille. He's getting old fast there. His hair's coming out and his teeth. . . It might as well be for life!"

At bedtime, as Connie was sloshing in the murk of drugged sleep, Skip walked lightly through the rooms of the ward and paused at the foot of her bed. In death his hair had grown out and he had regained his loose-limbed grace. "Come along," he called to her over the sleeping Tina. "Aren't you coming? Shuffle off with me, my dearie-o! Don't let them steal the best of you."

What was it, her Catholic upbringing that kept her from thinking about suicide? Just as contraception had always felt more of a sin than falling into bed. Somehow it was not in her. "I have my own way," she told Skip, muttering on the drafty back porch of sleep in the wind that blew through the sepia screens from the cold world's end where they piled the corpses. In the bleak moonlight she whispered to Skip. "I'm fighting too. Even now, when like you I bow, I lick their feet, I crawl and beg, I am biding my time. Wait and see what I do."

At lunch of macaroni and a little cheese she said to Sybil, "No trust? After all this time you don't know me?"

"How can I know my friend when I see her kowtowing to the Inquisition?" Sybil sipped her milk as if it were wine, looking down her arched and bony nose.

"We're at war, Sybil, don't you see that?"

"Some war! More like a massacre." Sybil snorted. "Soon

to be burned at the stake—the small stake. More cost-effective, as the grand master says."

"It's a *war*, Sybil. . . . If I could get out on furlough, I know I could run for it. The city's so close here. Once off this ward, we'd have it made! People come in and out of this building all day, outpatients, volunteers. If only I could make it to the elevators!"

"There's a lot more coming and going, yes," Sybil said thoughtfully, "but also more personnel. I have not yet seen the nursing station empty."

"You've been watching too."

Sybil smiled. "The volunteers, some are college girls. The hippie one who comes in Thursdays, Mary Ellen? Nurse Roditis told her that, quote, I *think* I'm a witch and go around hexing people, unquote. Mary Ellen came and asked me, quote, if I was into herbs."

"So what did you say?" She felt close to her friend.

"I said I was into this ward, although unwillingly. But I'm interested in herbs and have done some healing with them."

"Was she making fun of you?"

Sybil shook her head. "She told me lots of college students are interested in herbs. We discussed valerian, thyme, rosemary, comfrey. Finally she asked if I really was a witch, and when I assured her, she seemed quite pleased. She said several of her friends are 'into' witchcraft. She said she's trying to secure permission for one of her friends to meet me."

"You don't think she was . . . laughing inside the way they do?"

"No, Consuelo. She'd read a herbal and cured a leg infection with lovage compresses. We had the most civilized conversation I've had in ages. Except for yourself, of course. I was worried about you when they had that device in your head."

"Ah, I don't know herbs from weeds." She thought of Luciente feeding her that wild greenery and her mouth opened to tell Sybil. She shut it, then after a moment said, "My grandmother knew weeds to heal with. But even my parents made fun of that. It wasn't modern and scientific—like going in the hospital and dying of an infection!"

"Imagine, college girls studying witchcraft. She said there was a class in a women's school. I never heard of such a thing. If only I could have attended college, Consuelo . . . I am self-educated. I wanted to go to school, wanted it a great deal."

"Me too. I went for almost two years."

"I started part time. In night school. But it was expensive. I'd have to come home quite late at night, and then get up early to go to work. . . . I should have continued, Consuelo. I should have had the discipline!"

"It takes more than discipline. It takes money. It takes good public transportation."

"I wonder who teaches them witchcraft. Imagine"—Sybil's voice caressed her ear, tickling like a warm tongue—"a secret network of covens all over New York! Imagine the bars crumbling on the windows. Imagine the doctors fainting in the halls! The locks melting and running like thin soup to the floor!"

"Don't dawdle over your lunch, girls. Come on, make it snappy." The orderly Tony urged them along, swinging the keys in time to his transistor. He wrapped himself in music all day to insulate himself from the hospital, the patients, the boredom. "Tum di-tum, you just march it along."

"We can imagine all we like. But we got to do something real," Connie said plaintively. "I'm just trying to create some space by kissing up to them."

Sybil shook her head at the expression. "If we can figure out a way, I'm willing."

Dolly buzzed in, all in yellow. "Hi, Connie doll. Listen, I talked to Daddy. He says maybe he'll let you visit. How about that?" She kissed Connie, wrapping her in a cloud of perfume. "He says for sure him and Adele are going to visit you here."

"What, they need him to sign another permission?"

"He says he wants to see you. The hospital told him you're better. Look, I brought you a real chic wig. Black, the way you said you wanted. Pues, Tía? Give me a smile."

Valente and Sybil and Miss Green and even Tina, nodding out a little on the bed's edge, gathered around Dolly and her. Most of Dolly's precious visit got wasted on the wig. The wig was put on and she was commanded, among oohing and ahing, to stare at herself. Her bleary bloodshot eyes, her chapped and bitten lips, her hospital ashiness looked out from under sleek hair curled and combed just so, black and elegant. The wig felt heavy and she sat bearing it up on her short neck like a crown.

"Dolly, please!" She clutched her niece's arm. "Get me out of here. Let me come home to visit you. I don't want to spend Thanksgiving here. Please talk to them about letting me come home to you for Thanksgiving. I'll cook for you, hermana mía. Remember how I used to? We'll get Nita and have a real Thanksgiving!"

"Maybe, Connie. I got a convention coming up. I need the green stuff."

"On Thanksgiving itself? I wouldn't get in your way. I could sit in the library. I could take Nita to the movies. Or the zoo. I could take Nita to Central Park zoo and we could give the monkeys peanuts."

"Not to worry, Connie. Daddy says maybe you can visit him. You talk to Daddy. I wish I didn't have to work the holidays, but that's business. But now you look ten years younger!"

When Tina was taken off for testing, Sybil sat on her bed and sighed. "Good try with your niece. But it's true, that wig has some use. It covers the funny hole. You wouldn't get far without someone noticing that.

"What good does it do if I can't get out of here?"

She was standing in line at the nursing station the next night. "Nurse, please can I call my brother? I got the change right here."

"Where do you want to call?"

"Bound Brook, New Jersey."

"Calling out of state, you can't do that."

"But I got the change. Just to my brother. Look, see, please, he's on my visiting list."

"Has he been around?"

"No, but he promised."

"Why do you want to call him?"

Your life was everybody's business to rummage through. "I just want to talk about how his family is. To tell him I'm better. Maybe to talk about if they won't come and see me at Thanksgiving."

"Okay. But no trouble. I don't want you pestering your family from here."

There was a terrible line by the phone, nine people ahead of her. Talking to Luis was no pleasure anytime, but she had to work on him about Thanksgiving. They had to let her out for the holiday, they just had to. She didn't give a wink for a stuffed bird; they could stuff it with dollar bills and eat it with a sauce of Arpege. But she had to grasp the chance to run, before they operated on her. That one chance skinnier than a hair, than one of her own lost black hairs.

For an hour and twenty minutes she stood on one foot and then the other, waiting for the telephone. She was sweating with fear it would be time to line up for evening meds before she ever got her hands on the telephone. Finally she dialed. Don't let it be busy, she begged. Santa Marta, please let them be home and don't let it be busy and make Luis answer in a good mood, I beg of you, please!

"Hello?"

Carefully she pronounced the name the Anglo way, the way he liked it. "Loo-is? Hello, is this Lewis?"

"Yeah, who's this? Who am I talking to?"

"It's Connie. Your sister."

"Yeah?" A nice heavy silence like an avalanche of mud slid through the phone.

Desperately she forged on. "I'm calling from the hospital. They say I'm much better. Lewis, they say I'm much better and I feel really good."

"That's nice. You got in a good hospital now, you know that? It's a first-rate hospital. If they were making you pay for it, you couldn't walk in the front door, you know that?"

"Sure, Lewis. How's the family? How's Adele? How's Mike and Susan?" For an awful minute she thought she had the name of the new baby wrong. She had only been to Luis's home once since the baby was born. Maybe it wasn't Susan at all?

"Mike's fine, he's talking all the time now, give me this, give me that! He's his mother's kid, all right. Susan's teething, so she squawks all the time, but she's pretty as a picture. She's a real blond, yellow hair straight as a ruler. She's going to be a winner, this one."

"That's good, Lewis, that's wonderful. I wish I could see Susan. I wish I could see you. How's Adele?"

"She's fine. She got a new foxtail coat. Good-looking. She wanted mink but she's going to want that for a long time, if business doesn't pick up. It's a bad time for the nursery business, all over. People aren't spending money the way they did two, three years ago, construction is way down. Except for fruit trees. Lot of people are putting fruit trees in their yards in the suburbs. We've tripled our business in fruit trees. But that's like a one-time thing. People don't buy a new apple tree every year."

"Dolly came in to see me, she said maybe you might come?"

"Sure, Connie. Just it's hard to get the time. Weekends are the only time and the traffic is miserable."

"Maybe I could come to you, then . . . Lewis." She almost slipped and said Luis in her excitement. "Maybe for Thanksgiving I could visit you? I wouldn't be any work. I could help Adele. I'd love to see the babies."

"Yeah?" He didn't add anything, till the operator interrupted. She stuck in more coins. She had saved a good supply.

"At least maybe for a day, Lewis, for Thanksgiving, just overnight? It's so lonely in the hospital at holiday time. A real family holiday. Everybody goes home. The doctor says I'm much better. You could talk to him, Dr. Redding. Please, Lewis?"

"We'll see. You'd have to go back Saturday morning because Saturday night we're giving a party. But you could help around some. We'll have enough food to feed an army, we always do. . . ."

"I could help Adele cook and clean. You know I can cook real well, Lewis, remember? I can help you get ready for the party. It's a lot of work for Adele."

"Oh, she has a woman in once a week."

"But for the holidays, it's a lot of work. I can help and I wouldn't mind going back Saturday. I wouldn't mind at all. That would just be so lovely, to come and see you all Thanksgiving."

"Well, we might do that. I'll talk to the doctor."

"Dr. Redding, Dr. Redding, please?" She was trotting alongside to get his attention. "I talked to my brother, and him and his wife, they'd take me for Thanksgiving. I could have Thanksgiving dinner with them? It would be so nice. You said I'm better."

"Does your brother want you there?"

"He said yes. He said he did. He said I could help his wife." She trotted alongside. "He said he'll call you about it."

"He hasn't. We'll see." He dismissed her with a brusque

nod. "Morgan, has Moynihan taken a reading on her this week? I want to keep her monitored."

As Dr. Morgan took her off to Miss Moynihan's EEG machine, he commented on the cologne. "Is that for me?" he said, laughing at her as if she were an idiot. "How nice!" He made fun of her all the time because he wasn't afraid of her; she was too small to scare him the way Sybil did and Alice had.

For the EEG testing, she was taken off ward and up two floors. Always in the elevator her heart beat quickly and she imagined the opportunity of going down instead of going up, and out into the streets, whose gutters were full of the torrents of cold November rain. Miss Moynihan had made her leave her wig and purse behind, but she could still bolt if given a moment, a door.

Miss Moynihan was going to use the second room, with the ten-track machine on her today. Connie was so used to the routine by now she sat docile as at a beauty parlor while Miss Moynihan combed apart what little hair she had and marked her targets, used the jelly and the tape to glue the electrodes on, then slapped a gauze pad over. The wires led off to the chart on a machine near her head as she lay down and Miss Moynihan slid a rolled-up towel under her neck. Then Miss Moynihan turned the lights very dim. She had a patter she used that was supposed to relax the patients. "Now, here we go today. You're an old hand at this by now. Just relax. But don't you go to sleep on me. Just relax and get a little beauty rest. . . ."

Miss Moynihan sat outside the cubicle at the machine, whose ten pens scribbled away as the accordion piles of paper raced out from the face covered with dials. Miss Moynihan spoke in a carefully flat tone to her. "Close your eyes. . . Open your mouth slightly. . . . Open your eyes. . . ." As the pens rushed on, she wrote obscure notations that always made Connie terribly suspicious.

She had her favorite fantasy as she lay there. Miss Moynihan would be called away. She would be called to the phone. A family emergency. Did she have a family? Yes, patient gossip had it that her mother was dead, her father worked for the subway, her older brother was a building inspector, and her younger brother was still in school. . . . "Try not to move your eyes so much or I'll have to tape them. Relax. Open your mouth again slightly and keep it that way."

Miss Moynihan would be called to the phone and she would sit up at once, pull the electrodes off, and quietly walk past the two desks in the outer room, where sometimes a woman sat and sometimes no one at all, turn right, and bolt down the stairway at the end of the hall. She could see herself doing that again and again. . . . "Try to relax, Mrs. Ramos. Just let yourself go. Relax."

She would walk south to Harlem through the beautiful clean rain. Miss Moynihan's father could not stand Acker, the patients said. Romeo and Juliet. A doomed romance. Miss Moynihan had beautiful soft gray eyes, in which everything seemed to dissolve. She bustled about, efficient, hard, bouncy, but in her eyes chaos swirled. Connie decided Miss Moynihan was hoping to get pregnant. With so many beds in a hospital, it must be easy for them to make love. . . . Miss Moynihan tapped on the machine, hard taps, as if she could read her mind. They tapped that way sometimes. She never understood why. Did Miss Moynihan think she was falling asleep? Suppose she suddenly went over to Mattapoisett—what would Miss Moynihan's machine show? Was Luciente dead? Why did she never feel her anymore?

It was the week before Thanksgiving. Captain Cream had had the final operation and sat about with a bandage on his head. He had to be dressed and he ate so slowly he drove Tony wild. He ate almost as much as Alice. Connie had the feeling, watching him, that he would go on eating all day at the same maddeningly slow rate as long as they stuck food in front of him. He would go on doing whatever he was started doing. If he was taken to the toilet, he would sit there until somebody remembered to fetch him off. Alice slumped in the lounge, withdrawn and creepy. Orville, with an implant, made jokes no one else found funny and giggled all day. Alvin called them the three stooges, but he did not seem to find that funny himself. Alvin was scheduled for surgery the next Monday, along with Miss Green. He would have been done already, but Dr. Redding had won his invitation to Dr. Argent's hunting lodge, and took off a long weekend.

Connie worked at being a model patient. She did jigsaw puzzles, she watched television, she entered all conversations, she asked advice and agreed, she kept her wig straight on her itchy scalp and tended it like a prize poodle. She volunteered and volunteered. She was ward housewife. Next time she asked she got permission easily to call her brother.

The line was longer, everyone with the same problem, whining, begging, trying to charm. Only one thought fizzled through the whole spacy line. When she got to the phone, the damn number was busy. By the time she got back near the head again, it was lights out.

The next night, after an hour and ten minute wait, she got through. "Lewis, it's me, Connie, again. I was just wondering about Thanksgiving?"

"Yeah, maybe Christmas. How're you doing?"

"The doctor says I'm better—did you talk to him? What's wrong with Thanksgiving? Christmas is so far away." By Christmas she'd be operated on. "Remember, I was going to help Adele cook and clean and get ready for your party? Please. Lewis, please!"

"You've never proved much of a worker, Connie. There's a lot of work to do. We'd probably do better having the cleaning woman put in an extra day."

"I'll work, Lu—Lewis, I'll work! Ask them here if I don't clean up the whole ward. If I don't sweep and mop up and dust. I learned a lesson, please let me show you. I want so bad to get out for Thanksgiving!"

"Guess it's lonely in the hospital, huh, Connie?" He was playing cat and mouse with her.

Her hand sweated on the greasy receiver. The gray butter of human anxiety. "Please, my brother, let me visit you. Let me help Adele. Let me see my nephew and my niece. I'll clean and cook. I'll do the dishes. I'll make the house shine!"

"You never were much of a housekeeper, unless they taught you something. Besides, we're fixing the house up with a tropical motif, going to put plants everywhere. You don't like to work around the nursery, remember? You said the sprays gave you a headache."

"That was years ago! I'll work so hard you'd have to hire four men to do the work I'll do for you. Just let me out of here for a couple of days. Just let me be with you a little!"

"I'll take it under advisement. Don't call again. I'll let the hospital know if I decide to give it a try." He hung up.

Shaking with anger, she left the pay phone. She despised herself for begging to be given the privilege of scrubbing Luis's floors in Bound Brook. Claud would have stopped speaking to her if he'd heard that conversation; he'd have taken off like a shot. But it is war, she thought. I am conducting undercover operations. I am behind enemy lines and I must wear a smiling mask. It is all right for me to beg and crawl and wheedle because I am at war. They will see how I forgive. That made her feel stronger.

Sybil was waiting for her in the lounge. "What did he say?"

"Maybe, he said. He wouldn't let me off the hook by letting me know one way or the other."

Sybil touched her shoulder lightly. "Well, Thanksgiving together . . . I've had worse."

Only Alice, Captain Cream and Connie were let out on Thanksgiving furlough to relatives. Connie put on her old turquoise dress that fitted a little loose, and straightened the new wig on her head. Everybody was clucking and cooing over her except Sybil, who hung back, and Alice, who sat like a wrapped present in the hall, waiting. Sybil managed to catch Connie for a moment to whisper, "I hope you . . . fly away."

"I'm going to try."

Briefly, before the attendant could catch them ("No PC!"—physical contact—the slogan of the ward), they kissed. "I hope I never see you again," Sybil whispered. "My dear friend, run!"

Luis's house had an upstairs, a downstairs, and a level in between, most of it open space without doors or walls, like a big hospital ward. Rooms, rooms upon rooms. She was led up stairs covered with gold carpeting that must show dirt easily, to a room on the top floor. She had a bathroom all to herself, with a shower and a toilet and a wash basin and a mirror, a full-length mirror on the back of the door. She had not seen herself entire in months. The basin was like a vanity table, everything white with gold trim.

The room had twin beds, and she felt dizzy at the thought of choosing one or the other. For a moment tears burned the inside of her eyes. She blinked. Why should a bed make her cry? For months she had not chosen anything. Luis dropped her little overnight bag on one bed, so she decided to sleep in the other. She felt relieved. So much space around her, it was almost frightening. It made her dizzy, it distracted her as if it were freedom instead of fancier imprisonment.

The room had one window, covered with filmy blue curtains and white and gold Venetian blinds. Quickly she pried two of the slats apart to look out. Ay, too bad! She stared down two stories onto a concrete paved area floodlit by a fixture high on the house. An outdoor fireplace was set into one side of the area, before the yard sloped away into shrubbery. No way out through this window.

The yard was elegantly planted, with borders swooping in and out in drifts of pine and juniper, but in the night and the cold, it looked only bleak. The ground was frozen and bare. Through the glare of light surrounding the house to protect it against burglars, she could not see whether the night was clear or cloudy. She hoped it would not snow. That would make it harder to get away. She wished that Luis had invited her out a few more times in the past so that she knew something of the area. Which way would she walk to get to public transportation? She must figure that out.

Without knocking, Adele opened the door. "If you want to set the table, we're going to have pie and coffee before we turn in."

They were crazy, for they did just that: drank coffee from a blue and white electric percolator just before going to bed, along with a boughten apple pie. The pie tasted wonderful. She could have eaten the whole thing. A terrible desire to eat and eat and eat seized her throat. Food that had flavors. By shifting to the right in her chair she could see the refrigerator in the kitchen, huge and golden brown. It kept drawing her sleepy gaze, all that golden space crammed with food. She had seen it when she got out the nondairy creamer for their coffee. She had seen the turkey defrosting. The freezer was stacked with steaks and roasts and chops, with vegetables in bright cartons. She had seen gallons of milk, a pound of butter, vegetables in the crispers, salad dressings half used, real eggs, orange juice in cartons. She imagined herself rising slowly from her chair and with her Thorazine shuffle—she had been especially heavily doped that day in preparation for her furlough—stumbling into the kitchen to the refrigerator, sitting down on the floor, and pulling out one item at a time until she had eaten everything in the whole golden box. It all called to her in wonderful soprano siren voices: the jar of olives, the chunky peanut butter, the salami, the liverwurst in the opened package, the jar of maraschino cherries, the cheddar cheese, the packaged dip, the bacon, the eggs, the chocolate pudding from the dairy case, the soda, the big round bright pieces of fruit.

They seemed to eat very quickly. Luis talked nonstop about his day. He spoke quickly and he talked a lot and he didn't like interruptions: in that he was like the brother she had had all her life. But this middle-aged overweight businessman in the dark gray suit and the wide tie with its narrow dim stripe, the round moon face bulging into jowls, the forehead that ran well back to the middle of his scalp, the fat fingers with a lodge ring that remained braced on the table as he talked as though he feared if he let go of them they would fly up—did she know him from someplace?

" 'They all got brown spots on their leaves,' he says to me. 'They're no good. I paid you six hundred to do the foyer and they all got brown spots.' 'That was a special price I gave you,' I said. 'They're worth twice that now.' 'All covered with brown spots,' he said. 'Listen,' I said, 'I could have done the job with plastic. We have a beautiful selection of plastic. You wanted live ones. Now look, the world is full of diseases and bugs. You could've signed up for my service. My boys come around every month regular as clockwork and they mop off the leaves and they exterminate and they put in the fertilizer. We keep it up. Something kicks off, we replace. It's insurance. But you weren't interested. Now you complain to me that some pest has got into your greens. Of course some pest got in. What did you think—you can put up a sign and say no insects allowed? You don't keep up an investment, it's money down the drain.' " Luis told the story with satisfaction. "Let that fool paint the leaves green. Trying to cut corners with me. When I do a job like that at a competitive price, I expect the service contract."

Adele sat taking little nibbles of pie and nodding her head and making soft noises to accompany the loud fast rattle of his voice without interrupting it: um, Adele said, um hum, oh dear, mmm. She looked critically at her nails. Mostly she kept her eyes near his face, while her mind drifted high as a kite on some other wind. Once she smiled quickly, a loose bedroom face, and then smoothed her features over.

Adele blurred into Shirley, Luis's second and Italian wife, responsible for getting him into her family's nursery business. Somehow Luis had emerged from the marriage with a chunk of it. He was that way. Shirley had dark brown hair and a full pouting mouth and a full-blown temper. She had lasted as long as she had because of the business. Yet she had sat there many years saying um hum, oh dear, uh huh, mmm. And Carmel before her. All Luis's wives came to sound the same, nodding at him, but each one was fancier and had a higher polish. Each one was lighter. Each one spent more money. Carmel had been for hard times. Shirley was for getting set up in business. Adele was for making money in bushels and spending it.

When Adele noticed that Luis had run down for the moment, she asid, "No gardenias this time. They have too strong a smell. It gives me a headache."

"Okay, no gardenias. Yeah, they smell like cheap soap." Luis nodded, looking pleased. He collected distinctions, judgments, he always had. At eleven years old he was saying seriously, "You know, a Cadillac is a better car than a Chrysler?" Their family's ancient gray Ford had given way to an only slightly less ancient rust-colored Hudson. Her father had driven maybe the world's last Hudson. It was chocolate-colored and the body was already rusting into shreds when they got it. It suggested a lump of dog shit on wheels.

An hour after they had all gone to bed, she got up. Then she discovered that Luis had locked her in. She pushed and pushed on the door and then she tried to stick a comb in between the door and the jamb to push the catch back. It would not slide in. She turned back and slowly undressed. This was only Wednesday night. She had Thursday and Friday. He might forget to lock the door. She might find a key that fit it. He might get careless. A knife might work. Weary, heavy with drug, she let herself fall into the strange soft bed and dissolve into sleep.

"You're dreadfully slow," Adele complained. "My

cleaning lady gets that done in forty-five minutes."

"It's the drug. It slows me down. They gave me a real heavy shot so I can hardly move."

"It seems to me you move fast enough when it's time to eat." Adele was consulting a list. Everywhere she had lists—of groceries, of dry-cleaning, of jobs to be done, of people to be called. All morning, while Connie was cleaning and making desserts from the recipe books Adele shoved at her, not trusting her to cook on her own as she knew perfectly how to do, Adele was writing lists at a desk she had at the end of the kitchen. Every list made more work. Connie gripped the handle of the vacuum till her hand ached and took a deep breath and did not allow herself a word. She swept the yellow carpeting while before her the tropical fish Luis always kept swam to and fro in their glass prison in the living room, under the murmur of the bubbler.

Breakfast had been bacon and eggs and toast with strawberry jam and lots of real coffee from the blue and white percolator. All morning whenever she could sneak a chance to do it, she made and drank coffee. How wonderful she felt. Lunch was the next high point. Adele was talking on the phone and told her to help herself to leftovers. First she had a cheese and salami sandwich with a big mug of coffee, sweet and light the way she loved it. She heated the milk first. Then she ate a lot more cheese and salami without bread, so it wouldn't fill her up too fast.

Each time she opened the door to that paradise of golden possibilities, she felt buffeted by choice. Deciding was so difficult she could hardly move her hand. Too much. She felt like weeping with joy. She went back and forth from the dinette to the refrigerator, carrying each time one new treasure—a piece of leftover apple pie, more cheese, this kind white and blue like the coffeepot and strong-smelling, a golden delicious apple, chicken salad in a bowl. Finally Adele marched over, five phone calls later, and said, "You can't still be eating lunch? Really! Lew said you were here to help me, and I have to watch you every minute, just as if you were the hired cleaning lady!"

Connie put on the turkey according to a recipe Adele had clipped from a slick women's magazine, having filled it with a mix of nuts, cornmeal, mushrooms, green peppers, and raisins. Adele had her cover the poor bird with aluminum foil, although Connie knew that would spoil the bird and steam the skin. She obeyed. She felt drunk with food. Her time sense was altered by all the coffee. The world seemed to have slowed down as she speeded up. On the ward, hours passed and she never knew where they had gone. Now she felt as if she were running and when she looked at the clock an hour later, only fifteen minutes were used up. The drug and the caffeine battled in her, and she felt high and fast.

Candied sweet potatoes made from a can! As if she didn't know real ways to cook sweet potatoes. Eddie had loved yams. She remembered the time she had told Luciente that with some money and a decent kitchen, she was a good cook! How many ways she had learned to cook in her life: Mexican, Puerto Rican, soul food, and what Professor Silvester called continental. All good food. She wished she could be cooking a feast for Luciente and Bee. She pretended she was making a Thanksgiving dinner for Luciente's whole family, and for Sybil and Tina Ortiz too. They would all meet and sit down to feast together and they would drink wine and make jokes and maybe she would even, only politely for the season but with feeling, kiss Bee one last time. Then she would be the one cautioning Luciente to remember that the food was not nourishing, was not real, out of your own time!

She and Adele put all the boards into the dining room table, making it very long, and then covered it with snowy linen and set it with china and real silver plate and silver-plated salvers for breads and rolls and crystal goblets, except for the little children, who got ruby-tinted glasses for their milk. Luis came in to open the wine himself with a fuss, a sparkling rosé.

Now Luis sat at the table's head in a chair with arms, carving the huge turkey with an electric knife he flourished wildly. The strange stuffing he had already piled in a big bowl. On his right and left were Mark and Bob, his sons by his second marriage. Next to Bob, Dolly was dressed up in a jade green pants suit with a ruffled copper chiffon blouse, looking gorgeous and wound tight enough for her head suddenly to fly off. Nervousness ticked in her throat like a bomb. Delicately she ate green olives from a glass dish. Neither Shirley nor Carmel was there, of course, left to their own devices. Luis liked to command the attendance of all his children at Thanksgiving, Christmas and Easter, having the money to back up his commands. But Nita was missing. Carmel had insisted she was too sick to go. Then came Celeste, Adele's eight-year-old from her first marriage, Connie herself, and then baby Susan in her high chair on one side of Adele and the toddler Mike on the other side.

Luis, big with pleasure, lorded it now over his full plate and the dinners of everyone else. "Mark, you take more potatoes. That's how come you're so skinny. Makes you weak. That's why you didn't make the football team. Now, you try out for wrestling, listen to me—you can be skinny in wrestling. You wrestle in your own weight class, see?"

Mark grew red in the face and his fork slumped in his hand.

"Now take Dolly. She doesn't need to eat to get fat. She just looks at the potatoes and she gains weight, right?"

"I'm not fat, Daddy. I've lost all the weight I need to."

"It won't last. It's heredity. Look at your mother. If I didn't work as hard as I do, I'd be as fat as she is."

Luis was fat. He'd been fat for twenty years, but he refused to admit it. He talked about weight all the time. He wanted his women to be thin for him, she thought, wondering if she could ask for more turkey yet or if she should wait till it was offered. Dolly sat nervously poised for further attack from Luis. She had grown up thinking her parents married; then had come the period when Luis was proving legally he had never married and she was a bastard. Shirley's parents would never let her marry a divorced man. But then Dolly had become the child of his first marriage, and since she was eighteen she had been supposed to call him Daddy. Adele was Anglo and they didn't care how many times you got married, just so it was legal. So Dolly had slid into being his legal up-front daughter again. If only he could have divorced Connie, his sister, or made her illigitimate, how happy Luis would be!"

"Look at your aunt pack it away now. Eats like there's no tomorrow. If you ate like her, Mark, you'd make the football team for sure. Bob, why aren't you eating your sweet potatoes? Those are the best part of the meal."

"They are not. I don't like them, Dad. They taste funny."

"There's nothing funny about the way they taste. At your age you don't know what's good. . . . Celeste, what are you doing?"

Celeste jumped. She was happily swishing her candied sweet potatoes, cranberry relish, and broccoli into a multicolored mush, pressing it all together and sculpting it into castles with her fork. "Nothing."

"Adele, she's playing with her food again. That's a disgusting habit. You ought to have that put on your head to wear."

Adele blinked from her serene, faintly smiling cocoon. Connie watched her sideways, sure she was on something. No wonder Adele got on so well with Luis. She was hardly ever in the same room with him, no more than his fancy guppies swimming behind glass. She tended her two youngest with a casual smiling absentminded air, all the time off somewhere screwing seven-foot bronze angels on sunset clouds. She could not help speculating what Adele was on. Adele might just be incredibly stoned, but Connie didn't think so: she was too far off. Downers, most likely.

"Susan?" Adele focused on her baby in the high chair. "Why, she's a little darling. She ate her pudding all up!"

"It's Celeste again. Making mud pies with her food!"

"Oh, Celeste," Adele said with a sweet smile. "You can play afterward. You know that upsets your daddy." Her long thin hand laden with rings floated like a scarf through the air and sank to rest beside her scarcely touched plate.

Dolly refused seconds, which Luis seductively tried to press on her, pretending he was only teasing. Mark was still toying with his first serving. The twelve-year-old Bob ate dark meat and more dark meat, steadily ignoring everybody. He was chubby and darker than anyone else except her, with small chin and black eyes, the Indian nose. Once when he cast a quick survey down the table, she flashed him a private smile; his eyes widening with surprise, he smiled back. Mainly he seemed to be pretending nothing was real except him and the turkey. He raised a screen of strong protection between his father on his right and himself. You will not hurt me! You won't get through! the screen said. Indeed, Luis seemed to sense the barrier and he pretty much left Bob alone. He tried once. "That Cesar Chavez guy—I see they got him in jail again. Huh? You still got his picture on your bedroom wall?"

But under repeated prodding, Bob would say only, "I like him. He's got a nice face."

Connie smiled again at her tough nephew, who went to an Italian parochial school and had a picture of Chavez on his wall. At the table were those wrestling with Luis and those like Bob, Adele, herself, who were noncombatants. Bob and she rivaled Luis in how much they ate and their pleasure in eating. Adele picked politely. She was patting the baby's face with a napkin and cooing, while she floated in a sky-high hammock behind her eyes.

After the pumpkin pie, the maple nut ice cream and the coffee, Luis herded them into the living room she had decorated under his supervision with pots of pink and yellow chrysanthemums, big spidery blooms as big as baby Susan's head. Mark, Bob, Celeste and Mike galloped off to the family room one level down to watch TV, but Luis was serving drinks to the adults in the living room. Connie was excused to begin cleaning up. Dolly offered to help. Connie knew what kind of help she'd be, but looked forward to the company.

"No," Luis said. "Connie can clean up just fine. You stay with us. I don't see my big girl that often, do I?"

Dolly glanced at her little jeweled watch, then at the numberless blob of clock on the wall that Connie could never read. Vic was to come and pick Dolly up to take her back to the city, once he got done having Thanksgiving dinner with his mother in a restaurant near Leisure World retirement community.

Connie had run the glasses and dishes through the dishwasher and was just starting on the second sinkload of pots, when Dolly burst into the kitchen, weeping. Luis had been teasing her about how she had been talking about marrying Geraldo and nothing had happened.

After Dolly had wept on Connie's shoulder as so many, so countless many times before, blown her nose, and put her makeup back on layer by delicate layer in the small bathroom off the kitchen, she settled in a chair. "Why did you want so bad to spend Thanksgiving here?" Dolly asked her. "I wouldn't if I didn't have to."

"How come you have to? At least if you go to Carmel she doesn't make you cry."

"Yeah, Carmel keeps after me, she just makes me mad."

"How come you didn't bring Nita? Is she for real sick?"

"Carmel's pretending. She doesn't want to be alone on

Thanksgiving. Nita has a little cold, a drippy nose, is all. Carmel says she has her the rest of the time, she gets to keep her holidays. She only did it to spite him. I get caught in the middle. I have to get back to work. He always wants to collect everybody together like some crazy sideshow!" A moment later she was sniveling again. "How can he say I'm fat? How can he? . . . You know Adele's only nine years older than me? Just the difference between me and Mark!"

After Adele had put the little ones to bed, she wandered into the kitchen, where Connie and Dolly were putting the dishes away out of the dishwasher here and there, by chance.

"You put the good crystal in the dishwasher!" She was morose now, tense. "You could have broken it all! You don't do that with crystal. You wash it by hand, of course. Are you so lazy? Or I suppose you've never seen a good piece of crystal before." She was talking to herself. She puttered around the kitchen in low-pitched sulky anger. Dolly giggled softly; Adele appeared not to hear. We are not three women, Connie thought. We are ups and downs and heavy tranks meeting in the all-electric kitchen and bouncing off each other's opaque sides like shiny pills colliding.

She stuffed a bread knife into the hem of her dress and walked carefully upstairs, aware of its swinging and bumping. Again that night Luis locked her in. Lying stiffly on the bed, this time she heard him turn the key in the lock. She went through the empty drawers of the dresser, she went through the shelves of the medicine cabinet, finding aspirin, toothpaste, antiperspirant, shampoo, a room deodorizer. The bedroom window was closed with an air conditioner. The bathroom window opened a foot and a half after she worked on it with the knife for half an hour. Then she leaned out into that drop, two stories to concrete. No vines, no convenient fire escape, no porch or garage roof to drop to. She was still trapped. She worked on the doorjamb till she was drenched with sweat, but could not get the hall door open.

Friday was a big workday and also her last full day outside the hospital. Saturday she was to clean in the morning and then be carried back to Manhattan well before the party. Friday morning she spent cooking dishes for Saturday's buffet—three large cakes and two mousses for dessert. At two o'clock Luis came home to fetch her, taking her off to his nursery and greenhouses. The other places were just retail outlets. Here she had worked three months for Luis, transplanting, spraying.

Luis drove her over in his white Eldorado, which felt as big as the patient lounge. He had the radio on but after a while he shut it off to launch at her. She sighed and tried to dampen herself to endure.

"You seem pretty quiet this time. Not like the old Connie. Did they finally teach you a lesson in keeping your mouth shut?"

"I been helpful to Adele. Haven't I been working hard?"

"A lot harder than you're used to working. If you can call that work. You liked the food yesterday, didn't you?" He chuckled.

"I cooked it. Didn't I do a good job?"

"With Adele standing over you, sure. And careful to hide the chili powder. Yeah, you've been toned down a bit, taken down a peg or two. I bet you'd be glad for a job in the greenhouse now."

"Sure I would, Lewis. If you'd sign me out, I'd go to work tomorrow." She was craning her neck, trying to figure out where they were and how near public transportation. Maybe at the nursery she could get away. She knew exactly how to get back to Manhattan from there; she'd done it every day for three months. She had slipped the money out of her purse, in case he took that from her, and secreted it in her bra, feeling like a spy, a secret agent. It wasn't too comfortable. The stiff paper rubbed her breast. The nursery looked as it had when she'd worked there, except it was winter now and much less stock stood outside in rows, only what they grew themselves. Most of the stock was shipped to them in spring from the South, from Ohio, even from Texas, brought in by truck.

The greenhouses were full. Luis's top man, Richie, and his secretary came running after him as soon as he stepped through the door. Luis turned her over to Gino, the sixty-year-old grizzled Italian who ran the greenhouses, saying, "Keep an eye on her. She's crazy as a bedbug and she's likely to try to bolt. I don't want to be responsible to that hospital for her escape. So keep one eye on the door. I'm taking her coat to lock up, so she wouldn't get far. . . . Now, I want you both to pick out good plants for my house, for the party. We're having a tropical motif.

No gardenias. And I want perfect specimens. No curled leaves, no bug damage, nothing. You go over them and you look and look hard. I want about thirty good ones. No rubber plants. Take a big Norfolk pine. No coleus, no begonias. Take some Dutch amaryllis. Everything's labeled on the end, Connie, if you don't remember. Take a big pineapple and a few of the other fancy bromeliads. Take a careful look at the flowering maples and see if any are good enough. No cactus! Some jackass always backs into them. Gino, you pick out orchids yourself. Collect everything by the loading dock and I'll have the truck deliver it. One of the larger figs might be good. You look at them and pick out whatever's blooming best or got fruit on. There's some miniature citrus. Take a look, see if the butterfly lilies are out. Maybe a coffee tree. No Venus flytraps, none of the gruesome ones. Some fool always sticks a cigarette in. Now get moving. And use your eyes. You may be doped up, Connie, so you move like you've got lead in your britches, but I want you to use your eyes. Nothing but the best, you hear me?"

Gino helped himself to a cough drop and said nothing. After Luis left, he squinted at her, asking in his hoarse voice, "You work here one time?"

"Yeah, five years ago. For a while."

"You remember where things are? Okay. You take what he said to the loading dock. I'll look it over good for him. Listen, we got *no* white flies in here. We got the cleanest greenhouse in New Jersey." He spat into a bright handkerchief that reminded her of Luciente. "I got two thousand things to do besides worry about the boss's party. So you pick out the plants and I look them over when you finish. Okay. If you want to run away with no coat, it's sixteen degrees out there and you're crazy for sure. So you better just go to work. Yoy'll never get past the gate anyhow unless you can fly."

She picked out smart-looking plants, the ones with the shiniest leaves, the most graceful drooping foliage, the showiest flowers, the most exotic fruit. As best she could, she hauled them to the locked doors of the loading dock. A couple of times she had to yell for help, till Gino reluctantly assigned her five minutes from one of the other overworked, underpaid greenhouse employees. The pesticides had used to make her sick. She had worked long hours till her back ached and never stopped aching day and night, and it had taken her so long to come and go on public transportation she had had no time to spend with her own child. All for two dollars an hour and bad headaches. The poisons could kill if she breathed them, if they only touched her skin. Even when she wore a face mask, they got to her.

Snow was beginning, swirls of small flakes idling in the air and sticking in the crotches of bare trees in their rows outside. The only thing she could find was a smock of thin cotton, but she put that on. So she'd catch a cold! Her coat was locked up in Luis's office, but she'd go as she was. She moved slowly, ever so casually toward the door. But as she stepped outside, Richie called to her, "Where do you think you're going?" Again and again she waited and made a move, but always Gino or Luis or Richie was watching.

On impulse she walked back into the shed where poisons were stored. The cabinet was locked, but she looked behind the door and the key was still on its hook there. Like a joke, she had always thought, like having a safe and writing the combination on the wall. She unlocked the cabinet. A few of the poisons were new to her. There were the fungicides they used: zineb, Captan, sulfur. The pesticides: Sevin, malathion, Kelthane. Some came ready-mixed and some were powder or oil. Parathion: that was the most deadly in the nursery in the old days. Gino had warned her about wearing the gloves with all of them, but the girls told stories about people dying just from touching parathion. She had never used it. She was not allowed to. But she had seen Gino using that oil.

She grabbed up a small bottle and filled it with the brown oil, her hand trembling. Slowly she poured it, holding her breath. Perhaps even coming this close might kill her, but then they were going to kill her anyhow. But this was a weapon, a powerful weapon that came from the same place as the electrodes and the Thorazine and the dialytrode. One of the weapons of the powerful, of those who controlled. Nobody was allowed to possess this poison without a license. She was stealing some of their power in this little bottle. She put the big container back where it had been, locked the cabinet; then she thought better and opened it again and wiped everything with the hem of her dress. Fingerprints. Then she backed out, putting the bottle in the pocket of the smock, until she should get a chance to put it in her old plastic purse.

Quickly she went back to work, choosing plants. Her hands kept trembling. She wondered if she was dying of poison. Perhaps the shaking of her hands was the first stage of poisoning. Perhaps handling the bottle could kill her. She felt the brown oil radiating a sinister influence all around it.

Never had she done such a thing, grabbed at power, at a weapon. She did not intend to go Skip's way. Yes, she had stolen a weapon. War, she thought again. She would fight back. But her hands trembled and trembled and she found her knees buckling till she could hardly focus on the plant before her, large and leathery, almost as big as herself, whose name she had forgotten.

Supper consisted of leftovers. Adele toyed with her food, smiling again. "Did you have a good day? Oh, too bad. Yes. Um. Of course, yes, he's getting old. Mummm."

Connie looked hard at Luis. When she went to the kitchen to fetch the coffee and dessert, she could pour some of the poison into the coffee. It was brown and oily. It would work well in coffee. For all the meanness he had laid on her all the years of her life, for Dolly, for Carmel. Her purse lay within reach. She could do it.

Luis was laughing at his own joke, his head tilting way back. As he laughed, for a moment out of control, almost boyish, she saw in him that older brother she hated to remember she had adored. Up to the age of ten, she had adored Luis with her whole heart. He had seemed to her that prince, that peacock wonder he always remained to their mother. He could fight, he could talk his way in and out of trouble, he could speak English better than any of them, he could stand up for her if he wanted. Yes, Luis the street kid she had adored. Luis the young hoodlum had touched her heart and set a mold on it. Something of what she had loved in Martín, something of what she had loved in Claud: the grace, the anger, the sore pride, the refusal to swallow insult. The army had changed Luis. When he had come back, he had contempt for the rest of them. His anger and unruly pride had been channeled into a desire to get ahead, to grab money, to succeed like an Anglo.

Who knew what being poor and being brown would have done to Martín if he had lived? Perhaps he would have hardened like Luis. She could not believe that of his tenderness, yet she could remember Luis at fourteen stealing a bright scarf from the dime store for her to wear Easter Sunday, laughing as he pulled it from the leather jacket no one knew how he had come by. How beautiful he had seemed, the glint of teeth in his brown face, his eyes burning with anger or joy, the arrogant overacted thrust of his shoulders. Jesús had been scared he would go bad, they would lose him to the streets. None of them had guessed they would lose him to the Anglos, entirely.

After supper she steamed a label off a fancy herbal shampoo in the bathroom and pasted it on her bottle. When the bottle dried, the label stuck. She would take it back to the hospital with her alongside a shoebox of old cosmetics Adele gave her—lipsticks in frosted colors no longer fashionable, the wrong shade of eye shadow, a half-finished jar of cold cream containing oil of the palm. Adele also gave her a beige cardigan with embroidered flowers, shrunk in the wash, a pair of panty hose, and a pile of old *Vogues* and *New Yorkers*. It reminded her of the sort of things people gave you when you cleaned for them. She did not get to taste the dishes she had cooked for the party, but she discovered from the scale in the bathroom off the master bedroom that she had managed to gain four pounds from Wednesday night to Saturday noon. She did not mind. How I spent my vacation: I ate.

As she sat in Luis's big white Eldorado idling sluggishly through heavy traffic, she realized several weeks had passed since she'd gone over. Was Luciente dead? She could not bear to think so. She was the one who was dead. She could not catch anymore. She was hardening herself as Luis had done to himself, but not for money. To succeed in her war. To fight back. She closed her eyes and saw her weapon, disguised as shampoo.

Nineteen

THAT Monday Acker announced that Alice and Captain Cream were to be released Friday to welfare hotels. Alvin was taken away to be operated on, along with Orville. Sybil, Miss Green, and Connie were given yet another battery of physical and psychological tests and scheduled for meetings with the doctors on Wednesday.

"It means we'll be done next," Sybil said out of the side of her mouth as they stood in line for the meds.

"It means that's what *they* want," Connie said.

She and Sybil waited for an opportunity to do their laundry at the same time. Then she asked Sybil, "If you had a chance, would you be ready to try?"

Sybil nodded. "Tina tried in a laundry cart. I've been thinking—is there any way to start a fire?"

"You think you could make it outside?"

"I'm ready to try, Consuelo. I cannot permit them to operate on me if I have any way to stop them. It's a kind of death."

"Don't go back home. I know you never lived anyplace else, but you're in a . . . circle there where they keep getting rid of you."

"The volunteer Mary Ellen I mentioned to you? Her friend gave her a newspaper, a newspaper just for women, that had an article about witches. Real covens that worship Wica! Imagine that, Consuelo. With an address. If I got

. . . out, I thought I might seek their aid."

"That sounds better than going back to Albany for sure."

The next morning when Miss Green was in the bathroom and Sybil was making her bed, Connie darted in. "Here. Take this!" She pressed into Sybil's palm the wadded-up money she had got from Dolly, less what she'd spent on phone calls. It came to thirty-one dollars and sixty-two cents.

Sybil sat down on the bed's edge to stare. "What are you going to do? Why give me this?"

"Shhh. Hide it."

"Don't give up, Consuelo. Just because you couldn't escape from your brother's house!"

"Don't ask what I'm going to do. Only, Wednesday, tomorrow, be ready to run. There'll be a lot of confusion in the afternoon, when the doctors see me. Run then. Run and never let them get you again!"

Valente paused, stood in the hallway looking in. Connie left at once and went to make her own bed. At breakfast Sybil mouthed to her, "Consuelo, you frighten me. Don't give up. Please don't give up!"

"I'm not. For me this is war. I got to fight it the only way I see. To stop them. Don't ask me more." Her voice stuck in her throat. "I wish you a good life, Sybil. Hate them more than you hate yourself, and you'll stay free!"

Tuesday night, in spite of the sleeping pills she lay awake, her eyes wearing themselves raw on dim shapes. She tossed, she thrust her head into the pillow, she counted and tried to blank her mind. Her thoughts ran round and round like dogs trapped behind a fence, to and fro until they had worn a bald track in her head.

She tried to open her mind to Luciente. In weary boredom, in fear of the next day, wanting a little something nice, she tried. Her mind was rusted shut. It would not open. She pushed on herself, she tried and tried. Sweat stood out on her forehead, sweat gathered under her arms and under her breasts. Once she almost felt something, a presence. That made her go on battering her mind. She lay panting as if she had run up a flight of steps. Please, she begged, please! What had been so easy was hard and painful, hard as dying. Dying into distance. Where there had been only air, something solid stood, solid as bone, as prison walls. But she went on. What else did she have to do this night? What else but touch her fears like the beads of a cold, oily rosary, again and again. She went on trying.

Finally she felt a brush of presence, hard, hard and heavy. Yet she could tell almost at once that this time the pain was coming from Luciente. No, the pain was from the terrible effort. Luciente too strained toward her. Together at last they forced weak contact.

"I feared you were dead," she thought at Luciente.

"I feared they had done something . . . final to you. Tried . . . many times!"

"Bring me over!"

Luciente tried for a long time. "Very hard . . . need help. A moment. I'll call Diana or Parra or Zuli. . . . Wait!"

Finally, roughly, she stood shaking in the meeting-house. As on the nights of the feast and of Jackrabbit's wake, many people circulated, but dressed now in ordinary clothes. Their voices were subdued.

Luciente hugged her tight. "How long! We missed you running hard. To reach you has been . . . like trying to walk through walls!"

"Yourself? How did you get out of the burning floater?"

"What?"

"At the front. With Hawk."

Luciente peered into her face. "I don't comprend. Hawk's over there." She pointed. "What stew is this of floaters and fronts?"

"We weren't together at the front? Fighting?"

"Not in my life, Connie. Not in this continuum. . . . With that device in your brain, maybe you visioned it. You've been redded for visioning over the last months, grasp, from all this going over."

"Pues . . . never mind. It felt so real. . . . How are you, Luciente?"

"I feel in you some large resolve. You plan some action?"

"I don't want to talk about it, please. Just tell me about yourself. Bee. Dawn. How you are."

"The Shaping controversy builds. I think we'll call a grandcil this March to decide it. I've been arguing myself empty. It's one choice to breed carrots for our uses—especially leaving wild and variant gene pools intact. Is another to breed ourselves for some uses or imagined uses!

For all we know, a new ice age comes and we might better breed for furriness than mathematical ability! I speechify! Pass it." Luciente hugged her again. "I feared never to see you. Hard bringing you over. We're fading contact."

"How is Bee?"

"Look!" Luciente pointed. "Bee is explaining about agribusiness, cash crops, and hunger."

"He's teaching a class?"

"A memorial. Tonight." Luciente waved at the booths, the tables, the holies and exhibits. "It's winter games. . . . Traveling spectaclers are visiting us this week. We all played roles. Divvied into rich and poor, owners and colonies. For two days all us who got poor by lot fasted and had only half rations two other days. The rich ate till they were stuffed and threw the rest in the compost. I know in history they didn't, Connie blossom, but it's not right to destroy, we just can't do it. We've been feeling a class society where most labor, others control, and some enjoy. We had prisons, police, spies, armies, torture, bosses, hunger—oh, it's been fascinating. Now we're discussing to know better before they go on."

"Is this a feast?" She stared at the people wandering through the room and out into the square, stopping to examine objects laid out, watching holies, arguing over graphs and exhibits.

"No, no, a memorial. Nothing to celebrate, fasure. In winter we make time for studying, communing. Often villages send out a traveling group who go around till they get worn with being on the road. . . . We've been chewing on—Bee, Otter, White Oak, me—going around with a skit on Shaping. This troupe is from Garibaldi on Mystic, where they make pasta, computer poppers, and breed grapevines. A beautiful place, Otter says. When person was eighteen, stayed a month during harvest working and coupling with Vittorio, who's with the troupe. Otter is crazy with pleasure to see per again. . . ." They were strolling among the booths, hand in hand. Bee was using a very small holi projector which produced one moment a box of a children's breakfast cereal from her own time called Sweetee Pyes and the next an image of braceros picking lettuce. He looked at once so serious, frowning at the Sweetee Pyes and rumbling deep in his chest, and at the same time so fine, with the delicate tattoo of the bee rippling on his arm, she lost track of what Luciente was telling her.

Hawk came dodging toward them. She greeted Connie and then burst out, "Luciente! I've fixed. It's time to travel. I'm going on with this troupe. Bolt's coming with me."

Luciente put her hands on Hawk's slight shoulders. "Do they agree?"

Hawk quivered with excitement. "They say we can learn the parts of two people who want to go home. I'll learn Italian and get to see villages, and when I find one that warms me, I'll stay on and work."

"When do you go?"

"Thursday morning. Tomorrow they're doing an opera. They say I sing well enough for the chorus, if I start working on the music."

Connie remembered Hawk setting out for her week in the woods. "How are you going to travel?"

"By dipper. Then, when we're further south, by bike."

"Do you own a bike?"

"Own? Like I dropped a rock on my own foot?"

"A bike that's yours."

Hawk scratched her ear. "Any bike not in use, I can use. Tomorrow I'll say goodbye to everybody!" Hawk stood on one foot. "You think Bee would like my painting of per? It's not . . . top good, but it has a lot of colors in it."

"How not?" Luciente kissed her cheek. "If person should be so blind as not to want it, I want it."

"I'm in velvet we're done with taboo so I can say goodbye properly to my mothers. . . . Don't tell Bee I'm going—I want to tell myself, hold?"

"Hold." Luciente shook her hand and Hawk skipped off.

"I love winter," Luciente said as they strolled on. "Eating and getting fat and going tobogganing and ice skimming. Talking and talking and talking. I'm redding Chinese, sweetness, fifteen hours a week till even Bee picks up from hearing it so much. Also our base, we're monitoring last year's results from all over. And I play in a new mojai group every Friday night, last Friday we went on almost till morning. Mojai is music like this. . . ." Luciente began beating out a complicated rhythm over rhythm with two hands on the edge of a table.

"Shh, Luciente!" Morningstar rebuked her. "We're listening."

"I blather." Luciente drew Connie away. "Such hardness in your mind tonight makes me babble more than usual. I fear for you."

"But it was you, your people, who taught me I'm fighting a war."

"Then fight well, Connie!" They walked out into the cold clean brisk air. Luciente paused to grab a jacket and drape it over Connie's shoulders. Big disks of snow came tilting and turning down where already several inches lay thick, rounding all corners and softening straight lines, an expanse of white across the square marked only by the tracks of children playing.

Luciente touched her shoulder. "You want to ask if I still mourn. . . ."

"I wouldn't ask!"

"I know. But you want to feel how I am. Yes, I mourn. But I work too. It hurts, but I can't let the pain bind me. . . . Diana has helped. Otter has helped. Bee has carried me! . . . I want no new lover and I dread spring. . . . But look!" Luciente waved her hand at a snowball battle swirling around the statue of a funny bird dancing on one foot and a barricade of benches. Briefly Dawn ran through a pool of light, whooping and waving.

Lazy flakes drifted onto the arm of the borrowed jacket. "Luciente, do you think it's always wrong to kill?"

"We live by eating living beings, whether vegetable or animal. Without chlorophyll in our skins, we have no choice." Luciente caught flakes on her outstretched palm.

"I mean to kill a person."

"How can I face something so abstract?"

"To kill someone with power over me. Who means to do me in."

"Power *is* violence. When did it get destroyed peacefully? We all fight when we're back to the wall—or to tear down a wall. You know we kill people who choose twice to hurt others. We don't think it's right to kill them. Only convenient. Nobody wants to stand guard over another."

"In my time people are willing to stand guard. It's a living. I guess maybe it's power, too."

"You brood on killing someone, my friend?"

She nodded, disentangling herself from Luciente to

clutch her hands together before her breasts. She felt pride and shame wash through her. Mala, the woman who acted. To thrust herself forward into the world. Luciente was speaking, but under the rush of her blood, the words mumbled like stones in the bed of a river. Slowly people drifted from the meetinghouse and began taking shovels, brooms from sheds along the square and the paths. The shovels clanged against the stone, the wood scraped. The night began to fill with laughter and the sounds of shoveling. The children stopped their fight and began to clear the snow. In red pants and a dark blue parka, Dawn was wielding a broom, coming along behind Otter, whose broad single braid bounced rhythmically on her back. Bee was clearing snow from the path toward the fooder, as Hawk came running and sliding to work beside him. Her breath came out in white plumes as she talked and talked full speed to him.

She could hear Luciente speaking but she could no longer distinguish the words in the roar of her blood. Only dimly she could hear the scrape of metal on stone. Lips moved as if people were singing. Dawn looked over her padded shoulder at them. Dawn smiled and waved and began to sweep very hard with the broom, showing off, casting up a fine white dust. Flakes rested lightly on her black dome of hair, the hood of the parka cast back. One flake sat for a moment on the end of her delicate, sensuously curved nose, snow on her beautiful Mayan nose where Connie imagined that she pressed a quick kiss.

She lay flat on her bed, out of breath as if she had been dropped from a height.

"What is it?" Tina sat up, awake. "You okay?"

"Yes . . ."

"You cried out. What happened—you have a bad dream?"

"A good one. Tina, I dreamed of my daughter, safe, happy, in another place." She could still see Angelina's face ruddy with playing, her small arms fat in the parka feverishly wielding the broom, while the snowflake melted on her nose. "If only they had left me something!" she whispered. Still trembling, she thought, If only they had left me Martín, or Claud, or Angelina, if they had even left me Dolly and Nita, I would have minded my own business. I'd have bowed my head and kept down. I was not born and raised to fight battles, but to be modest and gentle and still. Only one person to love. Just one little corner of loving of my own. For that love I'd have borne it all and I'd never have fought back. I would have obeyed. I would have agreed that I'm sick, that I'm sick to be poor and sick to be sick and sick to be hungry and sick to be lonely and sick to be robbed and used. But you were so greedy, so cruel! One of them, just one, you could have left me! But I have nothing. Why shouldn't I strike back?

Yet her hands shook with fear. She lay cold and trembling, all the night.

"This operation is designed to help you," Dr. Morgan said. "To enable us to return you to society. You'll be able to hold a job."

"I feel a lot better. Why do I need this operation now? I went home to my brother's Thanksgiving. I worked real hard there. I've been good and cooperative on the ward."

"You've been better before, Connie," Acker said. Today Miss Moynihan was not sitting at his side but across the room next to her boss, Dr. Morgan. She and Acker did not catch each other's gaze. Her gray eyes were bloodshot and underscored by dark tissue. She had been crying; she had not been sleeping. Patty passed her a note and she shook her head bitterly, drawing herself tighter. Acker seemed more nervous than usual. He had a dark area on his left cheek, like a bruise. Who had hit him? Miss Moynihan or one of her brothers? "We know that you can't help what you do. It's as though you experienced a shorting out of circuits that causes you to move into an episode of uncontrollable rage."

"I haven't done anything wrong in months. I'm much better. Why do I need this operation right now, when I'm doing fine?"

"You've had periods of calm before," Dr. Redding pointed out. His fingers were propped together like steeples over his empty cup. "Long periods. But they always end the same way. Don't they, Connie?"

"It isn't the same. Really, please, it isn't! Look, I did something I'm ashamed for, my daughter. But I've paid for that again and again! Forever. How can I be uncontrollable? You been controlling me."

"You don't want to hurt someone close to you again,

do you, Connie? You have a recurrent disease, like someone who has a recurrent malaria," Acker said, looking pleased with himself. He glanced at Dr. Redding for approval, but Redding was talking in Dr. Argent's ear. Both of them had been turning over the pages of a proposal of some sort, and Argent was going down the budget line by line, making little notes to the side.

"But maybe the other thing worked. Maybe I don't need an operation!"

"We have a permission from the brother, don't we?" Redding asked Patty.

She made a little sitting curtsy toward a file on the table. "Yes, Doctor."

Dr. Argent put down the proposal, took the pipe from his mouth, and fixed Connie with a twinkly smile. "Mrs. Ramos, you're frightened by the idea of an operation. Isn't that right?"

"Sure, I'm afraid! I'm okay now, Doctor. Look at the ward notes."

"Your mother died after an operation. Didn't she, Mrs. Ramos?"

Ay de mí, he was playing a psychiatrist game. She would have to say yes. "Doctor, can I get myself a cup of coffee, please? I feel a little confused, a little sleepy. I didn't sleep so well last night on account of worrying about this." She stood up, but remained balanced over her chair. "Please, Doctor, can I get myself a cup of coffee?"

Argent raised a silvery eyebrow, his interest fading. "You've often been a little confused, haven't you, Mrs. Ramos?" He picked up the proposal again, reaching for his pen.

"You can have your coffee as you leave. We're almost done with you," Dr. Redding said, stretching his long legs under the table. "We can all use a coffee break. This is the last of them, isn't it?"

"Yes, Doctor," Patty said, consulting her calendar.

"Connie, we understand that you're frightened. Society is also afraid of you—with more reason, wouldn't you say? This operation is less complicated than the one you underwent in October. Now, you agreed you're better for that operation." Redding spoke fast, the words speeding into her. "You'll be the better for this surgical procedure also.

Then, like Alice, you'll be released. Surely you don't want to spend your life in a mental institution?"

"But last time I got better and they let me out without any operation!"

"And here you are again. Aren't you? Your brother . . . what's his name?"

"Lewis Camacho," Patty read. "From Bound Brook, New Jersey."

"Your brother . . . er . . . in New Jersey . . . Mr. Comanchee? . . has signed the permission. The procedure will be carried out Monday. In a month you'll be released. Consider that, Connie, and you'll realize your fears are as irrational and as much a part of the pattern of your illness behavior as your hostile episodes. Okay, let's break!"

The staff leaned back in their chairs and turned to each other as Connie got up, all except Miss Moynihan, who brushed past her in a hurry. Her face was twisted and she raced toward the staff ladies' bathroom. Tony had been standing outside, sneaking a smoke, wrapped in a plastic bag of music from his transistor radio. "They done with you?" he asked.

"I don't know!" She held up her hands. "I don't understand what they're doing. You ask them. They keep talking about my brother Luis. I don't understand what they want me to do."

"Wait here. Just hold on." Tony stuck his head into the room, where she saw past him the doctors pushing back their chairs and beginning to rise, small knots of conversation forming. Argent and Redding had their heads together over the proposal, plotting. Morgan hovered, ignored and nervous. Redding nodded briskly at the little notes. Five thousand more chimpanzees? Prisoners? Women on welfare? They had disposed of her. "They said I could have some coffee," she said out loud, and moved at once into the alcove where the doctors' big shiny coffee machine stood. Quickly she dumped the contents of the old pot, emptied a premeasured packet into the filter, and pressed the Brew button. Then she fished the bottle from her purse and dripped the oily liquid into the glass pot as the coffee began to fill it. She hoped they would realize this was fresh coffee, and not discard it to make more.

When Tony came out the water was still pouring down.

"Come on, Ramos. They're done with you. Leave the doctors' coffee alone, don't mess up now. You can get a cup on the patients' side."

"They don't want me anymore?" She blinked confusion.

"What do you think, they need all day to make up their minds about you? They're big-shot doctors. That Redding, he had his picture in *Time*. Patty showed me, she keeps a scrapbook on him. Dr. Argent, he goes up to Washington to testify before Congress to set them straight on things. You don't think they got all day to waste making up their minds about what to do with you!"

She washed her hands in the bathroom, she washed them again and again. "I just killed six people," she said to the mirror, but she washed her hands because she was terrified of the poison. "I murdered them dead. Because *they* are the violence-prone. Theirs is the money and the power, theirs the poisons that slow the mind and dull the heart. Theirs are the powers of life and death. I killed them. Because it is war." Her hands shook like a willow branch used by dowsers in Texas, a willow branch pulled by water deep in the ground. "I'm a dead woman now too. I know it. But I did fight them. I'm not ashamed. I tried.

She broke the bottle under running water without touching it and washed the pieces down the shower. They'd most likely find them, but it was the best she could think up. Then she washed her hands a last time and went in search of Sybil. When she found her in the lounge she said to her only, "Soon!" Sybil looked into her face. A tear formed and hung in her eye. Then she looked down and said nothing, alert, ingathered, ready. Connie went to her room. As she passed Valente, knitting, the attendant nodded to her.

She thought of Luciente, but she could no longer reach over. She could no longer catch. She had annealed her mind and she was not a receptive woman. She had hardened. But she thought of Mattapoisett.

For Skip, for Alice, for Tina, for Captain Cream and Orville, for Claud, for you who will be born from my best hopes, to you I dedicate my act of war. At least once I fought and won.

After a while she heard the commotion and they came with stretchers—four. Dr. Morgan was trying to cut down on coffee, and Miss Moynihan was being sick in the staff bathroom. I am not sorry, she thought, her heart pounding terribly, and she sat on her bed, waiting.

Twenty

Excerpts from the Official History of Consuelo Camacho Ramos

State of New York—Department of Mental Hygiene
Bellevue Hospital

CLINICAL SUMMARY

IDENTIFICATION: This 35-year-old Mexican-American Catholic woman separated from her husband Edward for the past three years has one child, Angelina, aged 4. The patient has been on Aid to Dependent Children since last May.

PRESENTING PROBLEM: This patient brought her child into emergency at N.Y.U., stating that she had accidentally broken her wrist. The child was bruised. When questioned by caseworker, the patient readily admitted beating her daughter, while drunk or drugged. The patient was incoherent, weeping, and exhibited bizarre behavior.

PAST HISTORY: This socially disorganized individual has been in an increasingly deteriorating state since the breakup of her marriage. Whereabouts of husband unknown. This patient has been in conflict with the law for two years. Convicted of aiding and abetting a pickpocket and given a suspended sentence and a year's probation last April. The patient refers to an illegal abortion, followed by severe hemorrhaging and complications, for which a hysterectomy was performed at Metropolitan. The patient has recent alcohol and barbiturate problems. Seems hostile and suspicious toward authority. Lack of control and frustration tolerance. The patient has a tendency to act out problems with violent expression and hostile and extrapunitive tendencies.

MENTAL STATUS: This patient is disheveled and appears to be older than her stated age. She readily admits needing help. She is cooperative but confused and occasionally suspicious. Has not demonstrated assaultive behavior on the ward.

STREAM OF MENTAL ACTIVITY: The patient is incoherent. The patient's thinking is extremely concrete.

EMOTIONAL REACTIONS: The patient's general mood is anxious and exhibits extreme guilt. The patient's affect is inappropriate, marked by crying without cause.

CONTENT OF THOUGHTS: Denies suicidal ideation. Denies delusions or hallucinations.

SENSORIUM, MENTAL GRASP AND CAPACITY: Sensorium clear. Oriented times three. Recent and remote memory appear weak. The patient has somewhat slow intelligence and answers questions poorly.

DIAGNOSIS: Schizophrenia, undiff. type 295.90.

State of New York—Department of Mental Hygiene
Rockover State Psychiatric Hospital

DISCHARGE NOTE

Dr. Messinger

HISTORY: This 35-year-old Mexican-American woman, Catholic mother of one daughter, was hospitalized at Bellevue because of child abuse, alcohol problems, confusion, and bizarre behavior, and admitted here February 8.

HOSPITAL COURSE: The pt. responded well to medication, although with pronounced side effects, swollen tongue, etc. Her behavior slowly normalized and the pt. exhibited decreased psychiatric signs and symptoms.

PRESENT MENTAL STATUS: Alert, cooperative, coherent, relevant, with no abnormalities of stream of thought or content of thought. Acceptable insight. Oriented times three.

PHYSICAL CONDITION: Ambulatory—no physical abnormalities. Can care for self.

TREATMENT PLAN: Pt. discharged to welfare hotel until welfare finds her an apartment. She will report to Aftercare Clinic at Bellevue weekly.

MEDICATION:
1. Thorazine 200 mg q.d. at 5 P.M.
2. Prolixin 1 cc IM every 2 weeks.
3. Artane 2 mg t.i.d.

CONDITION: Improved.

DIAGNOSIS: Paranoid Schizophrenia, type 295.3.

From Bellevue Admission Notes: This evening this 37-year-old obese Puerto Rican woman allegedly attacked a relative and a relative's fiancé with a bottle. Upon examination she was found lying on the floor, groaned incoherently, and proved disoriented as to time and place. She was hostile, uncooperative, and threatening. She was abusive to relative and relative's fiancé. Admit. Thorazine 1000 mg by injection. Restraint.

From Rockover State Admission Notes: This patient is a 37-year-old Mexican-American Catholic mother, separated from her husband Edward, whose child has been put out for adoption through the state agency. Has a history of violent psychotic episodes, including robbery, assault, and child abuse. Eleven days ago this patient attacked her niece Dolores Campos and her niece's fiancé. This patient is known to us and has been previously hospitalized in Rockover. After ten days at Bellevue, transferred here. Remained acutely psychotic. During hospitalization, she has been mute and withdrawn with occasional violent outbursts. She has been uncooperative, attempting to refuse medication, and has no insight into her illness. Has delusions of persecution by niece's fiancé and speaks of the State of New York as "murdering" a Negro boyfriend. This patient also constantly complains about the child put out for adoption. The patient has no consistent notions of right or wrong. She said that for the last two years she didn't drink at all. She smokes about a pkg. a day. She denies any drug addiction, although she admits use of barbiturates in the past. She claims not to have had any relations with men in the past three years. She doesn't admit any attachments to women either. This patient is a socially maladjusted individual subject to periodic dysphorias accompanied by fear, leading to violent episodes and aggressions. Admit to Ward L-6. Restrict to ward. Violence precautions.

Escape Report: After a fight with another patient on the ward, causing mild concussion, this patient wandered out of the hospital and was lost in the woods for two whole nights and days. She was recovered in a bus station in Fairview very confused and uncertain where she was trying to go. She was covered with mosquito bites. It was decided to place her on close supervision. . . .

From New York Neuro-Psychiatric Institute Notes: This 37-year-old female did not appear to have any motor difficulties. The patient appears to have learned to walk and talk at the normal time. Sent to Texas for birth records. Patient was delivered by midwife. No definite documentation of premature birth or birth traumas. History of blackouts and violent episodes in which patient felt as if she couldn't control herself.

. . . Mr. Camacho is a well-dressed man (gray business suit) who appears to be in his 40's. He operates a wholesale-retail nursery and has a confident, expansive manner. I would consider him to be a reliable informant who expresses genuine concern for his sister. . . .

LIST OF PROBLEMS AND TREATMENT PLANS

1. Repeated hospitalizations
2. Psychotic sy
3. Episodic violence
4. Lack of insight
5. Lack of motivation
6. Toothache
7. Cracked rib
8. Negativism

ORIENTED: Fully oriented
REMOTE MEMORY: Intact
RECENT MEMORY: Slightly impaired
RETENTION AND IMMEDIATE RECALL: Intact
COUNTING AND CALCULATIONS: Impaired (mistake in serial 7's)
READING: Read with ease
SCHOOLING AND GENERAL KNOWLEDGE: Commensurate. Claims to have 2 yrs college? Welfare records indicate only 1 yr., 3 mths. in community college.
INTELLIGENCE RATING: Average
COURSE OF MENTAL ILLNESS: Deteriorative process
ABSTRACTING ABILITY: Impaired
ABILITY TO MAINTAIN SET OR ASSOCIATIVE: Intact

. . . After the implantation patient was markedly better with no episodes for two months. Symptoms then recurred. Amygdalotomy indicated but not carried out because of incident. . . .

There were one hundred thirteen more pages. They all followed Connie back to Rockover.